ALSO BY ALICE ADAMS

Careless Love

Families and Survivors

Listening to Billie

Beautiful Girl (STORIES)

Rich Rewards

To See You Again (STORIES)

Superior Women

Return Trips (STORIES)

Second Chances

After You've Gone (STORIES)

Caroline's Daughters

Caroline's Daughters

ALICE ADAMS

Alfred A. Knopf   New York   1991

THIS IS A BORZOI BOOK
PUBLISHED BY ALFRED A. KNOPF, INC.

Library of Congress Cataloging-in-Publication Data
Adams, Alice, [date]
Caroline's daughters / Alice Adams. — 1st ed.
p.   cm.
ISBN 0-394-56825-7
I. Title.
PS 3551.D324C37   1991
813'.54—dc20   90-52908   CIP

Manufactured in the United States of America
First Edition

For

SYDNEY GOLDSTEIN

CHARLES BREYER

and

VICTORIA WILSON

with love and thanks

Caroline's Daughters

One

Caroline Carter and her husband, Ralph, as a couple are impressive, even imposing: perched at the top of a broad concrete flight of stairs, in one of San Francisco's prettiest, greenest and most elevated parks (the view is marvellous, hills and tall buildings, church spires and further high green parks), they draw a lot of attention from the stray passers-by, the dog walkers and strollers, on this bright April Sunday. For one thing they both look foreign, Caroline and Ralph, although Caroline has lived in this city for many years and Ralph is a native son. But now, out of the country for over five years, they wear mildly eccentric clothes. Caroline's heavy gray sweater (she expected fog) is un-American in design, as is the cut of Ralph's tweed jacket. Also, they are very large people, Caroline a tall fair woman, broad-faced, serene, with wide-set green-blue eyes and heavy gray-blonde hair—and Ralph a towering, massive man, once called "hulking" by a hostile press. Ralph is Caroline's third husband, and she his fourth wife—an unpropitious history, perhaps, but after twenty-five years this marriage seems to have taken: they look quite permanently married.

And, almost rich and almost old, Caroline is back in a city where for many years she was young and almost broke, where four of her five daughters were born, and where she enjoyed a number of lovers. A lively life, then, and in its way romantic, although Caroline is eminently a realist, a practical, sensible woman. Or so she sees herself, generally.

At the moment they are sitting there like tourists in the early sunlight, looking down the terraced hill and across the street to their own house—from which they have been temporarily expelled by those five daughters, who are giving a welcome-home party for Ralph and Caroline. A somewhat delayed welcome back: their actual return from Portugal, where they spent most of those five years, took place in January. In any case the daughters, Sage, Liza, Fiona, Jill and Portia, are "doing it all," bringing food and drink and even flowers—quite foolishly, Caroline thinks, her garden is full of flowers. It is the sort of party that has been discussed and discussed, and that Caroline has all along tried somehow to prevent, but has not. And now it is almost upon her. Upon them all.

The food will be almost entirely done by Fiona, the middle, highly successful food-person daughter: "Fiona's" is an extremely trendy, very popular (this year) California-cuisine restaurant, on Potrero Hill.

Everything about this project has contributed to Caroline's unease, now expressed in her restless posture, and her large strong hands that gesture helplessness from her lap. "I'd like it so much better if they were all doing it, and not just Fiona," she says, with a small worried frown. "Or if I were doing it all myself."

"If you were doing it all." Ralph laughs at her, gently. "Come on, Caro."

But Caroline insists. "Well, it is our house. Even if food is what Fiona does. Ostensibly. So funny, she really can't cook. I don't know, it just all seems wrong. Everything," she vaguely finishes.

"Our rich kids," Ralph supplies.

"I suppose that's part of it. To have two such extremely successful ones, in ways I never knew about or even imagined."

Ralph makes an ambiguous sound, expressing to Caroline the fact that she has said all this before, more or less. But she does not mind this comment from Ralph, whom she loves (usually); she has needed, repeatedly, to say how she feels about these particular daughters, the very rich ones: Fiona, at thirty-three the well-known restaurateur (does anyone say "restaurateuse," Caroline wonders?), and Jill, at thirty-one a very rich young lawyer-stockbroker.

"Well, there's always Portia," Ralph put in, now in his turn repeating himself. "We can count on her not to get ahead, I think."

Portia, twenty-five, is the one and only daughter from the marriage of Caroline and Ralph.

"Well, you're right about Portia," says Caroline, about this youngest, most problematic child. "And then there's Sage," she adds, with a sigh for her eldest daughter, a bravely unsuccessful, highly talented (in her mother's view) ceramicist, whose strange, small, intensely expressive figures sell rarely or not at all, in their occasional viewings, in local galleries. Sage, now forty-one, is the product of Caroline's very early (at nineteen) marriage to Aaron Levine, who died in that war, in 1943, before Sage was born. Subtle, dark Sage is the image of her father. She seems given to trouble: fairly soon after the demise of a spectacularly unfortunate love affair with a local lawyer-politico, she married a man named Noel Finn, who is overly handsome (again, in Caroline's view), a carpenter, some seven years younger than Sage.

"Sage will be the first to come today," says Caroline, who is now beginning to speak her thoughts aloud. "And she'll bring some present that I won't quite know what to do with. And there'll be some excuse about Noel."

Caroline is right, as things turn out, but before that happens she and Ralph get up and walk about, and they talk about how much San Francisco has changed since they left it in 1980 (Reagan's year, as they think of it), and how much they like their house, despite neighborhood changes.

Behind where Caroline and Ralph were sitting is a tall grove of waving pines and redwoods, enclosing a little play area for children. Sandboxes, slides—all at the moment unoccupied, amazing in this sunshine, this early fog-free morning. The long flight of stairs is flanked by terraces of grass, marked off with hedges and narrow paths. And below is the street, on the other side of which is a row of very attractive Victorian houses, all originally (just before the turn of the century) identical. And one of these is Caroline and Ralph's.

It is really Caroline's house. She bought it when she first came to San Francisco as a young widow in the Forties, an investment for which she used the last of her husband's insurance money. The house was in bad shape at that time, sagging and neglected; Caroline, who is skillful with houses, had it all fixed up—and in the course of that long process (she kept running out of money) she grew to love the house but could not afford to live in it. Also, her next (second) husband, Dr. James McAndrew, did not like the neighborhood, at that time considered "bad," too close to what was then known as "the Fillmore," an area where mostly black people lived. And so, with Jim, Caroline moved to a "better" neighborhood, and she rented out her house. (Liza, now thirty-five, and then Fiona and Jill came in an orderly succession during that marriage of Caroline's to Jim—whom she divorced in 1959 in order to marry Ralph, by whom she was then pregnant with Portia.)

As Caroline herself would have been the first to admit, she was stubborn and foolhardy about the house, rather than prescient. She did not have an instinct for real estate, she did not think in those terms. Her feelings about the house's drastic rise in value are ambivalent, to say the least (upper Fillmore Street was "gentrified," the black people "relocated").

She did have an instinct for houses, perhaps an atavistic inheritance from her English mother, the actress-playwright Molly Blair. She bought the house, really, because it was small and beautiful; she felt that it would suit her perfectly, and she was quite right. But Ralph, when they first married, did not want to live in the house for an opposite reason to Jim McAndrew's: for him the neighborhood was much too fancy, he felt (Ralph is a former longshoreman, later a political writer).

Then, in 1980, Molly Blair died, and a subsequent revival of interest in her work, publication of new editions of her plays, gave Caroline, her only child, a fair amount of money. And Reagan was elected. And Ralph had a mild heart attack. "Take it easy. Change your life," he was fairly forcefully advised.

For a combination of reasons, then, after distributing much of her money among her daughters, Caroline and Ralph took off for Portugal, where they spent almost five years—during which the tenants of the house were elderly friends of Caroline's, who died within months of each other this past year, a strong reason for the return from Portugal of Caroline and Ralph. They returned to a valuable and perfectly maintained house; sheer practicality helped to persuade Ralph to live there after all. Their south garden, a treasure, widely coveted in San Francisco, grew bountifully—just now, in April, full of roses and camellias, rhododendron, white wisteria.

"It's a perfect house for two people," in their sunnier moments Caroline and Ralph have remarked to each other. And, at darker times, "How can the two of us possibly occupy a whole house? with all the homeless people—"

In their walk about the park, marking time until the arrival of the daughters and the pre-emption of their own roles, in their own house, Ralph and Caroline have touched lightly on all these topics, including that of the beauty of their garden.

"It must be in my genes," Caroline has earlier remarked. "The way I respond to gardens. I absolutely fall in love."

"Except that I really like the garden too," Ralph tells her. "My Texas genes?" Ralph's parents, grandparents, great grandparents all were Texans, a fact often manifest in his voice. Especially as he ages, Caroline thinks, he sounds more and more Southern. Texan.

And they now return to the more pressing topic of their daughters.

So many! Whatever have I done to deserve five daughters? rueful Caroline has been heard to remark, and there does seem a certain illogic to that fate, in her particular case. (And it was in many ways the presence of all those young women in San Francisco—like many California offspring, those five cannot imagine life elsewhere, for themselves—that kept Caroline for all those years away in Portugal. "I simply don't want to be so *present* in their lives," said Caroline.)

"I sometimes don't think Sage really likes Fiona very much," Caroline next remarks. "Or for that matter Jill."

"How could she? All that money that both of them seem to have." Ralph tends to speak more succinctly than Caroline does; conversationally he does not wander, as he sometimes accuses Caroline of doing.

"But she and Liza always seem great pals."

"Everyone likes Liza. She's the most like you."

This is a remark that Caroline often hears, not only from Ralph— so often that she is tired of responding to it. What she might say, of herself and Liza, might be: We only sort of look alike, both being large, and she has three children. But we've got very different characters, lucky for her.

Ralph, that quintessential American, that most unlikely expatriate, was in fact quite happy in Lisbon, during those years. His solution—and this was a part of the overall unlikeliness of it all—was to domesticate himself, in ways hitherto quite unimaginable for him. He not only learned to cook, he went out to markets and he bargained, endlessly and successfully, in a language he could not speak, coming home with the largest cod and the smallest shellfish, at bargain prices. And this from a man whose life before that had been of the most intense and public involvement; in San Francisco he was known to be a not-too-secret political kingmaker—and a man who had always come home, to all those wives, expecting meals on time and clean clothes, a clean bed and a pretty, accommodating wife, and who had always found all that, except for very brief between-wife periods. "It's something new for me," was Ralph's explanation to Caroline. And, "I like the fish." She came to understand that he also liked the docks and the fishermen, the whole waterfront atmosphere; it was what he was used to, and missed.

Whereas Caroline, who had spent her life in domestic pursuits, now spent all her days in museums and galleries. She even did some sketches and some tentative watercolors from their small apartment, high up in the Alfama, the old quarter of Lisbon, near the Castel San Georgio. They had a view of the harbor, boats and the bridge, the Twenty-fifth of April Bridge, built to commemorate the Generals' Revolution, the end of fascism. And all around them geraniums bloomed, on balconies and terraces, every shade from white to pink, orange to deep scarlet.

One of the best aspects of Lisbon was its access to the rest of Europe. Ralph and Caroline flew to London or Paris or Rome, they took trains to Madrid or Barcelona. And so those Portuguese years worked out quite well—but nevertheless they both became quite restless, impatient. Travel writing was not his métier, Ralph decided, and Caroline felt that her sketches were hopelessly amateur. And then everything seemed at once to conspire to bring them home, most immediately the deaths of their tenants, the vacancy of their house.

They both, especially Caroline, had a sense that by this time their daughters were all right, or were at least settled on courses that they, the parent figures, would be unlikely to deflect. Sage had her ceramics, and her marriage to Noel. Liza was married to Saul Jacobs, a psychiatrist, and had her three babies. Fiona had her restaurant, Jill her law and her money. And Portia had her Bolinas shack, where (it was generally believed) she wrote poetry.

What could change?

"Well, of course you were right, there's Sage's car." Unnecessarily, Ralph points downward to the battered, mud-spattered, once-black, once-convertible VW. Sage is just getting out, alone, and maneuvering a very large box.

Tall, too-thin Sage is wearing white pants, probably Levi's, and something striped on top that is from Cost Plus, probably. Sage resists clothes, she tends to beat them up, to pour liquids over them. Her long, very dark hair is unfashionably pony-tailed. All in all she seems to be saying that she does not care, does not care that she is getting into her forties, that her husband is seven years younger and very handsome. But Caroline, looking at Sage as objectively as possible, still thinks that this daughter, this difficult eldest, is very beautiful, perhaps the only truly beautiful one. Ralph agrees: "Fiona and Jill are sexy but not true beauties." But they also agree that Sage should fix up a little more, as Ralph puts it. (Liza is very pretty but too fat, and Portia is, well, odd-looking; she looks like Ralph.)

Caroline calls out to Sage from where they are walking down the steps, and Sage waits for them where she stands, leaning against her dirty old car, with her big brown cardboard box.

"Noel had to go down the Peninsula," is the first thing that Sage says, with a quick downward twist of her mouth—once kisses have been exchanged among the three of them, out there on the sidewalk, in the very unseasonal hot sun. "Honestly, these damn clients expect maintenance too," Sage says, and then adds, with a lift of her small cleft chin, "Of course it's a lot his fault. Noel loves to feel indispensable."

"Darling. I suppose we all do, don't we?" At times Caroline still sounds just faintly British, more inheritance from Molly. Her father was a New Englander, a Connecticut Yankee.

"Men are like that, kiddo." Ralph likes teasing Sage, who has been known not to take it very well, possibly (Caroline thinks) because she was an only child for all those years, those six before Liza was born. And perhaps for the same reason Caroline is aware of being over-protective of this daughter. Still.

"Sage, whatever have you brought in that great box?" As they walk toward the house Caroline for an instant puts an arm across her daughter's thin shoulders. "Can't Ralph carry it in for you?"

"No, it's okay."

As they reach the front steps, from inside the house the phone begins to ring, and Ralph hurries in to get it.

"That could be Noel," Sage tells her mother. "Coming after all. Maybe." Her smile is brief, and wistful.

"Or Portia not coming at all," says Caroline.

"Well honey, I'm just sorry," they hear Ralph say as they enter. "We'll do it later. See you and celebrate."

"Portia," says Caroline to Sage.

"You're so always right," says Sage, with a little laugh.

"I know, it's tiresome, isn't it. Sage, do put that down."

"It's Portia, want to talk to her?" Ralph, from the kitchen phone.

"No, just give love."

Caroline and Sage then walk through the long narrow white Victorian living room, through the dining room to the deck, where at last Sage deposits the big square box. Very carefully; clearly its contents could break.

"Portia's car has died." Ralph has come out to stand beside them, on the deck that Caroline has so filled with pots of flowers that very little room is left for furniture, or for people. Roses, mostly. Two rose trees, full and white, and smaller bushes of yellow, peach and pink and lavender (Sterling Silver, a delicate favorite of Caroline's), but also two lemon trees, and three large wooden tubs of poppies and ranunculuses, all now in bloom. And smaller pots of thriving marguerites, all over.

Below the deck and down in the garden are still more roses, tall rose trees and bushes of roses, all placed at rather formal intervals, in tidy beds that surround a circular area of brick. In the farthest bed, at the very back of the garden, are two enormous twin camellias, now profusely flowering, dark scarlet. It has been so far an exceptionally sunny spring, leading to talks of drought, and Caroline has feared for her flowers, just now so lovely.

"You might as well open your present," Sage instructs, indicating the box, with a smile that to her mother signals pride.

Caroline works at the taped-down flaps, and then for no reason that she can think of (except that she always makes guesses, as she opens presents) she says, "I know, you've made me a birdbath."

"Jesus, Mother. I hate you, I really do."

Dismayed at the accuracy of her intuition (and, having had it, why on earth did she have to blurt it out like that?), Caroline sees that what Sage has brought is a birdbath: a wide, shallow, blue-glazed bowl, with tiny birds, a small frieze of birds perched here and there on its ridge. "But darling, it's so beautiful, that glaze—"

"But how did you know what it was? Jesus, Mother." Sage's thin lovely face is pulled into a frown. Her pale-brown skin is lightly freckled, her eyes troubled but golden, clear gold.

"I don't know, it was just a lucky guess. Let's put it over here. Look, it's perfect."

"All that noise has got to be Fiona," says Ralph.

"Besides, you always think of what I really lust for," adds Caroline, to Sage. "I did want a birdbath. I need one, and this is ravishing." She goes over to give Sage a quick light kiss.

Fiona's arrival is a big production, taking place as it does from her restaurant's big white van. FIONA is emblazoned on one side. And Fiona has brought along an assistant, a fat, very pretty young woman who immediately begins to unload a series of white food boxes.

"You didn't exactly leave me a lot of room," is Fiona's opening remark to her older half-sister, Sage.

"I didn't know you were bringing that truck, I thought the Ferrari."

"How could I get all this food into the Ferrari?"

"How many people did you think were coming?" asks Ralph, as boxes are passed into the kitchen, either stacked or piled into the refrigerator.

"Well, isn't Liza bringing her kids?"

"She only has three, and they're little," Caroline reminds her.

"Oh well."

Fiona's pale-blonde hair is very long; all three of Caroline's daughters by Jim McAndrew have wispy blonde hair, as he does, and they have his eyes, very large and pale gray. Fiona dresses smartly, always, "dressed for success," as the advertisers (and her sisters) put it. Today she wears very tailored pale linen, two shades of brown, and trim brown shoes—in which she now walks about the deck, inspecting flowers, then looking into the birdbath. "Terrific," is her mild comment.

Fiona is thin, very thin, but nature intended her to be otherwise, or so Caroline thinks, observing this daughter. Caroline sees Fiona's wide bones, quite like her own, stretching the pummelled, pampered skin.

Sexy Fiona, how odd that she seems to have no lovers, thinks sexy Caroline.

"Where's Jill?" Fiona then asks. "She's coming?"

"I guess, but we haven't heard from her."

"Some big deal in her life, no doubt," sniffs Fiona. To say that Fiona is ambivalently pleased by the success of her younger sister would be to put it mildly.

"Portia's car died," contributes Ralph.

"Lord, what else is new?"

"Well, it must be time for drinks, what would everyone like?" Caroline and Ralph say these things at almost exactly the same moment, then laugh at themselves for so doing.

Sage wants wine with some ice in it. "I know that's awful, Noel the purist would die, but it's just so hot."

Fiona wants a Perrier.

In the kitchen, faced with all those boxes of food, Ralph and Caroline exclaim to each other, "Look at all she's brought, it's terrible, we'll have to take it all somewhere—some shelter, a food bank."

"Well, anyway, here's Liza and her gang."

And indeed, trooping up the steps are two small children in impressively white clothes, followed by their parents: Liza, carrying a baby, a very small one; and Saul Jacobs, the father, psychiatrist, carrying several paper sacks and also a very large bunch of over-sized pink peonies. (And Caroline thinks, as she sometimes has before, how very much she likes this shrink son-in-law, this Saul—and how little she seems to feel for the children. Her grandchildren. They're quite nice enough, in their way, but after all only children. And she wonders, perhaps her strong affections for the very young are simply worn out, nothing left?)

Liza is as large as, in Caroline's view, Fiona was meant to be. In her invariable blue denim prairie skirt, her white lace Mexican blouse, blue beads, she bustles in and kisses everyone present in turn, with effusive greetings for all. "Mom, you look super, you look *home*. Ralph, don't you love your house? Does the garden give you enough chores to keep you happy? Skinny Fiona, what on earth have you brought in all those boxes, goodies to keep the rest of us all happy and fat? Darling Sage, you look so beautiful, where's Noel?" And, turning back to her mother and Ralph, "Where're Jill and Portia?"

"Portia's car," they tell her. "We haven't heard from Jill."

"Noel had to work," Sage adds.

By this time, Fiona's helper is carrying boxes out onto the deck, and, assisted by Ralph, Fiona begins to arrange an assortment of salads, cold pastas and thick cold soups. And cheese and fruit and pastry. Mustards, relishes. Breads and special butters, in crocks.

We'll never be able to eat all that, Caroline begins to say, and then does not, not wishing to sound unappreciative of her daughter's largesse. But it isn't really largesse, she reminds herself. It's "free," in the curious sense that expense-account meals are free, and certain trips. All are part of an extremely expensive bit of unreality, the unreality in which the very rich spend all their time, insulated, as though in capsules. Including Fiona and the absent Jill.

And then, more practically, she thinks, Well, Liza can take home some leftovers. Picnic lunches all week for the kids. And she thinks, At the rate Saul's going he'll certainly never be rich. (Saul donates considerable time, most recently to an emotional-support project for people with AIDS.)

A light confusion then takes over the party, and reigns for the next several hours, actually. There is not enough ice: how come Caroline had not emptied and refilled all the ice trays early on? (It is Caroline who demands this, aloud, of herself, Ralph not being given to that sort of petulant nagging.) The children want a variety of soft drinks, mostly ones not there. "I'm not about to go out to any market, so just settle down," Saul, their stern father, tells them. And isn't it time to eat? All the cold food will warm up in the sunshine and lose its flavor, according to Fiona.

Then from the doorway is heard a voice, high-pitched and quite familiar to them all: "This fucking van, where in hell do you expect a person to park?"

And there is Jill, her pale-blonde hair short and sleek, a small cap, a helmet. Jill, in pale-pink silk, looking slightly rumpled, and flustered—and, as Ralph has said, very sexy.

"I thought I left plenty of room. You do look fabulous, Jill."

"Hurry up. We're just starting, my kids will eat it all up if we don't."

"Where on earth have you been?"

Thus more or less in chorus is Jill greeted by her sisters. She chooses, though, to answer only Sage's somewhat accusing question. "I had some work to do," she tells Sage, and then, "Where's Noel? He's working too?" She laughs again, and seems not to expect an answer. "I will have a glass of wine," she tells Ralph. "It all seems so festive, I feel rather festive myself."

As though deliberately, the three blonde daughters have clustered together, Liza, Fiona, and Jill, all happily out in the sunshine, in their summer clothes, with plates of summer food before them. Sage, isolating herself somewhat, chooses a shaded corner of the deck, near a budding yellow rose.

Caroline is moved to go over to her, though not to say what is most in her mind, not to say, You're worried over Noel, you shouldn't be, he's just not worth it. Although that is what she would have liked to say.

And Caroline sighs, with the further self-critical observation, How much a mother I do seem still to be! So annoying, no wonder I haven't done much else with my life.

To Sage, though, what she does say is, "How's your work going these days? Do I get to come to your studio any time soon?"

Two

Sage is not sure why she feels that she must tell her mother and Ralph that she is just going for a walk, "I'll just walk around for a while, check out Pacific Heights," when she is actually going to see her stepfather. (Or, former stepfather? These designations have become unclear.) Nevertheless, that is what she says.

She is actually going to see Jim McAndrew, former husband of Caroline and father of Liza, Fiona and Jill. Who lives in a condominium not far from Caroline's house. Sage is off to see Jim, while Caroline and Liza are dealing with one of Liza's kids, who threw up. And Ralph and Saul are packing leftovers into Saul's old Ford wagon, directed by Fiona—as Jill buzzes off in her yellow Mercedes.

And Sage announces her walk. "I'll be back in an hour or so to pick up my car, but you guys will probably be taking naps by then."

"That sounds right."

Has she always, all her life, been in love with Jim McAndrew? Sage has wondered this, and she took it up, repeatedly if not very fruitfully, with the psychiatrist to whom she briefly went—at the end of a love affair with a man of about Jim's age, a married man, a father. Roland Gallo, a well-known local lawyer-politico, a semi-friend of Ralph's.

But it did not much matter what name she gave to her strong, surviving emotions in Jim's direction, both she and the shrink concluded. Entering her life when she was at the very tender, very vulnerable age of less than three, as the first San Francisco suitor of her widowed mother, Jim was and has remained for Sage the ultimately desirable and finally unavailable person. "Friends" is the word she generally uses to describe her connection with Jim, and very likely that is how he too thinks and speaks of it, if he ever does mention this connection. "Sage and Jim have remained the greatest friends; it's slightly odd, I suppose, but extremely nice, and quite natural when you think of it. After all, he was her father for all those years," is how Caroline has been heard to describe it.

Sage did not much like the lunch party. Or, she wonders, are her nagging, ill-defined worries over both Noel and her work enough to prevent her enjoyment of anything, even in this soft blue April weather? It is easier to ascribe the mild depression that she now experiences to the multiple presences of her sisters, her three half-sisters. Three halves: the very phrase suggests wrongness, no one should have three half-sisters, much less four.

Not for the first time Sage considers the fact that of all those women it is Caroline, her mother, who seems most truly her sister. Although she is indeed fond of Liza, and of the absent Portia.

Suppose she did a group of those female figures? Suddenly seeing that possibility, seeing the circle of small clay figures—perhaps at a table? chairs? No, standing would be better, more scope for individual postures—Sage stops in her tracks, stops right there on the sidewalk, which happens to be at the crest of a hill, the height of Pacific Heights. She stops to think, and to see.

How amazing, really, that she has not thought of this grouping before. Or for that matter not done it long before.

But now she will.

From where Sage stands, had she been looking down to the bay she would have seen a flutter of white sails, all over the blue. A Sunday regatta, through which, all slow and stately, a long black freighter moves deliberately outward, toward the Pacific, the East. Bearing exports, probably, to Japan.

Much closer to Sage, in fact she can smell them, are the thick dark woods of the Presidio, the eucalyptus and pines, the weird wind-bent cypresses.

She is or has been taking the long way around to Jim's condominium, where she is not due for almost half an hour (she called; she does not drop in on Jim, a busy bachelor-doctor). She takes this route both to kill the time and because she has always walked this way. Below her on Pacific Avenue is the row of large, dark and quite splendid houses, some Maybeck, a Julia Morgan, an Esherick, in one of which Roland the married lover lives, there across from the playground and the woods, with his view of the bridge and the bay. In the bad old days of the end of that affair Sage used to disguise herself in scarves and bulky sweaters (she hoped she was disguised) and to haunt the small area of playground just across from his house, trying to read messages from its handsome façade: lights in what must be the master bedroom (that most horrible, wounding phrase), or drawn shades. What was meant—by anything?

Just as these days Sage tries to decipher the bruises on Noel's upper arms (he bruises easily, he says, as she does): small round bruises, the size of fingertips. Fingers pressing, in some extreme of passion. Fingers belonging to almost anyone. Or, as Noel says (although she does not exactly ask him), something he bumped into, at a building site.

All of which has led Sage to rephrase an old question: was it in Roland Gallo's case the marriage, and in Noel's the possible involvements with "other women" that she finds so fascinating, so addictive? Roland was quite bald, thick-bodied, middle-aged. An essentially political person, a lawyer, involved in various local money-power structures, mostly big real-estate deals. Not much in common with Sage, intellectually speaking. (A few quite incredible tricks with oral sex, however.) Noel, although undeniably handsome, is not especially "interesting" either, and in sex, she has to admit, he is somewhat passive, a recipient of love.

Sage never gets very far with any of this, only further into her normal anxiety (she knows she's a woman who loves too much, and so what?)—and it gets her, geographically speaking, up to the massive glass doors of Dr. Jim McAndrew's building, which she has just now reached.

Their embrace at greeting, Sage and Jim's, is always faintly indecisive, and there is awkwardness over kissing: cheeks, never mouths are aimed for, but sometimes it all goes wrong and mouths do brush, accidentally. Rather than hugging, they sometimes grip each other's shoulders.

And then the ritual comments on each other's perceived condition:

"You look—"

"—great! thin!"

"—a little tired?"

"—really rested!"

Jim in fact looks worse than tired, he looks gray, and exhausted. And too thin, he has suffered the sort of weight loss that withers the skin. However, apparently aware of his effect, he quickly explains, "This great new diet. I know, too fast. I'd never let a patient do this, but I feel really great."

"You doctors are such jerks about your own health."

Jim laughs, acknowledging accuracy. "Of course we are, we think we can fix anything, including ourselves." And then, "But how're you? Still madly in love with that Noel, despite being married to him?" This is an old semi-joke between them: Jim believes that marriages have ruined his love affairs. All two of them; there has only been one wife since Caroline.

"Oh, I guess I am. For all the good that does me," Sage tells him.

"Well, sit down over here by the window. The view may do you some good."

And here we are again, Sage reflects, looking out at the same high green park that Caroline's house also faces, from another angle. And she and Jim are returned to their old roles; he is doctor-omnipotent, super-dad, with a small New England shading of irony. And Sage, with Jim, feels herself young and sad and bewildered, but at the same time she is a sort of wise-ass, with Jim.

She never tries to explain that sadness to Jim, though. She never says, Noel worries me a lot, I never know where I am, with him. My work isn't going very well. I never have any money, and I'm tired.

But it seems today that Jim really wants to talk to her.

And he starts right out. "I've been in this, uh, situation. This *girl,* Lord, she's younger than Jill." (Amazing that anyone could be younger than his youngest daughter, Jim's tone seems to say. Much less a girl with whom he has a romantic connection, or whatever.) "Well, I guess you could say I loved her, I was crazy about her, I have to admit it. I even thought, A new family. Hey, why not? A lot of guys my age do it, and I'd read these articles, and some of my patients, they go on about their biological clocks. Girls wanting babies. But she saw a lot of reasons why not, as things turned out, and it wasn't just my age. For one thing she doesn't like doctors. Gosh, I thought everyone loved doctors." (This is only half ironic). "For another thing she has this really pathological obsession about AIDS. No new relationship for her, she says."

Jim talks on and on, a boyish man in his early sixties, in the throes of an obsessional love. Sage's glance and her attention wander out to the terraced park, the dark swaying pines and redwoods, the eucalyptus. And she thinks of the time when she walked through that park in black blind mourning for Roland Gallo, who was only a few blocks away, but could not see her. As Jim has no doubt walked along those same paths.

She listens enough to grasp the essence of his story, though: a rational, older-than-middle-aged man, a doctor, a "success," is having a sort of semi-breakdown all over this thin, thin girl ("I even worried that she could be anorexic, I cared that much about her, wanted to run some tests"). This girl, who, like his youngest daughter, Jill, is also a big success, another lawyer, is clearly quite uninterested in him, in Dr. James McAndrew. Refusing sex, refusing finally to see him. So that Jim indeed went a little crazy, walking around on upper Grant, where she lived. And calling, calling, leaving messages on her machine. "I even fell in love with her answering machine," is Jim's small joke.

During the Sixties, when so many middle-aged men, Jim's-age men, were growing beards, buying turtlenecks and Nehru jackets, taking off after young girls, Jim was a stalwart, only mildly liberal husband and father, in clothes from Brooks. And that period was the nadir of his relationship with Sage, who was actively demonstrating for Free Speech, the People's Park, and was totally committed to the Anti-War Movement. "It's your methods, that's all I disagree with," Jim used (not quite truthfully) to complain. "You mean you think we're vulgar? Noisy? Well, you're fucking right, we are," Sage would cry back.

What he is going through now could be called a delayed mid-life crisis, then, Sage thinks. Apparently men can have them at any time, and repeatedly.

But why are you telling me all this? she also thinks, observing his pale bony high-browed familiar face (so similar and yet so much more distinguished than the smaller faces of his daughters, Sage believes). I am not in sufficiently good shape myself to hear so much of your nutty obsession, she thinks. And the real problem is that you old guys are just not used to being turned down, you've had it your way forever, all you middle-aged establishment successes. Young girls all tumbling into your tired old beds.

At the same time she knows she is being both selfish and unfair; for one thing, Jim has never been "promiscuous" in the sense that she thinks Roland is—fears that Noel is—and an impulse urges her to go over to Jim, to cradle him in her arms with murmurs of reassurance, of ultimate love. And then, as in Sage's childhood dreams, could the two of them run off somewhere together? Could they live happily and sexily ever after? Sage often believes that they could, if things were ever so slightly changed, changes that she cannot exactly specify.

"I've even thought of going to a shrink," Jim more or less finishes, running nervous medical fingers through his fair graying thinning hair.

"That wouldn't be the worst idea."

"I guess not to my son-in-law, though."

"Saul could recommend someone."

"I wonder if Caroline would see me," Jim muses.

"It's not quite the same thing."

Sensing a small joke, Jim laughs a little. "Don't think I don't know how trite all this is," he tells her. "If one of my patients told me this story, it'd be very hard not to laugh."

"Why don't you try laughing, then?"

He frowns. "Laughing? That nonsense? But I'm not sick."

"No, I mean pretending you're a patient. Your own patient."

"Oh. Well." The frown deepens as he tries to puzzle it out. "I sort of see what you mean." He brightens a little. "Matter of fact, a patient was telling me her story yesterday, very sad, mixed up with an alcoholic, and heaven knows I didn't laugh."

"Of course not," Sage reassures him.

Jim grins. "She wouldn't believe me when I told her how old I am. But I'm always very open about that. I just tell them right out."

Sage has been hearing this particular little vignette from Jim, the telling of his age, on most of the occasions that they have recently seen each other, she now reflects: the patient who cannot believe Jim's so readily admitted age. And for a crucial moment she now wonders: could he have misinterpreted all around—are they in fact surprised that he is not older than he says?

On the way over to Jim's, Sage now realizes, she had wanted to talk about Noel. She wanted from Jim the magic, impossible words: No, of course Noel isn't seeing anyone else, you're just very insecure, you're too used to trouble, when it isn't there you make it up (true enough). Or, she had wanted some large and quite "inappropriate" dosage of love from Jim.

"How about a drink?" he now asks her. "What a lousy host I am, I go on and on about myself and leave you high and dry."

There is so much truth to this—and a drink is so much *not* what she wants—that Sage begins to laugh. She laughs and laughs, bending over as she sits there, then cuts off as she feels her laughter out of control, she could as easily cry.

"Actually I have to get home now," she tells Jim, when she can. "I want to get a little work done before dinner."

"Work? But it's Sunday. Don't you know there's a name for people like you?" Somewhat heavily he chides her.

"I like to work, it's when I know who I am," Sage tells him.

"Well, I guess I'm rather like that too. I should stick to medicine, I do best at being a doctor. In fact Caroline said that to me rather often. Only very tactfully of course."

"Of course," Sage echoes.

By now they both have risen and are walking toward the entranceway. Where they repeat their small non-embrace routine. Affectionately.

"Well, I'm really glad you came by. You always do me good," Jim tells her.

"Oh, me too," Sage lies.

Driving home, passing Presbyterian Hospital, Sage thinks briefly of the years of her grandmother's dying there. Molly Blair, all shrunken and dying forever, and Caroline going to see her every day. Caroline brushing Molly's thin yellowed hair, and taking home Molly's hand-made silk nightclothes to wash by hand and to iron. (Sage, who hates to iron, was especially touched by this detail.) And Sage, visiting, would silently, secretly exhort her grandmother to die. She used to wonder if Caroline ever felt the same. She must have, mustn't she? Must have longed for her mother to die? But if so no one ever knew.

The house now occupied by Sage and Noel, bought by Sage with her inheritance from Molly Blair, is at the end of a small cul-de-sac on the eastern, "wrong" side of Russian Hill, a neighborhood once cheaply inhabited by working-class Italians, now very expensive, mostly occupied by Chinese, Vietnamese, Cambodian families who double or triple up, in the tiny rooms of those houses.

Sage and Noel's is a large two-story stucco box with an entirely undistinguished exterior, a sort of disguise, Sage sometimes feels the outside of their house to be. While inside Noel has performed miracles (or, almost performed; he tends to leave things unfinished): walls knocked out so that what had been a warren of tiny rooms now contains essentially one room per floor. Downstairs, a living-dining room; upstairs, big bedroom and bath. Everywhere large white spaces. Scant furniture, good Oriental rugs.

And that is how they first met, Sage and Noel. He was the carpenter whom a painter friend recommended to help her with her new house. "He's sort of offbeat, you'll like him. Very talented, good ideas. And fabulous-looking." Thinking that she did not especially need a fabulous-looking carpenter, Sage nevertheless called this Noel Finn and Noel came over, came over again for more talk, and plans. And then wine, excitement, more plans and eventually love, or something like it.

And now they are married, and the house is still unfinished, its suspended quality still (sometimes) afflicting Sage with gloom: Why must their house be so perfectly an expression of their life? she wonders. And she answers her own question: Because this house is Noel's work, he made it this way.

The small panel on her answering machine shows a bright-green 2. Two messages, one surely from Noel, with excuses.

Sage pushes Play, and instantly she hears loud sounds, banging, background shouts and then Noel's clear voice: "For Christ's sake, Bill, you fucker, cut that out, I'm on the phone." And then, "Sorry, babe, my asshole partner's deaf. And look, I'm sorry I missed the lunch, but we're really going at it down here. Got to go now, it's going great! See you later."

Oh, so he really is at work, is what Sage thinks. And then, How terrible that I should be pleased by the mere fact that he isn't lying.

The next message is fairly long, and entirely unexpected.

"Sage Levine? Jack Cronin. You won't remember but I'm the guy who bought that little woman-holding-cat figure from your show at that place down on Union Street?" (Sage does remember, it was her only sale from that show.) "Anyway, I'm in New York, and a friend of mine saw it and went a little nuts, I mean he really liked it, and guess what? He has a gallery down on Broome, in SoHo. So, do you have some slides? Would you be interested in something back here, and if so would you call him tomorrow? Calvin Crome," and he left a number.

Sage has been a ceramic sculptor for about fifteen years by now, and she has considerable dark knowledge of the probabilities of success in her field (she knows about the art world in the meticulous way that a jealous lover knows the faithless habits of his beloved). Still, despite all that information, her blood leaps at this message, this possibility of a New York show—and the woman whose face she sees in the mirror above the phone table, the woman holding the phone, is grinning, a bright grin that seems to cover her face.

And even with such a grin this woman, Sage, looks very pretty, she has to admit this of herself. She looks like a happy, very pretty woman.

"Baby, that's great, that's *great.*" Noel hugs her to his chest, but the face that Sage now sees mirrored, Noel's face, is frowning, preoccupied. He came up to the bedroom, where she has remained since the phone call, where she has been sitting and thinking, daring to imagine: a New York gallery. And so as she went to greet him, to tell him, and as Noel embraces her she can see the two of them mirrored there. And at his slight frown her elated spirits sink, just a little.

She asks, "But you don't think it's necessarily so great?"

He touches her hair very lightly, quickly. "Well, maybe not." He laughs, a light quick laugh. "But don't take me so seriously, babe. After all, what do I know?"

Noel's very dark hair is longer than men are generally wearing their hair that year, and his skin is very white and fine. His nose is narrow, finely molded, eyes narrow and gold. A Renaissance face, Sage thought, when they first met. The face of a Medici prince—a description that pleased him a lot, early on, that made him laugh with pleasure.

Actually they look quite a bit alike, Sage and Noel. Others (her sisters) have said this, and at certain times even Sage can see it, but she would not say this to Noel. He does not even like it when Sage has borrowed and worn a shirt or sweater of his (she no longer does this, ever), although they are very close to the same size. A small, slight man, Noel is even thinner, narrower than Sage is, a new experience for her: she has generally loved very large men. Roland Gallo is large, and so is Jim McAndrew.

"You're right," Sage now tells Noel. "I know I'm grasping at straws. Leaping for them in fact. But. Well. You know."

"I sure do." He gazes at her, but dreamily, his gaze somehow abstract. And then, returning to her, he advises, "Well, get some slides together, send them off. Why not? What've you got to lose?"

Sage smiles, feeling the melancholy of her face. "Not a hell of a lot, I guess."

Three

"Oh! Oh—good!" Saul breathes out, as he always does, as he comes. His words are slightly muffled in Liza's hair, as was her outcry a minute before: their middle child is uncannily alert to sexual sounds. "You're beautiful," Saul now whispers to Liza's ear, so that she makes a small half-laughing sound of pure pleasure. "I love you," she whispers.

Removing himself from her body, Saul now stretches beside her, his hard bones and tight skin against her much softer, very ample flesh. I am perfect for Saul, Liza has sometimes thought and sometimes said to him; a thinner woman with Saul would be a mass of bruises.

Liza pulls the covers up over them both. The fog has come in, a cold night succeeding the hot, hot April day. She should get up and see that the children are covered too, Liza thinks, but maybe she doesn't have to, actually? She wants so badly just to lie there next to Saul, savoring sated flesh. To lie in peace.

In the late Sixties, the years of her own late teens, Liza appeared to be the essential Flower Child, plump and blonde, streamy-haired, braless, in her bedspread or Indian-looking flowered fabrics. She was often half stoned on grass, and in a feckless, affectionate way she made love a lot, as everyone was enjoined to do, back then. With a lot of long-haired boys, who often gave her flowers to wear.

And then, one day in Presbyterian Hospital, where Liza was visiting her endlessly dying grandmother, Molly Blair, an intern came in to check on Molly (who usually gave him hell). Saul Jacobs, who took one look at Liza and had to have her, he was instantly crazy about her and not only that—he took her seriously, he insisted on marriage and began at once to talk about having children.

Even Caroline, who had done more or less the same, married impulsively not once but twice (Jim, whom she now regarded as in most ways an error, had been the single reasoned choice)—Caroline nevertheless thought this was a bad idea. "My darling, you're so young, and you don't have any money. It'll be really tough, these days, the expensive seventies. Are you really sure you want children?"

Liza laughed. "Didn't you want us?"

"Well, once I had you I did."

And so everyone who thought it would not work out was wrong, for the most part. And the parts of the marriage that worked less well were known only to Liza, who never spoke of them, not to anyone.

"If we didn't have children we could do a lot more screwing," Saul now whispers.

"We do quite a lot, don't you think?"

"Not as much as I want to."

"Me neither."

"We'll have to get away for at least a weekend this summer. Carmel or Tahoe, somewhere like that."

"Yes." But Liza knows perfectly well that this will not happen, something else will take precedence. Saul's patients. The children.

However, raising himself on one elbow to look down at Liza, Saul now says, "I mean it. Let's make a definite plan. Commit ourselves to a place for five or six days anyway. Pay for it ahead, so there'll be a penalty if we don't go." He laughs a little as he says this, knowing that Liza thinks him a little, well, thrifty, as she herself might tactfully put it. While he finds her, of course, a wild-handed spendthrift.

"Listen, I'm going to hold you to that, you'll be sorry," she tells him.

As she says this Liza sees a huge low motel bed, heavy draperies covering long windows, so that it really doesn't matter where you are; the point is, you can sleep as long as you like. That is Liza's idea of a wonderful trip away, she realizes, lots of sleep. She loves making love with Saul, he is better at it than anyone, more generous, imaginative and patient (she thinks his cock is very beautiful). That was why she married him, mostly: for great sex. But she has had enough sex in her life, she thinks, she really has. After all those years of marriage they still make love at least four or five times a week, but she needs more sleep; she is almost asleep right now. How nice of the children to let her sleep. How good of Saul.

In her dream, though, a hand is caressing her breast, and a voice murmurs near her ear, "So beautiful—"

She is not asleep, not dreaming, and Saul is whispering, "Why not? Couldn't you? Come on, lovely Liza, just turn over. A little variety will wake you up."

Turning, sleepily aware of at least a little response, some rush of warm blood to all the usual places, as she reaches back to touch Saul, Liza next hears a small voice from the doorway, inquiring, "Mommy, are you and Daddy planning to talk all night?"

"Damn," Saul mutters, flopping back, as Liza, turning again, holds her arm out to her child. "No, darling, and you're supposed to be asleep."

Although only two years older than Liza, Saul was married once before. And during all that time of Liza's feckless love affairs, and flowers and dope and hikes on Mt. Tamalpais, Saul was a serious medical student, who had married a very young nurse, the first woman who let him make love to her, and unhappily for them both she did not take to the experience. Not at all.

Saul's next sexual encounter was with Liza (he and the nurse had just separated when he wandered into the room of the cross old actress Ms. Molly Blair and found beautiful Liza), and from then on, as far as Saul was concerned, Liza *was* sexuality. She was his blonde erotic goddess, his muse. He had, indeed, certain objections to her character: Liza tended (as her mother did) to messiness; she was disorganized, often late and often extravagant. But none of that mattered, really, to Saul; he placed infinite and grateful value on their shared sexual life, and he also valued Liza's kindness, her considerable intelligence, her general good humor with the children, as well as with himself. In his own view, Saul is a difficult, somewhat problematic person.

Even Saul's sexual fantasies center around Liza; other women do not occur to him, in that way. And this fact, this sexual single-mindedness of Saul's, can be observed: Liza's jealous sisters, especially Fiona and Jill, and Sage, with a thrust of pain as she thinks of bad Roland, of wandering Noel, all those women took note of Saul's "pathological monogamy" (their phrase). "If anyone strayed from that ménage it'd have to be Liza," they have speculated, and they look for signs that she might.

"But she's probably too fat," Fiona and Jill have concluded.

Caroline too has taken note of Saul as a dedicated husband, and remarked to Ralph, "How wrong I was to urge those kids not to get married. You see? When I'm wrong I'm really wrong."

Liza's days, these days, are often spent down at the playground (across from Roland Gallo's house). She takes the baby and the middle child there, the older one being in nursery school, as next year this barely steady two-year-old will be.

And that playground and park, for Sage the scene of such lonely, jealous anxiety, for Liza is filled with happy nostalgia. "Let's go down to J.K. and turn on," the kids used to say, after school—and then they would, ambling or sometimes running down the hill to the park, Julius Kahn Playground, and to some special places off in the woods, the cypress groves. Someone always had some joints, several people had transistors, and they were all off and away, sucking down smoke and laughing and floating, off into the sky with Lucy, with diamonds.

Liza liked all that a lot. She liked her friends and the dope and the music, she felt perfectly happy then. In a permanent way she is crazy about that park.

She especially loved making out, making love with those boys, almost all of them, at one time or another.

Sitting now on the hard green bench, as her small child pushes a dump truck through some sand in the sandbox, Liza sighs for those years. It is not so far back, really, but so passed, now so totally gone, swallowed by the strange Nixonian Seventies, and now the awful Eighties.

And then she thinks, If I'm pregnant now I don't know what I'll do. (With Liza this is a frequent concern.) Could she have an abortion without telling Saul? And if not why not? Because it's his child too, that would be one reason why. But I cannot have four children in this rotten, rotting world, thinks Liza.

"Well, Liza, hi!" A white-blonde young woman, about Liza's age, with a child the age of Liza's sandbox child now sits down on the bench beside her, all bright smiles, as her child, a little girl, stumbles into the sand, down to Liza's child, a boy. *"Good* to see you again," says this woman, all teeth, all enthusiasm.

"Oh, good to see you!" But Liza is unable to remember this woman's name, or where they met. Some cocktail party, she thinks, and now she does remember: it was the sort of party that she and Saul never go to but this time for some reason they had to, and there was this woman, who said, when introduced to Liza (who has kept her own name—she has her own plans, for her name): "Are you by any chance related to Fiona McAndrew? The Fiona of Fiona's? Oh, her sister? How marvellous! Such a rich famous successful sister! How exciting!"

Well, small wonder that Liza could not recall her name.

"Isn't it funny, I thought of you this very morning," this Joanne now tells Liza. "We're going to Fiona's tonight, and I'm so excited! Do you think we'll see her there? Will I know her, does she look a lot like you?"

"I honestly don't know," says Liza—a covering answer. And then, "She's quite a lot thinner than I am."

"In her business? Wow, she must really work at it."

"I suppose she does."

This exchange of inanities could go on all day, Liza thinks, or for several days, except that the two small children just then begin to scream. One has thrown sand at the other, now both are throwing sand and screaming, eyes and noses wet, baby voices hoarse with passion.

"Oh shit," says Joanne. (To Liza, her most sympathetic utterance so far.) "I'll have to take her home to change, we're on our way to Roland's mom's. Lucky for me we live right over there."

Thus reminded, Liza now recalls that Joanne indeed is married to nefarious Roland, Sage's once-lover. Roland left the wife to whom he was married in Sage's time to marry this Joanne, to marry Joanne instead of Sage. Joanne, even younger than Sage, and so stupid— further cause for chagrin.

Watching silly Joanne as she plucks the child, now calmer, up from the sandbox, saying goodby and watching as Joanne starts off across the grass toward her splendid house, Liza remembers all that her sister suffered on infamous Roland's account, and she feels a renewal of that old rage as she further thinks, What a total jerk, choosing that dopey woman over beautiful talented Sage. And not quite consistently she also thinks, How lucky after all that he didn't marry Sage. And she adds, Noel's quite bad enough.

"San Francisco is the smallest town I've ever been in," is a frequent remark of Caroline's, and one that her daughters have sometimes put down to sheer snobbery, shades of English Molly. However, in one way or another, from time to time, they all come to agree with her, more or less. Particularly, Liza now thinks, when faced with coincidences of this very small-town nature: running into Joanne Gallo in the park, on the day when Joanne is going to Fiona's.

"I'm the non-achieving sister," Liza has had occasion to remark, though perhaps it is she herself who has created these occasions, through a bad habit of self-depreciation.

The usual rejoinder is, "Oh, but you have those great kids, and a really nice husband; in fact he's great, and attractive."

And all of that is perfectly true, Liza knows very well. And yet, and yet, these days it is simply not enough. Now women are supposed to have a great husband and children and run several corporations; be good at Leveraged Buy-Outs or design marvellous post-modern houses. Or run for public office. Or maybe all of those somehow at once. Not to mention being very thin and aerobically fit, a memorable cook-hostess-decorator. And fabulous in bed, multiorgasmic and tender and demanding, all at once.

"It's like the Fifties in spades," Caroline has remarked, of the present decade. "Only then we didn't have to have careers as well. We were just supposed to make all our own curtains and iron a lot of shirts, and do what people back then called 'gourmet cooking.' You know, all that cream-enrichment business that now you're not supposed to do at all."

Liza thinks her mother is quite right (as usual). Too much indeed is asked of women now. And men are not helping as much as they think they are, even Saul is not. And she, Liza, is asking too much of herself. Probably. Nevertheless.

The fantasy with which Liza comforts herself for this perceived underachievement of her own is that in another five years, say, when she will be just forty, and all three kids will be in school, then she will write a novel. And then more novels. Liza McAndrew, a novelist.

In the meantime she reads, and reads, and reads, her taste running generally to heavy Victorians, Mrs. Gaskell and Gissing and Trollope, Dickens—and, further down the line, Henry James and Edith Wharton, Elizabeth Bowen—and of course Virginia Woolf.

She keeps a notebook in which she writes every day. And this is a secret from Saul, one of her few: if he knew that she kept some sort of secret journal, he might suspect that she wrote about him, which, meticulously if for the most part lovingly, she does. She writes about everything, her mother and sisters, her father and his girlfriends, her stepfather. Her sisters' husbands and lovers, and their work, their successes (Fiona, Jill), or unsuccesses (Sage, so far, and Portia). Her friends.

Also, in an acerbic, occasionally mean-spirited way that would probably have surprised anyone who knew her, Liza writes about the current San Francisco literary scene. "Such as it is," as Liza herself might put it. She has found it interesting, for example, to note that the local writers, all male, who were so prominently billed as such ("LOCAL NOVELISTS X AND Y") in the Sixties, early Seventies—those who at that time spent all their days at Enrico's Coffee House (always hard to imagine when they wrote), now seemed to a great extent to have faded away. Their books if published at all do badly, are even ridiculed as sexist, macho stuff.

But Liza wonders: are these valid critical or even novelistic observations, or is she simply mean and envious, even of those old has-been writers? of anyone, in fact, who has published.

She thinks continuously, though, of her own novels, a long bright row of them, all fat and heavy and deeply satisfying. Complex and funny, and beautiful and wise. Books that everyone or almost everyone will love.

In the midst of this fantasy, however, today Liza is struck by the cruel realization that she could quite as easily be imagining children, a row of babies. Plump and handsome, funny and wise, and almost universally loved.

Sighing, Liza thinks, I cannot have four children. I cannot. I want to write.

Looking up from these not entirely encouraging thoughts, Liza sees a thin woman in jeans and a shabby red sweater hurrying toward her, a young woman whose heavy dark hair swings out as she walks, who walks happily. And whom at first, in her own abstraction and confusion, Liza does not recognize as Sage, her own Sage. Her favorite (she sometimes thinks this) sister. Half-sister. It is Sage, looking totally happy (further reason not to recognize her), Sage trying for whatever reason to repress that joy. Or perhaps only trying to calm down.

"Oh, I found you!" Sage sits down on the bench beside Liza, breathing hard, as though she had been running all over the city, looking for Liza.

"Sage, tell me, what on earth?" Liza laughs, and reaches to give Sage's shoulders a light quick hug.

"Well." Sage too laughs, clearly at herself, at her own too-obvious inability to contain this excitement. "Well, I can't even remember if I told you, Noel said not to tell anyone and so maybe I didn't. But I sent some slides to this man in New York, and he called me just now, and he wants to *give me a show!* Isn't that really fantastic? A New York gallery! A show!"

"Oh, Sage, that is so super." But even as her eyes tear over (surely with pleasure for Sage?) Liza hears a new, quite horrible interior voice that says, God, one more sister with some big success out there in the world. And I just keep on being a tired and semi-broke mother who's pregnant, probably. I'll never get to write books, even if I could write, which is dubious.

But, "Sage, that's fabulous," Liza says quite loudly, silencing those other, awful voices with her own actual kindly voice.

And Sage of course hears only the spoken words.

However, strange Sage, who is unpredictable, has already gone off in another direction. More precisely, she has gone backward, in the direction of Roland Gallo. "You know, I still even now think of Roland in this goddam park," she says to Liza. "People don't get over things, really, do they. Even getting this great news, I sort of thought of wanting him to know. That I'm not just the run-down kid radical he used to know."

With these reflections Sage's face has gone from near-ecstasy to a wild black melancholy. Only the intensity is constant.

As Liza thinks, No wonder men find Sage just a little wearing, certainly a man like Roland would have. He probably only meant to have some heavy motel hours with an almost beautiful young girl, whom luckily no one would know. And Sage is probably a little much for poor foolish Noel. Men are not really mad for complexity in women, or big intensity.

She wonders if she should tell Sage that she just saw Roland's dumb blonde wife, the ubiquitous Joanne. And she quickly decides that she absolutely should not, and how mean and stupid of her (of Liza) even to consider telling. Indeed, what sort of person, what sort of sister is she becoming?

Sage has now gone back to her excited, happy phase ("a manic-depressive on a very short cycle," Sage has described herself as being). "I haven't even told Noel this latest, about the show," she says. "Lord, what will he say?" Her eyes glitter, challenging, seeming to dare Noel not to be as happy as she is.

"He'll be so proud," Liza tells her, hoping that this is true.

"You can't tell with Noel," Sage muses. "I can never predict with him."

"That's supposed to make life interesting." This had come out with more irony than Liza intended, and so she adds, "You'll have to go to New York! What fun!"

But just as Liza is thinking how silly that sounded, even how false, Sage has got quickly to her feet again. "I've got to tell Jim," she announces. "It's Wednesday, he just might be at home, don't you think? Before golf."

"I guess."

"Well, *ciao.*" Sage laughs; they both dislike people who say *ciao.* And then she is off, running across the park in the direction of Jim's condominium. Her stepfather, Liza's father, whom Liza almost never sees.

At that moment, for no reason, Liza's child in the sandbox begins to cry. He sits there and screams, his face all red, his eyes and nose streaming.

Going over to pick him up, Liza reflects that this particular child is quite as mercurial as Sage is. She hugs and comforts him, and considers the oddity of genes—odd that a child of hers should be like Sage.

She reflects too on Sage's news, and she tries to imagine this new person, successful Sage. With a gallery in New York, and big sales, maybe.

The small boy in her arms stops crying and nestles his head against her, as Liza thinks, You're only tired, poor baby.

And just then she experiences the sensation for which all that week she has longed: the cramping twist that with her announces the onset of a period. And Liza thinks, Oh, thank God. Now I can write.

Four

For years now Fiona and Jill have begun their days with a phone call, one of them to the other. And who calls whom is not incidental, they both keep track. Promptly at 7 one of them will make the call and they will talk, sometimes for only a couple of minutes, sometimes for half an hour or more. This total accord in habit is possible because of what must be a genetic similarity, both are people who wake up mentally alert but physically very lazy. They are ready for talk, that is, though not for any more demanding activity.

And the topics for discussion have a certain ritualized quality, though neither woman is aware of this. They talk about their older sister, Liza; far more rarely do they mention either half-sister, Sage or Portia, or for that matter their mother, Caroline. They compare the weather from their respective vantage points, Fiona on Potrero Hill, Jill on Telegraph. Mutual friends, new clothes, trip plans, new novels (both are big readers, in fact Caroline and all her daughters read a lot). They ask each other about investments (Fiona asks Jill) and restaurants (vice versa). The fact that they rarely talk about men, romantic attachments and/or sexual ones is interest, in that such matters are or have been of consuming interest to both young women.

Are they now? Fiona at least has wondered.

In any case, the conversation that takes place a few days after the welcome lunch for Caroline and Ralph is fairly typical of their interchange, with some notable exceptions.

. . .

Waking to sunlight—as Fiona likes to point out to people who live in other areas, Potrero gets the first San Francisco sunshine—Fiona's first thought is that Jill should call her; it is her turn, isn't it? didn't she, Fiona, call yesterday? But no, they did not even talk yesterday, Jill had her exercise class, and it was Jill who called the day before. However, at just that moment the phone rings, resolving indecision.

After their usual, quite minimal greetings Jill says, "Do you think she could be pregnant? again?" It is unnecessary to identify the "she"; it almost always means Liza. "Miss Large. Honestly, she'll have to start going to those big-lady stores."

"She's not that fat, she can't be more than a twelve." Defending Liza always gives Fiona a shot of self-approval. "And Saul loves her like that."

"Jewish men, honestly. How do you know he loves her all that much? He may have some anorexic nurse hidden in the linen closet."

They laugh.

"Speaking of anorexia," Jill takes it up again. "Do you think Sage could have it? People can be too thin, and she's living proof."

"I think she just looks tired, she's always been thin." She's no thinner than we are, Fiona does not say.

"That terrible Noel. She seems to have some sort of fix on very dark men, doesn't she? Substitutes for a Jewish father?"

"My, we're being quite racist this morning."

Jill laughs, and insists, "But she does. I keep reading about her old pal Roland Gallo. Do you think he'll run for mayor?"

"I doubt it, he's too sensible."

"There's some heavy money on him."

"Sage could do a Gary Hart number. Come forward as the other woman."

"I think it's a little late for that." Jill sniffs. "He's got that dumb wife, and God knows who else. Better-looking than Sage, though, I'll bet."

Fiona is curious as to why Jill so has it in for Sage this morning, when they rarely speak of her at all, but she decides not to ask.

Instead she throws out, "I think they're coming to the restaurant. The Gallos, I mean. He's not related to Ernest and Julio, is he?"

"It's never been proven. God, Italian men must be worse than Jewish men. Macho crooks."

"Honestly, Jill, I'm glad Caroline and Ralph can't hear you."

"Me too, those old liberals can be pretty vicious. How's the weather over there?"

"Fabulous, absolutely gorgeous."

"Well, it's pretty good here too. Must be some sort of record."

"I guess."

Hanging up a half-minute later, Fiona wonders whatever is eating Jill, why is she so mean about Sage? To Fiona Sage simply seems in many ways an unlucky person. And Jill was down on everyone today. On everything except the weather.

And then Fiona stops thinking about Jill, and begins her own day, which like all her days is to be extremely strenuous. Not as strenuous, though, as when she first began in the restaurant business, when every morning she had to go personally to both the produce market and the flower mart, to get the freshest and best of everything. Now at least other people do all that for her. Still, Fiona works very hard. She does very little but work.

Potrero Hill is actually a cluster of slopes, like most of the hills of San Francisco: Nob, Russian, Telegraph, Pacific Heights, Bernal Heights. And Fiona's house is on one of the highest hills of Potrero. The lower two floors constitute her restaurant, and the kitchen was built into her basement. Fiona lives up above, in what was once an attic, and is now an elaborate decorator-dream of a penthouse, from which she has views of everywhere: both bridges and most of the rest of the city, its other hills. The Mission District, industrial South-of-Market, plus a great deal of the bay, and Berkeley and Oakland. On especially clear days she can see Mt. Diablo, over in Pleasanton—and out to the Farallon Islands.

In 1980, with her share of the Molly Blair money, Fiona bought what was then a very nondescript building. At first she simply rented out some rooms to friends, while she herself and her current lover would sleep in the attic. And then she and one of her friends, having simultaneously lost their downtown receptionist jobs, decided to start serving lunches and dinners in one of the downstairs rooms. She (the friend) loved cooking and had high ambitions in that direction, seeing herself as the newest Alice Waters. Mostly other friends came at first, and some interested locals. The ambitious cook, though, turned out to be possessed of impressive skill and imagination—and Fiona, through a lover in the wholesale grocery business, was well connected with growers in Half Moon Bay and all the way up to Napa.

And word got out. Someone wrote a review, and what came to be known as Fiona's was launched.

Fiona remodelled, she hired more people, she vastly expanded her menu, wisely never letting it get out of hand. Nothing more elaborate than she could cope with. The first cook, the friend, left to start up her own place in Beverly Hills, which did not do so well, but by then Fiona had found someone even better, a bona fide graduate of Chez Panisse.

These days the downstairs is a cluster of smallish, private-seeming rooms, and the basement is a state-of-the-art kitchen. And the attic is Fiona's penthouse, with a sundeck and sauna, hot tub, tiny kitchen and enormous red-tiled bathroom. Hugh bedroom, endless closets.

And those views.

But now in the penthouse there are almost never visiting lovers, any more than downstairs there are live-in friends. Sometimes Fiona feels this lack acutely, both of lovers and of friends. At other times she is simply too busy to notice.

In the hour succeeding her conversation with her sister, Fiona does the following things: aerobics, ten minutes, and isometric facial exercises, five. A shower, blow-drying hair. Doing her face and hands and feet. Two phone calls to New York—one to the editor of a magazine that wants to do a spread on Fiona's; Fiona wants her own favorite photographer, and this conversation ends in a standstill. And, second call, to a woman in Nova Scotia who grows chanterelles, and freezes them.

Then, in clean jeans and a red silk T-shirt, long hair tied back, Fiona goes downstairs to the kitchen, where the produce is being delivered, along with the flowers. And both are being checked over by Stevie, an apprentice chef, an all-around help (and, a fact that Fiona tends to forget, an investor in her business).

"Foxgloves!" is Fiona's shouted greeting to Stevie. "Give me a break!"

"But imposing. And scrutinize that purple. The depths." Stevie, a tall, heavy, long-haired blond young man (not so young, actually: he and Sage were Sixties radicals together, another fact that Fiona tends to forget)—Stevie sometimes talks in this campy way, Fiona has no idea why. He could be gay but she doesn't really think so; if he were he wouldn't talk like that, probably. Although it is clear that a couple of waiters have big crushes on Stevie.

And as usual he is right about the flowers, they look great. The purple is deep.

"Shit, you're right," Fiona tells him as with the slightest smile Stevie turns and walks off between the crates of baby lettuce, from Sonoma.

What a shapely ass, Fiona thinks. Well, how about Stevie?

And then she forgets about Stevie, and on the whole forgets sex for the rest of the day.

She eats some yogurt and granola, she drinks two cups of herbal tea.

In the restaurant area she confers with the bookkeeper, then checks the day's menu, and the evening's reservations.

Roland Gallo. Two, at 9.

For several reasons Fiona has been highly aware of this particular entry, this reservation. First, of course, she noticed because of Sage's awful old love affair, of which all her family eventually became aware; they all, in one way or another, have followed the career of Roland Gallo with more than passing interest.

Additionally, for Fiona, the very making of the reservation was odd: she took the call herself, for the very simple and stupid reason that she was passing the phone when it rang and inexplicably, inexcusably, no one else was near it ("Can't someone answer the fucking phone?"). And so, of course, in the voice of some underling, not "Fiona," Fiona answered the phone. And she had a very strange, strong sense that the person on the other end, the person billing himself as Roland Gallo's assistant, was in fact Roland Gallo himself—or else maybe a complete impostor: it is possible that no one will show, that happens, and you can't ask "Roland Gallo" to reconfirm. In any case it was a very odd exchange, enough to make Fiona seriously wonder for at least a full minute what will happen at 9 tonight. If anything.

The rest of the reservations are more or less routine, the usual mix of people whom Fiona knows or whose names she recognizes. Quite a few regulars, including some hard-core patrons who are there a couple of times a week. (This is a pattern that Fiona knows from experience won't last: the group will move on almost in a body to whatever is trendiest next, and go there twice a week. Fiona is perfectly prepared for these predictable defections, she tells herself.)

As always, there are several people on the list whom Fiona has never heard of, although it always pays to check very carefully, just in case she should have heard of them. Some hot New York playwright, for instance, whose fame has not yet travelled across the Rockies. But the truly unknown have usually reserved a long time in advance; right there is a tipoff to their lack of fame.

Fiona's office is strictly speaking not that at all. Her big desk and most of her files are up in the penthouse, in fact in her bedroom, discreetly hidden. However, the smallest downstairs dining room, the one requested for most private dinners (the one that Roland Gallo has requested for tonight), this pretty pink-toile room is preferred by Fiona herself and by her staff as Fiona's office, and it is there that she receives certain business callers, has certain appointments.

This afternoon there are two such: the first with her lawyer, the second with a young woman who wants an interview, Fiona has forgotten for what, and she can't for the moment find wherever she wrote it down.

Actually the young man who arrives very promptly at 2 is not Fiona's lawyer but an associate from that law office. The young man is lean and tan, obviously a tennis-playing type, in his new Wilkes suit and with his too-new Mark Cross brief case (not much imagination working there). He wants to talk about a new restaurant that just started up in Petaluma, and it is called Fiona's. Of all the unlikely names to find duplicated in Petaluma, as the lawyer remarks.

He goes on about this at some length. Petaluma Fiona's is also in an old house, several stories divided into small rooms. Kitchen in the basement. He quotes some specialties from both menus— similar use of goat cheese, radicchio, chanterelles, monkfish and yellow peppers. Pausing, he laughs. "And that Fiona is even a tall thin blonde with very long hair."

"Unlike any other thirty-three-year-old women in northern California," Fiona cannot resist saying. "In the middle Eighties."

Only slightly abashed, the young man then delivers his punchline, or, rather, his punch paragraph. It is fairly long.

There was such a case quite recently, he tells Fiona. A restaurant opened up down in San Bruno, called The Nob Hill. ("Pretty funny right off, don't you think? The Nob Hill, in San Bruno?") Named of course after the one and only San Francisco restaurant, The Nob Hill. Well, those guys apologized all over the place, offered to change the name, et cetera. But Roland Gallo would not let them off the hook, he kept right after them, and he came up with a very high five-figure settlement.

"Hey, why not six?" asks Fiona.

"Well, even R.G.'s got his limits, I guess."

There is a pause, during which Fiona is staring out the window as though coming to a decision. This small room faces east, and its eastern wall is all glass, a French door leading out to a miniature herb garden, and so what Fiona sees beyond the garden is the shining dark slate of the San Francisco Bay, boats, tankers and big white container ships—and the shining windows of Oakland. She could buy a boat, Fiona thinks, a nice big boat but still small enough for exploring, up the secret inlets of the bay and far up into the delta. Christ, she could live on her boat. She does not have to do all this stuff that she does.

"Would you believe," she then says to the young apprentice lawyer, who is smiling expectantly in her direction, "that I don't give a flying fuck what that dago pig Roland Gallo does?" Fiona had no idea that she was going to say that.

After an instant he recovers. "May I quote you on that?"

"You do and I'll sue, I'll have you out looking for work." And she adds, "And tell Stanley to stop hustling me, okay?" Stanley being the main lawyer, who wishes that Fiona would lead a more active legal life.

"You must be the thousandth person to ask me that question. I'm thin because I'm thin. I do not suffer from anorexia or bulimia—is that what you wanted to ask me? I am simply a very thin person. My two younger sisters are even thinner than I am. I eat quite a lot, in fact I eat all day. I love my own food very much. Obviously I would not spend my entire day doing what I do if I didn't like food, would I.

"But no, if that's what you want to hear, I do not have any special tricks for maintaining thin. I don't have a trainer or anything like that. I don't go to a gym or an exercise class, I don't have time.

"I eat quite sensibly and I walk a lot. I don't eat junk, not ever. I like wine but I'm not a big drinker. I only eat and drink what's extremely good, which is what I get here. And if you want my secret there it is, eat only the best."

The interviewer, who is quite as thin and stylish and even as blonde as Fiona herself, just sits there for a minute, in the pretty bleached-and-carved French chair that is so very good with all the toile. She sits there, in her smart brown linen clothes, her dark patterned hose and excellent shoes, she sits as though unable to believe what she has heard.

She smiles, and in a perfectly natural voice she says to Fiona, "Well, Ms. McAndrew, thank you very much." And in a deliberate way she gets her things together, gets up and walks out. Saunters out, actually.

Very strange, but on the whole Fiona feels better. So good, when you finally get to say what has been on your mind. So good for you; at least in theory.

Later that afternoon, taking a long walk around her neighborhood, Fiona notes and considers its changing character: Some small new shops, nothing spectacular, nothing that anyone would term a smart boutique, just some nice little stores. And a couple of newish restaurants, on more or less the same order (Fiona already knew about these restaurants, of course; she keeps track). Nothing that anyone in her right mind would call a threat to Fiona's. But still, Fiona views these small changes as harbingers of much larger future change. Potrero could become another Union Street, and look what's happening out on Sacramento Street, and even on Clement, not to mention the Oriental rape of North Beach. It is simply a question of the time frame involved, Fiona concludes, and she will have to try to figure out just how much time Potrero Hill has left. Like a doctor with a very old patient.

Which reminds her that she has not seen or talked to her own father, to Jim McAndrew, for quite a while.

And then she wonders: Could Jill possibly be so down on Sage because Sage is and always has been so very (so curiously) close to Jim? Is Jill jealous of Sage, because of Jim? Fiona doubts it, Jill is silly but not that silly, nor that hung up on her father.

Fiona is actually present during most of the dinner hours at Fiona's, on almost every night, five days out of the six they are open (the dark night is Monday). She manages, though, to make her presence there as unobtrusive as possible; it is not clear to anyone, not even to Fiona herself, just how this is achieved. For starters, she dresses quietly, usually in black or dark brown, with good safe jewelry. She looks very much like one of her own customers, and she is often mistaken for such, or for a hired hostess, by those who don't know her. Which is part of her intention.

And she moves about in a certain way. Never too fast, or too purposefully. She appears to wander, she could be just some woman in search of the ladies' room.

Because of the restaurant's reputation, and perhaps even more because of the worshipful regard in which food and wine, and food-and winesmanship are held in the Eighties, many of Fiona's customers seem to feel it necessary to make it clear that they too are highly knowledgeable in these areas. They've been boning up, they too know almost all about vintages and regions, about oils and lettuces, baby eels and special Wyoming cheese and Oregon pomegranates.

What these experts do not know is the contempt in which their semi-invisible hostess holds both them and all their information.

Watching one such couple tonight, as they ponder the wine list and get into a big discussion—"Won't a Beaujolais be a little ebullient with the salmon, or will it? I've heard the '85 is fairly docile"— Fiona would like to say to them, Have you dumb schmucks ever tried reading anything? Ever thought of brushing up on your Bach? And have you ever looked, really looked, at a non-balletic Degas?

But she obviously cannot say any of that to these people, to this feeble-chinned young man with his Talbot-catalogue girlfriend. For one thing, she has already sounded off enough for one day. And for another, she could be wrong: these two could both be full professors at Stanford, or Berkeley. For all she knows.

Roland Gallo's silly wife is sitting there crying her eyes out—more literally, she is crying her makeup off—in their private dining room, the room that earlier served as Fiona's study. Walking slowly past their door, Fiona looks in, then tries to pretend not to see, as she is all along pretending not to be Fiona.

She has never actually met Roland Gallo. Would he know her? Probably, somehow. There have been pictures of her, along with articles. Just as she would know him, anywhere.

It is now a little past 11, and the two Gallos have finished off three bottles of wine: a split of Dom Pérignon, a full bottle of white burgundy, a Montrachet. They are now both sniffing from big snifters of brandy, which is enough to make anyone cry, probably, after all that wine.

Once past their doorway—but not before her eyes met those of Roland Gallo, for one split second—Fiona quickens her pace. What flashy eyes that man has. So dark, and bright. Alive.

In another, larger room a dinner party for ten is still going on. And in another, empty tables are being cleared, as two good-looking middle-aged women continue their conversation, oblivious to the busboy. They look very happy, and very successful: Fiona wonders, should she have recognized them? In any case, too late now.

Fiona continues to the bar, a small dark-panelled room, with the requisite black leather chairs, the abundance of chrome and glass. Two young busboys whom Fiona understands to be in love are clearing up, one polishing glasses while the other attends to the chrome. They are both very small and dark—really sweet, thinks Fiona.

She is suddenly exhausted, and why? This was no different from any other day, or evening. Sliding into a chair, she slips her feet from their high black sandals, and closes her eyes.

"Well, this is the first piece of luck I've had all day." Roland Gallo (of course) has said this, he has sneaked in and sat down on the chair next to hers. And as Fiona opens her eyes quite wide, feigning surprise, at the same time she admits to herself that she knew he would follow her in there. Of course he would.

She says, "Please go away, I'm very tired. I'm resting." But she doesn't close her eyes again.

He must at some time have been extremely good-looking, even too handsome; God knows he is very attractive, still—and he clearly knows this, although he is perfectly, shiningly bald. But his high white brow, strong nose and fine mouth are impressive, and especially those eyes, deepset and wide apart, and so dark, so extremely, flashingly dark.

Right now he is fairly drunk, but still controlled. "I just want to know one thing," he says to Fiona, with a small twist of a smile that involves just the corners of his mouth. "Can you tell me why I didn't marry your sister instead of Miss Dumb Blonde Twat?"

"That's disgusting," Fiona tells him. "Disgusting. Your wife. I think you're too drunk to drive," Fiona tells him, although this is probably not the literal truth; he will get home all right, he is the kind who always will, and if he gets a ticket he can fix it.

"I'm sure you're right, but I'm going to drive home anyway." He smiles again, as he stands up. "Well, Miss McAndrew, I thank you for an exceptionally lovely evening."

"Oh, get lost," Fiona tells him.

Roland Gallo laughs, and then he bows, just managing the gesture. "I'll see you very soon," is his exit line.

After which, for the very first time that day, Fiona smiles.

Five

"How much money do you have, anyway?" the voice on the phone asks Jill.

And Jill, who is lying in bed, begins to laugh into the phone, at this serious, outrageous question. Still laughing, she holds the receiver away from her mouth for a moment, looking out into the darkened corners of her bedroom, as though at least some answer might be out there. It is almost midnight. A window across the room, her most westward window, is a few inches open; from down on the bay she can hear the faint short barks of the sea lions, and the longer, louder foghorns' moan.

She brings the receiver back to her mouth. "That depends on what day it is," she says into the phone.

"You mean you're richer on Wednesdays than on Thursdays?"

"No, stupid. The market. Don't you have any real money at all?"

"No, I'm very poor, I keep telling you. That's why I like rich girls." A pause, and then he says, "Now tell me what you have on."

"Well." Jill, who is naked, hesitates. "It's quite a fabulous gown, actually. Very pale pink silk. All pleated, these thousands of tiny pleats, and some very tiny rosebuds—"

"You're not wearing anything, Jilly. You're perfectly bare, I can tell."

"Don't call me Jilly, I hate that. And I hate you, Noel Finn. Where are you, anyway?"

"I'm out in my workshop, where do you think? Do you wish I were there?"

"No. Yes. Oh shit. *No.*"

The truth is that Jill wishes almost anyone were there, any man, and until fairly recently, she thinks, there always was some guy, and almost always someone pretty good. Some okay or fairly cute or handsome guy. She is not sure just what has changed—and it seems to have changed for all the women she knows, lots fewer men around, and it can't all be guys gone gay, or fear of AIDS. But she knows that then she was not reduced to these sleazy conversations with her half-sister's sleazy husband, for heaven's sake. She would not be there when he called, or not answering the phone. He could ask her answering machine how much money she had, if he wanted to know. "This is a very sleazy conversation," she says to Noel.

He laughs. "I've had sleazier, and I'll bet you have too."

Well, he's right there, and for an instant, it is fortunately just one instant, Jill is tempted to tell Noel about certain things that she used to do. Things that would really shock him, that he would never expect of her, Miss Successful Corporation Lawyer. Daughter of Dr. and Mrs. James and Caroline McAndrew. Noel is kind of a snob, she feels that—but he also has a way of making her want to talk to him. Or maybe she is simply lonely.

"What's the worst thing you've ever done?" she asks Noel. "Aside from cheating on my sister, that is."

"You're some lawyer, Ms. McAndrew. Okay. One, I don't cheat on your sister all that much. Nowhere near as much as she thinks I do. In fact she's very flattering, that way. And, two, sure I have done worse things than that. So now let's hear about you."

Sitting up, pulling silk-smooth sheets around her shoulders, Jill laughs, comfortably. "You wouldn't believe me," she tells him.

"Try me."

"No, I have to go. I just remembered there's a really good book on my table."

"Well, of all the—" He laughs, defeated.

"I mean it, I want to read for a while."

Jill puts the receiver down very lightly, and reaches to the table next to her bed for the book that she did in fact just remember, a nice new edition of *The Last Chronicle of Barset,* which is her mother's favorite book (Jill believes). She herself finds it hard to tell one Trollope from another. But she has always meant to read this one.

Most of Jill's reading is of magazines, she must subscribe to a couple of dozen, all very glossy, bright—and by contrast this book seems so heavy; she does not really want to read it at all, she finds. Annoyed, she puts the book down, and recognizes that she is more than a little turned on by Noel. She feels sexy and restless, her mind very lively, roaming all over.

And for both reasons, sexiness, restlessness, she begins to think about what she used to call (to herself) the Game, which is what she came so dangerously close to telling Noel about. How he would have loved that! The only man she ever did tell almost went crazy, he was so excited. He adored her for what she had told him, he said. As Noel would have.

The Game began in a curious way, one day at lunch with a sort-of friend of Jill's, a round-faced, pink-skinned, nebbishy-looking guy named Buck Fister (so wrong, he was the last person for a name like Buck). Buck was a big success in something odd, like lighting fixtures; no one was ever exactly sure what he did, a lot of people always said he made his real money dealing—the only explanation for so much funny money, these days. And he was usually good for some blow, if you felt the need.

Buck was always around in the places Jill was around, hanging out at lunch at the Balboa, sometimes the Elite at night, Campton Place or the Zuni Cafe. He used to call Jill a lot, apparently just to talk, he never actually asked for dates. He seemed to want to be friends (he could have been gay but no one thought he was) and every now and then they would do lunch, and always on him, Buck insisted on that, and usually in a fairly pricey restaurant. He was a pretty fun lunch, lots of insider scam on everyone, he always knew just who was in big trouble with money or drugs, who had just tested positive, he knew a lot.

Jill always wondered, though, just what he was up to: what did he really want of her, anyway? She knew there was something.

And then it came out, very slowly, very cool. He simply said for maybe the hundredth time that she was the spiffiest girl in town. ("Spiffy" was a word Buck liked a lot—oddly enough, a word that Jill's stepfather, Ralph Carter, also used. Ralph liked to tell Caroline that she was very spiffy.) And then Buck said, "I know guys who'd give a thousand bucks for a date with you."

They went on talking after that, and Jill laughed it off, but as soon as he had said that, Jill knew exactly what was meant. Later he said it again. "Well, you do have some curious friends," Jill told him. And, "Just how much would you get out of it, Bucks?"

Buck laughed too, as though they had just had a harmless, mildly sophisticated joke between them. Old friends.

A week or so later, though, he called her. "A friend of mine from D.C. comes through here a lot, and he says he's seen you around. Says he met you one night at Harry's but you wouldn't remember, probably. Anyway, he's dying for a date."

The mechanics of it, then, were very much like the old game of blind dates, a friend recommending a friend. You'd go out with the friend, and if you liked him, if you wanted to, you could easily end up in bed—in the old days Jill very often would. (But now no one would be quite so easy about it, probably, unless you handed out rubbers, something Jill really can't see doing. You certainly can't believe anyone's stated history; the straightest guy in the world might have had some swell gay fling. You can't tell, and nothing's all that safe any more.)

In any case, no one has that kind of blind date these days—and in this case, with the Game, ending up in bed is the main part of the deal. You both know that all along, all during the early part of the date, the dinner, whatever.

And after the first couple of times, Game times, Jill knew that the next day, in her office high up in the Transamerica Pyramid, she would receive a very large spray of roses, at least three dozen (there went a lot of Buck's profits), into which was thrust a thick envelope in which were ten C-notes. Romantic old Buck, such a valentine of a payoff.

And that was the Game.

"I just happened to have this overload of cash," Jill explained the first time she got all that money, at Wilkes, where God knows they were used to big notes—as she bought a great new dress, the shortest anyone had seen around that year, in dark-red silk.

The date. That first guy was very nice (clever Buck). A little old, early sixties, probably, and a little on the scrawny side for Jill's particular taste: she prefers men to be about ten or fifteen pounds overweight, no less or more, and she knows this prejudice to be a little odd, even very slightly kinky. But this guy had good thick gray hair, and he was a doctor, for heaven's sake, talk about reassuring.

It was all arranged by Bucks, of course. They met in the upper bar at the St. Francis, the Compass Rose. Jill wore a white gardenia. ("A touch of Billie," Bucks told her. "Billie never turned tricks, you stupid prick." "Oh, don't be too sure.") Then they had dinner in the English grill: it was clear that they were not to leave that hotel, where the doctor of course was staying.

Dinner was strange, to say the least, strange and for Jill intensely exciting, in some crazy way. As they talked and talked about absolutely nothing, Jill studied that man. John, he said his name was, and it could have been. Giving no thought at all to what she was saying (if he thought she was a real airhead, no matter), Jill tried hard to imagine or predict his sexual tastes. How she could really turn him on, make him wild, just as though she were really a hooker. As though she didn't care at all about her own fun.

And at the same time she was playing with the idea of backing off, out, away. Of course she could, no way to stop her. Why not? She did not need a thousand, really, and for that matter she certainly did not need to get laid, not back then. She was doing it with someone or other on far more nights than not, in those days. What was known as sexually active. Very.

Possibly this John knew a little of what she was thinking. He was fairly smart, for a doctor.

After dinner they went up to that crazy penthouse nightclub, and they danced. One dance. And then, perfectly easy, they went down just one floor in the big elevator outside. To his very large room. And almost immediately to bed, just some fairly perfunctory kissing, then undressing (he undressed her, an old-fashioned touch that Jill quite liked).

The interesting thing was that she had figured him exactly right. Precisely the touches that she had thought he might like really got to him, he went a little crazy. Very likely he hadn't done it for quite a while, a sick wife, or something. Maybe just no time, doctors over-schedule themselves so much these days.

Another interesting thing was that it was great for her. In fact so terrific—*major*—that she could remember it still.

Afterwards, as she was leaving, there was none of the usual, "I'll call you, I must see you again, very soon." Nothing like that, which was almost funny, and also a big relief. They both knew what they were doing. The Game.

Later guys were also okay, most of them. Almost all from D.C. or New York, a couple from L.A. Mostly over fifty, mostly too over-weight. Nothing quite as special, ever, as what happened with her the first time. Still, the situation, the sense of what she was actually doing, turned Jill on quite a lot. She did not choose to probe too deeply into why she found all this so exciting, she didn't need to. She was always primed with a little good white powder, but it wasn't just that, she knew, that turned her on.

How shocked her sisters would be! Even Fiona, but especially Sage and Portia, on what Sage would call feminist grounds. (Sage talked a lot about Feminist Grounds, as though all the feminists owned some enormous state park.) And some feminist Sage is, let-ting that lousy Noel get away with all that he does. And Portia is probably gay, Jill has for some time thought that. Portia has seemed not to like men at all, unless they were gay, except for the creepy kid she hung out with sometimes. Harold? Yes, his name is Harold.

Does she herself like men? Jill has wondered that, and she has been forced to conclude that she does not, or not very much. What she does like is sex, she likes screwing a lot, and she needs men for that. (She has done it with a vibrator, which works, so to speak, an instant O, but not much fun. Much more fun using a vibrator with some guy.) She wants men around to make love with and therefore she has to humor them, to put up with what she considers their basic simplicity. Even smart men are basically very stupid, is Jill's conclusion. Which is not exactly a feminist point of view, or is it? On feminist grounds, she is probably way off.

When she told one man about the Game, a lover named Crimmons, of all nerdy names, he got incredibly turned on. Crimmons was married of course and a senior partner in her law firm. At first she wondered why she was telling him all that, it was not exactly politic, but then, when he got so excited about it, wanting more and more, wanting every detail, she knew why she had told him. Just for that. His turn-on.

Now she will have to take a Dalmane, thirty grams. If it just puts her to sleep right away, it is now 1:30, so if she sleeps until 7:30 she will be okay for a meeting at 8. She hopes. She can skip the call to Fiona, she knows it's her turn to call and if she doesn't Fiona will call her. But Fiona can talk to her machine.

Jill is so thin that the ingestion of almost any food makes her feel bloated, as though whatever she had eaten were protuberant in her stomach, and visible, as if in the transparent stomach of a baby bird. (A baby bird is what Caroline thinks and says that Jill looks like, these days, with her very fine hair and long thin neck, and her wide, wide eyes. Jim McAndrew's pale-gray eyes, all the girls have them.)

Just now, having consumed three-fourths of a cornmeal breadstick, and several strawberries, a slice of orange and some tea, at Campton Place, Jill feels unpleasantly stuffed. She also has a heavier-than-usual Dalmane hangover. She is finding it hard to listen.

Her breakfast person is very young, her own age, probably, a red-haired lawyer from Memphis; this seems odd, Jill has never heard of anyone coming from Memphis. But he has no Southern accent: is he really from Memphis, what is this? Jill dislikes his hands, the red-brown freckles and reddish hairs. Dislikes his small blue eyes, and his voice, especially his voice, which is high and nasal. "Very vulnerable," he is saying, seeming to sum up what he has been saying all along. They are talking very hostile takeover. Some small company in Portland, Oregon.

Quite inadvertently, then, and very likely because she was thinking of the Game the night before, as she lay awake after all that talk with Noel, the Game comes back into Jill's wandering mind, and she thinks, Oh God, suppose Bucks had fixed her up with this guy, this red-and-pink-skinned twerp who doesn't even seem to be from where he says he is. Well, obviously that would have been the night to say no, just get up and leave, bow out, as she has always half imagined herself doing. Another tiny voice within Jill, though, is imagining how it would be if she did not leave, did not leave this particular guy. She is seeing herself in bed with him, this very young (too young!) man, knowing precisely what would excite him.

He asks her, "Are you okay?" She must have turned pale.

"I'm fine. It's just that breakfast always makes me sort of tired."

"Me too, as a matter of fact. I guess we're getting old."

"I guess," and they both laugh at the sheer unlikeliness of this.

"You don't sound like you're from Memphis," Jill tells him. "It's in the South, isn't it?"

"I'm from Detroit, originally."

As they are leaving, walking out through the pretty, perfectly appointed tables, linen and flowers, silver, crystal, porcelain, as they almost reach the doorway, Jill experiences a shock: there, sitting alone at a window table and absorbed in the *Wall Street Journal* (thank God), is Buck Fister. Bucks, looking much younger than whenever she saw him last, a couple of years ago—which was when she finally said, "I really don't want to do this Game any more, old Bucks. Frankly, with this plague around it's just too dangerous. Besides, I make plenty of money." And now there is Buck, looking terrific (for him), leaner and tight-skinned. Tan. Prosperous. Jill hurries past, not wanting any more contact with Buck, not now.

It is strange, though, that she should see him today, when she was thinking of the Game and of him last night (usually she manages to think of that small area of her past not at all, or hardly at all). But that sort of thing happens more and more as you go on in life, Jill has concluded. As though some sort of reliable radar signalled another person's proximity: she thought of Bucks because she was going to see him today.

In the lobby, standing beside the giant arrangement of dry desert flowers, Jill and the red-haired man shake hands. His name is already gone from her head, but not from her notes. Back in her office she will be perfectly prepared to deal with their meeting, to give it her appraisal.

He says, "You know, that's the greatest-looking dress I've seen in San Francisco." He seems to be speaking through his nose.

"Thanks. Actually I got it a couple of years ago." With cash, at Wilkes.

"I hope it wouldn't be out of line if I asked you to dinner?"

Not out of line, just out of the question, you nerd. "I'd really love to but I can't." Jill smiles. "I'm really sorry."

Jill's firm is considering a move from the Transamerica to one of the old brick buildings on Jackson Street, in what used to be Jackson Square, where the antique dealers and decorators were. Jill can't wait to move; she has never said so to anyone but the views from this building, this pyramid, make her sick, on some days sicker than others, a sort of shifting vertigo. Today, maybe because of the Dalmane, it seems unusually bad. It is horrible to look out at all that distance, out and down to the bay, all that terrible deep water, and closer up all those monstrous dark boxes, the other new buildings. Jill shudders, and sits down at her desk, which faces away from the windows, toward the door.

One of the messages before her is from her half-sister Sage, which is such a surprise that Jill picks up the phone to make the call right away. And then she hesitates: suppose Noel should answer? Well, that would serve him just right, the cheapo cheat.

Sage, though, picks up the phone on its first ring. "I need some advice," she says, sounding happy as anything, really high. "I need a good hotel in New York, and you go there all the time—"

"When I go it's on the firm, though, Sage. So I stay at the Meridien, or the Westbury."

"I'd like to be downtown. Sort of. Near SoHo."

"Well, look, Sage, I'll ask around. Okay?"

"Sure. Thanks."

Only after hanging up does it occur to Jill that she could have asked Sage why she was going to New York, why she sounded so excited, so happy. And was Noel going to, and for how long? But she couldn't ask Sage that.

Looking at her watch, Jill sees that, miraculously, she now has exactly fifteen minutes to herself—or, that she can take fifteen minutes. Which should be exactly right.

Quickly pulling several folders from a drawer, and opening the *Wall Street Journal* on her desk to the day's quotations, she begins to jot numbers on a pad of yellow paper. She then makes a few calculations on her handy brown lizard computer, and after seven or eight minutes of this she comes up smiling.

And she thinks, almost aloud: I have just barely under two mil, dear Noel, if you really want to know. And I'm only thirty-one, just starting out.

And she adds, I'm five feet seven, and I weigh in at just under ninety pounds. And so, what else would you like to know? Would you like to hear about a game I used to play?

Six

Portia Carter looks remarkably like her father, Ralph, as indeed all Caroline's daughters resemble their fathers rather than herself. "I must have very weak genes," Caroline has remarked, which no one believes to be true. Portia is very tall and often stooped, she has a look of being bent, like a tree. She has her father's large white face, long nose and large teeth. She is shy and somewhat strange; her mother and her sisters are divided between thinking her brilliant (the opinion of Caroline and Sage) and somewhat simple (Liza, reluctantly, and Fiona and Jill). Ralph has never been heard to pronounce on his daughter, it is only clear that he adores her. "She hasn't found herself," is a sentence on which they all might agree, concerning Portia; brilliant or innocent, or both, she gives a sense of floundering through life, with both more trials and more errors than most people seem to encounter.

She is not actually a poet, although she is occasionally explained as such. "I do write an occasional haiku," Portia has confessed to Sage, to whom she is closest, "but that's just for fun. It's a sort of meditative exercise." She allows the rest of them to think of her as a poet, since she believes that they like to, "poet" as a designation makes her more plausible. "I really don't quite know what I want to do," Portia has said to Sage. "Do I have to, already?"

For a living she does several things. She house-sits, with emphasis on plants and pets, and when not house-sitting she works for a young couple who do organic gardening. This last is back in Bolinas, in her cabin (her purchase with her Molly Blair money), what she thinks of as home. She also occasionally works, for no money, for a young man named Harold, who also lives in Bolinas, a refugee from a very high-powered East Coast alcoholic-politico father. Harold is trying to start a nursery.

Of all her occupations Portia's favorite is the pet- and plant-sitting, the houses. She likes Harold, likes helping him out, but she worries so that he may fail. She is over-identified with Harold, she sometimes thinks.

Plants and pets and houses, though, she finds extremely reassuring, especially going back to places; she is happiest when working on a more or less regular basis, as she does for a Mrs. Kaltenborn, an elderly, eccentric lady who lives in Bernal Heights but goes to Italy every summer for three weeks, leaving three cats and a house full of ferns and philodendrons, yucca plants and spathofilium. There are ferns especially all over the house, and one of Portia's chores is to see that the cats do not take bites from the fern leaves, which they like to do, and which always makes them throw up, an ugly green bile.

The oldest cat is eighteen, she is cross and demanding and extremely talkative, called Pink. She is Portia's favorite, for reasons that Portia herself does not quite understand. A tailless Manx, Pink walks with that non-existent tail held high, her long thin legs a little uncertain now.

The other two cats are Burmese, sleek and plump and fairly stupid; Pink dislikes them both. Portia believes that Pink remembers and recognizes her, which could be true. Portia also believes in a curious kinship between herself and Mrs. Kaltenborn; they seem to inhabit each other, which is to say that the absent Mrs. Kaltenborn seems (to Portia) to be present in Pink. Pink is a combination of extreme crossness and an affection that is just as extreme, as is Mrs. K. In any case, Portia feels herself quite permanently attached to both.

And that semi-shabby, architecturally eccentric neighborhood also appeals to Portia. The grander areas in which she sometimes tends house, or for that matter in which she visits her sisters or her mother—those places, Pacific Heights, Russian Hill and Telegraph, all quite intimidate Portia, they fill her with unease and loneliness. But in this tall narrow crooked house, impractically arranged, Portia feels a sort of recognition. The house reminds her of herself; like her, it is not quite right.

In fact Portia is possessed of an exceptionally acute sense of place, a heightened sensitivity to the physical facts of her surroundings. She once had an almost mystical experience, involving "place." This is what happened:

A few years back, when Portia was in her early twenties and just out of school, U.C. at Santa Cruz, she and some friends elected to drive across the country, to New York and back, in a more or less random way. (Portia paid for most of the expenses of this trip, her way of getting rid of a lot of her Molly Blair money.) Driving through Texas, they stopped in a town near Austin, called San Marcos, that for no apparent reason appealed very strongly to Portia. Quite literally it appealed: it cried out to her to stay there, everything shouted, the ordinary town square with its small, fairly ugly town hall, the streets of very ordinary two-story houses, with a few rare spacious beauties—and the river, flowing through.

Returning to San Francisco, more or less in passing Portia mentioned this town (of which she still thought, for which she yearned) to her father, only saying, "I really liked it there. Something about it."

And Ralph told her: "That's pretty amazing. San Marcos is where your grandfather was born, and I used to visit there a lot when I was a boy. They had the prettiest farmhouse down on the river, the most beautiful trees. Your blood must have recognized that place."

They both laughed, denying such a possibility, blood recognition, but to Portia that was exactly how it had felt, a surging of all her cells, with her warm blood, toward that place.

Portia "feels at home" in the Kaltenborn house, in Bernal Heights, to such a degree that she sometimes invites friends for supper, a rare event for her. She likes to cook in that narrow, hopelessly crowded kitchen, with its small vine-tangled deck just outside; she likes looking out to the rusting cans of flowering herbs, cracked terra-cotta pots of alyssum, lobelia and daisies. Ralph and Caroline have visited her there, and Liza and Saul and the children (Portia likes children, generally, and especially these half-nieces and -nephews). Harold has visited her there, and several times Sage. Never Fiona or Jill, however, who are simply too fussy about how things are.

To celebrate Sage's good news, the show of her sculpture that is definitely scheduled for October in New York, Portia is making an old favorite dinner for just the two of them; Noel conveniently has some business with clients, over in Orinda. (Portia is pleased, nothing against Noel, really, just that being alone with Sage is a special pleasure.) Salmon and asparagus and brown rice, an endive-and-watercress salad. Sage will bring some fruit for dessert. The simplicity of it all will make it more fun, with minimal chances for culinary disaster. Portia is a fairly good cook but easily distracted, prone to burnings. And Sage's cooking has gone markedly downhill since her marriage to Noel, quite possibly because he is such a chef, given to flamboyant French feasts, Italian banquets ("Retro-disgusting," is Fiona's harsh verdict on Noel's cooking. "A busboy's dream. *So* South-of-Market").

In Portia's mind these days Sage is already a big rich success. Large glossy photos of her ceramics in all the fanciest art magazines, and for Sage herself a new house, a big studio. New clothes and trips to Europe. Imagining all that for Sage, Portia's heart warms: How wonderful Sage will look in her new role as a woman who has arrived. How becoming success will be, since Sage has so surely earned it.

Bedazzled, literally, by such large generous thoughts, late in the afternoon of the dinner day Portia simultaneously recalls two small lapses of her own: she is not yet dressed and has no idea what to wear, and, worse, she has forgotten to get any wine.

In a hurried way she pulls on the better of the two sweaters she brought over from Bolinas; it doesn't matter, but she does wish she had something slightly better for a Sage celebration. Clean jeans. She finds her billfold and heads out the door, which does not lock. Sage will know that she should just go right on in.

Portia has spent so much time in this neighborhood that she has various neighborhood relationships, people she nods or speaks to, animals she stops to pat along her way. With the Vietnamese family in the corner grocery she has an especially elaborate connection— she really likes them. They are small and shy and highly ceremonious people, as Portia is tall and shy and also excessively polite. Thus any transaction between Portia and My, the mother, and other family members tends to be lengthy.

"I'm having some salmon," Portia now confides to My, who seems to be alone in the store.

"Ah, fish! You like white wine?"

"Well yes, I thought white. I guess some Chardonnay."

"Ah yes! very nice! Chardonnay." My has lovely large dark eyes, and a terrible scar across her chin. She is always very pale.

This business, then, takes some time, the purchase of a seven-dollar bottle of wine, more than Portia meant to spend, but the label has a nice drawing of California poppies, so festive. At last it is over, the sale, and after inquiries into each other's health and happiness (would My tell her if there was actually something wrong? would she tell My?) Portia is out on the street again, and hurrying toward her temporary home.

And there in front of her house is Sage's old black VW convertible (formerly convertible, the roof doesn't work any more). *Good,* thinks Portia, who knows that she is late. How good that Sage is there, is inside.

As she pushes the door open, though, she hears Sage talking to someone, and at first she thinks, A neighbor? How strange.

And then she realizes that Sage is talking to Noel, they are both in the kitchen. Sage and Noel.

Portia's unstable heart sinks, even as she is calling out, "Hi! You're here! How great."

Sage comes out of the kitchen by herself, looking wonderful in a red cotton shirt, her dark hair shining, lively, eyes brilliant. "Well, we're both here, as things turned out." In a breathless way she laughs. "And guess who's cooking."

"But I really—I was going to—"

"Sweetie, I know, but you know—" They exchange a long look, embarrassed half-sisters between whom there is no physical resemblance but much strong feeling, and intimate knowledge of each other. Each, just now, is quite aware of the other's feelings regarding Noel: Portia takes it for granted that Sage is still "madly in love," a condition that she finds it hard to imagine, outside of literature. And Sage knows that Portia has, well, reservations.

Noel comes into the room, slim and graceful, his dancer's entrance. He even bows, greeting Portia. "Ports! How's the kid? I hope you don't mind, I put a little marinade on your salmon."

And Noel goes on to make one of his splendid dinners. Portia's salmon, cut in cubes, becomes the hors d'oeuvre. Noel has brought along a chicken, some pasta, radicchio and watercress. Peach ice cream and cookies. Lots of wine.

He even manages to provide some time alone for Portia with Sage, while he is cooking; they are ordered to stay in the living room and let him work. "You ladies just stay out of it, be my guests."

And so Portia is able to say to Sage, alone, "Sage, this news is so great, I'm so excited."

"That's good, you be excited. I'm trying not to be."

They both laugh.

"But Sage, it's wonderful."

"Not necessarily, really. It's just a show, people have them all the time. I may not even get reviewed, no one may buy anything."

However, Sage is talking to herself, and her face belies all those stern lecturing words. She looks incredibly happy, her eyes and her voice are so warm, so pleased with her life—at this moment.

And then, leaning forward, she whispers, "I'm sorry about your dinner, but he means well, honestly. He just tends to take things over." And she reaches to pat Portia's hand.

"It's okay, really. And God knows the food will be better."

Noel makes a marvellous success of the celebration, in Portia's view, actually. Subduing her rebellious sense of having been taken over, she is able to understand that tonight, absolutely, he is making Sage happy, he is giving her a much more dramatic sense of being fêted, celebrated, than she, Portia, could have done.

With dessert, the ice cream and cookies, Noel opens champagne, and he pours and stands up, and raises his glass to Sage. "To my Sage, with all my love. To success!" And he bends to kiss her mouth, as Sage leans to him, closing her eyes. And then Noel sits down again and they all begin to eat and drink—again. By now they are all a little high. Laughing a lot.

Portia dreamily believes that she is in the presence of true love, and half-drunkenly she recalls her early childhood with Caroline and Ralph, her (at that time) just-married, much-in-love parents. How fortunate she has been all around, Portia vaguely thinks (but in that case, whatever is wrong with her? how could she have turned out so odd?). Looking across the room at handsome Noel, his ravishingly perfect nose, his fine mouth and golden eyes—and at lovely Sage, so lively, so perfectly happy—Portia is quite struck by their resemblance to each other. She has seen this and thought of it before but never so strongly, and so she says, "You know, you two really look more and more alike, it's amazing."

At which Sage laughs. "Don't say that, Noel will leave me."

Noel frowns, the smallest frown, but what he says is, "I'm deeply flattered." And then, "But I honestly can't see it."

Portia goes to bed that night with blurry thoughts of love and happiness, of money and success for Sage.

The next morning, though, she wakes to a grinding hangover— and total havoc in her kitchen. "Promise you won't stay up to clean, that'll make us feel too guilty," Noel and Sage both said, drunkenly leaving. And why? Why would her cleaning up last night make them feel more guilty than her doing so now?

Dirty dishes tend to multiply in the night; that is an axiom of Caroline's, an advocate of midnight kitchen cleaning, and Portia is sure that it is true.

Sitting down with a large mug of coffee, before starting in to clean what looks to be an impossible, horrible mess, Portia is then visited by several (for her) uncharacteristically unkind thoughts.

First, of course, she considers what is nearest at hand, the mess, and she thinks: How could Noel possibly have used so many dishes?

And then, with somewhat more distance from the evening as a whole, she thinks too of his perfect aplomb, the complete assurance with which Noel took over the evening. A woman would not do that, Portia feels sure. If two men were scheduled to have dinner together, a woman married to one of those men would not automatically assume that both men were really dying to spend the evening with her.

Although nowhere near ever married (she has not even lived with anyone, and only made love, not terribly successfully, with Harold), Portia is still quite sure that this is true. And it makes an interesting feminist point, she thinks. Could she possibly discuss this with Sage? With Liza, or Caroline? Most likely with Caroline, she decides.

And then she gets to work. She works for hours, cleaning up.

Seven

"Portia, I do think you're quite right," says Caroline to her youngest daughter, over the phone. "I think that men generally do assume that women alone are lonely and would rather be with men. But it's odd that a man as young as Noel would be so what Fiona calls retro."

As she speaks to Portia, who is in Bolinas, Caroline, in her kitchen, is looking out to her deck, the profusion of roses—and she considers the enormous pleasure to be derived from flowers, a pleasure that she knows is not shared by everyone. Portia, for example, although she works in nurseries sometimes, does not especially care for cultivated flowers, really, her preference being for flowering weeds, and grasses.

"Noel is retro," Portia tells her mother. "Retro-macho."

Caroline chooses not to take this up. "I have to admit that I used to have that same idea about women alone," she says. "When I'd see women alone in a restaurant I'd think, Poor things." (Caroline wonders if she is quite consciously making an effort not to discuss Noel. Quite possibly she is, she thinks.) "But now I usually assume they're having a good time, out together," Caroline continues.

"It's strange, this taste for mean men that Sage seems to have," Portia persists.

"They're not entirely mean. Noel is extremely complicated, don't you think? As I'm sure Mr. Gallo is."

"Extremely. Both of them. And I have to admit that Noel was

really nice at dinner. So proud of Sage. Don't you think they look a little alike?"

"No, I wouldn't have said so. But then I'm much more aware of her looking like her father. Aaron Levine was so handsome, really. But then all you girls—"

She is interrupted from this musing by a sudden scream by Portia, on the other end, who after a moment cries out, "A spouting whale! He's right out there!"

"My God, Portia, I thought you'd been attacked."

"Hardly. Listen, I have to go. I'm going out to the mesa to see the whale."

"Darling, it's okay. Goodby." Portia has already hung up, and run off across the mesa to see the whale. Leaving Caroline both to smile and to sigh. How enviable, just to whale-watch in Bolinas. Maybe she and Ralph should move there, after a few more years?

More practically, what Caroline is most wishing is that she did not have to go to a wedding party tonight, something huge and extremely elaborate, she fears. In one of the old Broadway mansions that now are schools.

For one thing there have been so very many parties, this spring and early summer of their return to San Francisco, hers and Ralph's. People are so curious about them both, after their five-year absence, Caroline believes; old friends wish to see if they have changed, and what the survival chances are for this improbable marriage. And friends also wish to insist that they themselves have not changed at all, they are not a day older than they were five years back. And so seemingly everyone from their various worlds has invited Caroline and Ralph to parties, and more often than not they have gone.

Ralph, a political man, a gregarious Texan as well, in a general way likes parties better than Caroline does, and she has deferred to this wish of his, his wish to be more sociable. Also, in Lisbon they were more or less isolated, thrown upon themselves, which was wonderful in its way (sort of), but they have had a large dose of that isolation.

At moments of low-ebb discouragement in Lisbon, days of not

much to say and weeks of perfunctory sex (if any), Caroline, remembering the passionate intensity of her love affair with Ralph, all that heady talk and all that incredible, matchless sex—Caroline has even thought that the transition from marvellous, illicit love to the dailiness of marriage is too much for anyone. In saner, wiser (and far more frequent) moments, however, she has concluded that she and Ralph have done very well indeed with that transition: they talk a lot, generally, and their average for sexual love is high, very high.

In fact, of her three marriages, the only one that went bad was the marriage to Jim McAndrew, whom she married largely because she thought Sage needed a father (so unfair to Jim, she later thought)—her only marriage not preceded by passionate love.

The mansion in which this wedding is held (the daughter of an old friend of Caroline's is marrying the son of a Marin County foreign-car dealer)—the place is very grand indeed: everywhere marble, pillars and floors, long vistas of marble halls, with appropriate statuary, and a central fountain playing, gently. And flowers, everywhere towering arrangements of the tallest, largest flowers. Huge heavy pastel blossoms, half hidden in showers of pale-green leaves.

Having decided against going to the church ceremony, which was to take place in a massive Episcopal church on Van Ness Avenue (not the cathedral, Caroline has somewhat snobbishly noted), Caroline and Ralph arrive at the reception at the marble mansion just barely past the specified time. And at the door they are given slips of paper with their table assignments. "Separate tables," Caroline whispers to her husband. "What is this? Assignation time?" "Only if you're lucky in the draw," he whispers back.

First, though, there is a lot of milling around in the hall. "Mingling." Waiters pass through with trays of champagne glasses, other waiters with white-napkin-wrapped bottles, for instant refills. And white-lace-aproned maids proffer trays of hors d'oeuvres, which Caroline notes are surprisingly good.

Everyone of course is at his or her most excessively dressed up: almost all the men in black tie (Ralph being one of the few in a plain dark business suit, that is as far as he will go: "I'm not renting a goddam uniform"). Older women wear long, extremely expensive dresses (what Caroline thinks of as Nancy Reagan dresses), with beaded or sequined tops, long swishy skirts. Long-legged young girls in pretty, short silk dresses, and high, high heels.

Caroline is wearing red, a red silk dress from Lisbon that cost about thirty dollars, she recalls with some pleasure. But now that she is here she feels the dress to be somewhat inappropriate; she knew as she put it on that you do not wear red or black to weddings, or for that matter white—but she also thought to herself, What the hell, doesn't anything go these days? Besides, this is not the actual wedding. She had under-estimated, though, the extreme, old-establishment conservatism of this group; stronger than any perfume is the reek of old money. But now once more Caroline thinks, What the hell? It's really a great dress, for a woman my age I look great—or as great as possible, for me.

And she is right, Caroline looks much better even than she thinks she does. She looks like a beautiful woman of sixty-five, or some years less, with her thick, swinging gray-blonde hair, her wide blue-green eyes and her smooth tan skin.

From somewhere she hears band music, old music, what she believes is a Forties sound, and she thinks, Just as well I'm not seated with Ralph, I might end up having a good time in all this, and I don't think it's his scene at all, and he hates to dance.

Married people should not be expected to go about so much together. Caroline had often thought this but has been unable to make any practical application of it, in any of her marriages. But it is quite unrealistic to expect two very separate, distinct and very different people to respond in similar ways to a given set of circumstances. To like the same people, the same parties. Even to want to go out together on the same given evening.

She and Ralph seem to have struck some sort of a balance, though, which may be all you can expect? (Marriage is still in a very primitive stage of development, according to Sage, and Caroline agrees.) At this particular party, then, Ralph, who insisted that they come here, is not looking about with a scowl, while Caroline, the reluctant guest, is lured by faint strains of sentimental music, from her distant youth.

The tables, of which there are thirty (Ralph counts), are in a long series of rooms, also marble—rooms all marble-pillared and bedecked with extraordinary flowers, down a small flight of stairs from the entrance hall. Somewhere there must also be a kitchen; in the course of things white-gloved waiters and busboys stream through, bearing trays of food (seven courses) and wines (five in all). Removing barely eaten food, on barely soiled dishes, and considerable untouched wine.

In fact some of the "help" have a very good time with all the leftover wine, quite a few of the busboys and waiters and the maids, who are moonlighting from various restaurants, including Fiona's. Many of them are in various sexual ways involved with each other, and they are mostly quite young, and they quite possibly have more fun in the long run than anyone present.

(There is also in the kitchen, somewhat late that evening, a small group who help in an enterprise called No Waste; these people go around to "charity events" and huge banquets and enormous private parties like this one. By prearrangement, of course, they collect as much untouched food as possible, which they then take along to one of the shelters for homeless people, or a food distribution center for people at home with AIDS. Very few people know about this enterprise, so far.)

One of the things that plague Caroline through that very long evening is the presence of so many half- (or less than half-) remembered faces. There are so many people who look quite familiar, and it is hard to tell in what context she might conceivably have known them: is that a woman whom she used to see in the Cal-Mart, or a social acquaintance, a person with whom she exchanged dinners, possibly, a long time back, in her proper Jim McAndrew days? Caroline kept up with a few Pacific Heights friends in her later time with Ralph, but not many. And even within a city sheer geography plays a very large part in the patterns of friendship, she has thought.

Is that very pretty white-blonde young woman in black (did no one tell her not to?) just now dancing by, quite close to Caroline's table (so close that Caroline notes a look of sheer panic, terror on that young face)—is that someone whom Caroline has met, or perhaps bought perfume from at Macy's, or did she see her in Julius Kahn Playground, watching babies in the sandbox, with Liza? No way to know—or is she simply a type? An Eighties blonde, too thin, in astronomically expensive clothes; lots of heavy gold jewelry.

At the large round table to which Caroline has found her way the same condition persists, vague familiarity all around, and now this applies not only to faces but to names: the names that she hears in the rounds of introductions are quite possibly all known to her, but there again it is also quite possible that she has only read them somewhere.

And the noise level is so high, such a din of voices and plates and silverware and music, the somewhat conflicting sounds of a small band at either end of the room—so much noise that a true conversation would be quite out of the question, even if anyone could be sure whom he or she was addressing.

But no conversation is fine with Caroline. She is perfectly content for the moment to smile and nod, to mouth what she hopes and trusts are the appropriate inanities—and no matter if they actually are not. She is content to eat quite a lot of the surprisingly excellent food. Lord God, this party must be costing the absolute earth, thinks Caroline, as she polishes off her mounded caviar, then spoons into the salmon mousse on endive.

But what she really likes best is the music, so marvellously sappy, so quintessentially Forties.

When Caroline was a girl, back in very conservative New Canaan, Connecticut, her mother, Molly Blair, a young widow, either was actually under considerable social suspicion, because of her actress profession, or else simply felt that to be the case. Being "English" was somehow helpful, although there seemed to be some ambiguity as to class, an ambiguity that Molly herself, from working-class Liverpool, did nothing to clear up. But Molly felt called upon to be very proper indeed, and extremely strict with her daughter. Thus Caroline, a big blonde, very eager adolescent, was not allowed to go to any of the racier faraway places to dance, not the Glen Island Casino, which was popular with some of her wilder friends, and surely not into New York, no dancing at LaRue or at the Plaza.

However, in nearby Katonah, a scant hour's drive away, there was a very nice little roadhouse (are there any roadhouses, these days, Caroline wonders?) with a small live band, on weekends. And Molly Blair, somewhat misguidedly, believed that going to dance in Katonah was perfectly okay, no trouble likely there. Or perhaps it was only the appearance of trouble that Molly feared: "Daughter of actress caught in raid." A very smart woman, she must have known perfectly well that a lot could go on in the back seat of a car, coming home from Katonah. Not to mention all the possibilities for parking in all those secluded lanes, almost anywhere in Connecticut.

The band nearest Caroline's table now is playing what she thinks of as Katonah music, which is to say early-Forties, pre-war dance tunes; it is all Caroline can do not to hum along. But her feet beneath the table do tap, a little. (In her day Caroline was known as a terrific dancer.)

And she is thinking how much fun all that was, actually, all that dancing and then all the kissing and groping and touching—and how terrifically frustrating, finally. No wonder I so eagerly followed Aaron Levine into his bed, thinks Caroline; he was just the first boy who really insisted. "I don't have time for this kid stuff," Aaron said, after they had spent several dozen hours doing what was known as "everything but." And of course as things turned out he was right, they had very little time.

Aaron at first was just someone's tall dark attractive friend down from Amherst; he was whispered to be "Jewish but terribly nice, and smart, of course they all are." A very good dancer, and a tennis star. It was even whispered that he was "fun to kiss, really sophisticated."

(Just now, remembering that particular phrase, boys saying it to her, "Mmm, you're fun to kiss," Caroline is wistfully positive that no one ever says that any more. Certainly she will never hear it again.)

And so Caroline and Aaron, in another phrase from that time, "got serious." They progressed from parked cars to Aaron's room at Amherst; Caroline by this time was a freshman at Vassar. And then, on some steamy afternoon in the spring of 1943, during one or another jubilant act of love, Caroline became pregnant, and so they got married, in Molly Blair's pretty house. And then Aaron went off to war, to Okinawa, where he was killed. And Sage was born.

But it all really began out on the dance floor at the Katonah roadhouse, dancing to something pretty and quite ridiculous, like "Dancing in the Dark." Which this band, at this preposterous party, is playing at this moment.

"Would you care to dance?" Unnoticed by Caroline, a man from across the table has got up and come around to stand beside her, just after the *filet japonais*. A tall dark bald man, shining skin taut across his bare skull, heavy dark brows and arrogant, sexy eyes. He too looks vaguely familiar—but, then, everyone does, in this room.

Murmuring some assent, Caroline gets up and follows him to a small dance floor (Katonah-sized), where other couples are making the same brave effort.

This man is an excellent dancer, graceful and confident, strong. Too bad there is not more room and a better band, thinks Caroline; they would have had so much more scope, she could follow this man through almost any dance, she thinks. What fun!

Believing, though, that women are supposed to make some sort of conversation, having been so instructed by Molly Blair, instead of just dancing, enjoying it, Caroline says, "I didn't get your name, I'm sorry, so hard to hear—"

"Roland Gallo. And you're Caroline Carter, formerly McAndrew, right?"

Caroline misses a beat and steps on his foot. "Oh, sorry."

He holds her more closely but Caroline has stiffened. Then she silently laughs at herself as she thinks, Am I supposed to be the avenger of my daughter's old broken heart? She smiles up at Roland Gallo. "Yes, I am Caroline Carter."

And he smiles back, a very sexy, acknowledging look. "I do know some of your daughters," he tells her. "As a matter of fact I met Fiona just last week, in her very spiffy restaurant."

"We seem not to go there," is Caroline's comment, as she realizes that this fact might seem a little odd to anyone else. "My husband dislikes nouvelle cuisine," she explains. As she is thinking, Oh, my poor Sage, this guy is a very sexy piece of business.

And then the dance is over, and Caroline and Roland Gallo exchange small regretful smiles, and push their way back through the dancers and then through tables to their own table, their separated seats.

Where at last the dessert is being served. The wedding cake.

Surely, thinks Caroline, after this it will be time to go home? However, apparently not. There is a general movement toward the dance floor, or floors, and just as Caroline has finished her last bit of cake, which was delicious, saffron-flavored, at her elbow she hears, "Caroline, couldn't we have this dance?"

It is not Roland Gallo (no such luck), but a tall thin man with wispy thinning blond hair whom at first she does not quite know but who is—dear God, how could she not recognize him?—Jim McAndrew, her second husband. The father of three of her daughters. "How terribly nice," she murmurs, assenting to the dance.

Jim is not a good dancer. Clumsy and insecure, no rhythm. Almost automatically Caroline finds herself taking over, helping out. As it was in their marriage. And what a joke, really, these relationship power struggles are, she thinks, when it matters so fiercely who does what, works at what, earns more. I do hope younger people manage to work things out better than we did, she thinks, though I don't see a lot of hope in my daughters' relationships.

"Well, how do you like San Francisco, now that you're back?" Jim asks, speaking into her ear; they are just about the same height, due to Caroline's heels.

"Oh, rather mixed," she tells him. "I love our house, but I sort of miss the homey old neighborhood. You know, out in the Mission. And I think Ralph misses it even more than I do. He's not exactly a Pacific Heights type, you know."

A little stiffly, "I suppose not."

Too late Caroline recalls that Jim does not know Ralph—oh Christ, of course not. He only knows what he's read in the papers about this "labor firebrand, this hulking radical." And he knows that Ralph was the man with whom he saw Caroline coming out of a motel on Lombard Street, fatally, late on a lovely spring Wednesday afternoon, when Jim was driving back from an innocent afternoon of tennis in Marin. And Caroline stood in that motel parking lot with Ralph Carter hulking beside her, Caroline smiling beatifically into the sun and not quite seeing Jim as he drove past. (This incident is one of Caroline's reasons for insisting on the smallness of San Francisco.) "It's great for us to be so near the girls," she says—mainly to change the subject.

"I mostly see Sage, or sometimes Liza and the kids. But Sage comes around—" Jim's voice trails off huskily.

And Caroline recalls what she has considered his somewhat mawkish affection, always, for her daughter, *her* daughter, when after all he has three of his own.

"Wonderful news of Sage, don't you think?" Jim goes on so warmly and happily that Caroline chides herself for negative views. Jim is simply being kind to Sage, that's all, and God knows Sage could use a little more kindness in her life, especially from men.

"It is great news; now Jill's the one I worry about." Caroline has not known that she would say this.

"Oh, why?"

"I don't know, she's so thin. She looks strained. Unhappy."

"They're all too thin. Stressed out."

"I guess."

Bumping around the small floor with Jim, for the first time Caroline thinks, And just where is Ralph?

And then she sees him: Ralph is dancing with the bride, in a far corner of the very small dance floor. Dancing to music that is slow and saccharine and very familiar. Tall heavy Ralph and the tall, very beautiful, truly radiant dark bride, small ringlets escaping from her smoothly knotted hair down her smooth olive-skinned neck. They are dancing, Ralph and that girl, barely moving, both smiling as though at some secret joke.

Caroline feels a sharp jolt, a lunge of heated blood: it is sexual jealousy, pure and simple and terrible, and instantly recognized as such—although jealousy has not really been experienced by Caroline for many years, not since the early days with Ralph, when she used to worry obsessively about all those former wives, all three of them, and those even more threatening lady friends. Along with the jealousy Caroline feels its frequent concomitant, strong sexual arousal, pure lust, so acute that she has to laugh at herself, though on the surface she is merely smiling, pleasantly, as she dances with her nice former husband, Jim McAndrew. But such craziness, and at her age! And all over Ralph, who is only doing what all gentlemen at weddings are supposed to do, he is dancing with the bride.

"It's really nice to see you," Jim is saying, as he steps sharply across her left instep. "Oh, sorry. Maybe we could—"

"Have tea or something? Well, that would be awfully nice. And now I must go collect Ralph. I'm sure he's forgotten that we have an early date with a contractor tomorrow."

"Some expensive bash."

"Well, what do you think it cost? You know, I'm not great at calculations," Caroline on the way home asks Ralph, rather tipsily.

"I'd say thirty thou, but Roland Gallo put it at more like forty, and he'd be more apt to know."

"You talked to Roland Gallo? You're friends?"

"Sure, we're sort of old buddies. I used to see him around City Hall all the time. His politics are quite okay, actually. He's just rotten with the ladies. But you mean you spent all that time dancing with him and you didn't talk?"

"Of course we did, but not about how much the party cost. Honestly, Ralph. Though of course it is interesting. All that money."

"Goddam right it's interesting. Thirty or forty thou for a fucking wedding? Lucky no one in that group's running for public office."

"Well, why didn't you just ask the beautiful bride how much it all cost, speaking of dance-floor conversations?"

This half-drunken and fairly heated conversation takes place in Ralph's old Mercury, in the brief drive between the marble mansion and the home of Caroline and Ralph.

Who, at their door, disembark with not quite sober dignity.

In their separate bathrooms (a marvellous new luxury for them, in this new house) they undress and wash. Caroline very much wishes she had not had so much to eat and drink, and she thinks, Are all men dirty old men, at heart? I suppose they are. But, Lord, that girl could be Ralph's granddaughter.

As Ralph in his bathroom is thinking, Roland Gallo, Jesus Christ. He's laid everything in town, including Sage, for God's sake. I always thought my Caroline was too much of a snob for that sleazy bald dago.

And then they meet in bed, very eagerly, where for the next fifteen or twenty minutes they experience the liveliest, the most intense pleasure of and from each other that they have known in many months.

Eight

E ven the weather is conspiring, Sage now feels, to make her
perilously elated: how can she expect to calm down and to
be simply, quietly happy when July, normally such a terrible
month of cold wind and heavy fog in San Francisco, this year is
brilliantly blue from early morning on, and warm, with the gentlest,
most seductive breezes? Even the usually gray San Francisco Bay
looks blue, and is festively strewn with white sails, and rippled here
and there with streaks of waves, like a small inland sea.

But she must calm down, Sage knows that. She has a lot of work
to do before her show.

Sheer physical fatigue has been most helpful for almost anything
that is wrong, in Sage's past upheavals, and so now she walks a
great deal, hoping for peace. She walks from her own house on
Russian Hill to North Beach, and up and down Grant Avenue, past
all the seedy old once-beatnik haunts, past uninviting small shops,
full of old stamp collections, dingy jewels, and a few new boutiques
of expensive, downtown clothes. Past new bars and experimental
restaurants, across Columbus Avenue and up through Chinatown,
where despite the jarring crowds, the sheer press of terrific over-
population, Sage is assailed by the most marvellous food aromas,
spicy, exotic, tantalizing—so enticing that she hurries home to make
a sandwich for her lunch.

And then to work.

· · ·

What she is working on, when, these days, she can and does work—
what she absolutely must finish before the show—is the mother
group, the woman with her five daughters that she first began to
contemplate, to imagine, on the day of the welcome-home lunch for
Caroline and Ralph (when Fiona brought all that ludicrous food
and Jill was so especially bitchy, Sage thought). This matriarchal
group will in no way be specifically *them,* and God knows not rec-
ognizably so, not really Caroline and her five daughters. Just six
related female figures, one of whom is considerably larger, more in
control and more beautiful, more reposeful than the other, smaller
five, who also vary among themselves as to size and shape, awkward
restiveness or grace (the most reposeful, most graceful of the smaller
figures is also the heaviest: is that Liza?). No faces are in the least
defined, just figures. Sage is all absorbed in this project, fascinated.
She is so pleased with its concept that she can hardly bring herself
to its implementation, a seemingly contradictory condition that she
has experienced before.

But she does. She surprises herself with the prolonged intensity
of her work, and with the amount that she gets done. By the end
of that afternoon, the largest figure, who is seated, is almost there,
large and reposing, with a quality of waiting, of peaceful expectation, that Sage had neither planned nor foreseen, but that she very
much likes.

And all the time she is thinking, thinking and saying to herself,
New York. A gallery in SoHo.

Noel is indecisive or in any case vague about whether or not he will
come along to New York with her. "It really depends," he tells her,
presumably meaning his work. "Do I have to decide right now?"

"No, of course not." And, saying that, Sage thinks of another
time, almost exactly two years back, when she had to go or felt that
she had to go to Los Angeles, to take some slides around to galleries
there (everyone said artists had a much better chance down there,
San Francisco being so very conservative, art-wise). And she wanted

Noel to come too, she wanted (she told him this) to make an interesting, fun excursion out of what could be otherwise just a chore, a
discouraging task. They could go to some galleries together; Noel
likes to see paintings, he has an extraordinary if quite untutored
eye. They could find some good restaurants, walk around. Make fun
of Rodeo Drive, its horror show of commerce. *Have fun.* Sage said
all that to Noel until she realized that she was pleading, and that
the true point (as extremely intuitive Noel had no doubt grasped)—
the real point was that she did not dare leave him alone. Even for
one night.

Which of course was crazy: if he was "involved" with someone,
as from various signs she often suspected that he was (those finger-
round upper-arm bruises, his more-than-usual impatience and
crossness with her), he could see *her,* whoever, at any time. He had
all day to be out seeing someone else. And if, as Sage suspected,
whoever it was was married, *she* was not free at night (or on weekends) either. And so to make sure that she, Noel's wife, was with
him every night did not make sense.

At that time Noel decided not to go, after all, to L.A., and so
Sage did all her business, all that discouraging legwork, in one day,
leaving early and coming home late and horrendously tired. To find
Noel asleep in their bed, of course, and annoyed that she woke him
up—coming in, kissing him good night.

But about Noel's coming with her to New York, Sage with some
interest now notes, she does not feel any such urgency. She is not
even entirely sure whether or not she wants him to come along.
How very interesting, she thinks. She is almost moved to call the
shrink whom she went to see at the end of her Roland Gallo debacle;
she can almost hear that classically Viennese voice, saying, "So. So
you genuinely do not care that he comes or not? That is very interesting, it is even very good."

Sage asks herself, is this new attitude because she has no special
suspicions of Noel, recently? For she has not, she has even had the
curious instinct that someone had turned him down, maybe a good
feminist who does not believe in screwing married men? Sage smiles

at that thought, and then she thinks, But it could be anyone at all. Even one of my sisters.

It might almost be better if Noel did not come to New York. Sage explores that idea for an instant, tasting it, and then wills herself to leave it alone. For one thing, if Noel got the slightest whiff of that feeling, which he surely would if she truly entertained it, he would in some way act on his perception: he would come to New York.

Perhaps, Sage often thinks, I am simply one of those people who do fairly well with work but not with love.

Which in the long run is surely better than the reverse? In her Roland Gallo days she felt supremely good at love, so in love and so loved that her work was all pushed aside, postponed.

And then, in the horrible, devastated post-Roland period, she could not work either.

But in her present semi-euphoria she is even able to remember only Roland at his best. Which is to say, Roland in bed.

Why me? was one of Sage's earliest responses to Roland's violent pursuit of her. Why me, for all those phone calls and flowers? (Roland in his way was an old-fashioned, classic lover.) Why me for such extremes of insistence that I see him? Even at the party at which they met, a gallery opening of the very lavish sort being done a lot just then—that night there were better-looking, younger women than Sage. But soon after that, in the early stages of their great love, Sage saw herself as inevitable for Roland, she even saw herself as fantastically, incredibly attractive: of course Roland Gallo would pursue her. Later still, she felt that he must have chosen her for a certain docility, and for a sensed potential for gratitude. Not to mention the very practical consideration that she lived a scant few blocks from his house—he then as now in his Pacific Street mansion, facing the playground, and she then in a small flat above a store, out on Sacramento Street (at that time even less fashionable than now, in fact rather shabby). Sage had the very small flat, easily taken over and possessed by Roland. What Sage remembers is standing on the top of her stairs, breathless from the sound of his knock at her door and the turn of his key (of course she had given him a key, even insisted that he take it). Those stairs were the most impressive feature of Sage's apartment—and Roland would run up them, would run up to her, both of them laughing. "Your stairs keep me very young," he had said. "Not to mention—" (Like many exceptionally sexual persons, Roland was quite chary, prudish, even, about sexual references in talk.)

And then they would move from their languishing kiss, down the short hall to her bedroom, to bed, where, almost as soon as they were naked, touching, Sage began to come—at first slowly, trying not to, postponing. And then she did, again and again. Explosions of light.

"I have a sort of weakness for Italians," a few years later, suppos- edly "over" Roland Gallo, Sage said to the very handsome young carpenter who had come to help her with her house, the house she had finally dared to buy with her inheritance from Molly Blair. He had come, this Noel Finn, to talk about what could be done, a studio, et cetera. But then he stuck around for some wine, and personal conversation. He was not especially attracted to Sage (that must have been the case, although Noel would never admit it), and therefore, as they talked, in that way, he confessed to a lot of love affairs, laughingly telling her that he did best with married women, preferably Catholics, much better than young chicks who wanted to get married, have babies and a house. He was telling her quite clearly: Don't get involved with me, I'm not to be taken seriously. Although he said, with his flirty, confident smile, "Would a South- of-Market Irishman do?"

And so Sage not only got involved, fell in love, but married Noel, despite both their intentions otherwise: they simply reached that point in the affair when it was time either to marry or to separate, and according to many observers (Sage's half-sisters and her mother, Noel's past and present lady friends) they made the wrong choice.

And all along Sage knew everything about him: Noel was much

too handsome, vain and unreliable. She also knew that in some mysterious way he was an imitation Roland Gallo.

The balmy weather most unexpectedly became a heat wave, two days of temperatures in the nineties—unheard of in San Francisco in July. No breeze anywhere, no fog. And even Sage, who normally hated both fog and wind, began to long for both.

"It's as hot as New York," Noel tells her over dinner, a shrimp salad that Sage intended to be better than it is, but at least it is cold (and then she remembers: God, she forgot the cilantro).

"I hope you don't get this kind of weather there in October," Noel continues—meaning that he isn't going along?

"I suppose I could," Sage tells him—perhaps meaning, It's okay if you don't come, I can make it alone all right. Or does she mean that?

He grins, showing strong white perfect teeth. "You're ready for anything, right?"

"I guess. Listen, is that the beginning of foghorns?"

It was. Faintly at first, and then with more assurance, the horns had begun their hoarse, inharmonious rounds as, edging into the bay, the first dark fingers of fog could be seen, and a slight breeze began to flutter the air—not yet quite cooling, but shifting the currents, promising cool.

The heat has not agreed with Noel at all. He looks sweatily pale, exhausted. His perfect nose is red at the tip, and his eyelids droop. Looking across the table at his face, Sage sees what she has never before observed there: she sees an intimation of age, of a lessening of his beauty. Someday, Sage thinks, he'll be just a plain aging man, good-looking (he'll always be good-looking, probably) but no longer such a dazzler. Fewer heads turning in the street to stare.

She finds some measure of relief in that thought—how could she not? Quite involuntarily she smiles.

"Feeling better?" Noel asks her.

"Yes. Really."

He smiles across to her, and with that smile all his beauty is instantly restored.

Nine

Now that Caroline is back, Liza talks to her mother so often that the two women sometimes lose track of the fact that they have not seen each other for a while. Liza even feels, sometimes, that she talks to her mother almost as she would to herself, so non-judgmental—and at the same time interested—does she feel Caroline to be. At other times she thinks that Caroline is less non-judgmental than simply preoccupied. God knows what is really on Caroline's mind.

In any case Caroline is the only person to whom Liza could say, as one morning she does, "Well, David Argent really got trashed in the *Times*. That almost makes my day."

"Honestly, Liza, he's really not worth a thought."

"I know, I really do. But for so many years he got all that terrific attention, like all those Enrico's guys. The so-called writers."

Caroline laughs. "Yes, one wondered when they wrote."

"One did indeed."

A pause, and then Caroline remarks, "I am a little worried over Sage. She's so high, over-excited. Come to think of it, I saw something of the same thing with Aaron, that terrific excitement."

"All my kids are like that. So far. But you think Sage could be manic-depressive? Saul says it can be inherited, at least a tendency. He thinks."

"Darling," says Caroline, reprovingly. "Of course I didn't mean that."

As Liza thinks that actually she did—that Caroline is worried.

"Jim might know how she is," adds Caroline. "I gather she sees quite a lot of him. Still."

"Well, that's nice," Liza tells her mother, somewhat distractedly. And then she asks, "Have you been to any more good parties?"

"Well, we did go to one in our old neighborhood. Mostly Ralph's old political pals, but very nice. Just around the corner from Liberty Street. With such a pretty garden, I nearly died of envy at all those roses. One surprise, of all people Roland Gallo was there. So odd, you see an unlikely person in one place and then they're everywhere, have you noticed? Anyway, his poor young wife got terribly drunk, quite sad to watch actually. I did not get an impression of much marital accord."

"Very likely not," says Liza. "I don't imagine marriage is exactly what he's best at. Does Ralph think he'll run for mayor?"

Caroline allows one of the discreet pauses for which she is noted, within her family, and then she says, "He won't say. In fact I have to tell you that I find Ralph the least bit worrying these days."

"How do you mean?"

"Oh, nothing specific. Just not entirely himself. Very tired. But of course I always forget how old we both are."

"Of course you do, since you aren't."

"You're sweet, but I'm really not thirty, which is what I seem to think I am."

Hanging up the phone (a child is crying upstairs), as she hurries to them Liza wonders, Do Ralph and Caroline sometimes still do it? I think probably yes, they do.

They were certainly active the year before they got married, Liza remembers, just after Caroline broke up with Jim and Ralph moved in. They could hear them every night, and all those sex sounds were new—they never heard Caroline doing it with Jim, although they must have, at least a few times. And Liza wonders if she and Saul will begin to taper off, and if so when.

At times I sort of wish we would, thinks Liza. I could use more sleep.

"You kids were supposed to be asleep!" she says to her children, in their bedroom. "It's naptime."

.   .   .

"My mother called, and I think she's really worried over Sage," Liza tells Saul that night, during what they somewhat ironically refer to as the cocktail hour, which is more often spent in some way with the children: talking to, reading to, playing with, trying to separate from children. At the moment, though, out of character, the two older children are sitting across Saul's knees, absorbed in a magazine. And the baby is asleep in her basket.

"Here we go again." Saul sighs, possibly remembering the many evenings that he and Liza spent with Sage, after Roland Gallo. Listening, giving advice, and more listening, listening, to all the repetitive rhythms of Sage's broken heart. "But I think she's really okay now," he says, hopefully.

"Well, maybe. Oh, and Fiona called. Such a surprise, she wants us for dinner. Thursday."

"Thursday's out. You know, my good works."

"Well, I'll go and tell you all about it." Liza smiles, and then adds, "An interesting thing about our family parties, have you noticed? There's always someone missing."

"Well, I guess I get to be the missing person."

"Darling, I'm not sure you count."

The more surprising missing person at Fiona's dinner turned out to be Jill, actually; this was considered odd in view of her known great closeness to Fiona.

Also, a second surprise, Portia brought along what with great relief everyone took to be her boyfriend. Harold, the young man with whom she worked at the nursery. (Harold, in what looked to be his prep-school graduation suit: dark blue, with wide lapels.)

But the main event of the evening was surely the food. "I'm still not sure what Fiona was up to, but if she meant to be impressive in a totally disgusting Eighties way she really succeeded," Liza later reported to Saul. From the lobster canapés through foie gras (in a cornmeal crust) and salmon mousse with a tomato coulis. Veal Orloff, which at that meal was a nice old-fashioned Julia touch. Spinach with prosciutto. Salad of arugula, radicchio, et cetera. Brie and Stilton. Grapefruit sorbet. Melons, grapes. Chocolate truffles. Coffee. Armagnac.

They were all somewhat subdued, no doubt in part by the sheer weight of so much food—and conversation rather dragged. But some of them made a certain effort—mostly of course Caroline.

"I keep reading these days about yuppies," she said. "You know, it's quite a new concept for us, they don't have them in Lisbon. It sounds quite disgusting, all that programmatic expensiveness."

At which Fiona told her, with a small tight laugh, "Mother, this has been described as the quintessentially yuppie restaurant."

"But surely you don't like being called that? I think it's most unfair."

"I'm afraid the shoe fits," Fiona told her.

But, Liza wondered, surely Caroline knew all that before? Sometimes she suspects Caroline of considerable feigned innocence.

Caroline tried again, conversationally. "Another thing that I very much dislike," she said, "is the use of the word 'elegant.' Suddenly everything is elegant, when it really isn't at all, if you see what I mean. 'Designer clothes,' and what an awful term that is, right there. Anyway, designer clothes are not elegant."

"They're just ripping off L. L. Bean," Ralph suddenly, surprisingly said. "Calvin Klein, Mr. Lauren, all that bunch, it's really straight out of Freeport, Maine."

Such a typical Ralph observation, everyone thought. So right on. But how did he know? One doesn't exactly imagine Ralph perusing the ads in *Vogue*. In fact all Caroline's daughters had sometimes wondered just that about Ralph: *how did he know?*

Fiona was all over the place that night, like a first-time hostess, jumping up and down, running in and out of the room, staying away for increasing intervals. Of course she was working, being hostess in her restaurant on what looked like a busy night, as well as entertaining her family, but still: Liza had a curious sense that someone was there whom the rest of them were not supposed to know about. "Fiona must be getting it on with someone wrong," was how she described it to Saul. "The hidden mystery guest."

Noel, in Liza's view, was at his most charming that night, which is to say that he was fairly quiet, and helpful in small ways to Fiona, courtly to Caroline and very sweet with Sage (too sweet? could he be up to something?). He and Sage looked marvellous together that night, with all that thick dark hair, those two very lithe thin bodies, their golden eyes.

Portia, in a gauzy flowered dress, looked, well, odd, in her sisters' opinions. "A little like a tall young boy in drag," Liza put it to Saul, later on.

"Later we got into travel talk," Liza reported. "I've often wondered, where would Eighties conversations be without food and travel? I always think of this at doctor parties, you know? All those rich doctors and their wives, going on about the boiled beef at the Sacher, kidneys at Claridge's. It's enough to put you off food entirely."

The ostensible reason for the travel talk that evening was to advise Sage about her trip to New York. The best fares for getting there, the various Frequent Flyer plans—as though that were what Sage was about to become, a Frequent Flyer. And then they talked about New York restaurants. Where her dealer should take her for dinner.

Later still, on the way to the ladies', Liza got somewhat lost, easy enough to do in that maze of Fiona's. She went past the tiny room that Fiona calls her bar, and was sure that she saw Roland Gallo there, although she was hurrying past. But Liza would know that shining dome anywhere, she thought.

And she wondered: Is that who Fiona is hiding from everyone? Protecting Sage from Roland, which would not be like Fiona? Also, Liza was sure that Roland Gallo was there alone, Joanne the airhead was definitely not in the ladies'.

Could Fiona be getting it on with Roland Gallo?

Ten

"What can I woo you with? I'm an old-fashioned wine-and-flowers man, and you're surrounded with both. I don't know what to do about you, I'm really upset. I don't know myself these days. I could write a book—now, there's a song for you. You've turned my life upside down. You see how silly I sound? But you can't keep turning me down. I won't let you."

Smiling Fiona, in her sunny penthouse bedroom, now streaming with rare brilliant August sunshine—Fiona turns off the tape to which she has just listened, as to herself she complains, Well, really, doesn't he have anything else to do but make these phone calls? He's been calling me all day.

However, at the same time another, interior voice is saying, Of course he's right. I can't keep turning him down. I really can't.

On another tape, a couple of days ago, Roland said, "I am mad, you know that? around the bend. I am seriously thinking of cashing in everything, the practice, my house, everything I own, and kidnapping you. Permanently. We could go to Capri, or maybe Taormina. Or Palermo. You'd like it there, it's beautiful. Flowers. I have a few connections, some cousins there. We'd stay there for good. I am seriously thinking of this. I am crazy about you, Miss Fiona McAndrew."

Of course he knows that she could keep all the tapes, that is another thing that Fiona thinks. The Gallo-McAndrew tapes. The *Chronicle* would pay a lot for them, if he runs for mayor.

But of course I wouldn't dream of doing that, thinks Fiona.

She also thinks of saying to Roland, straight out, Just how many times have you said all this stuff before, old pal? You're coming on as though the whole thing were entirely new, the very first time. For you.

Fiona would truly love to have a conversation with Sage along these lines, a real tell-all chat, the kind that men imagine women have all the time, when actually we don't.

I could never even bring it up with Sage, thinks Fiona.

Uncannily prescient, or something, Roland shows up at the restaurant, Fiona's, at various times all during the course of the day. There he is, just wandering through, or sitting in the bar with a paper. *But only when Fiona is there.* And how could he possibly know? She is in and out all day, in a way that no one could predict, not possibly. Has he hired someone, maybe someone who works for her, to clue him in, let him know about any plan or appointment of Fiona's? He wouldn't do that, would he? Fiona in fact believes that he would not, more likely he goes on instinct, and Roland's instincts are probably quite uncanny.

At times with severity, at other times with a sort of envious amusement, Fiona has observed the extremely sexual behind-the-scenes atmosphere at Fiona's. She has pondered this, and at some point she read an article about another famous local restaurant in which the same condition was described, a heightened sexual atmosphere. But no explanation was proffered.

Fiona has thought about this a lot, but has not come up with much beyond the inherent sexiness of food: there must be something excitingly permissive and generous about working with food? really getting into very good food, with hands and mouths? anticipation? smells?

She can't work it out, but all around her everyone seems to be getting it on with someone else who works there; the very air is full of sex, romance, with whispers and whispery, sexy laughs. Along with the cooking aromas, the wonderful garlic and fish smells, the lemon and rosemary.

Even the two young women who deliver flowers for Stevie every morning are lovers, one tall and black, the other small and fair.

In other words, everyone at Fiona's is doing a lot of sex. Except Fiona.

Does Roland Gallo know all that? It almost seems possible that he does. Almost. Or is Fiona getting a little paranoid?

She doesn't know.

"If she keeps this up I may have to have her disappeared, I'm that crazy about that girl," Roland confides, over a lunchtime Campari, in the bar of the Big Four restaurant. "I know you think I'm crazy, but I've really got it for her. Like, like nothing. I could throw it all over for that kid. Make tracks for Palermo." He flashes his widest, most Sicilian grin at his companion-confidant. Who is Buck Fister, an unlikely choice all around that even Roland cannot understand, except that Buck has a certain reputation for discretion; he does not talk.

As Roland himself might put it, With the deals that guy's got, he's got to be discreet.

Most recently, Buck has shifted from the engineering-illumination projects that no one ever quite grasped, that were always slightly mysterious (there were hints of union connivance), from all that he has gone into real estate, making the shift with a very loud noise indeed. His name is now attached to most of the largest property deals in town, residential-wise. Two-bedroom cottages, needing work, in Pacific Heights, for 995. Or, on Russian Hill, bargain condos at 950. Not to mention mansions for, probably, somewhere in the neighborhood of 3. And BUCK FISTER, in small discreet lettering on the black-and-white signs affixed to all those properties. (Like many profoundly vulgar people, Buck is a stickler for what he calls "taste." He likes things to be "elegant," and he uses that word a lot. He is a passionate if partially informed Anglophile—of course.)

And, to his occasional displeasure, his name is suddenly proclaimed in every column; he is at every dinner party, opening or ball, giving almost half of those parties himself, it seems. In his tasteful, elegant Nob Hill pied-à-terre.

Plump and rosy-faced, average-ordinary-looking Buck. Nothing you would ever notice or remember about that face, thinks Roland, who is something of a snob about good looks. You can't even tell which way Buck swings, to look at him, thinks Roland. Of if he swings at all. Buck's sex life is something about which there have been no rumors that Roland has ever heard. Or maybe he just hasn't heard them yet. It could be something wild, but Roland doesn't think so, he does not think Buck does anything very interesting, along those lines. He may be just one of those guys with a very low sex drive, whom Roland sometimes envies, sort of. Buck functions as a walker, an escort for very rich, older women whose husbands do not wish to go to the opera, but he is also quite often seen with very pretty young women. In any case Roland knows that they, he and Buck, make a most unlikely couple, as, leaving the bar, they pass into the dining room, with its portraits and hunting horns, its suggestion of private clubs, of "Englishness."

The Pacific Union Club, with its difficult, expensive memberships, its excellent food and its ludicrous rules concerning the presence of women, its terrific basement swimming pool, is just across the street, in the old Flood Mansion. It is to that club that both Buck and Roland most secretly, unadmittedly and probably in vain aspire.

Today, in addition to his loverly wish to speak of his beloved, Roland has what could be construed as a favor to ask of Buck: he has recently heard a rumor about Buck and a certain property that Buck owns, a big house, a mansion actually (though no one would buy it), out in Seacliff, near the Golden Gate. If the rumor is true, and Roland has every reason to believe that it is, then Buck could be very useful sometimes to certain of Roland's relatives who come to town, people whom Roland refers to and even thinks of as his distant cousins. To whom Roland, for ancient but unburied family reasons, old debts, has inherited some indebtedness—which he cleverly manages to over-pay, usually, thus incurring an indebtedness in his own direction.

"You know so many people," Roland in his most flattering tone begins (his detractors sometimes call him oily).

"Unlike you. You of course don't know a soul." Buck's somewhat crooked grin is very boyish. But a fleshy mouth is one of the things that keep Buck from being good-looking, Roland now observes.

"Well, some of my relatives, my cousins, have heard of you. And they come to town sometimes."

Buck answers with a very long look—a look in which much more is contained than in their usual, fairly prolonged conversations. "I'll give you a number," he says at last. "But nothing funny. Absotively, poso-lutely." (This last is a teasing putdown of Roland's own somewhat dated slang; it is not an expression of Buck's.)

Roland laughs. He is trying to be good-natured about fulfilling an obligation that he finds inherently distasteful. And all this business of women in houses is very dangerous, as Buck should know. "Of course not," he says to Buck. And, "These are not funny people, my friend. But thanks, old man." (This last was in Buck's own ersatz-English voice, and manner.)

Propitiously, just at that moment the first course arrives, spinach salads for both.

"You ever thought you'd grow up and order spinach in a restaurant, go out and eat spinach on purpose?" asks Roland, in the chatty, bantering mode he seems most usually to use with Buck. "If my sainted mother could see me ordering spinach—" He laughs, his dark eyes sentimental. But both the sentiment and the subject of food have led him directly back to his obsession, back to Fiona. "They make these terrific soufflés at Fiona's place," he tells Buck.

"It's a very good restaurant, she's doing a good job." Buck is sober, judicious. A man who knows good restaurants, as who in his world these days does not?

"She's got a nerve, though. Putting me off."

"True," Buck mumbles, chewing spinach.

What is it about Buck that urges Roland to run off at the mouth like this? Roland himself has no idea, he is not even entirely (posolutely) sure that Buck does keep his own mouth shut. God knows who Buck talks to. Some flabby-mouthed bimbo, that could be. "Your mother still living?" for no reason Roland then asks Buck.

"She's in a nursing home, actually. Just outside Boston. The best I could find." Buck smiles, deprecating his own efforts. (Although in actual fact his mother, called Rosette, in late middle age is lively and well and quite on her own, operating a small, highly successful bordello in Carson City, Nevada.)

It must be something like this to go to a shrink, Roland imagines, this urge to go on and on about yourself. At a certain point Sage used to write him long letters about her hours with that woman she went to, how much it helped. And as though writing to him were also helpful. Poor old Sage.

Talking to Buck is sure as hell not like confession, where he, Roland, was always controlling what he said (good Christ, he had to), leaving out some things, making up some innocent others. With Buck, Roland is aware of being just slightly out of control, and what is strange is that he enjoys it, Roland does; he likes this yielding to his own urge to talk, and talk. To tell Buck everything. Maybe he should try this Viennese shrink sometime—but no, you'd have to be sick.

"It's an interesting family," Buck next remarks, tidily finishing the last leaf of his salad.

"Family?" This is a word that Roland almost never uses.

"The McAndrews. Remember the old Andrews Sisters? You must. But those five girls, and their mother."

"Yes," Roland agrees, as he uneasily wonders where all this could go. He does not want to talk about Sage, although Buck surely knows that old chapter.

"You met the youngest?" asks Buck. "I think Portia."

"No, I don't think I have. I know perfectly well I haven't. Maybe I'm working my way down to her, so to speak."

Both men laugh, and Roland thinks, Good, now, that's enough family talk.

"You know Jill?" Buck asks.

"No, not really. I've seen her around, I think. Pretty girl." Roland has spoken in the tone of a man having no interest at all in the pretty girl under discussion.

Which Buck catches. "She doesn't do much for you, huh?"

"Well, you know how it is, I'm in love." Roland laughs.

"You don't think they look alike?"

"Fiona and Jill? Well, maybe the slightest. I hardly see it, though. Fiona's hair, it's so long, such beautiful hair. Fiona is a really beautiful woman, she just needs a few pounds. But why? You know Jill?"

"A little. I was thinking, you might have an easier time in that direction. I could even put in a word."

"Come on, Buck. I keep telling you, I'm serious."

"Okay, okay. Forget I spoke." He looks sideways at Roland. "I just thought, in case you wanted something a little younger."

"Look, fellow, at my age I can't handle anything under thirty."

Another oblique look. "Is that right? I've heard it's easier, the younger they are. But that's just what they say." And then he says, "But about this mayor thing. Let's talk."

"Well. Okay." Roland sighs.

A sexy atmosphere is one thing, thinks Fiona, as she goes down into the wine cellar for some Meursault that some people she knows especially ordered, and finds two young waiters down there, making out—but that's a little much, she thinks. And there they are, two skinny young guys, kissing, bending back, their hands all over each other. Transfixed, for an instant Fiona just stares at them. Didn't they hear her? She once read that sexual excitement dulls the hearing, but still, they writhe against each other, hands on necks, on butts. A first kiss, Fiona imagines, halted where she is, then turning to walk back to the stairs, heels clicking as loud as she can make them. Behind her she hears feet in sudden motion—at least, at last they heard her.

Fiona finds Stevie, confronts him. "Stevie, I can't! This is really too much, I can't deal with this stuff. You go down there, get the fucking Meursault—"

Stevie's large face is kindly, as always, but otherwise a blank: he is not taking sides.

As who would? Fiona a few minutes later thinks, momentarily alone. She sounded hysterical, a hysterical frustrated almost middle-aged woman. SHIT! She can hardly believe it. At thirty-three. Her mother, Caroline, never sounded like that. But then Caroline always had something going, probably, or almost always. Some husband or lover or someone.

Of course one of the problems is that all this stuff going on around her is pretty arousing. And so there she is, turned on and totally frustrated. Cross. She feels very cross, most of the time. A classic case. Maybe she should see Sage's old shrink?

Even Stevie's flower arrangements look sexy, Fiona now observes. Beds of moss with towering, spiky pink things rising upwards. What's with Stevie, anyway? With everyone?

Walking through her rooms, now crowded and lively, everyone grinning and eating and drinking, eating and simultaneously talking food, and talking wine as they drink, Fiona inwardly snarls and she thinks, The silly jerks.

She wonders if a health spa might do it for her, The Golden Door or that other sort of Zen place that's more strict, where you get bone thin. In Mexico, she thinks.

Or, there's always her handy vibrator. Which works, God knows it works, right off. But it's still a little depressing.

Oh shit, Fiona thinks. Maybe I'm just tired. Well, early to bed. Some treat.

She must, though, get through at least another hour of greetings. The stupidest possible chattering with friends and non-friends, friends of friends. She does all that, managing at the same time to think of her bed, her nice private bed, and her book; she has a good new book to read, a history of Venice that her stepfather, Ralph, just gave her. Fiona and Ralph have similar taste in reading matter, both preferring fact to fiction.

"I'm heading up," Fiona tells Stevie at last. "See you tomorrow." And she goes outside as though leaving the premises (as she does every night), and slips around the corner to her own private, secret door.

A dark wind has come up, and Fiona glances briefly at the sweep of clouds. She shivers and inserts her key. Which as always sticks.

"Let me help you."

Turning—had she meant to cry out? to scream?—Fiona sees Roland Gallo. Of course, it would have to be. His bald head shines in the streetlight, and Fiona sees the large bright whites of his eyes. And she thinks, I still could scream—but she does not.

With one hand he takes the key and turns it easily in the lock, as with the other he takes Fiona. He leads, guides, propels her up the stairs. To her own apartment. As she half resists, pushing at him, stumbling a little.

At the top of the stairs he turns her around to face him, and then, gently pulling her hair back, he begins to kiss her. Stopping once to breathe, to mutter, "Ah, good Christ!" Then more kissing, more violently.

This is what rape is, a voice within Fiona's mind informs her. Someone you know, even someone who knows you want him. But not so quickly, so easily.

"Roland, no. No."

"Yes—"

He pushes her down to the bed, always kissing—her mouth, her face, her neck.

As Fiona pushes up against his shoulders with both hands, twists her face from his—and feels flooded with a violent, crazy heat.

With a slow and curiously respectful motion, Roland reaches beneath her dress, reaches up silk thighs. "Ah Christ," he breathes. "The most beautiful—let me touch—"

Eleven

"**D**oes it count as rape if you come?"

Early this morning Jill heard that startling question from her answering machine, in her sister Fiona's voice. That crazy question, and then Fiona's deep familiar sexy laugh. A laugh that sounds, Jill knows, very much like her own. As do their voices. Different as in other ways they are, all three of the McAndrew daughters sound very much alike. And unlike both Sage and Portia. Sage's voice is rather high, at times strangely childish, and Portia's by contrast is deep, a little hoarse.

But. "Does it count as rape if you come?" Fiona asked that, and left the words on Jill's machine. So odd. They don't talk about sex in that way, for one thing. The word "come" has never been used in that sense before, in any of their conversations. And "rape"? What on earth is Fiona talking about? Did Stevie—? Or one of those sexy young waiters? They all look gay, but probably some of them are not.

Thinking all this, and playing, replaying Fiona's strange question in her mind, at the same time Jill is actually doing I. Magnin's, as she puts it to herself. A store that she never goes into any more, too *old,* really retro, but today something called her there, she felt this as she was passing those awful front windows, just now full of opera gowns, the worst. There was something inside especially waiting for her. Jill could always tell that, with stores.

She has already checked out Valentino, St. Laurent and Anne

Klein II, nothing for her in any of those places. And just as well, her cash picture is not the greatest right now.

The other women in that store all look so desperate, Jill thinks, and she hates (fears, pities) their desperation. They are all hunting, and all very uncertain. All believing that whatever they buy will make some difference in their lives. As she, Jill, to a certain extent must also believe, else why would she be here, so eagerly checking out racks, so avidly looking over this entire store? Clothes are a total hoax, one more rotten trick on women, Jill believes. Women end up with closets full of unworn, or nearly unworn, and unbecoming clothes. All bought on speculation, so to speak. And Jill hates this willingness in herself and in other women to go along with that gag, to read *Vogue* and to buy what they are told to. To buy what totally hostile, totally commercial-minded men tell them they should wear.

When she is older and stronger (Jill imagines old age as a time of much-increased moral strength) Jill plans to give all this up, "this" being most of what she is doing now, including her fancy clothes. She will wear jeans and runners, Shetland sweaters and maybe some kind of sheepskin, for cold. She won't care.

In the meantime, however, now, she sees the most perfect night-gown ever imagined. Conspicuously displayed on a plaster model, right at the entrance to Lingerie. A gown and peignoir of the palest pearl-gray silk, the gown cut low and narrow, the peignoir all foaming lace. Handmade lace; Jill or almost anyone could tell that a block away.

Jill can guess too that it costs about 750, crazy for a nightgown, but of course it's more than a gown. The peignoir with all that lace could be worn to the opera, and wouldn't that be good? "Ms. Jill McAndrew, in a gray gown and peignoir—"

It costs not 750, but 995, considerably crazier. But there is no way now not to buy it. Jill is hooked.

And no, she does not want to try it on. She can tell, the size is perfect for her. The petite. She hands over her platinum card.

So annoying, though, the length of these transactions. Jill is allowed too much time to think, and to speculate. Just what does it mean, this purchase? Why an expensive nightgown? She is not going back to the Game with Buck any more, she has less than no intention of doing that. And she isn't "seeing" anyone.

Does it mean, then, Noel? Is she finally going to say some sort of yes to Noel?

Jill's mind switches back to Fiona then, and she wonders again, just what did Fiona mean, with that flaky rape question? Who on earth would dare do anything resembling rape, with formidable Fiona? Whatever went on with her last night, however, with whomever, Fiona certainly sounded madly cheerful (as Caroline sometimes puts it).

Noel, though. How he would love her pale-gray silk, her lace. (By now they have talked quite a lot, about almost everything, even clothes.) And her lace is as romantic as a Forties movie, Noel's favorites. He loves all those old blondes, Carole Lombard, even Ginger Rogers (and so what is he doing with Sage, with her dark, dark hair?). Jill can see the two of them, herself and Noel, as in a Forties musical finale. She with her short sleek hair, her blonde cap perfectly shining above all that floating pale-gray silk. And beautiful Noel, with his shapely mouth, strong perfect nose and all that thick dark Irish hair. And Noel is wearing—she can't see what Noel is wearing, maybe nothing? lovely naked Noel, dancing and bouncing about? Jill is on the verge of a laugh, a giggle, really, when she remembers, or reminds herself: Noel is your sister's husband, you silly bitch. Whatever are you thinking?

However, the silly excitement, the cheap thrill of thinking of Noel in that way persists, as at last Jill receives her nice brown-striped Magnin's box, and heads for the elevator.

Stepping back to wait as a group of women emerges from the car, Jill suddenly recognizes—of all people, at that moment—her half-sister. Sage herself, in something green, her hair as thick and dark as Noel's hair is. (If Sage and Noel had kids they would be Jewish-Irish, Jill quickly thinks, all with wonderful dark ethnic hair, all thick and wild.)

"Sage!"

"Jill!"

The two women brush cheeks, not quite together.

"But whatever—"

"Lingerie! of all places to meet—"

"In that case I'm on the wrong floor," says Sage.

"Oh, me too. But I just bought this silly nightgown," Jill tells her. "I can't think why," she lies.

"Well. I need something for New York. Maybe I don't really but I think I do," says Sage a little wildly.

"I saw a yellow blazer on Four, perfect for you," Jill tells her, having automatically in that moment put Sage in the yellow coat, which would indeed be great on her.

"Yellow?"

"It's really big this season, it's all over. Great on you, with your eyes."

"On the other hand, I could get something in New York."

"Well, you could."

"Fiona said Bergdorf's was on the corner near my hotel."

"Well, in that case, you can't beat Bergdorf's." I don't have time for this conversation, I really can't stand it, Jill is thinking. And she also thinks, This rotten small town, in New York people don't run into their half-sisters at Bergdorf's elevators, do they?

And for once Sage is so chatty. "I guess I'm focussing on what to wear instead of the trip itself," she tells Jill—who could not be less interested, and who recognizes the good-patient tone that Sage has been using, ever since that shrink she put in time with, that dowdy doctor. After Roland Gallo. Ever since then Sage has been analyzing herself—so boring!

"Well, I've got to run," Jill tells her sister, half-sister. And why not? She does have to run, she's late.

"Well, great to see you. We'll talk."

"Yes, great! Good luck!"

A real downer. Running into Sage at just that moment was surely a lowerer of Jill's high spirits, a destroyer of all that fantasy froth. For one thing, Sage looked so bloody happy. So up.

Sage should have known what Noel was like when she married him. Jill has this thought some twenty minutes later as she contemplates the blank screen that she faces, a space on which her thoughts on a Midland, Texas, mineralogy quarterly are supposed to appear. Her very own serious, appraising, valuable thoughts.

But instead Jill is remembering the marriage of Sage and Noel, it must be nearly five years ago, up on Mt. Tam. So hippie, so retro-Sixties, the whole ridiculous thing, and everyone was already much too old for that.

High up on Mt. Tamalpais, a grassy plateau overlooking the bay, the headlands and back to the bridge, the distant city. Except that on that bright September afternoon, almost as soon as the wedding party arrived great billows of the purest white fog began to roll in through the Golden Gate, obscuring everything but the space where they were, the small sunny clearing that then seemed suspended in clouds.

Sage in pale-yellow silk. (Yellow is Sage's best color, has she forgotten?) Noel in a light-brown suit, managing to look like a man who does not wear suits, who is uncomfortable in suits—and a bright-red tie that somewhat later he took off, and he unbuttoned his shirt (the afternoon was hot but not all that hot, everyone thought, and they thought too, Did he have to unbutton it so far down?).

A woman judge performed the ceremony, some old feminist friend of Sage's, from what Sage insisted on calling the Movement.

A recorder group played Sixties songs. Beatles songs, Stones songs, songs from Aretha or James Brown or Dionne Warwick, or even the Beach Boys. Quite sweet, in a way, making everyone feel just slightly sentimental, a little tearful. Emotional, in a way that makes you hate yourself later on, you know you've been had, as by a very bad movie. That was Jill's reaction, and Fiona's too; they later said to each other, How dumb, how totally dumb.

Since Sage and Noel's romance had been fairly brief, about five or six months, this was the first time that several of the wedding guests had ever met Noel, including Jill. (Caroline and Ralph were already off in Lisbon, and had yet to meet him.) And Jill had two very clear, related impressions. The first of course had to do with his extreme handsomeness, that curved mouth, indented chin and all that thick dark hair made him almost too handsome, nearly pretty. And the second very clear idea that she had of Noel, right off, was that he was a really big flirt. A real male tease who would never, never in his heart be married. Jill felt this quite clearly despite the fact that on that day, certainly, Noel was all over Sage with affection, little kisses and small touchings. If you didn't watch too carefully you might think he was mad for Sage, which is what poor Sage herself must have thought, probably.

Jill, though, had picked up on a certain look, a look that Noel surely meant for her to think was meant for her alone (and recently he has said as much, in one of their increasingly long phone calls: "My wedding day, and I couldn't take my eyes off you, babe. My new sister. I thought, Oh, right!"). But Jill also knew that his flirty look could have landed on anyone, any woman, that is, whom Noel had sized up as the best-looking, or simply the most available, or the sexiest, maybe, in any group he landed in. At that moment. For Noel was a very momentary person, Jill knew that right off, along with all the rest she knew about him, just seeing him that first time. They were in some ways rather alike, she knew that.

Will Sage ever work that out? Will she ever get a fix on what Noel is really like? Probably not, Jill decides.

In any case, on Noel's wedding day, Jill just happened to be the best around, the best in sight, for the moment. Liza was pregnant (of course) and Fiona was in one of her imperious, Red Queen moods (Caroline used to tease her when they were teenagers, "Come on, Fi, please don't Red Queen it with me, I'm tired"). Fiona, cross and bossy, was not at her most attractive. And Portia was much too young, and that day especially nerdy in her pinkish Indian gauze, so Cost Plus. And there was Jill in her bare black dress. No one cares about black at weddings any more, it's all right to wear black. Jill had assured herself of that, since she wanted to wear that particular great dress—although if Caroline had been around she just might not have.

Anyway, Noel was managing to be wildly affectionate with Sage, while communicating quite another set of messages to Jill. Nothing really sleazy, though, nothing to put her off, make her mad. Noel's glances at Jill said, rather, Can't we be friends? And, We two have a certain understanding of how things are, now, don't we?

And then more looks. And after that, at all the so-called family gatherings, over the next few years, some idle but not really idle conversation.

Very little comes to Jill today on the Midland mineralogy publication, and so she simply gives it a negative report. Which it very likely deserved. Forget it, guys.

Walking home through Chinatown, along jam-packed Grant Avenue, among all the lagging tourists, fat and ugly in their polyester travelling clothes, and the fatter and uglier Chinese, shopping and stopping to talk—and oh, how long and loud they talk, those Chinks, Jill hates them all—she wonders why she walks this way. It's all so terrible, and getting worse, daily more Chinese, or whoever those people are, from wherever, and every day more tourists. The two major San Francisco industries, Jill with some asperity thinks: tourism, and taking in Orientals.

And then she thinks, Christ, I haven't fucked anyone for over a month, no wonder I'm turning into such a snarling racist.

She thinks, I hope, I really hope that Buck doesn't start calling me again with any big Game plans. I might, I really might just say yes. Maybe that's what my new nightgown's all about. Not Noel. Maybe it's really a brand-new uniform for the Game, when I always secretly hope for that first John to come back again.

Besides, I could really use a thousand bucks about now. I really could.

If she takes a long, foaming, scented bath, and then tries on her new nightgown, no one will call her. Jill is superstitiously very sure of that. It is her kind of logic.

And so she does just that. She lies back in a tub that is scented with bath oils and bubbles, she lies there admiring her breasts. So nice, small hard pink nipples just peering up through the foam. She loves her breasts.

But she is thinking of sex, distractingly. Of course she is. All the terrific men she's done it with. And it all seems so long ago, dear God! As though sex were something she just didn't do any more. As though everything were dangerous now. Which everything is, she thinks, the air we breathe is carcinogenic, probably.

Glancing around her steamy bathroom—but basically a beautiful room, all bright glass and steel and mirrors, she spent a fortune on this bathroom—Jill's eyes come to rest on the phone, in its cradle on the wall, not far from her head. Just as, jarringly, it rings.

She reaches for the receiver. "Hello?"

"Hello." It is indeed Buck, which is somehow not at all a surprise.

However, as they pass through the preliminary small talk, not having seen each other or communicated for quite a while, as Jill is thinking, Well, why not? Why not right now, tonight?—in a very slow way she realizes that Buck is not calling about the Game. No John.

For one thing, he is taking far too long to get to the point: if he had some guy whom he wanted her to "meet" there would be some urgency, some haste to get on with it. But no, tonight he runs on and on about nothing at all. New restaurants, stale gossip. As though they were big friends.

And then, as she has almost turned off listening to Buck, almost gone back to her own concerns, Jill quite clearly hears, from Buck, "slight cash-flow problem."

Buck Fister wants to borrow money from her? Is he out of his mind?

Without having consciously decided how to handle this, Jill instantly tells him, "Oh, me too. I was just thinking that today, low on cash. Do you think it's a trend? Are we all going broke, the whole country?"

A pause, and then a heavy, "Well, could be."

Jill decides to help him save face, a little. "It's just as well I'm low, though," she babbles. "I went to Magnin's this afternoon, God knows why, and the clothes, well, really I can't tell you how dreadful. Just the worst. Just made for all those Peninsula ladies. Stanford golfers."

Buck is unresponsive for a moment (he must be in bad shape), and then he asks, "Do you think the three of you McAndrew girls sound like your mother, or just like each other?"

Slightly taken aback—and besides, the water is getting cool and she doesn't want to turn on more hot, Buck would hear and know where she was, and she doesn't want to be that intimate with Buck— Jill tells him, "I have no idea. I really don't know how we sound, I'm so used to us all. But I think Caroline sounds more English than we do. Like her mom."

"I suppose. Never met the lady." And then Buck asks, "How well do you know Roland Gallo?"

"Hardly at all. I've seen him at parties, restaurants. We sort of avoid each other. Is he going to run for mayor, do you think?"

"I wouldn't be surprised." Another pause, until Buck's next question: "Is Fiona seeing anyone special these days?"

He cannot be wanting to fix Fiona up with Gallo. The nerve! Hiding a genuine shiver with a small false laugh, Jill gets up and out of the tub, still clutching the receiver as she asks him, "What is this, a quiz show about my family?"

"I just wondered."

Buck never "just wonders." Jill knows that as well as he does, but she does not at the moment feel inclined to pursue his questions. What's it to him, about Fiona? If he thinks Fiona would ever play his Game he's dead wrong.

For a moment then Jill experiences her cold and familiar panic: if anyone, especially anyone in her family—oh Christ!—should ever, ever find out, she would quite simply, actually die. She would have to. Which is a reason she has to be nice to Buck.

"Dear Buck," she now says. "It's been adorable but I've got to do my exercises, it's been such a day."

And with a few further endearments, and vaguer plans to meet, they both hang up.

Drying and powdering herself, applying lotions, Jill still feels a little cold. She feels very alone, and scared. Her life is so exposed, she sometimes thinks. She is running so fast she could fall, and there's no one for her to count on. Her mother, Caroline, is great, of course, but all Caroline really cares about these days is Ralph. Her last big love, old Ralph. And besides, she, Jill, is too old even to think about her mother, in terms of dependence.

Even her apartment, which most of the time she is crazy about, is very proud of, at other times seems precarious, perched as it is on a high edge of Telegraph Hill, facing out to the bay. It could fall, there could be an earthquake, or just a simple and terrible cave-in. It has happened before.

Sometimes now she can hardly bear the sound of the foghorns. They sound like prehistoric animals, huge ugly mammals out there in the water. Groaning, dying.

But she might as well at least try on her new gown, Jill decides. In fact she had better, she had better break this mood, or she'll never sleep. She wishes she had a little of the white stuff.

Slipping the silk down over her head, down her body, Jill then thinks, Oh, it was worth it, worth every fucking cent. Just the feel of this silk, so light.

Going over to the full-length mirror she sees—she sees that never at any moment in her life has she been more beautiful. Never so perfect.

A pity.

She sighs, and picks up the peignoir.

And then the phone rings—as she must have known it would. It had to.

"Noel?" She laughs. "Are you crazy? It's so late." She laughs again, a small excited laugh. "Whatever are you doing in North Beach? Are you crazy? Well, okay, since you're already almost here. But just for a minute, I really mean it. One minute, Noel."

Twelve

Of all her house-sitting jobs, the one that Portia likes least is in a million-dollar (probably more, by now) condominium on top of Nob Hill, very near the Pacific Union Club, to which Buck Fister and Roland Gallo so vainly aspire. The cathedral, Fairmont and Mark Hopkins, all that. Portia dislikes the neighborhood, the hotels and traffic, the Gray Line buses clogging and polluting everything. Even the cathedral seems to her austere, too new and cold. She is not even fond of the small park there, where uniformed nannies guard the large expensive English prams.

And the rooms themselves of this extremely pricey condo are truly terrible. Their owner, a deeply insecure, semi-alcoholic, emotionally battered woman (from New Orleans: as a young beauty she modelled at Neiman-Marcus, and married Big Oil in the person of a man who after various forms of "minor" abuse broke her arms, a farewell tussle that entitled her to three times the amount of alimony that he was protesting)—in any case, poor Janice Lee is as vulnerable as she is rich, and Portia feels sorry for her.

The insecurity and the money, though, produced these frightful rooms with their pseudo-comfortable, pseudo-English look: everywhere wicker and chintz, and towering glass-fronted bookcases filled with gilt- and dark-leather-bound volumes, all unread by human eyes. Even the bedrooms look like studies into which beds have been discreetly placed, in disguise.

It is awful here, Portia thinks, waking with Harold in what is the least "done" room, ostensibly for a maid—but Janice Lee never has maids, she can't trust them.

"Why do we do this, really?" Portia asks Harold, on that dark October morning. It is supposed to be Indian summer, but not so; a dirty fog obscures what could be a view of the bay, and the Bay Bridge, and a mean wind blows leaves about the little park.

"Do you mean, stay in this place or, uh, have sex?"

Actually the sexual act just completed, more or less, between them was indeed what Portia meant. Why do we do this? was a cry from the heart, or the flesh. Why? Why these clumsy pawings at each other's bodies, Baby Oil spilled all over the sheets.

However, given an out (it is so much easier, obviously, to complain about this place), Portia decides not to go into their sexual failure of rapport. Or, not now. And Portia knows herself to be a coward, with an exaggerated fear of hurting Harold. "This awful place," she says. And then she says what is also true, "I'm worried about Sage."

"She goes next week?"

"Week after. And she's been so up, so high on it all. And that guy in New York, he keeps puffing at her, blowing her up."

"How's Noel reacting?"

Portia looks at Harold, feeling the friendship that she counts on, with him, despite the floundering sex. "Good question," she says. "He seems to be suddenly terrifically busy, all over the place. Sage says she barely sees him, he's so busy. But she doesn't seem to care, that's how high she is."

"What a handsome guy. An Irish prince," Harold muses.

"Superficially speaking." Prim Portia, who suddenly wonders, Could Harold too be in love with Noel, and if so does he know that?

Harold stretches his legs out, longer legs even than Portia's are, and with one hand rubs at his stubbly blond chin (his sadly small, shyly recessive chin), and he looks around. "This place is quite ghastly, though. Holy heaven." And then he laughs, "Ports, I've got the greatest idea, why don't we just trash it? Take a little jewelry so the cops will think robbery? We'd really be doing Janice Lee a great big favor."

"Someone could probably work out that it was us," Portia tells him, dryly.

Easily deflated, Harold sighs and accepts her logic. "I guess," he says. "But still."

"You know what I most hate about this place?" Portia asks him.

"Let me guess. Let me count the ways."

"No animals. I can't stand it. No warm fur to touch."

"She's allergic, isn't she?"

"Most likely. It'd be just like her, poor thing."

After a few minutes Harold tells her, "But I have to say, I really don't mind all that much." And then he says, "You remember I'm having dinner with a visiting aunt tonight? You'll survive here alone?"

"Silly boy. Of course." But Portia, who had indeed forgotten the visiting aunt, had rather hoped that she and Harold could go over to North Beach for pizza or something, and she now experiences a certain pang; she in fact does not like to be alone in this particular place at night—infantile, regressive as she knows that feeling to be. For one thing, the phone rings at all hours, people who generally hang up, realizing that she is not Janice Lee. But she tells Harold, "It's okay, I'm having lunch with my dad. Family day for me, I guess."

Portia does not especially like Bruno's, the once extremely popular North Beach restaurant that is still her father's sentimental favorite. In the distant (to Portia non-existent, prehistoric) Forties and Fifties, it was popular with Telegraph Hill's new bohemians, the bright young men and women with little money and considerable taste, aspirations and a sense of local history—and with what came to be known as the Beats. It was popular with writers generally, some painters and a scattering of newspeople. And with a few old leftist political types, relics of waterfront, Wobbly days, including Ralph Carter.

A colorful mix, Ralph likes to tell his daughter, and, like many people of his age, Ralph finds it hard to resist alluding to prices then: the five-course meals for $2.50, the fifty-cent drinks (Portia believes he exaggerates, but he does not). Just sitting in Bruno's seems to bring a form of instant happiness for Ralph, and so from time to time Portia agrees: okay, they'll meet for lunch at Bruno's.

But she does not like waiting for Ralph, in this window seat of honor that he is always given—another reason that he cleaves to this place, obviously. Portia hates the exposure, the conspicuousness of being seated there just next to the hustling, bustling sidewalk, where anyone and everyone can see her.

How she wishes she had thought to bring a book or a magazine, anything to read. Lacking that, she studies the big shiny white menu, as if it ever changed, as if she did not know it by heart. But anything to avoid all those faces on the street, looking in at her.

Impossible, though, not to look up from time to time, as, even when you are terrified of heights (Portia is), in a high building sometimes you have to look down. And to nearsighted Portia, looking out, those faces all blur in a single stream, as she glances out at them, a scary stream of unknowns.

And then, in a stabbing flash of clarity, two well-known faces pass, and then are gone, but not before Portia has recognized Jill and Noel. She has seen Jill's sleek fair cap of hair, Noel's dark thick hair (so like Sage's), and their radiant, blind smiles; dazed with each other, they see no one.

Portia's stomach twists, and she gulps at her water. What *jerks,* she thinks. Ralph could easily have been here, Jill knows he comes here all the time. Anyone could have seen them. And then she thinks, Oh God. Oh Sage—as her old extreme love for her sister overwhelms her.

"Well hey there, honey. I'm not really late, now, am I?" With an anxious frown, a mouth-avoiding kiss, her father, Ralph, is with her. Settling down across from her, and in another instant checking out the room: no one he knows. Portia sees that in a tiny flicker of disappointment across his face.

"No, you're not late," she reassures him.

"Well, I guess it's time for my bi-monthly martini. You'll have a shot of that expensive imported water you favor?" Ralph very much disapproves of Perrier and its offshoots, something he mentions a little too often.

"No, I'll have a glass of wine. Uh, white." It might help her, Portia is thinking. And if it makes me feel worse that will at least be a distraction (the total illogic of this last escapes her for the moment).

"Your mother is home praying for rain," Ralph then tells her. "I have to remind her that in California dark clouds don't mean a thing, necessarily. But I think that woman lives for her garden these days." He grins fondly.

"That's nice," Portia tells him. She is thinking that at some point they will have to get to Sage, their whole family lately is talking so much about Sage, and how difficult now to discuss her—for Portia, with her new knowledge. She thinks, How could Noel? How could Jill? I do not understand the sexuality of grownups, Portia thinks, having momentarily forgotten that she is one; twenty-five is grown up, by most standards.

"—worried over Sage," her father indeed is saying at just that moment. However, the waiter then interrupts with their drinks, and a stern demand for their food choices.

Ralph, who always has linguini with clam sauce, today orders minestrone.

And Portia, who often orders minestrone, chooses a Caesar salad.

The two sips of wine that she has had so far have a somewhat giddying effect, Portia now observes. Well, good, she thinks. And she begins to tell her father in some detail how much she does not like the condominium of Janice Lee. "It's so bloody English," she tells him. "Why are so many insecure people such Anglophiles? Nothing against the English, it's not their fault, but I do wonder. Poor Janice Lee. Even the magazines that she gets are the English editions. British *Vogue*—"

"Would you excuse me for a minute?"

With her father gone, Portia has again no defense against her angry thoughts of Noel and Jill (her quite prurient thoughts, actually: by now they must be back in Jill's apartment, to which they were so clearly headed. They are naked there, together, having sex, doing everything that people do—about which Portia is a little vague). These terrible—reprehensible, embarrassing—and complicated thoughts twist Portia's face in shame, as she also thinks, again, Oh, poor Sage, after Roland she loved and trusted Noel, she seemed really happy with Noel.

Has Ralph actually been gone a long time, though, or has she simply felt his absence is long, alone with her painful imaginings? Portia cannot be sure, but as she begins to focus on waiting for him the time then seems long indeed.

When at last Ralph does return to his chair, he sits down heavily, not speaking for a moment. His large face is gray, and he tells Portia, "I have to say, I don't feel so wonderful. That martini, maybe. I'll have to cut down to one a month. I think—I think I'd just better get a cab."

"Sure, I'll come with you. I'd love to see Mother."

"Don't you dare, you'd scare the woman to death, taking care of me. No, I'll just go along, a little rest will fix me right up."

She can't call Caroline right away, that indeed would alarm her mother, Portia tells herself, forcing her steps to slow down on the short walk from Stockton Street, in North Beach, up to California Street, on Nob Hill. At Broadway she allows the light to change twice, three times, making herself just stand there among the tourists, the local Chinese, businessmen, women out shopping, children getting home from school—the anonymous throngs who blur before her distracted, nearsighted face.

But then she thinks, Suppose I run into Jill and Noel again? The way this day is going I really could. And that thought alone gives her license to hurry, Portia decides, back to poor misguided Janice Lee's fake-English retreat, her county spread of rooms, high up in the fog.

She dials from Janice Lee's "study," but there is no answer at her mother's house.

And no answer at Sage's either. Sage and Noel's.

And no answer at either place, still, an hour later, after Portia has done every time-consuming thing she can think of, in terms of cleaning up *chez* Janice Lee. Washed the kitchen and bathroom shelves, dusted and straightened up the floors of closets, polished various small needy pieces of silver, and washed and dried all the tiny Baccarat animals, from Neiman's.

When the phone rings a little after 5 Portia runs for it, almost trips, and answers breathlessly, "Hello?"

A woman's voice, "Hey there, lambkin. You feel like seeing anybody?"

Horribly tempted to say yes, yes, I would love to see almost anyone, Portia nevertheless explains that she is not Janice Lee. No, Janice Lee will not be back for another week.

At about 5:30 Caroline calls, sounding very tired but using what Portia thinks of as her English good-sport voice. "He's in Presbyterian Hospital, so lucky it's so near," Caroline tells her daughter. "A mild stroke, he's being monitored. They thought it'd be best to keep him there for a while, but you can imagine how Ralph liked that."

"But, but he'll be okay? really soon?"

"Well, darling, of course that's what we hope. But it's hard to tell."

"Shall I come over?"

"No, love, if you don't mind I think really better not."

Sage is not at home.

Nor is Harold. Dialling his number, Portia had entirely forgotten the visiting aunt. Of all times for an aunt, she rancorously thinks. And she thinks, senselessly, Why don't I have a true lover? Someone I could always trust and count on? (Someone with whom sex was wonderful.)

It would be very inconsiderate to call Caroline again, thinks Portia, and so she does not. She remains alone, and falls at last into a light and troubled sleep, broken by pornographic visions of Noel and Jill. And every now and then she wakes to foghorns, their heavy, grating, mourning sobs, far out in the bay.

At last, she allows herself to admit (she has no choice, at that undefended time) the true source of her panic: she is thinking, *feeling,* that Ralph might die.

When the phone does ring, at some cold black pre-dawn hour, her first conscious thought is, Oh Christ, all I need right now is some drunken Janice Lee old pal.

But it is Caroline, who tells her, "Darling, I am sorry to call so very late. But the head doctor just got here, finally, and I did think you'd want to know. He's really doing all right, the doctor says. He'll have to stay here in Presbyterian for a while, but he's really going to be okay. I think."

Thirteen

U nable to throw out the fall harvest from her deck, the dozens of too-full rose blossoms that must be clipped from the potted bushes to make room for more, Caroline instead floats all those stemless flowers, those masses of yellow, white, pale pink and lavender, in a large blue shallow Chinese bowl. How lovely they are, she thinks, stepping back to admire the luxuriance of bloom, of satin petals, of scent. Leaning down, she brushes her face against the cool petals, and sighs. They'll be gone by tomorrow, she knows that, or further gone than they indeed are now, but in the meantime how very beautiful they are. She has placed the bowl on a table, against the French windows that lead out to the deck, and now, crossing her kitchen, she looks back at her arrangement, and sees with pleasure the floral profusion, the waves of flowers.

She wishes she could take them to Ralph, at Presbyterian, but they would not survive even that four-block trip, Caroline knows that.

Ralph is not doing very well. While still in the hospital he has had two more mild strokes (and how can a stroke be mild? Caroline wonders). The doctors have been guarded; there is now a group of them, all hovering and circling. Like vultures, Caroline tends to think. They do not, they tell Caroline, try to predict the extent of the damage. (Amazing how little doctors turn out to know; she thinks that with some bitterness. For all their airs.)

But damaged he is, Caroline is certain of that. Even now he

is vague, and weak. He will come home damaged, not the person she is used to.

Damaged, or dead.

And at times, with great guilt, Caroline thinks that dead might indeed be better. How can she not think that?

But as though she had a choice, any choice whatsoever. As though Ralph did.

"Mother, those roses. So like you, I could see that bowl of blossoms anywhere and know it was yours." Liza is the most effusive of Caroline's daughters, she is cheering to have about. And today she has come over without any children; good Saul on his days off takes the kids on outings, even the baby. "I find them infinitely more interesting than golf," is his mild joke, presumably at the expense of most of his colleagues, including his father-in-law, Dr. James Mc-Andrew.

"I was wishing Ralph could see them—the roses, I mean—but then I remembered he's not actually mad for flowers," Caroline tells her daughter. "It's something he tolerates in me. Some English mania, he thinks."

"We've both married very nice men," is Liza's comment.

"Well, on the whole, yes, I do think so," her mother agrees, even as she wonders: *is* the Liza-Saul marriage as good as it looks? can it be? She is remembering herself at Liza's age, looking rather as Liza does now, somewhat overweight and underdressed (by doctors' wives' standards). Married to Jim McAndrew. A nice young fairly appropriate doctor's wife, who spent most Tuesday afternoons in motels, with a lively succession of lovers. (Tuesdays, the one day she had help and could leave.) Those afternoons were what got me through those long years, though, she has thought, through the rest of the days with those four little girls, and the nights with Jim, the bad sex or none at all. Until she met Ralph, who insisted on ending both the marriage and the parade of lovers, of which he was only dimly aware.

"Does it strike you that all your daughters are acting rather odd lately?" now asks Liza, somewhat surprisingly: she is given to gossip (thank God, they all are) but is usually more precise in her observations. Caroline has supposed that Liza's form of gossip is in some way connected to her literary aspirations: Liza "gathers material."

"Well, maybe," Caroline tells Liza. "Maybe. I haven't given them much real thought, except Sage. She's off next week, you know. New York."

"Yes. Oh dear. I think Dad's really worried about her."

Caroline sighs, and frowns, as she tends always to do over the intense, continuing connection between Sage and her stepfather. Slightly unnatural, it seems to Caroline. He is not even her stepfather any more, or so Caroline would prefer to think. Ralph is Sage's stepfather now.

Thinking all that, she voices some of it to Liza, as she has not quite done before. "So odd, Sage and Jim," she tentatively says. "I don't quite understand it. One would think they had rather little in common."

"It is a little weird," agrees Liza. And then she asks, "If they became lovers would that be incest, do you think?"

"Liza! Honestly." In a very nervous way Caroline laughs.

"Well, it does suggest itself as a possibility? I wonder if I'd be jealous. I guess I would. I mean, my own father. Saul would certainly expect me to be jealous, and God knows what another shrink would think."

"I'd feel very strange about it myself," Caroline admits, "very, very strange."

"Well, we're not likely to know about it if they do, so I guess we're safe."

Imagining (hoping) that to be the end of a preposterous conversation, Caroline sighs. "I really should get some sort of cleaning help," she remarks. "I get so behind."

"Mother, it's perfectly okay and you know it." Untidiness is a quality shared by Liza and her mother, and one that each appreciates in the other—so unnecessary, the fuss that most people go through, they say to each other.

"Sage will always be faithful to Noel, though, I'm sure of that," next observes Liza. "Have you noticed that women whose husbands play around are always faithful as hell, themselves? It's so awful, and I know it's true. It's as though an unfaithful husband paralyzes them."

"Well, I have noticed, and it is sort of awful, as you say. It's true of men, though, too, I mean they're faithful to unfaithful wives." Caroline of course is thinking of herself and faithful Jim McAndrew. "But I don't think Noel is actually as you say playing around, do you?"

"Actually I do," Liza tells her mother. "I didn't use to, I thought he just had that look. Mr. Available. He's a flirt, he really is. But he and Sage came by a couple of days ago, she had the kids' birthday presents, she's so great about that, and—I don't know, I could swear Noel's up to something."

"Really." I am so convinced by my daughters, thinks Caroline. They could tell me anything, especially this most talkative, most informative daughter.

"He's almost too affectionate, and at the same time rather impatient with Sage," Liza pursues. "Do you know what I mean?"

"Well, I think I do." That was a fair description of her own behavior with Jim a great deal of the time, thinks Caroline. The guilty affection, the impatience to be off with a lover. She knows very well just what Liza is describing.

"His timing is great, isn't it," Liza comments. "Just when Sage is really up. Well, maybe she'll be a big success and get up the nerve to dump him." Liza's smile, though, indicates that she does not believe this will be the case, not really.

"Let's just pray for her success, whatever." Is Sage so in need of our prayers? Caroline wonders.

"Oh, absolutely. But I still think Noel was mostly a reaction to Roland Gallo, don't you? Part of her recovery, don't you think?"

"I guess. Roland Gallo—" In a musing way Caroline finds herself repeating the name, and finds too within herself a shocking thought: if Ralph should die, went that thought, she, Caroline, could have some sort of an affair with Roland Gallo, maybe. How appalling, though! How dreadful the very process of her mind, and her heart. How could she!

I very well could, Caroline then answers herself. I damn well could have such an improbable fantasy, for that's all it is, and I must not blame myself.

"Roland Gallo's very sexy, don't you think?" is Liza's (possibly clairvoyant?) remark. "The old shit."

"I'm sure he thinks of himself as very young," Caroline tells her daughter, as she also thinks, Much too young for me, I'm sure he would think that. And she silently echoes Liza, The old shit indeed.

Partly to change the subject Caroline asks, "Are you managing any time for yourself these days?"

This means, Are you writing? How's it going?—which Caroline is much too delicately tactful, too discreet to ask directly. Always a non-intrusive mother, Caroline is perhaps most cautious, at least in this area of work, with this particular daughter, who most reminds her of herself. She knows that Liza spends a lot of time—that is, what time she can spend—with notebooks, journals, with what amounts to notes for being a writer. Which she herself had very often thought of doing, and not done. And Caroline has even wondered, Suppose Liza actually manages to pull it off, the successful sexy marriage *and* the nice kids, *and* some sort of literary success? How would I feel about that, actually? Caroline asks herself. Delighted, terrifically pleased (of course she would be all that) but at the same time more than a little envious; she can feel a little of the envy just thinking in this way.

"Oh, when I can," Liza says, in answer to her mother's question.

Which Caroline knows to mean, Oh God, how I wish I could find more time. How (at times) I wish I had fewer or maybe even no children.

"I am getting strange strong voices from both my younger sisters, though," Liza then says to her mother. "I don't know, I think they're both up to something."

"Oh?" Despite this sound of dubiousness, Caroline entirely trusts the instincts of Liza, and Liza's extreme sensitivity to "vibes," as she trusts her own instincts, her sensitivity. "You think they both have new lovers?" Caroline is quite sure that that is what Liza did mean.

"Well, yes. Guys they both are making a point of not talking about. Probably not even to each other. I get a sense of something really furtive. From both of them."

"You could be absolutely right. It's odd how they seem to act more or less in concert, don't they."

"Yes. Do you think it's all those early-morning phone calls? They sort of start off their days in the same direction?"

"I suppose, and then they're both so rich and successful. In more or less the same ways." Caroline sighs. "My yuppie twins. You know, I worry that something terrible could hit them both at once."

Very interested, leaning toward her mother, Liza's gray-blue eyes (Jim McAndrew's eyes) are wide. She looks so young, Caroline thinks, younger even than Jill and Fiona, who both are much too thin. Liza on this pleasantly warm October afternoon is wearing faded blue denim, a shirt and skirt. Not stylish in the least, Caroline admits, but very becoming. Liza looks extremely pretty. And rested, and well.

"Like, they both get pregnant the same afternoon, in separate motels?" Liza laughs.

"That's not quite what I had in mind. I was thinking of something more public than pregnancy. Some financial disaster, I guess I meant." Saying this, Caroline at the same time wonders, Just what made Liza think of motel afternoons, instead of night—a more licit time for conception, generally?

"Well, actually we could all be financially ruined, couldn't we. The way things are going. Though for Saul and me not such a very big change. God, how can we stay so broke."

"Well, us too."

When the phone rings just then Caroline jumps, as she has for the past few days. Ever since Ralph's hospitalization, that awful afternoon when he came home from lunch with Portia. So ill.

On answering, though, she hears her son-in-law's deep pleasant voice, but sounding upset. "Dear Saul, of course she's here," Caroline tells him. As she thinks, And thank God she is, and not off in some motel. "Just a minute," she says to Saul.

Listening to Liza's soothing, affectionate voice on the phone, Caroline then thinks, We haven't talked about Ralph at all. Is that strange?

"I guess I have to go." Returning from the phone, Liza twists her mouth in an apologetic smile.

"Chaos at home?"

"Chaos. Utter." And Liza adds, "Well, no one's perfect. Not even good Saul."

Walking together toward the front door, the two women are momentarily stopped by a rhythmic sound of chanting from outside on the street. They look at each other: what?

Opening the front door, they see, just passing Caroline's house, a tall thin tattered woman, actually gaunt, her no-colored hair as ragged, unkempt as her rusty clothes. Bent forward, as though there were wind. Carrying nothing. A bag lady with no bags. Slowly walking past. Chanting.

"Three hundred sixty-five. Days a week. Three hundred. Sixty-five. Do you know? Fire comes from dung. From shit. SHIT. SHIT."

Once in the course of passing by she has glanced up toward the two women in the doorway, her strange light-yellow eyes meeting Caroline's level blue-green eyes. And in that instant Caroline has thought, I know her. From somewhere. I'm sure I do.

"You never know what to do, do you?" is Liza's comment.

"No—"

"There's always the impulse to take them in. You know, at least one person."

Caroline, having just had precisely that thought, smiles at her daughter, helplessly. "So curious, really," she says. "I know her. From somewhere."

"Well, the way things are going you certainly could have. She too could have lived in Pacific Heights."

"I know. I think about that."

Caroline then begins to be haunted by that woman. Her eyes. Her strange chant. And the idea persists that this is someone whom in some context or other she actually knew. Not well, or very likely she could place her eventually; Caroline does not tend to forget people, only facts. And somehow, she is sure, she did know that woman.

In his room at Presbyterian Hospital, Ralph speaks almost not at all. Lying there, his extended arms attached to tubes, an incredibly elaborate monitoring screen mounted high above him, he acknowledged Caroline's presence with a look in her direction.

And so she talks. And talks, and talks.

"Liza came by today. Without the babies. Such a treat, really for both of us. She looks beautiful, I think. Of course she could do a little more about herself, the other girls say that, but, then, so could I. Always."

Realizing that she is talking to herself—and so boringly! dear heaven—Caroline comes to a halt, and looks out the window.

The hazy October day is coming to its golden close, as far out on the Pacific the sun sinks down, a sightless dazzle along the distant horizon. As, within the immediate hospital world, the noisy bustle of visiting hours, the footsteps, hurrying or slow along the corridor, the metallic creak of trundled carts, of IV stands laboriously pushed along. All those sounds now mingle in some dreadful and menacing disharmony.

On the other hand, I might just as well keep on talking, thinks Caroline. At least I drown out all that.

"Liza seems worried about her sisters, though," she tells the possibly not listening Ralph.

"I hope not me?" asks another voice from the just-opened door.

Startled, then delighted, Caroline has turned to see her youngest daughter, tall Portia, in the doorway, her smile hesitant and shy, even as she goes over to kiss her father, who himself smiles for the first time that day.

Portia then perches gingerly on the foot of the bed, avoiding the large double lump that indicates Ralph's feet. And she turns to her mother. "Liza's worried?"

"Oh, not really. Besides, I think people like to worry over each other, don't you? It makes them feel superior." And especially my daughters, Caroline thinks but does not say. How they all cluck over each other! "She mentioned Fiona and Jill," Caroline tells Portia. "And Sage. Not you." She smiles.

Some shade seems to cross Portia's face as she says, "Well. Jill." And she stops, regarding her mother as though asking for permission to say more.

"I haven't seen Jill for a while. Or Fiona. Have you?" Caroline adds, "Of course they call a lot."

"No, really not," Portia answers her mother. She still looks troubled and questioning. But then she brightens. "Sage leaves next week?"

"Yes."

Some sound then comes from Ralph, whom in a way both Caroline and Portia have forgotten (as hospital visitors tend to do; so much easier to talk to each other than to the patient). In a terrible, remote, hollow voice Ralph says, "When I'm home, pills always on the table."

Instantly grasping this frightful, cryptic but to her absolutely clear message (by "pills" Ralph means the assuredly lethal dose that they have always promised to make available to each other), Caroline hesitates for just one instant before she tells him, "Yes, darling, of course." As though he had asked for tea, or a special cookie.

She looks then at Portia and decides, or hopes, that Portia has not understood.

And she goes on talking. "This morning in front of the house there was this quite frightening woman. Poor thing. Chanting something. Something about three hundred sixty-five days a week. I just thought, She must have had some really awful job, don't you think? Or just an awful life. And some more about fire coming from dung. But is that at all true, Ralph darling? People do burn dung somewhere, don't they? Or they used to?"

But Ralph's eyes are closed, and his breath is deep and hoarse. Portia is gazing sadly at her father.

"The strange thing is," says Caroline to no one, "I'm sure I know her."

"I think he's asleep," says Portia.

Fourteen

The golden, brilliant, vibrant October weather goes on and on, that year. Drought is mentioned, but in the lovely warm blue air it is hard to worry. Clear pure sunlight brightens the pastel-painted architecture; sharp-edged shadows darken Victorian cornices, descending eaves. In the city parks, especially the better-tended ones of the expensive neighborhoods, Nob Hill, Russian Hill, Pacific Heights, the grass and beds of flowers have a midsummer look.

Walking out on Sacramento Street, heading westward, into the sunlight, Sage is thinking how happy simple sunshine makes her. Probably I should not live in San Francisco, she thinks, with its winter rains and terrible cold windy summer fog. On the other hand, the perpetually sunny places are mostly awful: Florida, Palm Springs, Tucson. And she thinks, If only it could be sunny next week in New York, that would make such a difference. And at the same time she tells herself that it is surely infantile to care so much about weather, to depend on sunny days for feelings of joy and success. Her old shrink would disapprove, but Sage smiles to herself as she thinks this; she smiles tolerantly.

For at the moment she does feel very successful. Her life at last seems okay. Noel has been busy and apparently happy lately, affectionate if not ardent—and how much ardor should she expect, married now for almost five years? Sage expects too much, she knows that—she must stop. She has certainly observed that when she herself is occupied and focussed on her work, and especially when that work is going well, she gives much less time to her black, obsessive thoughts about Noel: is he seeing someone else, and when and where and who? She puts less pressure on him, and Noel must feel that; they get along much better.

And now she is going to New York next week, for her show!

She has just come from seeing her mother and Ralph in the hospital, where Ralph is doing somewhat better. He was mostly asleep while Sage was there but Caroline said, "As well as can be expected. Maybe better. He's really a tough old party, your second step-father." Caroline looked happy.

Right now Sage is headed out to the Cal-Mart to buy some salmon steaks, terrifically expensive, in a store for the rich (they don't take food stamps), but so reliably fresh, so good. And Noel has taught her a special salmon sauce, with cucumbers and shallots.

Sacramento Street, in its Pacific Heights incarnation, remains an indecisive mix of residence and commerce, of dissonant architectural styles: Victorian houses juxtaposed with nondescript two-story boxlike store fronts, or sleazy new stucco condominiums, miserably designed. Here and there the Victorian houses have been converted into offices or restaurants or stores, all with quite varying degrees of success.

Observing all this, Sage remembers her stepfather, Jim, talking about Sacramento Street. (Stepfather: she does not actually think of Jim as that, she does not think of him in any defined or named relationship. Jim for her is an idea of trust and love, a wave of warmth in her soul; thoughts of Jim affect her as sunshine does.) Jim used to predict that Sacramento Street would become another Union Street, all tarted up for tourists, with fly-by-night restaurants (Sage smiles at Jim's somewhat quaint turns of phrase). But Jim was more or less wrong, Sage decides, recalling at the same time that she has not seen or even talked to Jim for too long—a week? maybe even a couple of weeks. But it doesn't seem to matter, really, how often they see each other, or if they don't; whenever they do get together, everything is right.

What a good idea not to bring her car today, Sage decides. She walked from her own house on Russian Hill all the way to Presbyterian, where she met Caroline, and now, after picking up the salmon, she can take a bus home.

Just then she is assailed by the sight of a new boutique, a small shop in the basement of a large Victorian house, one she has not seen before but that is already, as a large sign proclaims, GOING OUT OF BUSINESS. CLOSING SALE.

Smiling to herself, quite sure that she will find something cheap and beautiful to wear to New York, Sage goes inside.

And there it is, a green silk shirt that has been twice marked down. Still expensive but closer to her range. And very beautiful, with tiny pleats and nice small covered buttons. Meant for her, she thinks.

In the dressing room, in green silk, confronted with herself in all those mirrors, what Sage feels is—attractive. Confident. Rather sexy. Almost beautiful? It is hard for her to go so far, but maybe. She imagines herself at the gallery opening with the so far unmet Calvin, then probably dinner somewhere with Calvin later on. Some nice small Village place, most likely.

Sage has not given much thought to the nature of her Calvin-fantasies. He is at this point a warm deep enthusiastic male voice on the telephone. Fun to talk to, jokey. He always calls her "sweetheart," which is a nice old-fashioned touch, she thinks. However, there in the heavily carpeted, mirrored cubicle, swathed in silk (the shirt is very long), Sage is quite suddenly aware of the erotic content of all that, all those fantasies concerning Calvin Crome.

Actually, though, why not? Why not have a little friendly fooling around in New York? A little evening-up of scores with Noel, who certainly has from time to time "seen" other women, maybe even now he is seeing someone. And all the better that Noel will never know what she does in New York. Sage does not want to punish him, really, just to even things up, a little.

In the Cal-Mart, clutching the new package that contains her beautiful shirt, Sage buys the salmon—so fresh, that dark-pink flesh of fish, so sensual. She then buys the cucumbers, and shallots. Some nice lettuces for salad, and frozen-yogurt custard, Noel's favorite, for dessert.

As she leaves the store it occurs to her that she is only a few blocks from Jim's; she can call him and come by for just a minute, a nice small visit.

First, though, she should call Noel, to see if a slightly later dinner is okay. (This is not necessary, but something tells her to call him. Tells her in fact that it would be all right to call him now. It is sometimes not all right.)

"Well, hi there, babe. Is this a gorgeous day?" is Noel's opening sally. And then, "Salmon steaks, fantastic. But look, they'll be just as great tomorrow, don't you think? I have this goddam meeting. Some new clients on Telegraph Hill. In fact you just caught me, I could be late. Oh, and your new pal Calvin called. Said to call him."

The whole point of Cal-Mart salmon steaks is their pristine freshness. Sage does not have to say this to Noel, he knows it as well as she does.

But this is only a minor setback, really, isn't it? The October afternoon that she views from the open phone booth on California Street is still extremely beautiful, the blue of the sky just deepening, a breeze of dusk just very lightly beginning.

And a phone call from Calvin. Another nice flirty conversation to look forward to.

"Okay, love," Sage says to Noel.

And then she dials Calvin's number, which luckily by now she knows by heart.

"So funny," she tells him, having quickly got through. "I'm calling from a phone booth. It's really beautiful out here. Do you think you'll ever come out?"

"Ah, sweetheart, who knows?" Not sounding quite as up as usual, Calvin next tells her, "Things aren't so great around here, actually. Trips are just about the last thing on my mind."

Aware of a quick droop in her own high spirits (she has to work against this dangerous volatility), feeling the slightest chill in her blood, Sage struggles for balance. "We all have those days," she tells Calvin. "But they pass—you know?—and it's all okay again." But how limp that sounded. How dull and unconvincing.

"Look, sweetheart, I'm telling you. Things are not good. I'm having to make a lot of changes. Very quickly. Don't ask me what's going on, it's stuff I don't even understand."

By now Sage is grasping the receiver so tightly that her hand hurts. Realizing what she is doing, she is still unable to loosen her fingers, as she thinks: I might have known.

"—postpone until January," Calvin is saying. "No big difference, really just two or three months. You've still got time to change your reservations, right?"

"But I hate January," is what Sage ridiculously says.

From New York, from Calvin she hears a short, not-amused laugh. "Sweetheart, I can't deal with your superstitions today, okay? You hate January. Jesus. I hate this October."

A few minutes later they have said goodby and hung up, and Sage, incredibly, cannot remember the intervening words. After Calvin said he hated October, then what? She cannot remember. She is sure, though, that she did not try to pin him down, did not say, as probably she should have, WHEN in January? Probably should have. She thinks. But can't remember.

On the sidewalk near the phone both, where Sage still stands, transfixed, the foot traffic is increasing. Late-afternoon shoppers, or people just out for a stroll, as the air perceptibly begins to cool. Pacific Heights ladies, all dressed up from their lunches, dates with each other in downtown restaurants, at which they drink a little too much wine, and tell secrets. And younger women in running clothes, or leftover summer cottons. People with little kids. And among all these regulars, the legitimate population of this highly respectable neighborhood, are the highly irregular street people, slow and shabby, grossly overweight, or sometimes sickly thin. Neglected, and mostly ignored. Almost invisible.

Sage watches as a tall, gaunt woman slowly passes the booth, a woman with wild yellow eyes (she is the same woman who passed by Caroline's house, whom Caroline thinks she knows), who chants—very softly, here on this populous street—"Three hundred sixty-five days a week, three hundred, sixty-five." Half hearing her, Sage is thinking that she herself could be a street person, so easily. The lines or walls that now separate her from them, from that woman, are so precariously thin, and imperilled. At any moment she too could be out there on the street, and cold. Neglected. She shudders.

But then, with a jolt, an upward lurch of her heart, Sage thinks of Jim. Jim, just a few short blocks away, out here in Pacific Heights.

Jim, whom she was thinking of a few minutes earlier, and all along meant to call. Whom she now imagines as her true direction. Everything that has happened has propelled her toward him, all of this hitherto terrible day. She will not even bother to call him, Jim is meant to be there for her, and surely he will be.

First, though, she reaches into her billfold, having decided that whatever she touches will be what she gives to that woman. She pulls out a ten—well, good. Passing the woman, who has halted momentarily, gazing out into the traffic, Sage pushes the bill into her hand—rudely? Rudeness was surely not her intention, but the gesture felt wrong, somehow. However, when she looks at the money, maybe the woman will be pleased? Sage can only hope so.

She has walked a long fast block from the phone booth when something, some very slight lightness, reminds her that a short time ago she had two packages, and now she has only the brown paper bag of groceries.

After one quick split second of panic she turns back, almost running toward the phone booth (passing the street woman, who has still not opened her hand to look at the money)—panic, although Sage is entirely sure that her box will be there. The blouse that she bought to show Jim.

And it is there. One more sign that she is on the right track, she finally and absolutely knows what she is about. She picks up the smart store package, along with the groceries, and starts off again, toward Jim.

How terrible it would have been, though, if she had not remembered for several blocks. Maybe not even until she was at Jim's door. Suppose she had rushed back for her package through the increasing dark, and got there too late? Someone having taken it from the phone booth—maybe even the tall thin chanting street woman. If she had actually lost the lovely expensive green shirt, all paid for and never worn. Terrifying even to think of, a look down into the abyss. The abyss that for Sage is never very far away. (Where the bag lady lives.)

But the point is (isn't it?) that she did remember in time. She has the blouse, and she is on her way to Jim's. She thought of the abyss, she recognized its presence, but did not fall. She does not have to live on the street.

Going to New York next week is not important. January will be perfectly okay. Beautiful snow. Very quiet. (Although she does not like snow, actually.)

Only going to Jim's and finding him at home is really important.

Arrived quite breathless at his door, the heavy mitered glass, she pushes the buzzer. And Jim is there, he answers almost at her ring, as though waiting. He buzzes the intercom and Sage calls up, "It's me, Sage. Can I come up?"

His hollow voice. "Honey, of course. Come on up."

At his door, though, Jim tells her, "The truth is I've got this real cold, that's why I'm home. Had to cancel some patients." His voice is thick and congested, his long nose red.

How perfect and fortunate, then, that she should come to see him! "I've come to take care of you," Sage tells him. "I've even brought dinner, see?" Reaching for his shoulder, so that tall Jim bends toward her, Sage presses a kiss into his cheek. "I'm not really interested in germs," she laughs—giddily, she feels. "Let's just kill them with drinks, okay?"

A brief laugh from Jim, who then asks, "What would you like?"

"Could we have martinis? Would that be fun?"

"Well, sure, why not? I think I have gin. I haven't had a martini, Lord, it must be fifteen years. Caroline liked them. Sometimes."

"Great! And I brought a brand-new blouse to show you!"

Jim's bathroom is very bachelorish, all black tile and polished brass. The mirror is a little hard to maneuver, hard to find herself there, but Sage can see that the shirt is actually long enough to be worn as a sort of mini-dress. If she doesn't put her jeans back on.

"Oh, pretty short dress!" is Jim's comment.

"But it's beautiful, don't you think?"

"It really is. I like green a lot."

Perched on his hard white linen sofa, Sage can watch Jim in the kitchen as he goes about making a pitcher of drinks. She sighs to herself, almost tearfully, with love. Her heart is swollen with the incredible, overwhelming, dazzling love that she has always felt for Jim. So much love that everything else is crowded out. Problems with Noel. Her postponed show. She is dizzy with love, before she has even one drink! But at the same time very happy. Happy.

"Well, here you go. Cheers, honey. This'll kill us or cure us, right?" Jim raises his glass, which is tilted in her direction.

"Cheers. Jim. Darling Jim."

Jim gives her a mildly questioning look that lasts only a moment. Then he sits down on his largest chair, and smiles. "Nice of you to come by."

"This is the best drink I've ever had."

"Good. Let's see, you go to New York next week?"

"Well, actually it's been postponed for a while. Maybe January. But I'm sure this is better all around. January, much better. I'll have more time to get stuff together." Sage feels her own smile to be brilliant, convincing. She can feel the brilliance, the warmth.

Outside Jim's apartment's long windows a darkness that has seemed sudden now descends. Only streetlamps are visible, blurs of yellow, and the occasional slow beams of passing cars. The park across the way would be entirely dark by now, the sole and secret property of whatever and whoever choose to spend their nights there. Dogs, stray cats and smaller animals. Rodents, lizards. And for all anyone knows people are sleeping now out there in the park, in hidden or not-so-hidden corners. Huddled singly or perhaps together. Cold. Afraid.

"Aren't you sort of gulping that?" Jim asks.

"Well, maybe I am. I guess I need another, though, don't you? And then I'll make our dinner."

"You weren't kidding about drowning germs, were you. But maybe it will cure this goddam cold. What do doctors know." And he goes off to make more drinks.

So in love! All her life she has been in love with Jim, Sage now sees this very clearly, and her old shrink used to hint as much, now that Sage thinks of it—in her murky Viennese way. Roland, Noel— they were nothing, really.

And Jim will make everything all right. He always has.

"You could sit here," she tells him. She pats the sofa, and smiles upward.

"And give you my cold for sure? I'll try not to." But he takes that seat.

Sage puts down her drink, and in another minute they are kissing, wildly kissing. Opened mouths, wet. Tongues. Hands frantic on each other's backs.

Jim's hands grasp at her waist, then one hand reaches up her thigh, beneath the short silk, touching the top of her panty hose.

But then, as though her flesh had burned him, Jim cries out, "Jesus Christ! Sage! Crazy!"

His hand withdrawn as though from fire, he has moved back, away from her, and now he tries very hard to laugh. Chokes, tries again, and coughs. At last he gets out a laugh. "Drunk! I'm really drunk, have to stay off martinis, pure poison!" With the back of his other hand, not the one that touched her, he wipes at his mouth.

She cries out, "Jim, I love you! No one else. Always—" But her heart is leaden, weighing her down.

Jim stands up, beyond her grasp. "Honey, I love you too. But the truth is I feel really lousy. I'm sick. I'm going to call you a cab, while you get dressed."

Automatically, almost, Sage bows her head down, down nearly to her knees; the classic pose of a scorned, grieved woman.

But also a woman who is about to be very sick. Who will vomit.

She jumps up, rushes to the bathroom, barely makes it, before leaning into the bright-black bowl and emptying herself of everything. Of bitter bile. Of nothing.

In the cab, Sage forces herself to sit rigidly upright, resisting the impulse to hurl herself to the floor. To lie there, sick and hidden. As everything flashes by, in the dark. Lights, cars, stores. Up hills, down hills. Toward home. Russian Hill. And Noel.

But I don't have any money.

That rational, true sentence prints itself across Sage's mind, along with a clear and reasonable memory: as she checked out at the Cal-Mart she noted only one bill, a ten, and a little change left. Pretty close, she remembers thinking that, pretty close, and remembers too the self-congratulatory note of the phrase, of that distant moment. A golden time, afternoon. And now, now she is hurtling along in a cab, she has given that last ten to a bag lady who seemed not even to want it, and Sage has no money to pay.

Pulling at her bag, a drawstring sack which is hard to open, Sage examines her billfold again and finds—yes, two singles that she somehow didn't see before. And in her change purse a couple of quarters, dimes, some pennies.

The cab's meter says $3.25. Already, and they have just reached Van Ness Avenue.

"Oh, I have to get out here!" she cries out. "Sorry! Sorry—stop!"

"Lady, you all right?" He is black, black-bearded, enormous. He could kill her, in a way she wishes he would. Just dispose of her, somewhere.

"Sick! No money. Here."

"Lady, you be sick I take you home."

"No—" Sage has pushed all her money into his hand, pushed down the handle of the door, and she is out, out on the street. She is standing there unsteadily for a moment, dazed, and then heading across Van Ness with the crowd.

And now she will have to walk up Union Street, up all that hill, and her feet hurt. She is limping along, she is not at all sure she will make it.

And she has left all her food at Jim's, she now remembers.

Jim, whom she now can never see again.

Fifteen

Some letters from Liza McAndrew:
Dear John Lee,
In case you're still in Mendocino, I still think about you, sometimes. In fact these days I spend a lot of time down in J.K., again, but now I'm there with my kids. Not quite the same, not at all. I sort of look for you there, though. I think how great it would be if you just showed up. Not bloody likely, right?
Love. Still. Anyway. From Liza.

John Lee, in 1968, when Liza was eighteen, was a hero to most of her friends, and especially to Liza. A dropout from Lowell High, a couple of years older than Liza and her friends, and a semi-dropout from his very middle-class black family (both parents successful lawyers), John Lee was in Paris during the May riots, had hung out with Danny the Red and been arrested (briefly). Had fought the police in the People's Park confrontation, again been arrested, held overnight in Santa Rita prison. Had smoked dope in front of City Hall.

John Lee got a job working nights at the Rincon Annex, the main post office, down on Market Street. Sometimes he would show up in the afternoons at Julius Kahn, usually with some really good dope. And then he and Liza, or whoever (John Lee was very popular), would take off for his place over on Haight Street for what John Lee called "breakfast," and some very fancy screwing.

He was a sexual as well as a political guru in those days. He spoke Sixties messages: against possessiveness, lasting involvements, exclusivity, as well as all the Fifties icons of togetherness, marriage and houses, cars and kids.

And John Lee looked quite a lot like his idol, Martin Luther King—a compact handsome man with flat slant eyes, and a resonant, compelling voice.

Everything John Lee said was received as gospel by his bevy of blonde followers, and they all suffered considerable remorse (big guilt trips) when inevitably they fell in love with him, wanting him for their very own, resenting the others.

Liza fared better than the rest; for one thing she had heard all that stuff before from Sage and her Movement friends, for another she had quite a number of alternative loves of her own.

But she still remembers his near-priapic skills. His interesting eyes and his voice.

Another letter:

Dear Jonathan H. [in Liza's high-school class there were four Jonathans],

I seem to read about you all the time these days. Is it true, are you really such a hot shot Montgomery Street guy? I guess you must be, there you are in the phone book, in that old firm.

I am spending half my time, still, down in J.K., but it's a little different now, with babies in the sandbox.

In case you're ever wandering by that way, there I am.

I wonder if we still look sort of alike.

Would it be fun to talk?

Anyway. Love, still, from Liza.

Jonathan H. in the late Sixties was a plump but handsome blonde boy who did just slightly resemble Liza, with his pale-gray California eyes and long straight blond hair. And this was a joke between them, once they became lovers: "We're the fucking Bobbsey Twins. Incest! It's terrific!" Like most dumb jokes, it was a great deal funnier when they were stoned, which they both were, much of the time.

Jonathan's name was Jonathan Hamilton; his extremely rich parents lived in an outer Broadway mansion, conveniently near to J.K., to which Liza and Jonathan used to repair for hours of sweet sex and dope and cookies from Fantasia. After high school Jonathan went up to Reed College, against the protests of his Harvard (both of them) parents, and then on to a commune near Vancouver. And then back home to a proper marriage to a girl from Belvedere, to a job in his father's brokerage firm on Montgomery Street. A house on Green Street, on Russian Hill, and routine appearances in what passes in San Francisco for high society.

Liza wrote a similar note to Jonathan K., a dark wispy boy, the shy and poetic prodigal son of a famous criminal lawyer who always feared that his son might turn out "queer," who used to beg Liza to come up to the family house at Lake Tahoe. Liza and Jonathan K. were terrific friends and only very occasional lovers.

She found his name very easily in the phone book, and saw that he was living in the Castro. She thought with great affection of Jonathan K.

And a note to Gregory Chan, who was busted for stealing socks from the Young Man's Fancy, which he did on a silly dare, and got thrown out of school. Whence he went on to M.I.T. A good friend of Liza's, a part-time lover, but she had heard nothing from or about him for years.

And she wrote to Adam Argent, son of the writer David Argent, whom Liza especially disliked (the father, not the son). She felt a little sorry for Adam. So embarrassing, to have a father chasing girls about your own age, and writing those awful sexist books, one after another.

For Liza, the first effect of having written those letters is a certain new spice in her Julius Kahn afternoons. Getting ready to go down there, in addition to the necessary cookies and sweaters and Kleenex and Pampers and wheel toys, these days she remembers to insert her gold studs or sometimes big silver loops in her ears. To brush on mascara and to spray a tiny shot of Chanel 19 behind each ear.

And there she sits, in the suddenly glorious October weather— in what is often referred to as one of the most beautiful pieces of real estate in San Francisco, the park within the Presidio, a pocket of city land in the Army's lovely woods, the cypresses, eucalyptus and pines that, should the Army leave, as is sometimes feared, developers would almost instantly decimate. In the meantime those beautiful acres of the most northern, western tip of the city, overlooking the Golden Gate and looking out to sea, to the sometimes visible Farallons—all that is occupied in part by ugly barracks and just as ugly, if larger, officers' houses. And by beautiful country-seeming woods. And the Julius Kahn Playground. J.K.

There sits Liza, on her green slatted bench, her children for the moment happily ensconced in the sandbox—Liza, waiting for almost anything, for anyone. Fat pretty Liza, in her old pale-blue denim skirt, her blue shirt, with her nice long bare brown legs in sandals, silver loops in her ears, her long fair hair clean and brushed.

There is much more of curiosity than of personal eagerness, though. This is not a young woman awaiting the arrival of possible lovers with any anxiety, she is not at all worried that they might not show up. Liza is neither an anxious nor a fearful person, nor is she in any sense lonely, and the chances seem good that she will never be so. After all, at birth she fell into a young family in love: Jim and Caroline McAndrew were surely somewhat in love, at first, and it was a family in which there was already a lonely, somewhat anxious older sister, Sage, who was eager to welcome and love this pretty new baby. (Sage's more negative, rivalrous feelings found their objects quite readily and soon enough with Fiona, and then with Jill; by the advent of Portia she was again welcoming, and possibly looking for an ally.)

Instead of any former lover, though, the person who now approaches Liza, teetering unsteadily on very high heels across the grassy meadow, is Joanne Gallo.

"Joanne. Hi."

"Oh, hi. You're not Sage or Fiona, you're Liza, right?" With one of her sillier laughs Joanne sits down on the bench, fairly near but not exactly next to Liza.

"No kids today?" Saying this, Liza then remembers that Joanne and Roland have only the one pale unhappy late-life child, poor girl.

"No, I had lunch with my art group. God, I feel so drunk, we had margaritas."

There is a long dark stain of something, possibly coffee, on Joanne's purple silk shirt (Liza, who tends to spill things, finds this endearing, sympathetic), and her dark-green skirt is all awry. Her hair is all over the place, white-blonde, too teased and sprayed.

Curiously, at the moment of Liza's noticing her hair, Joanne chooses to say, "I'm really blonder than you and your sisters are even, aren't I. But no one knows it's real. The truth is, my mother's Icelandic. An Iceland poppy, my dad used to call her, and some-times Roland called me that. So I really am more of a blonde than you, all you sisters."

"Except Sage." Liza speaks that name quite deliberately, looking directly at Joanne as she does so.

"Oh, Sage," says Joanne, with an unsuccessful flutter of one hand. "Sage is history. What's the name of the stockbroker sister? She's the one you ought to warn. I'm sure she's on his list. The next one."

Liza, having never spent much time with drunks, finds Joanne's slippage in and out of drunkenness unnerving—and that is what she does: within a single sentence, almost, Joanne will be focussed, sensible-sounding, and then as suddenly she is not sensible at all, or focussed. And what on earth is she talking about, these hints of Roland and Jill?

She must mean Fiona, which would explain quite a lot, now that Liza thinks back to the "family dinner" at Fiona's, and so she asks, "Do you possibly mean Fiona?" This direct approach may shock Joanne into some sort of clarity, Liza believes, or hopes.

But no. "Fiona who? The Fiona of Fiona's?" Conveniently drunk again, Joanne laughs, lightly, messily and unsuccessfully. Her face then crumples, doll-blue eyes tighten, and she is crying, small sad constricted sobs, small tears trickling through the vestiges of her makeup.

"Mommy, he threw sand at me!" Liza's small daughter just then from the sandbox shrieks, just before knocking her brother over backwards. He too begins to shriek.

So that all Liza can do by way of comfort for poor Joanne is a small pat on the shoulder, as she gets up and heads for the sandbox, to separate her murderous children. As she does so, trying to be a good fair mom, her peripheral vision takes in Joanne hurriedly getting up, her wrecked face hidden in Kleenex. Joanne, leaving J.K.

Liza's next quite unexpected visitant that afternoon in the park is Sage—Sage, with quite another story to tell.

"When I got all this bad news I went over to, uh, Jim's," Sage says, with almost no preamble. She is perched on the same green slatted bench beside Liza where Joanne sat, overlooking the sandbox where the two small children are now deeply involved in making a municipal garage, or so they say.

Sage smiles, a quick humorless twist of her mouth. "Poor Jim. I was really not in good shape, I mean I was worse than I thought I was. More upset. And he had a bad cold." Divulging this piece of information, which is to Liza quite unalarming, Sage looks as though she, like Joanne, might weep—and Liza at once understands several related facts.

The first is that Sage, who tends to be indirect, who is never confrontational—Sage in this way is apologizing to Jim for whatever happened between them, apologizing through the medium of Liza, who is supposed to tell her father that Sage is sorry—Sage did not mean to get drunk, did not mean to do whatever reprehensible things she believes that she did.

Liza finds herself not wanting to speculate about whatever scene took place between Sage and Jim. Her father. Odd: usually she is quite given to speculation about such scenes.

It would really be better, Liza believes, if Sage could just say, I threw up. Or, I talked too much. I told Jim stuff that I really shouldn't have, I told him that Noel is a shit, and probably un-faithful.

Whatever Sage did or said, though, Liza knows that she will keep it to herself, contained within her infinitely complex mind, her series of selves. Liza has sometimes imagined this much-loved, subtle and difficult sister as a series of rooms, leading into each other but all quite separate, discrete as to decor, to mood.

"Are you able to get any work done these days?" Liza now gently asks.

"Not much. You know, I'm pretty discouraged. I'd counted on the New York thing too much. I just feel—and then Noel—" Sage gestures her feeling of helplessness, spreading her hands before her, in feeble self-defense.

"But Sage."

"I know." Again, the twist of a smile. "I know. I'll go to New York in January, nothing so different. It could be better, even. I could have finished something new by then. I never did really get at that group of women I meant to do. It doesn't matter about now, really, I keep telling myself. I'm being very childish, I know I am."

Liza smiles. "As who is not."

"Anyway, that same night, after I got home from Jim's, Noel came in really late, and I made this terrible scene with him. Honestly, Liza, what's happening to me?"

"Maybe making a few scenes would be good for you. Everyone gets upset. It's not so awful to let it show, I don't think."

"You mean, good for me to let it out for a change? Liza, you're such a wise kid. Not to mention really kind." As she says this Sage's narrow gold eyes fill.

As Liza thinks, I really cannot stand all this weeping. Honestly, everyone seems to be in tears. When what I really came to the park for was some sexy encounters. Honestly.

"What's so funny about your stupid older sister?" Sage has asked, responding to Liza's smile. But her tears have gone, as suddenly as they came into her eyes.

"Oh, nothing," Liza tells her. "Just sometimes I remember coming here to J.K. when I was sort of a kid, you know, high-school stuff. Afternoons in the Sixties. All those guys."

Sage smiles again. But even now, relatively cheered, she has a damaged look. Earlier, as she came toward Liza, Liza took note of her lagging walk, her especially tattered black turtleneck.

"Those must have been really good times," Sage says, wistfully, probably enviously. "But now you have good Saul. Even better."

"Oh yes. Better."

"God, some afternoon," says Liza that night after dinner to Saul. A rare civilized interval during which neither of them is actually doing anything else as they speak. Dinner and the dishes are done, the children asleep and Saul is neither trying to read nor playing with any of his various electronic audio equipments, not recording or listening, retaping anything. And Liza is not turning the pages of magazines that she means to read later. They are simply talking.

"First Joanne Gallo. Honestly, that poor woman. A potential suicide if I ever saw one. And then Sage. If Joanne were a patient of yours would you tell me?"

"No, of course not."

"I sure hope she's someone's patient. If I ever saw a woman in bad shape. Sage is not exactly happy either but she has more going for her, at least I think so."

"Sage. I don't know, but I think you're right. She'll probably be okay. Depending on what you mean by okay."

"Do you say that just because you know she put in all that time with your colleague?"

"No, certainly not."

"Saul, don't you ever get really turned on by a patient? I mean, you must get an occasional really dishy young girl?"

Liza has asked this question before, in various forms, so that now Saul smiles—in a way that Liza has wondered about: is he being condescending to her? would he dare? "Not often enough," he now tells her, with that smile.

"The point is, you wouldn't tell me if you did, is that right?"

"Even more to the point, I wouldn't tell her. How dishy she looked."

"Like a priest. How sexy, I'm married to a Jewish priest. But, Saul, it surely must happen?"

"I suppose. Or so some people say."

"The irony." Liza sighs. "People observe that we get along, we seem to talk to each other a lot, and from that they probably conclude that you confide in me. That I'm privy to all sorts of juicy secrets, the way lots of doctors' and lawyers' wives are. Whereas actually it's the other way around, I tell you things." She sighs again, before continuing. "Anyway, I did get a clear impression that something went very wrong between Sage and Jim."

"I hope not. I think she counts on him. She needs him."

"Of course she does. After all, he began in her life as her father, really. But I got such an odd impression today, as though things had taken a sort of sexual turn. Between Sage and Jim." Liza gives a tiny shudder. "Needless to say, that made me feel a little odd. After all. My dad."

"True enough."

"If they actually did it, would that be incest?"

"Good God, Liza. What a thought. I guess technically not, literally not, since they aren't related by blood. God knows what the laws are about that, if there are any. But emotionally it surely would be."

"On the other hand, once you're grown up, why not?"

"Liza. God. I'm going to see to it that you never get a chance to remarry. God!"

A small pause, and then Liza asks, as she reaches to pull gently at the longish hair on his neck, "Do you not get haircuts because you hate to or is it really some vanity about your hair?"

"Oh, Liza—"

"Do you mean you don't know?"

"Maybe both things are true? That's what my patients and I often seem to say to each other."

"Well, really. Are you actually quoting a patient—to me?"

"Patients. I was speaking generally."

"Darling, you do have lovely hair, though."

But as she says that to her husband, Liza is also thinking, Why must I always be so flattering—to Saul and to all men, really? No wonder I used to be such a popular girl. Why can't I just say, Go get a haircut, you asshole? You really need one.

And she answers herself, Because I'm Caroline's daughter, among other reasons. Impeccable English–New England Caroline.

But anyway, she thinks, I could write a story about a woman who sits in the park with her children, and one by one her former lovers all come by, a great line of them, all telling her how great she looks these days.

Or, maybe no lovers come at all? But entirely other people, whom she did not expect to see?

Sixteen

"I do not understand women. Do not, do not, do not." Saying this, ruefully, less than half-ironically, Roland makes an elaborate, Italianate gesture with his smooth white well-manicured hands, and he smiles at his lunch companion. Again, Buck Fister. And again they are in their favorite corner banquette at the Big Four, atop Nob Hill, but not yet where they would like to be: at the P.U. Club, across the street.

"Do not understand them," Roland repeats, to Buck's sympathetic, answering smile. "They change, every mother-loving one of them changes. And me, I am so incredibly, monumentally stupid that I never, never, never see it coming. Each time I think, Ah, a new woman, with this one all will be different. And each time it's the same damn thing all over again."

"Sweetbreads," Buck murmurs, just lifting his head from the menu. "In that case," he says to Roland, "maybe you have to change? Find some whole new breed of lady?"

"Holy Mother, what do you think I've been trying to do? All kinds! Holy mother-of-pearl, years of all kinds of women, that's the whole point. It's always the very same woman. Of course marrying them is the worst mistake of all, but everyone knows that. You ever been married, Bucko?"

"No." Buck raises thin eyebrows, which gives him a look of smiling, although his mouth does not smile. "You thought sisters would be different?" he asks. "From each other?"

"Oh well, sisters. Half-sisters, actually. And a long time passed, quite a few other ladies in between. But that was not exactly intentional. Crazy me, I fell in love with them both. The mother, though, that's the one I really—but she's so old. Funny about women's aging, isn't it? Fair Caroline and I must be in point of fact of a similar age, but I would never—What I mean is, well, she'd have even less luck with a younger man, I'd imagine. Whereas I, with younger women, well, it's hardly a problem. I wonder if older women find this unfair."

"Very likely they do. Feminists, women seem to find almost everything unfair these days. I think I will have the sweetbreads, they're very good here."

"It's all very sad, I sometimes think," sighs Roland, looking far more satisfied than sad. "The fate of women is very sad," he vaguely repeats.

"You could do a campaign speech on that," observes Buck.

"I guess I have to make up my mind." But it is clear from Roland's tone (at least it is clear to Buck) that he has already made up his mind. Affirmatively.

Which Buck has grasped sometime before: of course Roland will run for mayor, his whole career has been headed in that direction. "You'll need some advice," he tells his friend. "What I mean is, advice that you take."

Roland looks both tolerant and inquiring.

"You've got to back off certain things," Buck tells him. "It's that simple. And you know what things. No more Sage or Fiona, or Beverly or Beatrice or Beedy—who was that girl with the really silly name?"

Roland laughs, very pleased. "Where'd you ever get that list?"

"I know things. But from now on you only fuck Joanne, right?"

"Jesus. Just plain Joanne." Roland's laugh is short, derisive, rather ugly. "Well, of course I know that," he says. "It's just a question of when do I start. Or, rather, when do I stop."

"You know perfectly well when to stop," Buck tells him. "Like now." And then, "Spinach salad, that's what I really come here for," he tells the waiter. "Yes. More Perrier."

"Me too. Everything the same," Roland orders, impatiently.

"About Joanne. She does not look like a happy woman. I saw her last week out at lunch, and she looked, well—"

"Drunk, probably. She drinks too much. She's got a real problem."

"You've got a problem. Joanne looks unhappy, and you need a happy-looking wife. Look at Nancy. Tell Joanne to look like her. To look up to you a lot and smile."

"Holy Mother, do you know what she'd say? Saints, I can hear her. 'But Ronnie loves Nancy.' Some shit like that."

"It may be shit but look what it does for his image. His image is fabulous, and yours could use some work. Make Joanne happy. Buy her a present or something. Today."

"Now, there's an original thought. But okay, I will. I might as well." Gloomily Roland forks into his salad, just spearing a dark-green oily leaf, as he thinks: I hate spinach, why do I always have it here? To make Buck feel good? Why am I spending my life making people feel good?

"On the other hand," Buck tells him, "there might be a reward for virtue. I might know of something, uh, interesting for you. Something, uh, novel."

"Come on, Buck. I don't use whores. And God knows I'm not interested in boys, you know that. I'm really a very simple guy."

Buck scowls, Roland has never seen such a scowl. "No one uses any of those words," Buck says. "Never. This is just a nice house, a private home, you might say. In a very nice part of the Mission. Perfectly safe."

"You're out of your mother-loving mind. A home in the Mission. Jesus H."

"Well, a considerable number of our friends in the Department don't seem to find it such a weird idea. It's very nice. Some very nice, very nice young people. Young women. Uh, girls."

"Under-age Asians, I'll bet. I've heard about that. Cops are so stupid, I've always said so."

"What you mean is you're not ready to give up your latest McAndrew."

Roland grins, widely. A tooth-flashing, self-stroking Sicilian grin. "Say, how about being my manager, in secret of course?"

Buck's smile is a little lopsided. Somewhat furtive, the smile of a man unused to smiling. "Fine," he says. "That's just about what I had in mind."

It is somewhat later, over their sweetbreads, that Roland remarks, "If I am in truth going to run, and you're going to help, I suppose we should talk about issues?"

"There are no issues. This is the Eighties, remember?"

"Italians can be very, very treacherous." It is Stevie who says this to Fiona—speaking not of Roland Gallo but about some nursery wholesalers, a family some miles south of San Francisco, in an area of broad flat sunny well-irrigated acres, next to the coast. Presumably, Stevie does not know about Roland, though the smile accompanying his remark about Italians might suggest that in fact he does know.

What has happened is that the two young women, the florists, who every morning delivered the flowers to Fiona's, so early, so fresh—these two young women, black Lois and small blonde Bonnie, once lovers, now have broken up, ended not only their relationship but their working partnership, their business, with Lois gone off to Mexico and Bonnie back to Louisiana, where she came from.

And so, mildly desperate, Fiona and Stevie have undertaken this Monday drive (Fiona's is closed on Mondays), down to seek out new suppliers. The Silvestris were last and most appealing on their list, but also very expensive. The Silvestri specialty is lilies, wildly various, glamorously hued and fashioned lilies. Fiona's favorite was a giant but most delicately petalled pink, each petal improbably but beautifully edged in a pale apple green. Whereas Stevie took to an almost cocoa-brown variety, streaked with gold. All lovely, really lovely, and rare. "No one else on the coast can match our breeds," Julio Silvestri told Fiona, with a grin that reminded her strongly of Roland—but, then, almost everything these days reminds her of Roland. Fiona is very much in love.

However, as Stevie makes his possibly pointed remark about the treachery of Italians, Fiona thinks, You're goddam right, and I'd just better watch out, I know that. "I know," she tells Stevie. "We'd better ask around. About flowers."

As they drive northward, the land rises; to their left are smooth grassy bluffs, overlooking the glass-smooth gold-blue October-afternoon sea. There is such an extraordinary shimmer on the water, such a haze of gold far out at the horizon—it is all so amazing that Fiona, who is driving (her blue Ferrari), asks, "Mind if we pull over? I never get to see the ocean."

"San Franciscans don't, have you noticed? It's the bay we all look at. I think the sea frightens people. They might jump."

Swinging dangerously across the highway, Fiona finds a small road, where she parks the car, and they both get out—to walk silently across the bleached, cropped grass. To stand looking down and out at the sea.

Just below them is a narrow uninviting beach of coarse yellow gravel, no sand, and the bluff is red, eroded, deeply creviced: there is no way down. And the glistening stretch of water is changing even now, the gold darkening, like wet silk, with long purple shadows.

Italians are treacherous, and none so treacherous as Roland Gallo is with women, is what Fiona is thinking. And no matter what he says, why should I be any different from the rest, finally? The only thing that would make me different would be if I dumped him first. But—

But, as she thinks this, perfectly rationally and constructively, Fiona is assailed by a wave of erotic longing, a literal long flash of heat across her thighs (and she wonders: is that what so-called hot flashes are? older women remembering sex? she will have to ask Caroline). At that moment the desire, the pure lust for Roland is so strong that Fiona's knees weaken, almost buckling, as in a very specific way she thinks of him, of what he specifically does— repeatedly, repeatedly, in the same way every time, and each time is new for her, all her flesh becomes new, all melted, all liquid gold.

Unthinkingly she reaches for Stevie's arm, and just as automatically he moves away.

"Sorry—"

"Oh, sorry—"

Recovering first, Fiona remarks, "The sunset is gorgeous, though, isn't it."

"Sure is. Worth the trip, as they say in the Michelin guide."

"Oh, right."

Fiona is thinking, I really can't dump Roland yet. Or, not quite yet. Or, maybe I can?

She asks Stevie, "You been to Europe recently?"

"Not for a while," he ambiguously tells her. And then, "But I'm getting a real lust for Italy again. Maybe Sicily."

"Why on earth Sicily?"

"Because I've never been there."

He doesn't like me at all, Fiona suddenly thinks, and this new thought or perception bothers her not at all, not at that moment.

They turn back to the car and start off for home.

"My own darling, my adored, I count the minutes until I see you, but tonight there is an emergency. Political. A meeting. I will call, or call again, despite my hatred for this cold machine. Distorting your voice—"

"Roland, love, I couldn't be sorrier, but something's come up with my stepfather. He's not doing so well, we're all gathering around."

"My angel, the gods are against us. This afternoon has become impossible. I am devastated."

"Darling Roland, I know it's unromantic as hell but I've got this filthy cold. No, I absolutely cannot see you. Out of the question. I can't even go to the hospital to see Ralph."

Considering the high general intelligence, and the highly developed sexual intuitiveness of both Fiona and Roland Gallo, it is probably surprising that this exchange should continue beyond three or four messages, but continue it does—perhaps in part because both people are too vain to imagine the secretly subversive intentions of the other. It continues for weeks, and then months, with infrequent intervals of time actually spent together. Seized hours of the most marvellous intensity, as always.

Indeed, as they frequently say to each other, they are most

perfectly matched, in a sensual way, thin blonde young Fiona McAndrew and aging, dark Sicilian Roland Gallo.

They are also agreed on late afternoon as being the perfect time for love. Hours that are especially beautiful, that sunny October and then on into a November of drought, in Fiona's penthouse. Late sunlight brilliant blazing copper in all the windows across the bay, dazzling Berkeley, Oakland, San Leandro.

Dazzling copper sunlight on all Fiona's taut white skin, and on Roland's graying chest.

This pattern could have continued, those postponing messages on answering machines, repetitive and for the most part silly, those far rarer intervals of love—all that could have gone on indefinitely. It needed some shock to end it, a violent shock that was ultimately provided.

Seventeen

Although she eats so little, Jill cares a lot about food—more, actually, than Fiona does. Her favorite mode of intake consists of tiny bites, from a lot of creamy, rich, highly seasoned dishes. Watching her, anyone might think that she was eating quite a lot, although a look at her plate would inform the observer otherwise.

Her favorite meal is breakfast. And recently a new restaurant has opened in the financial district that serves marvellous breakfasts— Louisiana food: hush puppies, beignets and all manner of wonderful warm Southern breads. Not to mention the delicious breakfast casseroles of shrimp or crabmeat or oysters, or all three, in a creamy rich béarnaise.

Jill is there at the counter at Maxine's, eating (or, rather, tasting) crabmeat in béchamel, with hot buttered cornbread, when she hears the news of the stock market crash, that bad October Monday morning.

One of the things that Jill has so far liked about this restaurant is that no one else, no one she knows, that is, has thought of breakfast there. Who could handle all that rich food first thing in the morning? is the general view, among people who happily eat lunch or dinner at Maxine's. But Jill of course can and does handle it, she is enjoying her breakfast, when her peripheral vision catches a guy she does not like at all. He likes her even less, and for the stupid tired old reason that she turned him down: one night when they were simply having a boring conversation in a bar on Union Street

(Jill thought that is what they were doing), he used that tired old Seventies line, My place or yours?—and he meant it, the stupid jerk, he even got ugly about it, later on, and he badmouthed her all over town. Jack, she thinks his name is. A thin monochrome guy with a strange very unattractive lipless mouth, and darting pale humorless eyes.

And now he comes up to her, of all people, this Jack, to tell her, "Well, eat up, kid, this meal may be your last. The market's down fifty-seven points so far, and going fast."

"Very funny, what else is new?" But Jill is somehow sure that this is not a joke. Jack is not a joker, his awfulness is in another style.

"Lucky for me," he now tells her. "I mostly got out last week. Just a hunch I had."

"Well, hooray for you." Jill is not the only person to find Jack especially hateful that day.

At least he does not sit down beside her, he goes on down the counter to accost another non-friend (probably) with his good news. With his *Times* and his *Journal* rolled and tucked under his arm, his Burberry arm.

Jill very rapidly calculates that she could lose about 750 thou. Not exactly a million but goddam close. And close to all she has, not counting the paltry fixed assets, like the equity in her condo, the time-share place in Tucson. Her car, stuff like that.

For once she is quite unable to finish eating.

By noon Jill has found that her calculation was amazingly accurate, as she might have known it would be. She has always excelled at lightning arithmetic with large figures.

She is supposed to have lunch today with Buck, of all people. And one of the things that Jill instantly thought, in one of those clusters of automatic reactions, undifferentiated, that arrive in the wake of disasters—she thought, Now I can be a real hooker, full-time. I'll have to. I'll get in touch with Margo St. James. Join COYOTE.

Another thing that she thinks, seated there at her wide impressive desk in the Transamerica Pyramid, with its golden, spectacular view of the bay—she thinks, I'm sick, I've never thrown up before and now I have to.

Which she does, hunched over a bowl in the lavish restroom. Violent, repeated spasms, over and over, until nothing comes up but the nastiest, bitterest bile.

Could anyone do this on purpose? she wonders. Do it often? I'd a thousand times rather be fat, be fatter than anyone, thinks Jill.

After calling to break the date with Buck (easy enough: his secretary sounded as though she expected the call, as though this were a day on which anything could happen, and probably would), Jill's next rather curious impulse is to go home. To go, that is, to see Caroline. And Ralph; she thinks he's home from the hospital, isn't sure.

Caroline's house as always smells faintly of roses, and today it smells too of some lemony furniture wax that Caroline likes to use when she waxes, which is not often. "But it's so therapeutic," Caroline has said. "I should do more, all that scrubbing and rubbing."

If she, Jill, now told Caroline, I've lost almost all my money, would Caroline suggest some brisk furniture polishing, as therapy? Or making chicken-soup stock, as she is also now engaged in doing: the house smells too of that rich, highly personal broth of Caroline's, her special mix.

So far Jill has only said, "I was having a lousy day. I thought I'd come by."

"Well, darling, I'm so glad you did. And actually me too, all this with Ralph is just so worrying. He's back in Presbyterian, you know."

Caroline does look distracted, her normally smooth face is strained, and for the first time Jill notices that her mother has lost some weight, which is curiously unbecoming; both Caroline's face and her body look older, a little tense, without those extra pounds.

Jill notes too that the house is much too clean, for Caroline. All that obvious effort with the vacuum, with mops and rags and brushes bespeaks time on her hands, and tension, nervous energy to burn. Normally what is called an "indifferent" housekeeper, in her case an accurate description, Caroline has worked too hard at cleaning, so that every surface shines, with too high a gloss. Too much is reflected from glass-topped tables, silver vases and picture frames, in the high sheen of wooden surfaces, the rosewood table, Molly Blair's big walnut desk. It is simply not a good sign, all this cleaning by Caroline.

"Actually he's doing rather better, though," Caroline tells Jill, of Ralph. "But it's so back and forth, up and down. I keep having to readjust."

Readjust to the possibility of Ralph's dying, or not dying: she must mean that, and Jill tries to take it in, even as in another part of her mind she wonders: Should she tell Caroline about losing her money? Maybe not, after all?

Jill on the whole likes Ralph very much, she always has. At first, when she, Jill, was a very small child, he was sort of someone their mother knew, and then, when Jill was four, and Fiona six, they got married, Caroline and Ralph. In a non-close way Jill is fond of him (God knows nothing like Sage with her huge disgusting permanent crush on Jim McAndrew). And the real point is that Caroline is crazy about Ralph, she always has been. Fiona and Jill have figured that he was the first big sex figure for Caroline, that Caroline and Jim, their dad, did not get along so wonderfully, in the sack. And so Ralph's illness must be really horrible for Caroline. Loyal Caroline, who always puts such a good face on things.

"This bag lady," Caroline is saying now. "She kept pacing the sidewalk, with this awful chant about fires and dung, the end of the world. And I sort of knew I knew her, or at least I used to see her. Obviously in some entirely other context. And finally it came to me, of course one night, or rather early morning, when I woke up and couldn't get back to sleep. I suddenly remembered."

Her name was Mary Higgins Lord, and she was married to the head of surgery at one of the hospitals, Dr. Bayard King Lord ("the most ridiculously redundant name," Caroline had giggled to her then-husband, Jim McAndrew, who did not find the observation especially funny). And Dr. Bayard King Lord, who was quite as pompous as his name, dumped Mary Higgins Lord, his wife, whom almost everyone, including the doctor, insistently called Higgsie—for a much younger, blonder horsey type (so original, Dr. Lord), and "Higgsie," instead of taking it well, being a sport about it all, as discarded wives of her caste were known to do—quite out of character, Higgsie went mad, what was described as a total nervous collapse: there were rumors of scenes at parties, in restaurants, tears, endless tears, and all that from Mary Higgins Lord, hitherto such a model of control, of perfect children and parties, meals and clothes.

Caroline was of course one of those surprised, and sympathetically appalled—as she is now appalled, imagining the anguish involved in such a descent. Before that descent, she remembers fearing certain parties because of knowing that Higgsie Lord would be there, in all her black-and-pearl perfection—making her, Caroline, feel invariably a mess, a little overweight and showing it, her hair distraught, nails (from so much gardening) not right at all, her dress at best last year's. Perfect Higgsie Lord, with her never-to-be-forgotten yellow eyes.

"And the damn thing is," Caroline concludes her story, "now that I've remembered who she is, of course I don't see her any more. Although I'm not quite sure what I'd do about it if I did."

"It's a very scary story." Jill feels that this is not a great day for her to hear about how a perfectly okay woman fell through the cracks.

"Jill darling, you look so stricken. You mustn't take my story to heart. I didn't mean it to be an object lesson."

"But—" Jill is about to explain, to say, Look, I'm almost broke, I'm wiped out. But the doorbell rings.

They both jump, so concentrated are they on each other—and Caroline frowns as she gets up to answer.

In another moment from the front hall Jill hears the voice of her older half-sister, Sage. "I was on my way out to a place on Geary to get some paints Noel needs, and I thought I'd swing by," Sage is saying, as Jill thinks: I really don't feel like seeing Sage, I'm not up to Sage right now. Why do I have to keep running into Sage?

Then, "Jill must be here," she hears Sage saying, from the hall. "The only gorgeous yellow Mercedes in town."

As Jill thinks, She doesn't much like me either. Would she like me any better broke? Will she?

Sage is wearing her habitual black turtleneck, silver loops in her ears and black pants. Black Reeboks. Well, no wonder Noel likes lace so much, is Jill's almost automatic thought. Lace and silk, no wonder.

"I've got the very worst cold," is what Sage first says to Jill, "don't even come near me," as she extracts some Kleenex from her pants.

"Well, how's it going?" Jill very politely asks (too politely? maybe).

"Actually things are better than I sound or probably look. I was pretty undone at first, my show being cancelled. I mean postponed. So suddenly. So unreasonably, I thought. But now it all makes a little more sense, and I'm getting some work done. And Noel has been really wonderful."

"Darling, that's absolutely great," Caroline tells her.

No wonder I haven't seen him for a while, is Jill's silent thought. He's busy being wonderful at home. Being so supportive and protective, taking care. Being everything he really isn't. And how will he feel about me when I'm down, maybe out on the street?

"I felt so terrible, really totally discouraged," Sage is saying to her mother. "And then, out of that feeling, I'm doing some stuff I really like." After a small sniffling pause she adds, "It's a sort of phoenix syndrome. Hard to explain."

"Darling, you don't have to explain. But that is interesting. I can't wait to see."

"Well, Caroline, it'll be a while." (Sage always calls her mother by her first name, just as she calls Jill's father, her stepfather, Jim). "Caroline, you look awfully thin. Are you okay?" Sage asks.

"Oh yes, it's just the effort I make, all this readjusting. I was telling Jill, Ralph getting better and then worse, back and forth to the hospital."

They get along with each other much better than I get along with anyone, Sage and Caroline do, Jill thinks. They admire each other, especially Caroline admires what Sage does, her "creativity," whereas they both think that what I do is sort of immoral. And they're probably right, and they don't even know the half.

If she told them about her lost money, they would both be very sympathetic, they are both very "nice." But Jill decides not to tell them. She does not want their sympathy, and she surely does not want to appear to ask for it. Not from her mother, and definitely not from Sage. And she thinks, Oh God, suppose Sage found out about Noel, Noel and me? Suppose he should tell her, as part of his being "wonderful"? And suppose she should tell my mother, suppose Sage told Caroline? If Noel tells I will kill him, Jill decides; with my last cent I'll have him offed, Jill thinks.

And it is pretty bad, she further thinks; fucking your half-sister's husband is worse than turning tricks, it really is.

"Ah, Caroline, that's really hard on you." Sage has gone over to give her mother a quick warm hug. "All this with Ralph."

Jill has never before thought much about Ralph. Early on she and Fiona used to snicker about his accent, his general corniness; but as adolescents they recognized (without snickering this to each other, or certainly to Ralph) that he was a lot less uptight than Jim, their father, Ralph is a fair-minded person, they both dimly perceived (but how could Caroline find him so *attractive*).

And now, confronted with his illness, Jill uncomfortably realizes that she cares about Ralph, she would hate it if he died—that is caring, isn't it?

On the other hand, it might be interesting to see what Caroline would do next.

Perhaps to change the subject, Caroline then tells her daughters, "I got a card from Jim, is that not funny? He's down in Mexico *snorkeling,* he was apologetic about not being around to help. Medically, I guess he must have meant."

Sage flushes a dark unbecoming scarlet, as she mutters, "I haven't seen him for a while."

Jill begins to laugh: the very idea of her dignified middle-aged doctor-father snorkeling—in Mexico—is somehow funny.

Both Caroline and Sage regard her with some incomprehension, so that Jill feels she must explain, "It's just an odd picture, don't you think? He's so tall and pale. Such a doctor."

"Presumably he's not snorkeling in his lab coat," suggests Caroline.

"The truth is I'm a little hysterical," Jill now tells them both. "The market went sort of crazy today. Went way down, that is. I think I've really lost a lot of money."

"Jill dear, how terrible, why didn't you say? How awful." Caroline and Sage speak almost in unison, their very dissimilar faces expressing similar concern.

But this is not their kind of problem, Jill knows. They are both very nice women, and they mean awfully well, but they live in an entirely other world. They are basically anti-money, anti-business. Even technology, they seem against that, they don't even have any kind of computer, either of them. Though how they think the world would function if everyone were just like them—

"Well, I'll really be all right," Jill tells them. "I'm not exactly out on the street. Not yet. And lots of people were hit much harder than I was."

"But it's no fun, losing money," Caroline sighs. "One of the joys of not having any, I suppose." (Which strikes her daughter Jill as a very smug remark indeed. Very unimaginative.)

A short time after that Sage announces that she really has to run along, Noel needs his paint. "But why am I running around after paint for Noel?" she laughingly, rhetorically asks. "Marriage makes no sense, it makes you senseless. You and Fiona have the right idea, Jilly."

"And Portia," her mother reminds her.

"Oh well, yes. Of course Portia. Well, goodby; lovely to see you both."

Caroline goes to the front door with Sage, as Jill (digesting that "Jilly") is left to wonder: Why did I have to hear so much about how well Sage and Noel are getting along? That skinny little bastard, I'll get him yet. One way or another.

And then the phone rings. From the front hall Caroline calls back, "Would you get that, darling, please?"

Jill, answering, identifies herself to a man who then suggests that she and her mother come along to the hospital. Right away.

Eighteen

When Portia was a small child her father, Ralph, used to take her down to Mission Street (they were living then up on Liberty) for treat excursions. From his boyhood, so much of which was spent visiting relatives in Texas, Ralph retained a strong nostalgia for anything Mexican: colors, smells, sounds, food. Especially Mexican people, for whom he felt a ferocious, sometimes despairing affection. "A whole lot of Texans don't feel this way, I know," he said to his half-comprehending young daughter. "Some of the worst racists you're ever going to find are Texans, on the subject of Mexicans. Some of them up in high places in our government, sad to say. I don't exactly know why, but I feel exactly the opposite. To me they're the gentlest, loveliest people. I'll take them over those mean-hearted rednecks any day. If I'm not around Mexicans for a really long spell I miss them. I go over to Mission Street, Dolores, Valencia, for my own special kind of fix."

Ralph knew all the best *tacquerias,* the chili parlors, and he knew where the best Latin bands were, where sometimes he could persuade Caroline to go. (Caroline protested, "Darling, I have to tell you the truth, it's just not my beat. Even in the Forties I was not so marvellous at the rumba, or the tango.") But Portia took to the whole Mission District scene. The Mission was her Mexico, and later her South America. And later still, as Vietnamese, Cambodian boat people began to arrive, the Mission was also her Southeast Asia.

For all these reasons, then, Portia sometimes house-sits for the

Fuerte family, who live out on Guerrero, off Army Street, for free. Mostly, she very much likes them. Betty Fuerte works part-time in the Galería de la Raza, and Eduardo is a rather scholarly importer; together the Fuertes travel all over Mexico for artifacts, which then are sold at a far-from-enormous profit, from a converted warehouse on York Street.

The Fuerte house is curiously Southern, with verandas and side porches, a small orchard out in back and very little room inside; the house is also used as a storehouse for unsold *objets,* going into any room you can trip over a *piñata,* or stumble into a pile of holy relics (lapsed Catholics, the Fuertes do not treat their plaster saints with much reverence).

Simply walking through the small bare streets of the Mission, though, or along broad, very crowded Mission Street itself, Portia feels the sort of flutter in her blood, the purely visceral happiness that another person might feel in Paris, in Amsterdam or Tahiti, depending on taste. (This "flutter" has more than a little to do with intense early feelings for Ralph; Portia is of course aware of this, but she chooses not to make too much of it.)

Her friend Harold likes the Mission too, or he says he does, but Portia senses his liking as being more abstract, a theoretical affection. His true mania is for Israel, he is crazy about Jerusalem, the Old City. ("It's so extremely beautiful, and besides I like Jews much better than WASPs. At school ALL my best friends were Jews." "I think maybe I like Third World people best." ("You mean Arabs?" Which led to a familiar and quite unresolvable argument.) Harold also likes Greek islands, Dubrovnik and anywhere in Italy. A privileged child, in a way, he spent most of his adolescence in travel.

Another reason that Portia is especially happy at the Fuerte house is that she and Harold do not, cannot possibly sleep together there. (This is something that Portia admits to herself but, again, does not examine.) The bed is quite simply too small for two exceptionally tall people. A couple would have to be wildly in love, or at least in love, and fairly small, to make it in that bed. Portia, curled contentedly alone, has naturally wondered about Betty and Eduardo, who are both on the short side and fairly plump. Any explanation is possible, she believes. They seem very fond of each other.

Thus, not going to bed together, when Portia is at the Fuerte house and Harold comes to visit, they spend a lot of time walking about in the Mission. They go to various take-out taco places, they have silly arguments about which one is best. They like to sit around in the large but object-cluttered living room with store-bought enchiladas heated up on Betty's nice brown earthenware plates, and pale cold Mexican beer in tall blue swirled glasses.

Appropriately enough, Portia has been there at the Fuertes' for the weeks of Ralph's most recent crisis, which began on the day that Caroline and Jill were summoned to the hospital.

"It's not as though there were three choices," Portia tells Harold; as often with this close friend, she is half speaking to herself. "Of course actually there's no choice at all. I mean possibilities. Possible outcomes."

"None of them swell."

"Right. He's not going to come out great."

"No. Not what we'd call his old self."

"No. If he as we say comes through, it's a question of how much damage."

"Right."

"And which would be better, dead or damaged."

"Christ. But as you say we have no choice. But since it's Ralph—" Harold is enormously fond of Ralph, in fact he loves Ralph, partly by way of contrast to his own father, a John Birch Society, alcoholic Wall Street lawyer, a great success. "Since it's Ralph we have to think that anything's better than no Ralph," Harold tells Portia.

"Poor Mom. Poor old Caroline. She must feel all different ways at once."

"At least."

"We should know a lot more in a day or so. She says."

"I'm not sure how much longer I can take working at Podesta, speaking of days."

"Do you want me to talk to Fiona? She's always in trouble with flowers, probably you could help—"

"No, she scares me to death. And Jill."

During the past week Harold has often gone to the hospital with Portia, at first with some ambivalence (his more or less normal state), torn between wanting to help Portia and not wanting to be what his mother quite often describes as "very *de trop.*"

It began, though, to seem to Harold that he was very welcome; even Jill and Fiona, usually so intimidating, so impeccably blonde and hard-edged sexy, were glad to see him, Harold felt. (He was always happy with Caroline.) He began to see that he was a sort of buffer, separating family members from too much raw contact with each other, in a very bad time for them all.

No one but Caroline stayed in the hospital for very long—that terrible room, poor Ralph all tubed and computerized, medicated into insensibility. The others all came and went, they stood about with long sad faces, whispering, and at the approach of doctors they all scurried out, leaving Caroline to deal with authority.

"Dad must really hate this," Portia had whispered to Harold, more than once. And, "You're awfully good to come."

All the others and especially Caroline have whispered thanks, including Fiona and Jill—though Harold is still quite afraid of them both.

"I couldn't work for Fiona," he now tells Portia.

"You wouldn't. A nice sort of fat odd guy named Stevie does most of the stuff with flowers. You might get along with him."

"You mean, because he's so odd? Or fat."

"Harold, please don't be so touchy. I can't stand it. Not just now, okay?"

And then the phone rings.

The news of Ralph is, though, guardedly, good. Unaccountably in tears, Portia comes back to tell Harold. "He's going to be okay," she weeps. "I mean, not die. Not yet. Caroline says the doctors say the worst part is over. But what can they mean?"

"I don't know."

Nineteen

For a variety of reasons, and he has to admit that Caroline was always among those reasons, Roland Gallo has taken to dropping in to see his old acquaintance Ralph Carter—although they were never exactly intimates. First off, Roland was looking to Ralph's well-known political savvy: in a word, how did Ralph view his, Roland's, mayoral candidacy? could he win, or was he liable to fall on his face, not to mention all that money down the drain? And besides, Roland has always liked old Ralph (Roland tends to forget that they are very nearly of an age, he and old Ralph). He likes the country harshness of Ralph's very Texan speech, and Ralph's extreme courtesy, in a bad, rude world. He appreciates Ralph's wit and sharpness—he values Ralph as that great rarity, an honest man.

Furthermore, late-afternoon visits to Ralph tend to put Roland home fairly late but with the most legitimate, time-honored of all excuses: he was actually, literally visiting an old sick friend. Joanne could call him there if she would like to check it out.

And, then, there was Caroline.

At the close of his first few visits, as Roland departed she would come up to the front door with him, to thank him and to say goodby. On these occasions they would exchange the same brushing kiss that everyone does these days, perhaps with a little more warmth involved than was quite usual. Roland liked her, and she was grateful for the visit, probably. But one day, somehow, their mouths slid together, and met, and held, surely not by accident.

But the next time he came to visit Ralph, as Roland got up to go Caroline seemed nowhere in sight, as he hesitated, looking around. He descended the stairs as noisily as he could, and then, at the front door, he heard her voice calling down, "Oh, Roland, sorry, I was on the phone, but you can let yourself out, can't you?"

And the next time a neighbor was there.

Roland thinks about that semi-kiss, though. He was (curiously) very turned on by it, and he observes in himself a series of sexual fantasies concerning Caroline. A little more flesh than he is used to, but that might be very nice. And talking to her, making plans to get together, then somehow doing it—and hearing whatever she would say to him in bed. Hearing his sexual self praised in that high-toned voice. The truth is, he really wants to make love to Caroline.

Making it with Caroline would be like getting into the P.U. Club, he thinks to himself with a laugh—and regrets that there is no one he could say that to.

But how to suggest it to Caroline? Even assuming that she might possibly say yes. She would not mess around, Roland is quite sure of that; if she says no she will mean it, no for good—and if she says yes, well, well hooray!

She should get out more, Caroline knows that—and still, even when the weekly Guatemalan woman Nelia comes to clean (a gentle woman, whom Ralph clearly likes and trusts), even with Nelia there in the house, Caroline mostly stays home. She putters—and now for the first time she understands the meaning of that word. She polishes silver that is not even in use, she dusts invisible corners.

And she takes long naps. Sleeping poorly at night, she allows herself to collapse in the guest bedroom, where sometimes these days she sleeps, for an hour or so in the afternoon.

Her dreams, which are vividly, undeniably sexual in nature, inform her of one thing that is clearly wrong: sheer deprivation, hunger. She suffers the loss, the lack of love, until now such an active element in her life.

How do her daughters manage? Caroline wonders. She is thinking especially of Fiona and Jill—who, as far as she knows, are not "with" or "seeing" anyone. But of course they manage with the knowledge that eventually someone will show up, they're both so young. Also, although she chooses not to dwell on this, it is clear to Caroline that those two daughters "relate" to men in ways that are quite unlike her own. She finds it hard to imagine either of them in love—or, perhaps "in love," but not feeling whatever it is that she, for example, feels for Ralph.

However, finding that this line of thought is making her very uncomfortable, Caroline turns her attention instead to thoughts of Liza—at which she smiles; and Sage, to whom she gives the smallest worried frown.

But before she can even consider Portia the phone rings.

How did she know that it would be Roland Gallo? For in the instant before picking up the receiver and hearing his voice, Caroline did know just who it was. And she almost knew what he would say.

"Caroline? Roland Gallo here. Well, how're *you?* I was wondering, possibly, could you—lunch someday, like, tomorrow?"

Having said, No, terribly sorry, never go out to lunch these days—and hung up, and struck anew with the ferocity of her own needs, obviously so great that she does not dare even have lunch with Roland Gallo, whom in many ways she does not even like, Caroline bursts into unaccustomed tears.

From Caroline's bedroom, Caroline's and Ralph's, the sunset has faded to a dusky, ashen blue. As Ralph still sleeps, and she sits, dry-eyed, beside him with her tea, Caroline simply watches the sky—still in early evening fairly light, streaked with dark clouds, above the eastern horizon. In her further view, great purposeful, powerful jets rise up from the international airport, heading south, moving with infinite deliberation up and across the sky. One can even, occasionally, confuse a plane with a bird, from this perspective their size is about the same, and sometimes a large bird will seem to move so slowly, so majestically as to emulate the motion of a plane.

In the middle distance the lacy spires of a church are reminders of Notre-Dame, or Chartres—and not far from that sacred stone is an extremely strange cluster of very tall, very delicate structures. Like children's toys, Caroline has thought, the Erector Sets (such a funny name, actually) that are surely meant for boys but that she could never resist buying for her girls, who loved them. Especially Sage, who was always building something. These structures, in her view, so delicately balanced that sometimes they sway or very slowly swing about, like masts, sometimes catching a wink of sunshine— they are actually cranes, Ralph has told her, building cranes, in the midst of the Western Addition. They have risen there like swamp weeds, so Caroline imagines, from a bog of bureaucratic arguments. They are quite crazily beautiful, and Caroline has thought how she would miss them, should they ever finish whatever work they are supposed to be doing, and go. They are part of her ravishing land-scape, the most beautiful painting that is her view.

These days Ralph has moments or even hours, almost, of lucidity. A total return of all his old intelligence, his sharpness. But these intervals can be neither predicted nor summoned, they relate to no known exterior stimulus. Ralph, as always, responds to no will but his own.

And now, just as Caroline is about to submit to the end of her sunset observation, to relinquish her birds and the spires and the building cranes to the coming night—as she starts to get up and go downstairs to heat up their soup, Ralph comes fully awake.

And with an announcement: "Very interesting news on the tube this afternoon. You catch any of it? No? Well, it seems this guy named Buck Fister is about to be indicted by the Grand Jury. All manner of unsavory charges. Interesting. I've never liked the fellow, I was just saying so the other day to Gallo. But I'm sure Gallo had no idea what he was up to."

"Who is he, this Buck Fister?"

"Actually I hardly know the fellow. Friend of Gallo's, though I never did understand quite why, or I didn't want to. But he's been running some kind of a call-girl operation. A very fancy one, it looks like."

"You mean Roland Gallo could have been involved?" Shuddering, Caroline experiences a small vague nausea, as though she has eaten something a little off.

"Oh no, nothing like that. That wouldn't be Gallo's style at all, I wouldn't imagine. He's a rather old-fashioned gentleman in his way, wouldn't you say?"

"Well, yes, I would have."

"Your true womanizers don't run to whores. That's more for neuter types like Fister."

"I'm sure you're right, darling," says Caroline. "Ostensibly, what does this Fister do?"

"Real estate. This town's prime industry, right? Every whore and pimp in town is into real estate."

"But that isn't what Roland Gallo does. I don't see why you keep mentioning him in connection with this fellow, this Fister."

"Because they're pals, that's all. They have lunch together. Herb Caen sees them at the Big Four together and talks about it. And that's one more black mark on the page against Gallo running for mayor. If they really nail Fister, and it looks like they're going to, it's not good at all for anyone who knows him. Has lunch with him."

Pulling herself together (after all, there was nothing, really, between herself and Roland Gallo, nothing happened), Caroline says, "Well, it's really lucky that we don't know this Fister, and don't know Gallo any better than we do, don't you think so, darling? And now are you ready for some really super minestrone?"

"Sure, sweets. But first a kiss."

Twenty

"It's terrifically cold in New York," Liza, on the phone, tells Sage. "You can hardly imagine. Saul and I were there at those meetings about this time last year. Oh, I nearly froze! And then all the buildings and everyone's apartments are so overheated. But the snow is wonderful, so beautiful in Central Park. We walked there—"

"Actually I don't much like snow. You remember at Tahoe, when we were kids?" Sage in fact finds the very idea of snow terrifying, and especially in New York: the whole city could be buried, smothered in snow, all of life there frozen. Though perhaps in that way preserved, like the slaves and domestic animals in Pompei. But she is horrified at the thought of a snowstorm in New York while she is there.

And she leaves the day after tomorrow.

San Francisco, just now in the throes of January rainstorms, is bad enough, the soughing, powerful winds, water pelting the windows of Sage's house. All this weather seems an omen, a warning of worse things to come, in New York: if this is so nearly unbearable, how possibly can she even consider a still more treacherous climate, colder weather, snow? Sage feels that she is being asked this, is being accused in this way. How can you deliberately fly into your doom? is the question.

"I think you'll have a wonderful time," pronounces Liza. "You'll love the snow. You probably didn't like it at Tahoe because Jim overdid it, with skis and all that. But now you will. Just take along a lot of warm clothes, if you're warm enough you'll be fine."

"Oh God, I hate to pack. I'm so bad at packing, the very idea of packing drives me crazy."

"It is awful," Liza agrees. "Actually I hate it too. But I'll tell you my secret method. Allow an enormous hunk of time just for packing. That really works out, for me. Hours and hours."

"But. But I still don't know what to take."

"Saul has an idea about that," says Liza, who is not generally given to quoting her husband. "It's to do with displacement. We tend to displace other anxieties, other fears onto what to take on a trip. Women do, mostly. It really comes down to what to wear. How we want to present ourselves. As though it mattered, deeply. We're all so brainwashed when it comes to clothes, don't you think? It's actually quite interesting."

Liza thinks almost everything is interesting, thinks Sage, with some annoyance. Liza is so objective, no wonder she and Saul get along so well; they're basically scientific, both of them. Liza may think of herself as a literary person, but she's really a scientist.

"The point is, I suppose," continues Liza, apparently unaware of sibling hostility, "you have to work out what you're really scared of. And then you can pack."

"Thanks a lot. But that's easy enough, in my case. I'm scared of my show. I'm terrified."

"Well, there you are. Just convince yourself that what you pack won't really affect how your show goes. Try to tell yourself that it really doesn't matter."

"But it does matter. Everything matters. To me." And Sage makes an incoherent sound of pure helplessness.

"Well, call me back if you need anything. If there's anything I could do."

"I'm afraid not, but thanks."

And that is quite true of Sage: to her everything does matter. And almost everything frightens her, in one way or another. Her show is only the start. There is also the terror of unknown New York weather, so cold it might strike her dead—or so Sage feels its threat. And the city itself is a source of increasing panic, with its muggings, murders, its very streets filled with rage and hatred, with murderous impulses.

Furthermore, Sage is frightened of her meeting with Calvin Crome, now such an important person in her life. He is capable, she has so far perceived, of a considerable spectrum of behavior, and in her experience this is not a good sign.

She is frightened too of leaving Noel alone in San Francisco.

She is frightened of Noel, who is far more unpredictable than anyone, ever in her life.

Years back, after her time with Roland Gallo, Sage discussed her fears with her psychiatrist, her fears that Roland Gallo would leave her, as he did in fact eventually do. And they discussed her older fears that her mother would marry Jim McAndrew and have more children. Her fear that Caroline and Jim would divorce, and that Caroline would marry this huge new scary man with the funny accent, Ralph Carter. "You see? Whatever I most fear seems to come true, I am not really so irrational," Sage pointed out. Anna Weldon: "It's perhaps the intensity that is irrational."

Sage had of course lost the fears that revolved around Roland, and in time she did cease her mourning for him, but she remained very much that same person: the woman who had loved Roland to distraction, always terrified that she would lose him, was very much the same woman who now loves Noel, a far more dangerous man. Loves and fears him, mortally.

Packing, Sage now regards her open suitcase with panic, as though nothing she could possibly, imaginably think of to take with her could protect her from the violence of New York, from cold or snow. Nor could anything conceivably equip her for an exhibition of her work ("exhibit": the very word is horrifying). The small, highly personal ceramic sculptures now all nakedly exposed—if not broken in transit. She has not even been able so far to call Calvin Crome to see if they got there all right; this seems such an amateur question, full of juvenile or at best adolescent anxiety.

She carefully folds a heavy white sweater and places it in the suitcase. Then takes it out and puts it back on the shelf.

Because she is concentrating on warmth, the question of what to wear to the opening itself is almost buried in her avalanche of anxieties, but occasionally it surfaces, like an iron post in deep snow. Dangerous, immoveable.

The green silk shirt, so happily, optimistically bought for the specific occasion of her opening in New York, is now irrevocably associated with the horrifying hours at Jim's—of which Sage is still barely able to think. (When she does think back to that afternoon, it seems to her that that was the beginning; that was when everything terrible that she now feels commenced. When she fell into this dark, panic-stricken decline.)

On the other hand, it still is a beautiful shirt. No one seeing her in that shirt would imagine her to be a woman who would fling herself insanely, sexually upon her stepfather. Former stepfather. Whoever. Drunkenly. Crazily.

She does not, then, have any idea what to wear to the opening, and for dinner with Calvin Crome. And she sees that packing could take her even longer than the entire afternoon that she has allowed for it. Even longer than the day and a half that remains.

In the meantime the ferocious rainstorm continues, dark and gray, gathering momentum rather than abating. Sage wonders that her small house can withstand it, that she herself can. And what would they ever do, she and her house, in a major earthquake, which is constantly predicted, which could happen any day.

Looking westward from her bedroom window, in the direction of the mountains, the Sierras, Sage thinks of the snow that must be there by now, covering Donner Summit, relentlessly falling all over Lake Tahoe and the far Nevada slopes.

When the phone rings it is hard to hear; Sage cannot instantly identify that sound, above all the pounding, incessant sounds of weather, in her house.

"Hi, sweetheart, it's me. Your old reliable buddy. Old Crome."

"Oh, Calvin. I can hardly hear you, we're having this rainstorm. Really violent." Sitting down on her bed, beside the table where the phone is, Sage notes that her heart is beating very hard, and she thinks, He sounds strange, could Calvin be drunk?

"Well, January. We've got a fair amount of snow, but actually I love it. It calms the city down, slows everything. Everything shoddy looks beautiful."

"I don't like snow very much."

"Well, pack up your snow boots anyway. It's supposed to last." And then he says, "I hope you're sitting down? I've got some news that's really pretty amazing."

"I am sitting down." And you're going to tell me the show's postponed again, or cancelled forever, Sage thinks, and guess what? I don't even care. As long as I don't have to fly into snow. Fly through storms, thinks Sage.

"—your first sale," is what Calvin is actually saying. "Really funny, in a way. How it came about. Well, I was there in the gallery, setting things up. Your pieces look fabulous in this space by the way, if I do say so. And suddenly, unannounced, in flounced B. B. Hoover, you know, the big real-estate dame, with her entourage, those creeps. Anyway, she fell in love with your *Family*. Had to have it."

"Jesus." Sage feels that she is listening to a story about someone else, about other, quite unknown people. B. B. Hoover, whom you read about in trashy magazines, could have nothing to do with her, with Sage, and her simple though laboriously achieved small pieces.

"Jesus is right," Calvin goes on. "Jesus Mary AND. I even argued with her, I said I hadn't absolutely set the prices yet. A big lie, of course. So she said—she insisted, that's a lady who's never heard NO—Hoover said she'd give me thirty thousand down. DOWN. And to let her know the final price. She was a little gassed, or coked or something, but I checked with her bank and the money's quite okay."

"God."

"Indeed. The very hand of. So. So far you're about fifteen thou ahead. Want me to wire it to your bank? Unlike other dealers, I'm prompt. You could upgrade your flight. Make yourself a bit more comfortable. No point going steerage when you don't have to.''

Waiting for Noel in the pricey new Fillmore Street restaurant at which she is taking him to dinner (''No, it's not too early to cele-brate, Calvin's convinced me, the money's in the bank''), Sage sees her image reflected in the multi-mirrored room, herself in the green silk shirt. (Why not? she thought, after Calvin's call; it's her best color, jinx or not.) Sage is glad that no one can read her mind as she thinks, I really am beautiful. At last. I really am. My hair, skin, with this color—I look great.

She has ordered a glass of white wine to help her wait, some premonition having warned her that Noel will be late.

But Noel is not late. There he is, just now striding down the aisle of the restaurant, in his old cords. Wearing his work clothes as though they came from Wilkes. And frowning—even from this dis-tance Sage can see his terrific, handsome scowl. His black-Irish scowl.

As Sage thinks, If he doesn't notice at all how I look, if he doesn't say anything, I don't think I can bear it.

Sliding into the booth, still frowning, Noel instantly says, ''I don't suppose you saw the afternoon papers.''

Her heart drops, as she thinks that if something really awful had happened, Reagan killed, an earthquake, then of course Noel would not notice her, how she looks. She must not take everything so personally. ''No, I didn't,'' she tells him.

''Well, it's not good news.'' To the waiter who has just delivered Sage's wine Noel says, ''Do you think I could have one too?'' His voice is unnaturally challenging, meanly ironic, a mood Sage knows.

''Whatever's happened?'' she asks him.

''Well—'' And now Noel does seem to see her. ''That a new blouse? It looks great. And—hey!—congratulations.'' But before Sage can respond to any of that he frowns again. ''More news about Buck Fister,'' he tells her.

''Who?''

''Jesus, Sage, don't you read? You're supposed to be the big intellectual in our group. The papers have been full of nothing else, don't you think about anything out in the world?'' And then, in one of his familiar but still startling reversals, he leans to kiss her. ''Sorry,'' he says. ''I'm a little upset.''

''Well, I guess I do sort of remember. He's someone in real estate?''

Noel laughs, shortly, angrily. ''Ostensibly. Turns out his real shtick was hookers. Call girls. Hustling sex.''

''Well. But—'' But what on earth can this have to do with us? Sage would like to ask this, although even as she phrases the question she knows that it does indeed have something to do with them. Something terrible.

''This afternoon it said where some reporter'd got hold of one of his notebooks. Names and addresses of friends of his. Roland Gallo, that's the most conspicuous name.'' A name that by tacit agreement has not been mentioned between Sage and Noel, not ever, so that now Sage feels its force, even as she wonders: But so what? Roland has some sleazy friends, he always has, so what?

It is very much on her mind that so far Noel has said nothing, really, about her sale, beyond those vague congratulations. Isn't that what they are doing tonight, supposedly celebrating? ''How do you feel about this restaurant?'' she now asks, by way of exploring his mood.

''Well—'' He lifts his head to look around, and Sage sees that his eyes are not quite focussed; he looks feral, an animal trapped in that room. ''Expensive restaurants all look alike these days,'' he then says, in the soft, controlled voice (so contradicting his look) that Sage knows is dangerous.

''That's interesting, of course you're absolutely right,'' she babbles. ''You could close your eyes and open them in another place, and the food too, I really don't know why anyone goes anywhere these days.'' Running down, she stops talking and looks at him, sees that he is staring distractedly around the room, as though at any moment he might rush out into the street. He looks trapped, threatened, desperate.

When at last he speaks to Sage, Noel's voice is a whisper, barely audible above the restaurant noise. ''Jill was in the book too,'' he tells her. ''Jill was on his list.''

In the stupefied way of someone repeating bad news, Sage repeats her half-sister's name. "Jill," she says, unemphatically.

"Jill McAndrew. Young corporation lawyer. Your sister," Noel confirms.

Your sister Jill is in trouble.

That is Noel's audible, intended message, but Sage hears his true declaration as loudly as though he had shouted it. He has said, I'm in love with Jill, I've been fucking Jill, I only care about Jill.

That was absolutely in Noel's voice, but Sage is only allowed to respond to his actual words. She says, "That's too bad, poor Jill. But she doesn't necessarily know him very well, do you think? I mean, Jill knows a lot of people, I'm sure she does."

As her heart clutches, and she thinks, You lousy rotten prick, my own half-sister, how dare you? how dare she?

Having probably heard all or almost all of what she did not say, Noel glares across the table. "You bitch. Cunt. You don't even care about your sister's reputation."

"But." Have her heart's valves closed? She feels that. "But it just said her name was in the notebook, didn't you say? It could just mean—"

"You don't care. Your sister's name is implicated in a call-girl ring and you're only thinking about your fucking art show, your trips to New York. Your money from some alcoholic real-estate broad."

"But Noel—"

Having always foreseen doom, Sage has always known that one day Noel would get up and leave her. Just walk out.

Which now he does.

With a quick flashed look of total defiance, defiance both of Sage and of the room at large (some people of course have begun to turn and listen), Noel stands up, throws his napkin on the table. He turns and rushes toward the door.

But Sage cannot let him go, she will die if he goes.

Throwing money down on the table, too much money but no matter, Sage runs out after Noel, out to the sidewalk in the rain, just reaching him there.

"Noel, you can't—don't—"

"Crazy bitch—"

She is clinging to him fiercely, as though the pressure, the urgency of her body could stop him—and knowing as she does this how appalling, how infantile, hysterical and utterly futile is her gesture. But still she can't let him go.

Noel is much stronger, and even more charged with purpose than Sage is. He pulls her hands off and then, because she still presses against him, he pushes at her body, and then he leaps aside, away from her, as she falls back against a building, then slips down on the rainy, skiddy sidewalk.

Sage gets up very quickly. Not hurt, she thinks. A man who was standing there watching seems also to decide that she is all right, or perhaps it is to spare her shame that he moves on.

As though she had simply slipped and fallen for a moment, as anyone could, in this rain, Sage manages to walk along, as though she were quite all right, so that if anyone saw what happened they would not stop, not offer help. She is vaguely aware that her arm hurts, but she still needs to talk. Far up ahead on Fillmore Street she thinks she sees Noel, darting fast between traffic. But maybe not, maybe that is not Noel—and in any case Noel is gone.

Wherever he now goes (to Jill?) he will stay for several hours, and then come home to Sage, creeping in, crawling into her bed, their bed, carefully making just enough noise to wake her. And then in loud unnecessary whispers (who could hear him, possibly, in their house?) he will tell her what an awful man he is, how despicable, stupid, illiterate; how can she put up with him? To which so far there has only been one answer, which Sage has always given: No, darling, you're none of those things, and yes, I do forgive you, I know it's difficult, I know I'm difficult too. Please, only love me.

But: but this is a little different. Whereas before he has rushed out of the house from some drunken quarrel, which was bad enough, sufficiently hard to bear, he has not before pushed her away. Not pushed her down to a sidewalk.

He has not before told her very clearly, in effect, that he loves, is making love to, someone else.

And now, as she comes to a halt on the dark rainy sidewalk, Sage for the first time imagines another set of responses to his throes of self-castigation; she imagines saying, You knocked me down, you rotten bastard, I don't care if you didn't really mean to do it, or if it was partly my fault.

And she thinks, I really don't want to talk to Noel tonight. About anything. I don't want to hear his voice.

Providentially, at that moment a cab swerves past, a free cab. Sage hails it and gets in, gives directions to her house on Russian Hill.

Arrived at her front gate, she tells the driver to wait.

Upstairs, now entirely galvanized, Sage in seven minutes accomplishes the packing that she had thought would take her a day.

Back in the cab, with her bag, she directs the driver to the airport.

"What time's your plane?"

"Oh, I'm not sure."

"You know what airline?"

"Uh, United."

"Well, it's good you've got no definite time, this traffic's murder. A little rain and all the drivers in town go apeshit, you know that?"

"I guess."

To herself Sage is saying, He knocked me down, he really did. Even if I was asking for it, as he might say. And he didn't stop to see if I was okay.

Her arm in fact does still hurt quite a lot; she is dimly aware of pain, an ache, but this pain contributes to her mounting exhilaration, sharpens it, as the cab maneuvers through the dark and rain and the dazzling lights, the swish of tires on wet concrete, out onto the freeway.

He won't know where I am, thinks Sage, and he won't dare call Caroline, or Liza; I might have told them, he'd be too ashamed.

A little later she thinks, No wonder I feel a little drunk, I had that glass of wine and no dinner, I hope they serve something on the plane. I hope I can get on a plane, any plane. Tonight, I'll probably have to go First Class, she thinks, with the smallest smile.

She does not think about flying into storms, into snow. She is not now afraid of this trip.

Twenty-one

"She was in shock, but still, to sustain a compound fracture. And then get herself on a red-eye flight for New York—"

"She did get to go First Class," Liza interrupts her husband.

"Even so. But then to go to your own gallery opening, well, it's pretty amazing. Of course the ortho department at Columbia-Presbyterian is absolutely tops, really lucky she got there and got to Kiernan, he's the best. Does mostly knees but he's first-rate—"

"Lucky her new friend Calvin took her there," puts in Liza.

"Oh indeed. Compound fractures can be very tricky. Have to be reset, ugly stuff like that." Saul, like many psychiatrists, is extremely happy (he is happiest, Liza has thought) when dealing with or discussing problems that are strictly medical. Such a relief to have a concrete issue, Liza imagines, rather than the nebulous, often contradictory dark strands of neurosis.

"Sage has always been extremely brave," puts in Caroline, her mother. Then adding, thoughtfully, "In her way."

The three of them, Liza, Saul and Caroline, are having an old-fashioned picnic (so they all have termed it) in Julius Kahn Playground, on the grass—from which they are protected by several very old-fashioned steamer rugs, one of Caroline's most durable legacies from Molly Blair. The heavy wool protects them from the still-damp, still-cold earth; they could in fact be said to be celebrating what is at least a lull in the season of rain, if not the onset of spring. The day is warm and bright, the sky a pale washed blue, with giant billowing white clouds along the horizon, above the cypress-and-eucalyptus woods, and out across the bay, above Marin.

The two women are dressed in a way that suggests a hope of spring, Caroline in flowered cotton, pink espadrilles, and Liza in her usual denim skirt, with a lemon-yellow T-shirt, more or less the color of her hair. Even Saul, in his khaki pants and sleeve-rolled blue workshirt, looks as though he believed in a change of weather.

This being a Wednesday, Saul has his day off—and Caroline, somewhat to Liza's surprise, had announced it as her day off too. "The nice Guatemalan lady comes, Ralph loves her, she can get him anything he needs." It seems to Liza (in fact she is sure of this) that a couple of weeks ago her mother said she never went anywhere.

However, at the moment Liza is too preoccupied with the vagaries of her sisters to give much thought to her mother's possible inconsistencies.

Today Caroline has outdone herself in the matter of sandwiches, as her daughter and Saul (the clear if unacknowledged favorite son-in-law) have told her. Crustless cucumber and watercress, breast of chicken, cheese and ham. With sturdier fare for the children, fried chicken, peanut butter and raisins, their favorites. And a big lemon cake for everyone. "I must be in a really retrogressive Molly phase," Caroline has explained. "So English, at her best with sandwiches and cakes. Absolutely hopeless with vegetables, or fish."

Now the baby sleeps in her canvas basket between her parents, and the two others are off in the sandpile, from which from time to time they return, to report to the grownups.

"You haven't heard any more from Jill?" Liza now asks her mother.

"No, and I must say it is a little worrying."

Jill called Caroline and simply said that she was staying with a friend, that she felt like lying low for a while. She had taken some time off from her firm. She would check back in, which so far she has not done.

"Well, at least there's nothing more in the papers." For several days, perhaps a week, there had been photographs of everyone listed in Buck Fister's book, of Roland Gallo, and of Jill—Jill, in a bathing suit, even, at someone's Woodside party; Jill, laughing and very sexy. Recalling all that, out of her multiple reactions Liza sighs, and then asks her mother, "But weren't you even tempted to ask her how on earth she knew Buck Fister?"

"I didn't think I could, you know. None of my business." Caroline has always had a strong regard for the privacy of her daughters—too much so, they have all at one time or another thought. They have sometimes wished to be asked more, all of them. To be more certain of her interest.

"I couldn't have resisted asking her." Although Liza now reflects, the fact that Jill should know Buck Fister is not actually so odd, not in itself; Jill, as the phrase once went, gets around a lot, she is out almost constantly, in restaurants and bars, at gallery openings, she goes to all sorts of parties with all sorts of people. Liza thinks of all this with what she has to admit is another small breath of envy, her own life being so very much more restricted, necessarily. For the moment (she hopes it is only for the moment).

The absolutely unmentionable question is: just in what way did Jill know Buck Fister, who is now under indictment for running a ring of call girls?

Caroline, although she seems in many ways a contemporary of her daughters, is nevertheless of another generation; she must find it simply peculiar that Jill would know such a sleazy fellow, know him well enough to be entered in his engagement book. To have had lunch with him, probably.

The further possibility, that Jill could actually have been one of Buck Fister's "girls," would not even enter Caroline's mind, Liza thinks.

It has, though, entered Liza's mind, and, she has to admit, with a certain air of plausibility: Jill might easily think a little minor hustling was fun, or far out, or off the wall. However Jill might put it. And God knows (and Liza knows, they all know) that Jill loves money, deeply, passionately.

Or is she, Liza, simply fictionalizing her sister's life? It comes to her rather easily, Liza notes: She can see Jill in some very posh hotel suite (it would have to be posh, for Jill) with some guy who was lined up to have sex with her. For money. Some john. Very easy to imagine. Jill in fact would be terrifically turned on by the whole scene. She would probably come, even if, supposedly, real hookers never do.

But this cannot be true, Liza next thinks. It is only my own very sleazy imagination. Not to mention disgusting rivalrous-sibling feelings.

"The point is," says Caroline now, "I really don't know where she is."

"These are the best sandwiches," Saul tells her, in his serious way. And then, "Have you asked Fiona?"

"Asked Fiona where Jill is? Well of course not, I couldn't. What an idea." Caroline laughs nervously at the very idea of using one daughter to spy out another.

"She might know, though."

"Even so. And come to think of it I'm not exactly hearing a lot from Fiona these days either."

The park is relatively unpopulated at this hour, despite the beautiful fresh new weather. At the moment only one other picnic group sits gingerly on their blanket, some distance off: two very blonde young women, probably au pairs, speaking either Swedish or German. And much farther away, in another part of the playing field, is a small cluster of people, impossible to tell just how many, all huddled on the grass.

Thus, as soon as she enters from across the way, from her dark Pacific Street mansion, Joanne Gallo, coming across the park, can be seen by Caroline, Liza and Saul. Very clearly. Joanne on what must be very high heels is stumbling nearsightedly along the damp ground, her small sad thin daughter pulled along beside her. Both mother and daughter in pink.

"Oh God, Joanne Gallo," Liza whispers to Saul, who gives her an ambiguous look.

"Oh, is that—?" whispers Caroline (much too loudly, as she much too obviously stares, in Liza's judgment).

Joanne seems not to see them, although their group blanket lies directly in her path. But then, as she is almost upon them and as Liza is thinking, Shit, now I have to introduce her to everyone and she'll probably stick around—just then Joanne seems to see them. All at once her face contorts, as though with conflicting expressions, and she mutters a greeting that seems (curiously) to be addressed to Saul alone, and then she veers off toward the swings and slides, walking as though blind, and still pulling her child along, who also seems unsteady.

Liza has instantly understood that Joanne is a patient of Saul's, and so she only remarks, "How odd." Saul not only does not gossip about his patients, he will not even tell Liza who they are; she finds out sometimes inadvertently, and uncertainly, like this. So that now she thinks, Well, good, I hope it's true. Saul will help her if anyone can.

Caroline, though, seems uncharacteristically interested in Joanne. She who has been accused by her daughters of a fundamental lack of interest in most people—this same Caroline now remarks, "What a very odd-looking young woman. Honestly, white lipstick? And she looked so unsteady, could she possibly be a little tipsy, do you think?"

"I suppose she could be," is Liza's guarded response. She feels that under the circumstances (Saul) she should not say that she has fairly often seen Joanne Gallo fairly drunk, although that is indeed the case. Although she and Saul will never discuss his patient, she feels the need for a certain discretion.

Saul is simply staring into the distance—in the direction opposite to that taken by Joanne Gallo, Liza notes.

"It's interesting that there hasn't been any more in the papers about Roland Gallo." Liza cannot help saying this, and then she notes a distinct lack of response from her husband and her mother. "I mean," she runs on alone, "I do wonder what that big friendship between him and Buck Fister was all about. And I wonder if he'll run for mayor. What does Ralph say?" she then asks Caroline.

"I don't think Ralph has seen him for a while. He hasn't mentioned him."

"Sage should go up to U.C. to get her arm checked out as soon as she's back," Saul now says—as though Sage had been the subject of his scowl. "But I suppose they'll tell her that at Columbia."

"Her arm must seem the least thing on her mind," Caroline begins to beam. "The show going so well, it's all quite marvellous, and startling."

"It is marvellous," Liza agrees, although it occurs to her that it is a little strange that they are only just now getting around to Sage's success; and they have been together, the three of them, for well over an hour.

At Sage's opening, described by Sage in phone calls to both her mother and to Liza (and also to Noel? no one seems to know just how closely in touch they are), five more pieces were actually bought. "And not all by Ms. Hoover's pals either, that would make me feel truly meretricious," Sage has said. Bought by perfectly okay people (in Sage's judgment) who for whatever reason came to the opening and who very much liked Sage's small groups of figures. "Despite the totally crazy prices this Crome person has stuck on them." This was said with a great laugh from Sage, a laugh not entirely under-stood by Liza; she takes it as a reference to Mr. Crome, rather than to his prices. "Crome person," though, is surely a suggestive phrase. Something must be going on between those two, Liza thinks, and she also thinks, Good, just what rotten Noel deserves. She now asks her mother, "You haven't heard from Noel?"

"Not since those two rather peculiar calls."

Noel called Caroline on the day of Sage's supposed departure to say that he had been out a lot, had Caroline heard from Sage? This was odd, in that Caroline had heard from Sage that they were having dinner the night before she left, to celebrate that first crazy sale. Also, if Sage had called Noel, she could have left a message.

And then Noel called again a few hours later to say that he had indeed talked to Sage. Too bad about her arm, he said, but great about her show. He might fly to New York to help her celebrate.

But between those two calls Sage herself had called Caroline to say that she had taken the First Class red-eye, as she put it, and that she had fallen and hurt her arm at the airport; Calvin Crome had taken her to Columbia-Presbyterian, her arm was okay. She might stay a little longer in New York but she hoped Noel wouldn't bother to come. "It's really not his scene," she said, somewhat ambiguously.

From all of which Caroline and Liza had (separately) worked out that Sage and Noel were not exactly in close touch.

"But there's really no reason I should hear from Noel," now

muses Caroline. And then, "I did hear from Jim, your father. Speaking of odd phone calls."

"Oh?"

"He said that Sage called him from New York, which I would not have thought unusual. But he sounded so happy about it. He said he hasn't heard from her for a month or so, I guess that was the unusual part."

"Their whole connection is unusual," is Liza's comment, as she reflects that it is also unusual for Caroline to talk quite so much about her other daughters; Caroline must be quite seriously concerned about Sage and Noel, is Liza's verdict.

"My Liza has a pornographic imagination," Saul tells Caroline.

"Well, Saul, come on, you must admit it's a little intense. My father and Sage."

"Just don't give me your theories about it," Caroline addresses her daughter. "More cake?" She gestures with her knife.

"I think Sage will have some trouble adjusting to success, that's my real theory," Liza tells them. She is looking at Saul, although she knows better than to expect an opinion from him.

And his response is true to form. "Well, maybe. She could."

Liza laughs. "Such tremendous fun for the rest of us, though," she says.

And Caroline, "Yes, how we can bask in reflected glory. Well, if you two won't have more cake I will. I can't just take it all home to Ralph."

"I'd better check the kids," Liza tells them.

The children, though, are fine, playing so cheerfully with three others, probably the charges of those blonde au pairs, that Liza decides not even to go over to them; if they see her they could quite suddenly decide that things are not fine, they do not like their new friends after all, and they urgently need their mother for arbitration, or more cookies, or something. And so Liza moves back to stand in the shadow of the little clubhouse.

Standing there for a moment, unseen by her children, her mother or her husband, Liza thinks, as she fairly often does, of her total failure in attempting to woo back (she had to admit that this is what she was doing) any former lovers, if only for an afternoon of talk. Not one word from a single one of them. An interesting fact,

Liza is not quite sure what it means. Most likely, she thinks, it means that I'm supposed to stay very faithful to Saul, and to confine my fantasies to paper.

The horizon clouds look both larger and darker now, with menacing areas of gray, shading into black. And although the air is still warm, Liza can clearly feel that threat of cold. Soon enough she will have to gather up the children, toys and Pampers. Her life.

What I really need is a lot more time alone, she thinks, and she sighs for what is most unavailable to her.

Returning then to Caroline and Saul, she sees them in what looks to be urgent conversation, and she hesitates, aware of several impulses, and impressions. One impulse tells her to leave them alone, to let them say whatever they have to say to each other. Another thought, an impression, is of how very attractive her mother is, and she thinks, Caroline could probably still have lovers if she wanted to, couldn't she? It must be hard on her, with Ralph so sick; it's unlikely that they can do it any more.

But at that moment Saul sees her and gestures her over, so that Liza has no choice except to join them.

And so she is in time to hear this urgent speech from Caroline: "I've been having this curious fantasy," Caroline tells them, her sea eyes large and intense, very serious. "I mean, it comes to me like a message. It's a vision of homeless people taking over, marching on the rest of us and occupying all our houses. All that space where we all now sit so warm and smug and protected. I mean, who could blame them?"

"You're remembering the Thirties," Saul tells her, gently. "The marches on Washington."

"Actually I don't remember those marches. I was a very protected Connecticut girl, remember? But I do sort of remember my father talking about how anyone who wanted a job could find one, I guess he really believed that, it's a basic Republican idea. And I remember those shacks under the George Washington Bridge. People living in orange crates. Hoovervilles. My father blamed those people for living there. And I knew he was wrong, I really did. And maybe when I have this fantasy about their marching, taking over, I am sort of thinking about those people."

"This is what I like best, a dream I don't have to interpret." Saul smiles, very sympathetic to Caroline.

"Actually I know perfectly well what it means," she tells him. "It means I've got to find something useful to do. Cut out all this bleeding-heart hand-wringing. You can see I'm quoting Ralph, such a bad habit," she adds.

"You could have worse," Saul tells her. "I think you're talking about a violent sense of injustice. As though the imbalance were so great that it must correct itself."

"That's exactly what I do mean."

"Well, it's how I feel myself."

"Ralph sees only political solutions, that's the problem with him. With talking to him, I mean. He's so opposed to what he calls charity, he says it's bandaiding, prolonging the pain. I don't mean he's ungenerous, of course he's not, you know that. But."

"He's an old lefty. Semi-Marxist."

"Oh, I know, and I'm simply not political in that sense, aside from voting. And the peace marches in the Sixties, but of course they were so much fun."

Attending to this serious discourse between her mother and her husband, Liza has also been watching the group in the far corner of the playing field, the indistinct people who have now got to their feet, are standing about in the waning sunlight. Three young black men, and two women, they look to be. Having picked up their blanket, they still have not moved on, they all have an indecisive look, and stance. These could be homeless people, maybe plotting their march on the rich? Liza starts to say this but then does not; it has a frivolous sound, although in a way she means it.

She continues to watch, as, "mysteriously," those people replace their blanket on the grass and sit down again—as though, having discussed alternatives, they conclude that for the moment they have nowhere to go—or so Liza imagines.

She is prevented from further speculation by the shrill sound of impending children, her own—she would know their voices anywhere, from any distance. Just as, she is certain, they would always know where to find her. To track her down, no matter what she was doing.

Twenty-two

"I hate food. And I especially despise people who think about it all the time, and these days that includes almost everyone. Except for those thousands of people who're really hungry, hundreds of thousands, and of course they're thinking food too. No one should have to think about it. All these people every night, worrying themselves crazy over which fucking restaurant to go to, and then, when they get there, what to eat. What the hell difference does it make? Dover sole or medallions of pork in juniper berries, clams flown from Ipswich, for Christ's sake, what's the difference? No difference, it doesn't matter, it's only food."

Fiona's vis-à-vis at lunch, a thick-necked, bald, owlish man with round rimless glasses, whom she first met about ten minutes ago, looks less startled by this blast than might be expected. His expression of very mild boredom, resigned annoyance, suggests that for him such a scene is part of his territory: he works for Bonny Fairchild, the restaurant chain.

This particular new Fillmore Street restaurant in which he and Fiona have agreed to have lunch is now owned by his chain, and it is, in fact, the same restaurant in which Sage and Noel enacted quite another scene and finally did not have dinner, a few weeks back—a coincidence unknown to anyone present, although Fiona's tirade has drawn a certain amount of attention, as Noel's did on that dark and fiercely raining night.

Fiona is not only unaware of attracting attention, she could not possibly care less, as she herself might put it; she is only half thinking of what she is saying, as she continues in that vein.

What in a deeper, more concentrated way she is actually thinking is, why does almost everyone she meets or just sees on the street turn out to be bald? why this Easter basket of round pink or ivory heads, and none of them Roland's?

"If there's anything that makes me sicker than food it's people who know a lot about it, it's really more disgusting than just knowing wine, although that's fairly dreadful. So boring. It's just food! just stuff to push into your face."

But you could pretty much say the same of sex, Fiona thinks, not for the first time. Just an odd part of one person's body shoved into another, differently shaped person. A lot of skin-to-skin friction.

And then she thinks, Oh Christ, I can't stand it, I really can't. I am losing my mind over that dirty rotten crooked dago prick. Who is probably off somewhere doing stuff for the Mafia. His family.

"A person can get pretty tired of the restaurant business, like everything else," is Fiona's lunch companion's comment.

Which leaves her no choice, really, but to simmer down and to consider, against her principles, what she would like for lunch.

Roland, after their weeks of mutually planning not to see each other, is now quite unavailable. Out of town, on business; Fiona has even called his office, as though she too were conducting business. It is as though they had been competing for unattainability, and Roland had won. Fiona has even been forced to admit this to herself, to admit that she longs to see him.

"But what do you really do?" She once asked him that, of course in bed (wherever else were they, ever?), in an interval of calm.

"I'm a lawyer, angel, you know that. A little dabbling in city politics. A few business interests, some real estate. Nothing original."

"Is that all you do? It seems to me that these days lawyers are all over the place, doing other stuff. My sister's a lawyer but she's really in investments. A lot of lawyers I know own wineries."

Roland laughed, happily, peacefully, and smoothed the small area of gray hair that remained to him, around his neck. "Of course I have some things that I inherited out of town. Tied up with some relatives. On the East Coast, mostly."

"Darling, are you Mafia?"

"You read too many books. Bad movies. No one's Mafia these days."

Since her phone calls to his office Fiona has had a couple of postcards, proving that Roland is or was indeed out of town, but cards from somewhat odd places: Mamaroneck, New York, and Princeton, New Jersey.

Fiona assumes these places to be covers, as it were; he was probably actually in New York—or, more sinister, Jersey City.

In any case she is suffering his loss, or his lack in her life, with more rage and pain than she would have thought possible. If she ever sees him again she plans to really make some trouble.

"Yes, I'm very tired of the restaurant business," Fiona now says to the man with whom she is having lunch. "I hate my restaurant. Fiona's. God, what a silly name. I don't know how I got into it. Sheer accident, is how it feels."

"Well, you're young, and you're not locked into your restaurant. Even if it does have your name."

Knowing what is to come (she knew it pretty clearly when she made this lunch date, she who almost never goes out to lunch), Fiona still feels a powerful excitement. "What else would I do?" she asks him, a quick, false ingenue.

And he says, in words that she could almost have put in his mouth, "You could retire. A very early retirement. Sell out."

Fiona laughs. "I'm under forty. Think of the money I'd need. For the rest of my life." She laughs again, thinking of Italy. Sicily.

"I am thinking of the money you'd need. And I'm thinking of the money you could get." His voice is low and very controlled, but controlled with an effort, Fiona feels. He too is excited, thinking of major sums. Of very big bundles.

She then wonders how they must look together, she and this stocky, bald person with his thick round glasses. His rising voice, his quickening breath. Are they taken for lovers, she wonders, lovers in the excited throes of some sexy plans? She says, "Actually I wouldn't dream of selling."

"Not even for—" He mentions an outrageous sum.

"You're talking funny money."

"That's right, I am. But you think about it."

"Frankly, I wouldn't dare give it another thought."

"Well, that's pretty definite."

"I mean it. Honestly."

"So, Jilly, what do you think? Could I live for the rest of my life on that much funny money?"

"Actually you probably could. Especially if you did it right now, with the market so down. And please don't call me Jilly, I hate it." Jill's voice, from wherever she is (she still won't say), is indistinct; however, Fiona notices that when giving financial advice Jill is more focussed than at any other time in this so far not easy conversation.

And so Fiona tries to keep her own on that topic. "Would you do all that stuff for me? Outfit me with a really super portfolio? A great position?" She giggles, but hears no answering laugh from Jill.

"I doubt it," Jill tells her. "I may retire too. God, I probably already have."

"Listen, Jill, there's been more and more in the paper about this silly Buck Fister. Christ, what a name. Of course it turns out that he was into more than a little dealing too. But no more about any of his friends. Not even Mr. Roland Gallo." Fiona has managed not to stumble over that name. "And definitely nothing about you. He's refusing to talk about his friends, the paper says."

Their connection weakens, some odd noise comes on the line, as though waves were attacking the wires, and salt. "—not the problem," is what Jill then seems to say.

"Sweetie, you're really being sort of dumb, I can't help saying that. You obviously need some kind of help, as they say. Look, you could come here and stay with me. Stay here. God knows I've got lots of room, and I swear I wouldn't tell Caroline, or anyone."

"Thanks, that's good of you, it really is. And watch out, I just might show up."

Was there a catch in Jill's voice? In any case she sounds terrible, to her sister Fiona.

And Jill is indeed being dumb. It was dumb to have left town at all; Fiona assumes that she is out of town. Just because her name was in Buck Fister's notebook. It amounts to a semi-confession, as though Jill were actually saying, Yes, it's true. I did a few tricks for Buck, that's how I knew him.

Because Fiona knows that Jill would think it was funny, far out, off the wall, the very idea of fucking for money, with some strange guy. Some john. It would really turn her on. Fiona knows her sister. But at least Jill could make a better pretense, at least she could stick around and pretend she hasn't done anything, barely knew that Buck Fister.

Would she, Fiona, do it? Suppose Buck Fister had come to her instead, with some sort of proposition? Say, a thousand a night. Fiona has given this some thought, and decided that on the whole very likely not. It just wouldn't turn her on, the way it would Jill, and that is pretty much what it came down to. And, then, these days she'd be too frightened, not only of AIDS but of all the really violent nuts around, the fanatics of one sort or another. A john could turn out to be some big-shot religious fundamentalist, the way things are going.

She is fairly sure that she is right about Jill, though; always she has had this sort of gut knowledge of this particular sister, her closest sister.

And she wonders how many people, if any, could work that out, about Jill: could, or would, Caroline?

No. Caroline would not. Hustling, sex for money, is simply something that no daughter of hers would ever do, would be Caroline's reaction. Nor, for that matter, anyone else whom Caroline would ever know.

And where the hell is Jill anyway? Fiona now wonders. Could she be off travelling with Roland? Fiona does not seriously entertain this thought; on the other hand, R.G. does seem to have a certain penchant for her sisters. For her whole family: he once even said that he thought Caroline was very attractive. "I really dig your mother," is what he said.

And why is Sage still in New York? Not that Fiona really cares, but it is a puzzle, it can't still be all that trouble with her arm.

And where is Noel?

Fiona has an uneasy sense of all the world around her flying apart, familiar signposts vanishing. Nothing making sense.

It is very frightening.

"Actually Death Valley is pretty boring. Unless you're absolutely gone on sand." Roland laughs. "But the hotel is really nice. Nice pool, a pool with a view of sand. And the palm trees are nice."

"It sounds like a movie set. Thirties gangsters. Molls."

"Baby, you've got gangsters on the brain." He coughs. "The food is great, of course you don't really care about food, I know. It's just not my idea of where to come on a vacation."

"Then why—?"

"Business, really. A client heard this place might come up for sale, and he wanted me to check it out. But guess what? It's not for sale. Nice place, though."

"What is your idea of a great vacation?"

"I thought I told you. Place name of Mondello, just outside Palermo. You see? I'm just your basic Sicilian. But I thought I told you about Mondello."

"No."

"Well, someday, sweetheart, as the song says. Well, I guess I'll head out to the pool. It looks good from here."

After saying goodby to Fiona, telling her that he'll be back in S.F. soon, that they must see each other—Roland, who is not in Death Valley but in Las Vegas, now puts down the phone. He is in a very large room, a suite actually, high up in Caesar's Palace. During this rest between phone calls (he is bracing himself for the next two, to which he does not look forward) he contemplates the view, which does not include a swimming pool but does in fact look out to the desert. Sand, used by the Army for artillery testing. Nuclear tests. Not many rabbits running around through that sage any more, Roland noted on his drive in from the airport.

I must be slipping out, Alzheimer's here I come, is what Roland is thinking now. Mother of God, it was that other chick I told about Mondello, out in that sunset motel that she liked so much. Jesus. I ought to have my head examined. He works his shoulders up and down, in a shedding-of-trouble gesture, then stiffens his posture, then dials.

"Hey, Bucks. Good. Well, listen, fella, see that you keep it that way. Buttoned tight. No, of course I didn't know about that. I did not know. I just thought a house, maybe a couple of houses. Out in Seacliff. High-class. Not under-age Asians, for Christ's sake. And not anything super-fancy like girls—like someone's daughters. Jesus. Man, you're all over the place. Yes, I am angry, because you weren't straight with me. You even suggested helping me out in a certain direction, putting a word in, you said. Yes, you did, I remember. And there was her name in your fucking book. Listen, man, I'm giving you fair warning."

Hanging up, Roland is breathing too heavily. Hyperventilating, probably. Sitting still, he enforces calm, measuring his breath.

And then he dials again, this time to Philadelphia, to one of his cousins. "Of course I know him," says Roland. "We have lunch. Had lunch, I should say. But he has lunch with a lot of people. So do I. I don't think he talks a lot, he's not supposed to. Hell, he doesn't know very much. Yes. No. Well, I don't exactly love the idea. Whatever you say, you're the expert. But I want to be out of town."

Hanging up, Roland frowns, then does his shoulder maneuvers, and then takes some deep breaths again. And again.

He wonders what Caroline's reactions will be, if anything happens. He wonders if he will ever see her again.

Fiona, who took her call from Roland in her bedroom, the penthouse, at its conclusion lies back on her super-king silk-strewn bed, quite exhausted. Although she had no wine at lunch (two bottles of Perrier) she feels that it wore her out, somehow, that encounter with bald Mr. Owl-Eyes. And then the call from Roland, which was strange, and entirely unsatisfactory, she would like not to think about it, but is inwardly muttering, Rotten dago prick.

The weather outside, all that endless sky full of weather, is problematic, indecisive: a huge sweep of the clearest, purest blue, and an almost equal area of dark clouds, just over Oakland, resting there with no apparent menace. And there seems to be no wind, no action in the trees across the way, the tall eucalyptus and pines, nor in her careful plantings, the delicately flowering bushes on her sundeck. Plants that she can never remember the name of, that are tended by Stevie. "If I didn't you'd kill them," is Stevie's explanation for his perseverance in this task.

For this reason Stevie has a key to Fiona's suite, as she sometimes thinks of it, and she often forgets that he must pass through her rooms fairly often. But there is never a trace of his passage, except for the thriving, obviously well-tended plants, all green and glossy, never a dead leaf or tiny stray volunteer weed in their large, ornately garlanded (Italian) terra-cotta pots.

Today, however, Fiona notices a folded section of that morning's *Chronicle* on the low round table that is next to the sundeck door. Getting up from her bed very quickly, Fiona sees that it is the food section, taken up mostly by photographs of the restaurant in which she just had lunch, and that the caption is BEST PLACE IN TOWN, SAY CRITICS.

It is quite a long piece, using most of the words most familiar to Fiona: Fresh, innovative, visual appeal, presentation, unusual spectrum, vigorous approach. As well as: Firmly textured, subtle use of. Delicious, enticing, seductive, exotic. Writer David Argent is quoted, "The greatest food adventure since peanut butter."

Reading all that in a rush, and then reading it again, taking everything in, Fiona experiences a rush of the most sickening disgust, and on several levels: disgust at the general asininity of food talk now, as well as at this particular local restaurant critic, whom she knows, and who, perhaps a year ago, wrote an almost identical piece about Fiona's. Disgust at David Argent, who never misses a chance to appear in print. That whore, thinks Fiona.

But worst of all, the deepest and most nauseating chagrin is at herself for caring.

And, mingled somehow with all that raging contempt, that general and quite particularized anger, is quite another set of emotional sensations, some of which are distinctly physical and all of which have to do with missing Roland Gallo, in very specific ways.

She would even like to scream and break things, to kick in those big clay pots and throw dirt around.

But someone would hear her, someone would come up to see whatever was wrong. Stevie, probably.

And at that thought, the thought of Stevie, a new impulse prompts Fiona to pick up the intercom next to her bed and to call downstairs. Where, at last, she connects with Stevie.

"Stevie, I really need to talk to you. Could you come up for a minute?" This request has a perfectly normal sound; making it, Fiona has kept her voice level. It is only unusual in that never, never has she summoned Stevie or anyone up to her penthouse. No one, ever.

Stevie takes his time getting up there, of course. And at his knock Fiona simply calls out, "Come in," and remains where she is, propped up among the pile of pale silk pillows on her bed. Her shoes, green lizard, are down on the floor, and her feet in their sheer green hose thrust forward. But when Stevie comes in she retracts her feet, pushing them modestly under the coverlet. She is not sure why, some vague sense of disapproval that she always feels from Stevie. He is such a puritan, really, like all those Sixties people. Movement people. Like Sage.

He is as always immaculate in his starched blue work clothes, loose on his overweight tall body. Even his jeans are sharply creased, a contrast to his scraggly red-blond beard, his long thin hair. He says, "You summoned?"

Does Stevie dislike her? Curiously, this has never really occurred to Fiona before—but, then, she has not experienced much negative emotion in her life. Attractive and energetic, Fiona has forged ahead, and has not often stopped to consider her effect. And so for someone very close to her, someone important in her life—for such a person as Stevie to dislike her would be novel. Interesting, even. She tries it out. "Are you mad at me, Stevie?" she asks him.

Stevie frowns, and then simply stares at her for a minute. "You didn't get me to come all the way up here for a ludicrous, irrelevant question like that, now, did you?"

"Actually not. But sit down. Pull up a chair."

"Why? Do I have to?" He is smiling but not very nicely, Fiona feels.

"Christ, Stevie, I don't care. I just wondered about the piece you left up here. That so-called restaurant review."

"I wanted to be sure you saw it. Obviously. That simple. I've had this feeling that your attention has as you might say wandered of late."

Of course he is absolutely right. Her attention has indeed been wandering, wandering off and all around Roland Gallo, for months now; that is the simple, observable truth. "That's not true," says Fiona nevertheless. "I've had a lot of things on my mind, but one of the main things is how we're doing here. Always."

"Whatever you say, boss lady."

"You're not worried?"

"Not really. Or not enough to make me look for a new investment."

Stevie's early investment in Fiona's amounted to a few thousand, his savings, some little stash that he got when his father died and his brothers sold the house in Seattle. This was when Fiona was starting out and suddenly needed whatever he had; he was working for her even then, doing odd jobs, flowers, like that—she tends to forget the details of that transaction, only that she was surprised that Stevie had any money at all. But occasionally Stevie reminds her that he is to some extent a partner in her business. That her business is to some extent their business.

She asks him, "Suppose we just sold out?"

Stevie for a moment simply stares; he always seems to be staring out through a tangle of pale-red lashes, like a bird. Fiona wonders if she has succeeded in shocking him, if only a little.

Then he smiles, and Fiona realizes two things: one, that Stevie is not shocked or surprised at all; and two, that his smile is not at all friendly.

He says, "I understand, I guess. This is your way of telling me that the person from Bonny Fairchild suggested a major sum, is that right?"

"Well, yes, but how—?"

"I keep up. Your book is an open book, so to speak." And, again, that not-nice smile.

Seized with a powerful need to get something from Stevie, an urge to arouse him in some undefined way, Fiona blindly attempts, "I could take you off to Italy, how about that? Early retirement for us both." She had meant this as a sort of joke, of course she had, but as she says it Fiona thinks, Why not? Me and Stevie, why not? Early on she had wondered if Stevie could be gay, but then he had a big romance with one of the waitresses, a dropout from Mills, who confided to Fiona that Stevie was "really something else, sack-wise." And Sage had once explained Stevie in the sort of psycho-babble she sometimes uses: "He's basically nuts about women—and very accepting of the feminine in himself."

He is not, though, accepting of Fiona. He laughs in an unpleasant way, he says, "That might be your idea of a good time, but not mine. No way." And he turns and quickly leaves the room.

As Fiona thinks several things: one, she has never seen Stevie quite so unpleasant before; and two, this is her first experience of being disliked (she thinks).

Twenty-three

"Hi, Jill. My name is, uh, John. I guess you don't remember me, it's been quite a while—"

"Who the hell are you? Who gave you my number?"

"Well, actually Buck—"

"You're crazy! I don't know any Buck! I'm not Jill—" She slams down the receiver so hard that the instrument falls to the floor, then she grasps at the kitchen counter where she was sitting when the phone rang. She holds the cold white marble as hard as she can, but still she is trembling, violently, she cannot control this seizure, these chills. All her veins feel swollen with cold, her forehead could explode. Oh, how dare that John call? She could really kill Buck, the vile, the sleazy betrayer.

Still cold, Jill stands trembling in her kitchen, and then runs into her bathroom, where she vomits into the toilet. Then crawls into bed. To cry.

That terrible episode was a few weeks ago—two weeks? three? Jill is deliberately losing track of time. Of everything she can. Losing track.

She has now left town, and is staying in a quickly rented house in Stinson Beach—not in Sea Drift, she hates Sea Drift, all those expensive design-controlled houses jammed together. She is in a house just past the slummy part of Stinson, the *calles,* dead-ends where seedy old hippies live (the sort of people Sage might know, shabby old Sixties radicals), or just plain poor people. Jill's house is right between all that mess and Sea Drift. Belonging to neither.

A wonderful house: if she were not feeling so crazy, so persecuted (still), she could be happy in this house, Jill thinks.

It is not on the beach but somewhat back from it, in an area of wild grass, and sand. The roof slants sharply upward, the rear wall is two stories high, a huge-paned window that gives a view of hills, mostly green, deeply crevassed and scattered with trees. Just below the hills is a wide lagoon, a quiet dark stretch of water surrounded by dark, high rushes, from which large strange birds emerge, to flap across the surface, or else to soar up, suddenly skyward, and out to sea.

Jill spends a great deal of time simply gazing out at that view, at those shadowed, gently sloping hills, at the peaceful lagoon, at flights of seabirds. In that way she absorbs some peace, she believes; a slightly different rhythm enters her blood.

She has told her office that this is a leave of absence, not bothering to ascertain whether or not that leave was granted. She only let fall a few resonant, relevant buzz words; she mentioned overload, super-stress and a possibility of Chronic Fatigue Syndrome.

She has not called in.

She makes indeed very few phone calls—and Jill has thought of the extreme contrast in that way between now and then: her record, she thinks, was the day or, rather, the hour in which she made forty calls, forty calls in an hour. This is hard for her to believe but she kept score, that day, a running score on her notepad.

Anyway, these days very few calls. A few to her mother, Caroline, just to say that she is okay. She really likes Caroline, even if they are so different, even if Caroline can be a considerable pain. Even if Caroline is her mother.

And a few to Fiona, about whom she has feelings vaguely similar to those that she harbors for her mother. She is attached to Fiona despite rather than because of their being sisters; Fiona is more like a friend, a somewhat combative, somewhat rivalrous, basically affectionate friend.

And sometimes she calls Noel. He always threatens to come out to see her, but so far he has not. Mainly, Jill understands, because Sage is still in New York.

Jill knows a lot about this odd paralysis that seems to afflict married men when their wives are out of town. The guy, no matter how habitually he strays, is then seemingly pinioned to his house, his home. Even when there are no practical considerations like small children, or pets. The best way to keep husbands at home is to leave them there, has been Jill's longtime deduction, now once more proven by Noel.

Sage has not told anyone just why her stay in New York is so prolonged, as far as Jill knows (she might have told Portia but no one has spoken to Portia). Sage mentions work and treatments for her arm at some hospital there—both quite credible to Jill, and to Caroline, whom Sage calls regularly. But not to Noel, who insists that Sage has always said she can only work at home, in her studio (the studio that he built for her), and that really nothing could be the matter with her arm. He suspects, he tells Jill, that something is going on between Sage and "that dealer guy with the funny name." Meaning Calvin Crome, whom Sage has indeed mentioned to Caroline.

Jill, who has not said this to Noel, does not think so; he is only judging by his own motives, what would most likely keep him in New York.

If Sage were having a relationship in New York, and that is how Sage undoubtedly would put it, she would most likely call Noel and tell him right out, "Noel, I'm having a relationship with my dealer, Calvin Crome. I want a divorce, but when I come home we can talk about it." That would be Sage's style, that awful Sixties "openness," that stupid talk-about-it school of thought.

And so there is Noel, consumed with jealousy, and probably staying home for more or less that reason. Thinking that Sage might show up. Afraid to leave. It's fairly funny, really, Jill finds.

When she is not meditating on the eastern view, Jill takes long walks, in a number of different directions, and with different ends in view. She goes to the beach, just up and over a sandy ridge, past a small grove of cypresses, wind-bent and strange, like weird sculptures. And then just ahead is the rough blue Pacific, with uneven lines of foam (like giant crazy coke lines, Jill has thought), striations of darker, almost purple water, out in the depths.

Arrived at the beach, she can take either direction: to the right, up past Sea Drift and all those crowded-together, over-priced houses, to the end of that spit of land, the channel separating Stinson from Bolinas, where Portia might or very well might not be.

Or, in the other, leftward direction, back toward the town of Stinson Beach, past the shabby *calles* of the relatively poor to the several crazily expensive houses up on stilts, there on the sand. (Earthquake fodder, Jill has thought of those houses.)

Every night, for the sunset, Jill takes one or the other of those beach walks, choosing more or less at random.

More practically, each morning she walks from her house into town, about a mile and a half, to shop for whatever she plans to eat that day. And for the newspaper; she does not turn on the radio for news, and there is no TV.

But even during these scenically diverting and energetic walks, always a new and changing landscape through which Jill walks very fast—still she is aware of a heavy, almost dizzying apprehension which has been with her, like a strong and resistant virus, since the first revelation of Buck Fister's address book. When she saw her name among his "friends." Her fears are very imprecise, non-specific, and thus worse: she fears that anything at all could happen now. It is not exactly that her imagination pictures further head-lines, "Buck Fister Names Young Lawyer as Former Call Girl. Daughter of—Graduate of—Sister of—" On the other hand, some-times she does imagine exactly that, and when the phone rings she imagines just such a message.

Or, maybe she does in fact have a virus? Could she conceivably have AIDS, in some early form? She has meant to go and get herself tested but always she has managed to put it off. She is uncertain as to first symptoms, other than those terrible dark blemishes, Kaposi's something. But those come later, she thinks.

Of course she does not have AIDS, but she does not feel well at all, she feels constantly fearful, menaced. Ill-prepared for whatever should happen next.

The general store at the crossroads is sometimes crowded. Jill is always afraid that she will see someone there she knows, from some-where—even Portia, from Bolinas—and she will have to explain or invent an explanation for her presence in Stinson Beach. To say where she is staying, all that. As a defense against such a person, such inquiries, she has taken to wearing her large dark shades, and a dumb-looking flowered scarf that she found in the house, covering her hair. And she hurries through her tiny list of purchases: lemons, bran, eggs, frozen Weight Watchers' pizza, frozen W.W. zucchini lasagne. (Noel would die if he knew what she ate out here, Noel the big gourmet cook.) And then at the checkout stand a *Chronicle*. Generally she scans the headlines for a minute while her bill is being added up, and often that is as far as she gets with the paper until dinnertime.

Thus, it is there at the checkstand of the Stinson Beach general store that Jill learns of Buck Fister's death. His killing. Murder.

PROMINENT REAL ESTATE BROKER SLAIN OUTSIDE SO-MA CLUB.

Instantly certain that Buck is the broker in question (and why? it could have been someone else, some one of hundreds), Jill drops her eyes to the story. And yes, it was Alberto "Buck" Fister (Alberto? Buck is/was Italian? that is surprising, somehow)—well known, highly successful though recently under Grand Jury investigation for alleged involvement in a prostitution operation—who was shot at close range by an unknown assailant or assailants as he left the new club, Heavy Duty, on Folsom Street, in the early hours of yesterday morning. Mr. Fister had come in and gone out alone. There were no witnesses. He had a drink at the bar, had talked to no one. It was the bartender's impression that he was meeting someone there who did not show up. A mother, Mrs. Rosette Arnold, of Elko, Nevada, listed as the sole survivor. No friends were available for comment. Dead on arrival at Mission Emergency Hospital.

"That'll be twelve seventy-nine."

"—what?"

"Twelve seventy-nine. Oh, and seventy-five for the paper. You want the paper?"

"Yes."

"Out of twenty. Thank you, and have a nice day. Say, don't forget your groceries!"

The public beach is a short two blocks from the store, from the crossroads at the entrance to town, and it is there, in the women's room provided for picnickers, that Jill repairs with her paper, and with the groceries she almost forgot.

In her booth, seated on the closed toilet seat, she reads and re-reads that item, as though closer scrutiny might yield further information. Which it does not. No witnesses, no clues. The bartender's name was Clancy Barnes. No suggestions as to motive.

Anyone at all could have wanted Buck dead, including me, thinks Jill. Or, it could have been what they call a random killing, the kind we all dread for ourselves, just a wrong-place wrong-time death. Some crackhead driving past and not liking your face—and who in his or her right mind ever liked Buck's face, all those mean little features crowded into the middle of the circle of his head, especially those tiny pig eyes. A pig's face, and now a dead pig.

But suppose it turns out not to have been Buck after all? That quite irrational fear, which she knows to be irrational, nevertheless sweeps through Jill's heart, like a chilly wind. Suppose this is all an elaborate plot for Buck's escape, a plot contrived by Buck himself, so that he can show up somewhere very far away, having evaded both the Grand Jury and all the local people like herself who wished him dead? All the whores, like her.

But that is mad, truly mad. It must have been Buck.

Refolding her paper, Jill stands up and walks quickly out of that building, out into the manzanita thickets that thrive in that low-lying sandy area of the park, out through the thickets to the open beach.

On the sand she stops and for several minutes she simply stands there, breathing hard, as though she had run, her paper still clutched to her side.

The air is fresh and cool, faint smells of gasoline fumes from the highway mingle with beach smells of salt, and dead fish. As foghorns blend with the sound of a bulldozer, from a building site farther up the beach. Fog, massed and gray, obscures the western horizon, as, closer in, gray waves curl and foam at the edge of the beach.

Would anyone imagine or believe that she had anything to do with this, with this careful murder of Buck? Jill finds that she does not believe for an instant that the killing was random, if anything it seemed very well planned indeed, what the papers like to call a gangland killing. On the other hand, it is crazy to fear that anyone might in any way connect her, accuse her of having done it. For one thing, she actually is innocent, she only wished him dead, and she has not been so foolish as to say so; no one knows how much she hated Buck, how she wished him dead.

Except Noel. When she told Noel about the tricks, of course she also mentioned Buck, in an accidental way—and Noel, along with being so incredibly, wildly turned on by the very idea, Jill doing it with strangers in strange hotel rooms, for money—along with all that terrific excitement and a part of it, maybe, was Noel's white-hot rage at Buck, street-Irish anger, turning Noel into a fighter, glaring, eyes on fire. Like a dark little rooster: Jill now remembers this secret thought that she had of Noel, her private smile as he ranted and swore at Buck. (Cocksucker, motherfucker—funny that these are the worst things men can find to say about each other.)

And once Buck's address book was more or less published in the paper, Jill did tell Noel how she hated Buck, could kill him. How she wished that she had never known him.

No one, though, aside from Noel knows any of this.

Looking back down the beach to her left, eastwardly, the San Francisco direction, Jill is seized then with a strong, urgent need to get back to the city, not to her own place but just to somewhere in town. Away from here, no matter that she has paid for two months more. She is still a lot richer than most people are, she might as well spend the money.

Turning in the other direction, toward the beautiful house that she quite suddenly dislikes, Jill begins to run.

A good runner, although she does not much like running, too sweaty, Jill veers down to the packed wet sand at the water's edge and then starts moving along very fast, elbows in, her short fair hair flattened to her head (she has dropped the silly kerchief somewhere), as sandpipers scatter and skitter off in all directions.

By the time she reaches the dunes, the high ridge that marks the path back to her house, Jill is fairly winded. She stops—panting and sweating, thinking, I'm not in great shape, that was not very much of a run. After a moment she starts up and across the dunes, toward the cypress grove that separates her house from the beach.

And then she drops instantly flat on the sand: through the trees, in the driveway next to her house, parked next to her new car, is an old Studebaker. Custom-striped, green and white. Noel's car.

Pressing her body into the cold, resisting sand, Jill very carefully raises her head and she sees—Noel. Noel approaching his car, and at the same time looking all about him; he has obviously just knocked at her door and found her not there. Actually with all that glass he could just look in, which undoubtedly he did, he could see her not there. Noel, in his crisp clean khakis, clean matching shirt, stands there in the sunshine, looking slightly disappointed, a very small frown on that excessively handsome face, but on the whole he looks happy, Jill notes, recognizing his habitual expression of pleasure in himself.

And why? Just what is he so happy about? Did he come all the way out here to tell her about Buck's being dead, imagining she would not know? (And actually she might not have; she doesn't always bother to get the paper.)

At that moment Jill remembers that she has left the newspaper along with the small sack of groceries back in the restroom. No matter.

DID NOEL KILL BUCK? Jill does not really think so.

Has Sage come home?

If he even moves an inch in the direction of the trees that now protect her, Jill will get up and run, all her muscles are tightly poised for that run. Before he has time to realize who she is she will be out of sight. Her heart is beating so hard that it jolts her body, she feels it could shake her to death.

Noel looks at his watch, and then, in the manner of a person who has come to the end of the time allotted for a given project, he moves decisively toward his car. He opens the door, gets in, and in another minute or so (to Jill, a long, long time, many beats of her heart) he is gone, as dust from his hasty exit rises on the unpaved, rutted road.

She forces herself to stay where she is for a moment more, then gets up and rushes for her house, now propelled by all her earlier fears, redoubled.

Once inside, although quite out of breath, she picks up the telephone and punches numbers.

"Stevie? It's me, Jill. Look, I really need to speak to her. Thanks." A pause, during which Jill breathes, and waits, barely glancing through the far window at the green shadowed hillside.

Then, "Fi. Listen, I really need to stay with you for a couple of days, okay? I'll be there in, oh, maybe an hour. Don't tell anyone, okay? Not Caroline. No one."

Twenty-four

"Of course, taxes. You understand that when a piece of property changes hands—even by inheritance, as in this case—the rollback from Prop. 13 is eliminated, and the old rates apply. But it shouldn't be too horrendous for you, fortunately, as you know. You're staying there now? The place is really sliding down the hill, is it not? Mrs. Kaltenborn never—But I should say no more than—"

In a beatific haze, in this shabby room on Pine Street, lower Pacific Heights, Portia listens to this barrage of lawyer words and instructions, from a dark, sad-faced young woman: long nose, small pointy chin, large mournful eyes and heavy dark hair. Mrs. Kaltenborn's lawyer, who has just revealed to Portia that Mrs. Kaltenborn, who was eighty-nine, died "peacefully, in her sleep" on a boat from Venice to Dubrovnik. And that she has left her house to Portia.

Dazed, Portia is aware that she is taking in no facts, beyond the major fact of this incredible inheritance. Her familiar anxiety over incomprehension (she tends to be vague and often inattentive, to miss things—Portia knows that) is opposed and at last overcome by sheer pleasure, a controlled gratitude (she could easily cry and she probably will, later on). How amazingly kind of Mrs. Kaltenborn, how totally unexpected for Portia. An *acte gratuit*.

What feels like spring sunshine streams in through long dirty windows, falling on the lawyer's long brown hair, and on Portia's shoulders, warming, like a blessing. The lawyer, Hilda Daid, must be Iranian, or Lebanese? She seems most remarkably nice, but how could she not be, as the bearer and the instrument of such a lucky piece of business?

The letter in which she summoned Portia to her office, telling her of the death, could have been a clue of sorts to Portia, but it was not; vague Portia, digesting the sad news of the death, only wondered why she should be so summoned—and was pleased that the death had occurred so peacefully, even romantically: she was glad that Mrs. Kaltenborn had been to Venice, of which she had spoken to Portia with love and longing. But Portia did not see why she herself had to visit this lawyer, this "Hilda Daid." Was something wrong in the house? something missing, books that Portia had forgotten to return?

As Portia approached the lawyer's office, the relative shabbiness of the neighborhood was reassuring. This was not like being summoned to the Transamerica Pyramid (to Jill's horrible, terrifying office), or to one of those spiffed-up brass-trimmed old brick places on Jackson Street.

And the building that housed the offices (all women, Portia noted from the sign) was a run-down, once-elaborate Victorian: paint peeling from the windowsills, all the fancy trim now broken, neglected—conspicuously *not* gussied up with bright pastels, as in the many gentrified neighborhoods of Victorian houses.

At first Portia assumed that the tall, very dark young woman who came to open the door was an assistant, and even as the woman said, "I am Hilda Daid," the pronunciation threw Portia off: Eelda Dah-eed was not the name that she had heard, reading Hilda Daid. But then, as they entered the book-piled, grimy-windowed, sunny room, Portia and this woman of almost her own height, Portia understood that this was indeed the lawyer, there was no one else around.

And as they sat down on opposite sides of Ms. Daid's amazingly cluttered desk, the lawyer spoke these amazing words: "You are, you know, in effect the sole heir. The heiress." And she smiled.

"But that's just amazing, she really shouldn't, there was no reason—" Portia stumbled about, at the same time fighting to subdue that small urge to cry; she found herself very, very touched.

"Well, she just must have liked you a lot." And now Portia can hear the shade of an accent, something foreign in Ms. Daid's speech.

The accents are slightly more English than American, but not really English either. She could be an exiled Middle Eastern princess, Portia thinks. English-educated and trying to sound like an American lawyer. To be one.

"She had no relatives at all," this exotic lawyer continues. "That is fortunate. Sometimes, you know, they contest, even when the will is as airtight as this one is."

"No, uh, instructions?"

Ms. Daid laughs, a small shy laugh, and she tells Portia, "She just said, 'Portia will know what to do with it.' " And she shows Portia the line added in Mrs. Kaltenborn's familiar spider writing, at the bottom of the legal document.

"Well, that's really strange, unless she just meant in a quiet way to remind me that I know how to take care of the place. And if I ever get any money I'll know how to fix it up."

"That's a start." Hilda Daid smiles.

"And actually I do have this sort of shack in Bolinas, and if I sold that I could do a little fixing up in Bernal Heights."

"Well, there you are."

Portia frowns. "Somehow I don't think that's what she meant. Or, not all she meant."

"Well, perhaps not."

"Did you know her very well?" asks Portia.

"Not so very. In fact that part was also a little strange. She has heard certain things of me, certain difficulties that I and my family had, and she knew the lawyer who was helping us with all that, even she knew someone at the horrendous INS. And then next I understood that I am her lawyer. An *acte gratuit,* I felt."

"Exactly what I—Well, she is, I guess you would say, quixotic?"

They both laugh, tentatively, briefly, neither yet quite sure of the other's real meanings, or language.

"She reminded me a little of some old American leftists I knew in Jerusalem," Hilda Daid told Portia. "Emigrés. How they talked! How hopeful and good they were."

"You're Israeli?"

A smile. "No. Lebanese. I grew up in Jerusalem, though. One of the niggers." Another, briefer smile. "And then I went to school in England," she says.

After a tiny pause, during which Portia has been wondering what to say next, she asks Hilda, "You've been here long?"

"Three years. We had some relatives. Here and in England. They were most kind, all of them."

Should she leave now? Nothing about the conversation and nothing in the demeanor, the body language of Hilda indicates that she should; only Portia's innate shyness, which is extreme, makes her wonder, Should I go? She says, "I've never been to Israel. My father has, though. And he's an old leftie. But not Jewish. A Texan."

"Actually I should not have said that Lebanese are niggers," Hilda Daid contributes. "Actually we are more like Indians. Native Americans."

"My father's been involved with Indian movements." Portia relaxes, a little. Maybe it's all right to stay and talk? Maybe Hilda enjoys it too, and does not have something else very pressing to do just now?

"Does he know Mrs. Kaltenborn, your father?" Hilda asks.

"No, and he's not very well, he's pretty sick now. But I'm sorry, I wish—" I wish I could ask Hilda to dinner, is what Portia is thinking. On the way home I could stop off at Real Food and get some fish and things for salad and cookies and—Good God, this is crazy. I feel crazy. I feel in love with this woman I don't know at all, I just met her, and she is so beautiful, all that dark skin and so much heavy hair, and her eyes. A woman. So, I am a lesbian? Well, that would explain quite a lot.

"Well—" says Hilda Daid, looking at Portia.

"Well. Oh, I'm sorry. I was really enjoying, I forgot—" Portia feels a humiliating blush on her face, as though all her thoughts were there too, for Hilda to read.

"Oh, I too very much have enjoyed," Hilda tells her.

By now they both are standing, the two thin young women, quite similar as to height—and perhaps it is that very accidental similarity (so few women she knows are that tall) that encourages Portia to say, "Maybe sometime you could come to the house for dinner? It's really nice, but of course you must have been there."

"Actually I have not. She always meant—but not. And I would like that very much."

"I suppose you're busy tonight, though." Bringing out that sentence was for Portia an act of enormous courage. She had to throw out all the words in a rush, with all her breath.

Hilda Daid's dark skin has darkened, a flush of blood appears in her cheeks. "Tonight would be very nice for me."

"Oh, really? Well, great! Well, you know where it is? Should I draw you a map?"

"I have in fact this street map that serves me very well. I rely on it always." A smile. White teeth.

"Well, that's great. Great! About seven?"

"I shall so much look forward. Thank you."

"Oh, thank you!"

And Portia, the heiress, walks out of the seedy office and into the bright pure sunlight, the new spring day. How handy that this building is so relatively near Real Food, she can so easily walk. And she does, in that oddly mixed neighborhood, new cheaply built speculation condos, with their unseemly combinations of wood and plaster, juxtaposed with the graceful old Victorians, some quite gaudily restored but others not, left to rot away in their tree- and plant-crowded yards, beds of flaming orange California poppies and broken pots from which hardy geraniums strive, neglected and thriving.

In Real Food, as always, Portia buys much too much. She is irresistibly tempted by tiny new lettuces, small new green spinach leaves, fresh herbs and new potatoes, by whole-grain breads and nourishing cookies, and fish, the most beautiful swordfish. She leaves the store with an almost bursting brown bag. She decides to get a cab on Van Ness, then remembers that her car is parked on Pine Street, near the lawyer's office. Near Hilda.

Driving home, she sobers up a little, even with the heady thought that it is indeed "home" to which she is driving. Her house. And she admonishes herself that she must not confuse the person of Hilda Daid with the fact of home ownership. Hilda Daid is simply a very nice shy intelligent and appealing young woman, who happened, simply happened to be the bearer of great news. And to be very beautiful.

It does, though, make quite a difference to think that she actually owns the house. And a cat, for Pink is now solely hers (the other two have disappeared), as surely as the house is. Thinking this as she walks from room to room, Portia stares fixedly at walls and windows, as though expecting the difference to be manifest there. (Ostensibly, though, she is looking for the cat.) And then, understanding what she is doing, her own nutty expectation of change, Portia further considers the larger sense in which nothing is ever owned, perhaps least of all houses, with their curiously autonomous lives, their ineradicable personal characters. As could be said of cats.

Nevertheless, in immediate, practical terms, she does own this house, and now she goes to the phone to dial Caroline's number, to tell her about it. To tell Ralph.

Just as she approaches the phone, though, it starts to ring, and the voice that Portia, answering, hears is her mother's. "Portia, I've been calling and calling—"

"Oh, but I was just going to call you! I got such wonderful news—"

"Darling, I can't talk right now. Could you just come along to the hospital? right away."

In Ralph's spare white hospital room, with its narrow, oblique view of the bay, warehouses and dead wharves, Portia finds her mother and two of her half-sisters. Sage and Liza.

And Ralph, who lies there apparently asleep, with his mouth partly open. Breathing hoarsely.

Caroline looks bad, Portia thinks, as she kisses and embraces her mother. Her skin is pale and dull, her eyes surrounded by dark puffy circles, and her whole body seems to sag. She looks old, and Portia has always seen her mother as young, quick and vigorous, intensely alive. "You look sort of tired," she is unable not to say.

"I really am tired," admits Caroline.

At Caroline's elbow, now crowding toward Portia for a kiss, a long hug—Sage looks wonderful, a new person. In blue silk, her yellow-green eyes all wide and alive. Portia's quick glance takes in new bright-blue shoes, a very New York touch, Portia thinks.

And then Liza. She and Portia exchange a quick embrace, as though they saw each other more often than in fact they do. Liza, like Caroline, looks very tired, and Portia thinks, These two have been the ones doing hospital duty, it's fallen on them. Where have I been?

Going over to her father, Portia presses her mouth very gently to his cheek; she realizes that she is terrified that he might suddenly wake, as though he were now in some infinitely dangerous realm from which he would only emerge with horrible news. And she senses then a terrible truth, which is that beyond a certain point no one really wants a very sick person to recover. The watchers, who have already begun to cope with the idea of death, albeit unwillingly, do not wish to turn around, so to speak; they are like heavy trucks on a narrow and difficult course. What they are already doing is quite sufficiently demanding, difficult—no more can be asked of them.

All that passes quickly through Portia's mind, as she stands and stares at her father—who is simply not there any more. And looking over to Caroline, who is barely not weeping, Portia wonders, to what extent will Caroline be able to recover? to be her "old self" without Ralph.

And just what was their connection really like—was it really as good as it looked? Caroline has such a tendency to put a good face on things, all her daughters know this.

And then Portia thinks, My God! I didn't call Hilda! Oh! oh *dear!* She has spoken the last "Oh *dear!*" aloud, and as Caroline looks over, Portia tries to explain. "I have to phone someone, I forgot."

"There's a booth just down the hall. Where I called you. Do you have some quarters?" Caroline, always solicitous. Always a mother, Portia thinks.

"Uh, Hilda, this is Portia Carter. I'm really sorry, you remember I said my father was sick? Well, he's in the hospital, Presbyterian—"

"I would be so happy to discuss with you but it so happens that I have with me a client." The somewhat curt voice of Hilda.

"Oh, oh, I'm sorry. I didn't mean—look, I'll call you later, Dinner, I can't, I'm sorry."

"Of no importance," says Hilda Daid, and she hangs up the phone.

"Darling, are you all right?" Caroline asks this, as Portia re-enters the room.

And Sage: "Ports, you look ravaged, honestly."

Liza: "How could you lose weight, you skinny kid?"

Portia tries to explain, a little. "I'm really okay. Honestly. It's just been such a day. I went to see Mrs. Kaltenborn's lawyer, in fact that's who I was trying to call. She's a Lebanese. It turns out that Mrs. Kaltenborn left me her house, can you imagine?" And then to Portia's horror the tears that all day for one reason or another have threatened pour slowly down her face. "Oh, I'm just so·tired," she further tries to explain.

"Oh, but Portia, that's so very nice, no wonder you're touched, how really sweet of her." As usual, things make some sort of sense to Caroline.

"Ports, that's super, you love that house. I like it too, it's great. God, remember the night we were going to have dinner there, and Noel came along and took over?"

Of course Portia remembers that night, but it is such a bad memory of Noel, she wonders that Sage would bring it up. Unless she and Noel are through? he's gone? She looks at Sage with that question.

And Sage answers, "We're splitting. I'll tell you all about it." How keyed up Sage looks, Portia thinks. All nerves. Sage could easily cry herself, or she could go back to Noel, Portia thinks.

Very quietly Caroline then says, "I think we should all go now."

One by one they go over to Ralph, very lightly to kiss his apparently insentient cheek. How small he is, Portia thinks, as she follows her sisters, kissing last, and observing the shape of her father's white body beneath the sheet—and recalls the giant of her childhood. The gentle, mostly kindly giant.

Caroline goes last. Very quickly she bends to Ralph, and very softly she says to him, "I'm going now, darling. And I think that you could go too."

By which they all understand that Caroline has given her husband permission to die. She has released him—from herself, from them all. From his life.

Twenty-five

"Well yes, dear Liza, there is considerable relief involved. And no, I don't feel guilty about feeling relieved. Thank God I'm a simple person, relatively speaking. And I find that I simply follow the good advice that I've been giving to widowed or dumped-on friends from time to time over the years. Exercise, keep busy, entertain, try to make new friends. Honestly, darling, I'm really all right. Yes, of course I'm eating properly, what an incredibly silly question."

This particular conversation was between Caroline and Liza—but it could have been between Caroline and any one of her daughters, all of whom are being as Caroline sees it far too solicitous. Far too concerned about their mother's widowed condition.

And so for their comfort she gives them this litany of mostly lies, the only truth being that Caroline is quite all right—in her own fairly eccentric way—and that she does not feel guilty about being all right.

She does not do any exercise, because she hates it. All her life, Caroline now believes, she has exercised against, as it were, the naturally large soft shape of her own body, against that body's natural direction and toward the pleasure of some husband (or, while she was married to Jim McAndrew, those lovers). She has jumped around and stretched and pulled, played tennis and badminton and skied, has even attempted golf. All for those men, essentially; the only exercise that she really enjoys is walking, which she now does quite a lot. She does not think of walking as exercise.

And she does not keep busy, except on specified days when she works as a volunteer cook at the Women's Shelter, in a church basement a few blocks away. (Horrid work, Caroline thinks: slicing and chopping and clearing up in an ill-equipped, ill-smelling, very small space. The other volunteers seem carried along by a sense of mission. Not so Caroline, who thinks she can hardly stand it, and wonders why she does.) Otherwise she lolls about, which is exactly what she has always told everyone else not to do. She often goes back to bed with a nice cup of tea, a nice book. Not exactly what anyone would call keeping busy.

Nor does Caroline "entertain," or "see people," and God knows she does not try for new friends (to the people at the shelter she is polite, never warm or cordial; "Doing good work does not necessarily improve people's characters," she has said to Liza).

"I've seen people, most of the people I know, quite recently. All those parties when we first got back, I saw everyone we knew, several times. And now everyone's been so terrifically nice and kind, honestly, it's obscene, all those flowers. But it just doesn't seem to me that I have to see the people themselves. All that business of going out to dinner. The truth is, I don't feel much like talking about Ralph, or being careful not to talk about him, if you see what I mean." Again, to Liza.

The only untrue part of that statement is minor, concerning the flowers: Caroline actually does not find their abundance obscene, she adores having all those flowers. She carefully attends to their needs for fresh water, for trimmed or mashed stems, in some cases liquid food. Of course she recognizes that the amount of money spent on such an abundant floral display might have done more human good, spent otherwise; however, it was not, and so she might as well enjoy the flowers. Which she does, and she does all she can to make them flourish, and last.

"My daughters are not only terrifically solicitous, it seems to me quite hysterically so, they are also most wildly anxious to tell me all about themselves. I suppose in fact they always have been, but these days it does seem more pronounced, they go on and on. And on."

Caroline does not literally speak those words to anyone; she has no present friend with whom she is on such terms. Nor does she have the sort of sentimentality that would encourage conversations with a dead husband. It is perhaps to some ideal, imagined friend (as a child might have, as Caroline as an only child undoubtedly did have) that she voices these semi-complaints about the confessions of her daughters.

And in the meantime she goes on listening.

Sage says, "It's all so curiously depressing. I had no idea, I always thought I wanted to be successful, and now I am, I guess, but this doesn't feel like success. It's more like being hit by something on the street, some terrific burden that I don't know what to do with. Cal's been a big help, and in another way Stevie too, but still, I don't know, I keep thinking that this is not what I meant to do. Do you see what I mean at all?"

Liza's problem, very curiously, is somewhat similar: she has just sold a short story, her first, to a very trashy magazine. For three thousand dollars. Initially she sent it off to *The New Yorker,* from whom (from a pleasant-sounding woman) she got an encouraging letter. Another first: she is used to printed rejections. And then in her dentist's office she happened to read the trashy magazine, simply called *You,* and there was a story by a good writer, one she has long admired. And so rather whimsically she sent off her own story, and to her vast surprise they took it. For all that money.

Liza, though, is considerably more lighthearted than Sage about this strange success, as well as more objective.

"It's too funny, really," she tells her mother. "How it all happened, I mean how I came to write it. But at some point I guess I was getting a little down on motherhood and life in the park. Anyway, I sat there in J.K. and I thought about all the guys I used to see around there, you know, old Sixties pals, and I thought it might be a kick to see some of them again. So I wrote a few notes, just saying I'd like to see them, if they were ever around. I don't think I was really up to anything, but maybe I was." She looks at her mother in a speculative way.

Caroline has remained impassive—although somewhat tempted to "share" her own experiences of maternal boredom, she does not do so. "Perhaps," is all she says.

"Well, the funny part was that no one showed up. Not one answer," Liza continues. "So, I began to think about how it might have been if a couple of them had. And that was my story. Honestly, it's not as crappy as that sounds, though. You'll see. And I have to admit, I was excited about the *New Yorker* letter, that woman really liked it, I think. Why does everyone venerate that magazine so? STILL. But they can't write letters to everyone who sends them stories, I know they don't. I do have mixed feelings about being in *You,* though. Maybe I should have tried somewhere else too. On the other hand, all that money is nice, I'm working on persuading Saul to take off for a week in Mexico. He still feels guilty about the time we were supposed to go away, the time we almost made it to Carmel."

"Liza, that's terrific, and I can't wait to read your story."

"It'll look even better in print, I can't wait for that. Even wedged among all the singles-condom advice and brand-new diets. But it is encouraging. I'm going to put myself on a schedule somehow, try to write every day."

"You should, you know. You could use the money for help. Sitters, so you can work."

"I've thought of that, in fact I know it's exactly what I should do. You know I'll never get Saul to Mexico." But Liza laughs as she says this, as though referring to an amiable weakness.

A pause, and then Caroline asks, "Have you heard anything from Jill?"

"Only indirectly, from Fiona."

"Well, me too."

Fiona has clear and serious problems of her own, these days. In a word, Fiona's is suddenly in a very clear decline. The regulars have fled to trendier, newer places, and new enthusiasts are few and far between. For all of which Fiona has various explanations.

"Aside from the fact that this is almost always what happens," she tells her mother, "our basic problem is with the neighborhood.

We're too expensive for it. There're not too many yuppies on Potrero. Yet. So people don't walk by and think, What a swell restaurant, we'll have to check it out, the way they do on upper Fillmore. People have to make a big effort to get here from Pacific Heights or Mill Valley, for Christ's sake."

And then she says, "But what does all this matter? The point is, we're losing money hand over fist, so to speak. In a way it's sort of funny, I mean I always knew this would happen. I knew that I was successful in a way that did not make sense. Those other women, like Alice and Patty, they really care about food, they know food in a way that I absolutely don't. In fact at this point food bores me shitless, I hate it. I'd like to eat nothing but baked garlic and Acme bread and salad, that's all I really like to eat."

Caroline laughs. "Sounds very good to me; you know, I adore garlic too."

"Maybe I'll move to Sicily."

A pause. "Why Sicily?"

"Oh, I don't know, I just thought of it. In connection with garlic." And then, "Well, that's not quite true. I actually had this big love affair with a sort of Sicilian type, a married man, natch, very what we used to call prominent. You probably know him. Anyway, lots of talk about Sicily."

"Oh." A fairly long pause, before Caroline asks Fiona, "Well, how do you think Jill is, these days?"

"I guess about the same."

Because she knew he would have hated it, Caroline had no funeral services for Ralph. Thus there was no specific, familial occasion at which she would have seen Jill. Still, the fact was, she had not seen her daughter for several months, and according to Fiona, who seemed to be in touch with her sister (her twin, Caroline sometimes thought the two of them so linked)—Fiona said a little vaguely that Jill was "sort of depressed, but really doing okay." Caroline was instructed not to worry.

And Caroline for the most part very sensibly did not worry.

She assumed that Jill herself was worried over money. Such a perilous career, hers seemed to be, to Caroline, who understands very little of high finance, its wheelings and contortions. It all looks quite crazy, to Caroline.

And then there was the matter of that odd person who seemed to be a sort of acquaintance of Jill's (Caroline hoped no more than that) who was murdered outside some club in the Mission District. That Buck Fister. Just when the Grand Jury was about to indict him for "running call girls," a most unsavory phrase, and an ugly story all around. Amazing, Caroline finds it, that one of her daughters should know a person who was murdered! Not to mention that connection with what used to be called "white slaves." Caroline can well understand Jill's being depressed, brought down by any such involvement, however slight.

The police have been quoted as saying that the killing looked "professional," whatever that could mean; Caroline takes it to describe a crime beyond their capacity for solution.

But *was* Jill's involvement in whatever was going on so very slight, Caroline has been unable not to wonder. Why, really, was Jill's name in that man's little black book?

Caroline has always had a very dark sense of this particular daughter, a sense of some wildness, some feral greed and a sexuality that is both rampant and slightly askew, "kinky" would be the contemporary word. But Caroline does not choose to examine this intuitive impression of Jill. She would be absolutely unable to say why she thinks this of Jill.

These days Caroline would much rather think of Portia, with whom she is at least for the moment very close—first, for the blood-strong reason that Ralph's loss is one that they share. And second (more happily, much), there is Portia's acquisition of the narrow, funny house in Bernal Heights, the house and its needful, long-neglected garden, about which Portia and Caroline endlessly, these days, converse. (Not to mention the cranky old cat, with her arrogant walk and her loud, endless comments on life.)

And then there is Portia's new friend, the mysterious dark Hilda Daid, the young Lebanese lawyer. It is fairly clear to Caroline (again, she could not say why) that these two young women have now become lovers, and she rather believes that soon, any day now,

Portia will make this announcement to her mother. It is called "coming out to your mother," Caroline believes.

And she thinks, Oh dear, why is it that my daughters always have to tell me things? Why don't they just let me guess?

This, then, is one phase of what could be termed Caroline's new single life. Her post-Ralph life. Herself as a widow, a word she much dislikes and would never use. This is the phase, as she later thinks of it, of peace and self-indulgence. Of lying about with tea and new novels, magazines. A time of solitude, really, except for all those turbulent conversations with her daughters.

Sometimes, though, her whole balance seems to shift, and she feels herself very near an abyss of pain, of loneliness and longing. She feels the black loss of Ralph. She will wake then at night to his absence in her bed. To the total lack of his large, most loved and familiar shape. His body, now totally gone.

From such a night she will wake exhausted, and hopeless. Feeling old, and fat, and irrevocably alone.

At those times, of necessity she begins to follow some of her own prescriptions, starting with exercise. Walking six or eight miles a day (that much mileage is "exercise," according to Caroline; just walking about in her usual aimless way is not).

A huge fogbank now has covered what seemed to be the start of true spring weather. Every day the papers predict that in a couple of days the fog will lift, and it does not. It is not very cheering weather, but perfectly okay for walking, Caroline tells herself.

She finds it hard, though, to walk with no object other than exercise, and so she invents distant errands: she walks far out on Clement Street to a nursery, in search of some new shade plants, and some summer-blooming bulbs for her garden, and for Portia's. She goes over to Real Food on Sutter Street, a Portia recommendation. And sometimes she walks downtown, to Union Square.

Striding along with her usual briskness, arrested here and there by sheer curiosity, Caroline in a gradual way becomes aware that she does have an objective, though; she is in fact looking for someone, or something—all these very long walks have the nature of a search. Seeing that this is the case, that she is indeed looking (not yet knowing for whom, or what), at first she thinks, Well, what a silly old jerk I've become, I must be looking for Ralph, in some stupid unconscious way. How *dumb.*

But that is not true. Almost as soon as she says to herself, I'm looking for Ralph, Caroline knows that she is not. And she continues to wonder: for whom? for what?

Often, almost anywhere along the streets where she walks, Caroline encounters homeless people. Muttering old wrinkled black men; haggard, chalk-faced young women; old women with wild crazy hair and crazier pale eyes; middle-aged men in business suits with the shifty, humiliated look of middle-class failure. They reach out for money; some more enterprising souls have set up on the sidewalk, with signs ("Homeless and hungry, willing to work") and cups. Caroline passes out whatever she has, which is sometimes very little—and then she begins to make a point of taking along more quarters and single dollars, as she starts out on her walks.

At some point she begins to understand that in a way she is always expecting to see, somewhere, the thin bent woman who went chanting past her house, a year or so back, just before everything began to happen, as Caroline now thinks of it. The woman who she came to believe was Mary Higgins Lord, former wife of the famous surgeon.

Or was she, after all, "Higgsie"? It begins to seem more and more possible that she was not, and as Caroline encounters this confusion, this possible mistake in identity, she becomes more and more anxious to find this woman again.

And of course does not see her, anywhere.

Twenty-six

"What an incredibly beautiful mushroom."

"Sure is. But it's got to be poisonous."

"You mean all the prettiest ones are lethal? How trite of nature." Not especially wanting an answer, Sage kneels down on the mat of damp leaves and pine needles, twigs. "Besides, I'm not planning to eat it, it's too lovely." From her distance she examines the top surface of the mushroom, which is cream-colored, runnelled with yellow, its center a star of the palest blue. "Really, look at it," she says, intently.

"I would, but my knee," Jim reminds her. "If I get down I'll never get up. I'm a very old man," he says, with a disbelieving laugh.

"I forgot," and obligingly Sage rises to stand beside him, as they both look down at the mushroom.

The trail up which they have been hiking is not very clearly really a trail. Or, as Jim has earlier remarked, it could be just a deer trail; as he delicately put it, he has seen deer droppings.

Starting up again, Sage says, "You'd think I'd remember where we are, we used to come here all the time. Though of course that was about twenty years ago. About."

"Trees grow a lot in that time," Jim reminds her, puffing a little as he speaks.

"I guess so. Besides, we were usually stoned."

After a few minutes Jim manages to ask her, "Where is Noel now, do you think?"

"I don't know. Lurking, I guess you'd call it. He phones a lot, but he doesn't say where he is. The bizarre part is how friendly he sounds. As though he were off on a trip and just checking in. With the wife."

"You told him definitely, though?"

"Of course I did. I pointed out that he'd broken my arm, for God's sake."

"You've got to keep repeating it to him, saying you're really through, you mean it," Jim scolds. "Don't let him pretend you're just getting over some little spat."

"You're right, I know you are."

Although in a way she has very much liked Jim's scolding—it gets them back to a safe, familiar emotional plane—Sage still does not really want to defend herself. She does not want to explain her curious paralysis, in terms of Noel.

She feels, though, that this hike has been a very good idea. Months back, even after she had emerged from the initial trough of shame into which that crazy drunken time with Jim had plunged her (the night of the green silk shirt, she has thought of it as), she still thought often and troublingly of Jim. She had thought of calling him, even, to say, Look, all that was crazy. I do love you but you're my father, for heaven's sake. I was just so let down by everyone else that night, by Noel and by Cal, whom I hadn't even yet met, back then. But the business about the show being postponed, everything was terrible for me then.

Sage has said all that in her mind to Jim, but she then came to believe that the best solution would be (if possible) a simple return to their old connection: doing something familiar together, like this hike. She had even thought of a movie; when she was a little girl they went to movies together a lot, when Caroline was busy with new babies, or whatever. But this hike is just right. If only she can carry it off, and not say any more about Noel than she already has. Not bring up that terrible night with Jim. How relieved he will be if she doesn't!

Sage believes that, wherever Noel is, he is there with Jill. And if she thinks of it, if she thinks specifically about Noel and Jill together, she feels sick. In New York, at least, for the most part she managed not to, and when she did think of Noel then it was only with fury: how could he, how could he push her down in the street outside a restaurant? And in a way for Sage there was much relief in that rage. They had both been enraged, he had looked at her with pure hatred.

However, as she now imagines Noel ensconced somewhere with Jill, somewhere not too far away, probably, she feels sheer helplessness. No more power.

She and Jim have now paused once more in an almost sunny clearing, and Sage says to him, "It's interesting about sexual jealousy, isn't it. What an awful weapon it can be, I mean. If you can keep someone jealous all the time you have absolute control of them. I think it was almost deliberate, the way Noel made me jealous, and kept me jealous, and then taunted me about it."

"How do you mean?"

"Oh, every way. Always making some play for whoever we were with, if she was even half attractive. Telling me about people coming on to him, women he worked for. According to him he always turned them down, but of course I didn't always believe him. I wasn't meant to."

"The truth is," Jim brings out, "I know quite a lot about sexual jealousy, I've had some heavy doses."

"That's what you get for consorting with young girls." Sage did not mean to say this, but was then unable not to.

"Actually it was your mother who gave me the really worst time." Jim looks uncomfortably into the thick dark woods to one side of their clearing, as though someone (Caroline?) might be listening there. Facing Sage again, with a reluctant smile he tells her, "She was sort of a flirt in those days, I guess you'd say. There was always someone around she seemed to like. Of course I doubt if there was anything really going on—"

"Probably not," Sage agrees, as at the same time she thinks: If there's anything Caroline is not it's a flirt. She's serious. Probably one hell of a lot was going on. For some reason Sage finds this cheering.

"But Noel's a whole other story," defiantly Jim tells her. "Bad news. You've got to get rid of that guy."

"I know."

They take up their walk again, and quite soon the woods ahead of them begin to clear, smaller trees and bushes, more sky. And then they are at the actual crest, the spiny ridge that marks the top of Mt. Vision. What they now face is the sea, the shining, spreading Pacific, with long green complicated fingers of land reaching out into the water, curling around it. Turning back for a moment to face the other direction, they see wide flat Tomales Bay, and the smooth low shape of green hills on its farther side.

"Marvellous! so beautiful!" Sage and Jim simultaneously breathe.

And then, because by now she has to, Sage says, "You know, I've felt so awful about that night I came over, I mean—"

Jim's frown is very deep. "Sage, please. We were smashed. Martinis! Please don't think about it."

"Well, I don't exactly dwell on it," Sage lies. "Just sometimes I do think about it, and I worry."

"Well, not to worry. I'd say our luck has improved a lot since then, wouldn't you? Both our luck?" By now Jim is smiling with relief, glad to have finished (he thinks) with that major topic and happy to introduce another. "I've been wanting to tell you," he says, with some enthusiasm. "Remember that time, oh, maybe a year ago? You came over, you'd been to some lunch thing, I think, at Caroline's? And I was really down? I think I told you about this girl, we weren't getting along?"

"I think I remember."

"Well, it's okay now," Jim announces. "I mean we're together, and I, uh, I really like her, and she seems to like me too. Pretty good for an old guy, huh?"

"Jim, that's swell," Sage tells him. "I'm really glad."

"Well, what do you say we start back down?" He looks at his watch. "No point hanging around up here, do you think?"

"I guess not."

"And you've got this nice new friend out from New York. That's great."

"Well, sort of," Sage tells him.

"I think I'll have a martini, care to join me?" Roland says, smilingly.

"Oh God no—"

"Such violence. You have an allergy?"

"No, not really. I just never drink at lunch, remember?"

"Oh, right. And you still don't."

"Roland, please don't talk like a moron," says Sage.

"I'm sorry, I've had a lot of very upsetting events in my life recently. And, then, it was a surprise. Your calling, and then, uh, this."

"Well, I guess. Hearing from me."

They are seated, Sage Levine and Roland Gallo, in a small new garden restaurant, on Russian Hill. The choice was Sage's; this is a place that she heard about in New York from a friend of Cal's. They face each other from opposite sides of their small white table; again, Sage's choice. Roland would have taken the place adjacent to hers but Sage very firmly said, "No, I want to see you. That's the point."

Now she says, frowning into her empty water glass (the drought: you only get water if you ask for it), "Tell me about your upsetting events. I mean, if you want to." Saying this, she remembers a long time ago when Roland said to her, "It's amazing how I talk to you. Never before in my life."

"Well, that's a rather large order," Roland tells her. "As you know, I'm a very political man, and so certain secrets—well, that may be the point, I'm overloaded with secrets. Mine and some other people's. But lately certain events, there was something I put in motion, I mean, that had an outcome that I didn't at all foresee, that would be one way to put it. But, thinking back, I wonder now if I shouldn't have. Foreseen what happened." He smiles, or, rather, his wide mouth smiles. His eyes are black and worried.

The thought flashes across Sage's mind that he is confessing to her: he is telling her that he was responsible for the death of that man, that friend of Jill's. Buck Fister. The thought is so clear and so immediate that Sage believes it, although at the same time she thinks, How could I possibly know that? I don't even know those people, what can I be thinking?

She asks him, "Do you know my sister Jill?"

He pauses, looking away. "I don't think so, no. I've met another sister, Fiona, and come to think of it also your mother."

"We must seem an odd group."

"I suppose." But he seems not to want to consider Sage's family—and returns to his own. "My wife, well, she's also a worry to me. I'm a terrible husband, I know that."

Sage laughs. "Are you saying I should be glad we didn't get married?"

"Well, now that you say so. But, my very dear Sage, are we really going to have that sort of conversation? Must we? I should warn you, I'm much too old to be what people call open. I'm a closed Sicilian book."

Sage laughs again, appreciating him almost against her will. "I just wanted to see you," she tells him. "I thought it would be fun to ask you to lunch. To see you again. And that some of the things I worry about might come clearer."

He spreads his hands, palms upward, in a very Latin gesture. "I'm all yours," he tells her.

"Well, actually it was nice of you to come." Looking across at those somewhat stagy, dark, dark eyes, at that arrogant nose and shining, domed bald head, Sage wonders why she is feeling such a rush of affection for this man, whom she has always thought of as deeply injurious. As *bad.* At this moment she simply likes him very much, strange as it is that she should. She tells him, "I did feel terrible about your not marrying me, but maybe you were right, I mean it wouldn't have been a good idea for either of us."

He acknowledges this with a small gesture of his head, then says, "I'm sure marrying Joanne was a very bad thing to do to her."

There is a small pause before Sage asks him, "How about running for mayor? Will you, still?"

At that his whole face shifts, and seems to sag. His eyes droop as Roland says, "No way. It's out, for every possible reason. First off, I'd lose my shirt, financially, and I wouldn't win. I had to announce this. It'll be in the papers later this week, in fact."

"That's too bad."

"What's really bad is that I would have been a terrific mayor. The power would have brought out my better qualities. Look what happened with Harry Truman, if you'll pardon the analogy."

Sage is unable not to smile at this, in part because of the incredible difference in personal styles—plain, uxorious Harry Truman, from Missouri, and flamboyant, faithless Roland, the dashing Sicilian.

"I really had great plans," he tells her. "I had a plan for the homeless, and even ideas about AIDS."

"You did?" When she and Roland were lovers, Sage remembers, they never had political conversations, other than his conventional teasing of her Sixties views, her marches and protests. Although what he actually said was, she now remembers, "You people are right, of course, but you don't have a clue as to how to get things done. Take it from an old pol." She can hear him saying that.

And now Roland asks her, "Have you been out on the bay lately? Seen all those empty wharves? Just imagine them all turned into good clean living quarters. Dormitories, family condos, all types. And think of the work that would involve. Put people to work making houses for themselves. I really like that."

"God, Roland, you sound like some kind of commie-pinko radical."

"Well, maybe I am at heart. You know, I always told you that basically I agreed with what your people were saying. And maybe I've even been radicalized a little more by Reagan."

"I love it."

"Well, the guy's such a total old twit, he gives ideology a bad name."

"That's what Michael Harrington said."

"Who? Oh, that socialist."

"Right." This conversation is becoming heady stuff, to Sage. First, her queer discovery of liking Roland, *liking* him, feeling this odd affection. And now this beatific, genuinely socialist vision of his, about which she knows he is absolutely sincere.

But what about the very strange flash she had, when he told her about setting in motion something very bad, regrettable—and she instantly thought of the murder of Buck Fister? *Why* did she think that? Is everything that she now perceives of Roland, including that message, simply more craziness of her own? *Could* she be falling in love with Roland all over again? (It would be so like her, she knows, to sexualize almost any strong emotion; she does that repeatedly.)

All those thoughts have been very scary indeed, and in a brisk way she now asks him, "And AIDS?"

"Again, some abandoned buildings converted into AIDS hospitals, and several hospices. Apartment-type places. And more research money, piles and piles. Don't ask me where all the money's going to come from." He grins, very quickly. "No wonder those guys, guys with AIDS, are so mad at the administration. They really got shafted, and they're dead right about why. It's because those assholes in Washington think they're a silly bunch of queers."

"Which is almost as bad as being a woman, or black."

"Well, probably worse." And then he says, "What an odd conversation we seem to be having. This is not quite what you had in mind, I'll bet."

"You're right, but, then, I keep telling you, I didn't really have anything specific in mind. I wanted to see you, and I must say, you're a big surprise."

"May I take it, a not entirely unpleasant surprise?"

"Oh no, in fact—But really, Roland, do I always have to feed your ego?"

"Be nice if someone did." That was a plaintive old tune, very recognizable to Sage.

"Come on, now," she tells him. "Just when I've been thinking how nice you are."

They laugh, in mutual surprise.

"And this is a very nice restaurant you've brought me to," Roland tells her, with an appreciative look around at flowers, watercolors of flowers, and palest-pink walls.

The restaurant is in fact to be the eventual successor to Fiona's, in terms of an extreme if temporary popularity. But Sage is always to remember it as the place in which for the first time, after so many years of passion, then of rage and pain, she began to like Roland Gallo, to see him as an exceptionally complicated, contradictory and humanly flawed person, whom she cares about, in his humanness.

Late that afternoon, after Sage has visited her mother and stayed much longer than she meant to (Caroline seemed a great deal more interested in hearing about lunch with Roland Gallo than Sage would have expected—curiously enough), Sage comes into her own house on Russian Hill to the sound of the phone ringing.

Noel. She is sure it is Noel, it must be. And she is right.

"No, Noel, tonight isn't good for me. Well, I'm busy. A friend from New York. No, I'm not. No, of course you can't, you wouldn't get on at all. Well yes, as a matter of fact, he is. Well, what's wrong with friends? Noel, please, I have to go now. No. No, I just don't feel like talking right now. I'm sorry. No, no, I don't think so. No, I'm sorry. Well, goodby."

Noel's insistence that they see each other, *tonight,* is quite out of character for him—but, then, Sage reflects, he has usually not had to insist, with her. Sage was reminded of Jill and Fiona as tiny children, two- and four-year-olds, who never took no for an answer.

But Noel is not a small child, he is a very spoiled and now very angry strong, adult male. And Sage is frightened. Suddenly really scared.

She considers calling the police, but does not. Asking for protection would make her sound foolish, she believes, a "hysterical woman." In the midst of a "domestic crisis"—she has been told that cops hate both those categories of trouble, especially in combination.

And is she in fact hysterical? Paranoid, even? Noel has no history of violence, unless you count pushing her down on the sidewalk that night, when she broke her arm. And Sage does not exactly count that, she feels that in some way she provoked it.

In an agitated, quite unfocussed way she walks about her house, in and out of rooms.

Realizing her total lack of direction, she tries to concentrate on something simple, like the choice of a restaurant for dinner that night with Cal. But she is unable to think of a place, no restaurants in that city of thousands of restaurants come to mind. Except, quite crazily, Fiona's. Which is out of the question. Or is it? Caroline did tell her that Fiona was worried, her regulars were falling off. So maybe—

Sage picks up the phone and taps out the number.

And gets Stevie. "Stevie, how great!" she tells him, very much meaning it. His warm voice has come through to her like a much-needed present. "I've missed you," she says.

Stevie says he has missed her too, they must get together, seriously. And yes, she and Cal can have a nice table at 8:15, and yes, he himself will be there. "This someone important to you?" Stevie asks, a somewhat strange question for him to ask, unusual—but quite okay, Sage thinks.

"Very important," she tells him, "but maybe not in the way you mean. He's an art dealer, and he likes my work. He's gay."

"Well, I think I can handle that."

They laugh again, old good friends, and Sage hangs up feeling considerably better, cheered, at the very idea of Stevie.

She still jumps, though, at the sound of her telephone, and she thinks that it must be Noel, again, and considers not answering.

But she does answer, and she hears not Noel but Cal, sounding most unlike himself. He must have eaten something terrible, he tells her, he is not at all well. No, he doesn't think he needs a doctor, the crisis is over, he's sure. Rest and hot tea will do the trick, he knows. And he couldn't be sorrier about tonight—will she be okay?

Reassuring him that she will, she could use some rest herself, Sage on the instant of hanging up wishes that she had insisted on coming around to his hotel to see how he was (ostensibly). The truth is that she does not want to be alone in her house. *Does not.* She is frightened. Even another phone call from Noel would be more than she could handle, much less all the normal night noises that are very frightening to a person alone, a frightened person.

Various possibilities come to mind. She could after all just go to a hotel by herself, check in for the night: who would know? But that seems a little extreme, an admission of panic. Or, she could call Caroline, and go stay over there. But they just saw each other, Caroline would be alarmed.

Then she remembers that the first thing she should do is call Stevie at the restaurant, to say they won't be coming—and then she thinks, Why not? I can go by myself, and see Stevie. Stevie in one way or another will surely help.

Twenty-seven

"It must be wonderful for you, having such a, such a *voice*. You'll be great at readings and lecturing and just plain talking about your work, all those things writers do. In your own voice. Why, I'd know the sound of your voice anywhere, anywhere at all," Joanne Gallo quite improbably says to Liza. Out on the grass, at the Julius Kahn Playground.

At first, what most confuses Liza is the fact that her new editor at *You*, kind, hyper-intelligent Kathy, has in quite a different context said more or less the same: "What comes across most clearly in this story is a fresh, distinctive voice," wrote Kathy, in that first and memorable letter. Joanne is surely not talking about Liza's literary voice; she refers of course to the actual voice, the literal sounds of Liza's speech. But the coincidence seems more than strange.

And since this conversation, if that is what it is (so far, more like a monologue by Joanne), is taking place on a mid-morning, a balmy cirrus-strewn blue April day, Liza thinks it unlikely that Joanne is drunk; this is not a post-lunch or cocktail-hour encounter. (Although Joanne sounds, well, not right.) In any case Liza is less concerned with Joanne's sobriety than with her own children, who are all wandering off in separate directions, at varying speeds. The baby, a terrific crawler, is on hands and knees, heading for some very attractive yellow weeds that would no doubt make her very sick. Jumping up, Liza moves fast, at the same time saying to Joanne, "Well, thanks."

"Even on an old tape I'd know your voice right off." Joanne now speaks in a crooning, private way, addressing only herself. And then she asks, "Do you girls all sound the same, you and your lovely sister Sage?"

Inattentively Liza tells her, "No, I think Sage and Portia just sound like themselves."

"Sage, what a lovely name. What a name from the past, but simply, absolutely lovely."

At that moment Liza, who has managed to pick up the baby and tuck her under one arm, sees that the older two are pulling each other's hair, for no apparent reason. Their faces are red, noses streaming. Rushing over, Liza with her free hand manages to separate them, a not-easy task—as at the same time she has two thoughts: one, this isn't like her children, there must be something in the air, like pollen; and, two, what on earth is eating Joanne Gallo? whatever is she talking about, all this about voices?

Liza settles back on the grass, with her three children more or less all over her, still sniffling.

"What I can't figure out is when and where you would go to do it, you and Roland. I just can't figure that," sings Joanne Gallo. "When and where, where or when. When to fuck, where to fuck. Some problems!"

"Fuck!" echoes the oldest child, enthusiastically. A mysterious word, it is very powerful, she knows; all the kids at nursery school say it a lot. Her parents say it rarely.

"Joanne, I honestly don't know what you're talking about." But as she says this Liza's stomach clutches with guilt, as though she had in fact made love with Roland Gallo. As she has indeed imagined doing, seeing him here in the park, sometimes. Thinking about him and Sage.

"I'll admit he does give great head, fantastic head, I used to come three or four times, did you?" Now Joanne's tone is conversational, almost rational.

"Joanne, look, you've really got it wrong."

"Oho! No, no I don't. Not wrong. I'd know your voice any old where, I heard what you said to him."

"Joanne, where do you think you heard my voice?"

"On Roland's tape. He keeps all his phone tapes, it looks like. The one where you talk about fucking in Palermo."

"Joanne, I have never."

Joanne is drunk, after all. As she moves closer Liza catches winy breath, sees unfocussed eyes, crazily blue.

Joanne cries, "I'd know your style, I'd know that voice anywhere. I know you! And why do you think he decided not to run for mayor?"

"I—"

"I told him I'd have the tapes played over KPIX!" shouts Joanne. "All of them, all the ones he's too dumb to throw out. Shit, he's as stupid as Nixon, and just as vain. And you, you've got a pretty filthy tongue in your head. Shit, I thought I was a dirty talker, he complains that I am, even if it used to turn him on. But you, honestly, you—"

By now all three of Liza's children are shrieking in panic. This is their first view of a raging adult, a grownup out of control, and they find it terrifying.

Preoccupied as she is with their comfort, stretched three ways for hugs and pats and murmurs of love, another part of Liza's mind still attends to Joanne, and in the midst of all the shouting the obvious answer comes to her: What Joanne must have heard was a tape of Jill talking to Roland Gallo. Or possibly Fiona. For one thing, they both have so-called dirtier mouths than Liza does.

But she cannot say any of that to Joanne, of course not. And when she can speak at all above the subsiding wails of her children she only says, "You know, you've got me confused with someone else. I've honestly never talked in my life to your husband on the phone. And barely anywhere else."

"Fucking liar."

The oldest child, now staring with interest at this more controlled grownup conversation, now takes this up, a new chant. "Fucking liar, fucking liar," she sings with pleasure, as the second child, with even less real sense of the word than the first, tries to sing along.

"Oh, come on kids, shut up. I don't like that song," Liza tells them. And, to Joanne, "I'm sorry, you're just wrong. All around."

Joanne manages to get to her feet, and with a long baleful look at Liza, she starts off across the grass to her own house. Roland Gallo's house.

Watching her unsteady progress—Joanne is wearing heels, a narrow black skirt—Liza is moved to go and help her along; it is terrible to see another person, a woman, in such dire straits, and when Joanne thinks of it later, presumably sober, how deeply humiliating this will be for her, for poor deluded crazy drunken Joanne.

However, both because of the children and because of Joanne's very possible response, extreme anger, Liza does not go to her; she stays where she is on the grass, and her lively, busy mind runs over the interesting scenarios, possibilities suggested by Joanne, who has now moved out of sight.

Just suppose, thinks Liza, that as she, Liza, once assumed, Jill had at one time indeed been a call girl: could she have met Roland Gallo (so to speak) in that capacity?

Liza plays with that idea. She envisions Jill in a posh hotel room, lying there waiting in some very fancy nightgown; she envisions the entrance of R.G.—whom Jill of course would instantly recognize from all his pictures in the papers. R.G. the family villain, the demon lover of Sage. What would Jill say—and what would Roland?

Next Liza wonders if she should tell any of this to Saul. This is a tricky problem, which she now ponders in all its complexity, as she gathers up her children and their gear (this gathering is an even trickier problem, both in physics and logistics), as she tries to start off for her house, for their lunch.

But is this information that he should have? Should he be told about a drunk and seriously delusional Joanne, at such an hour of the morning? Liza decides that it could, conceivably, be important, and she decides too that she can easily pass it off as gossip: silly me, you know how writers are, but guess who I saw in the park, and guess what she said?

More or less pulled together, trailing Pampers and toys, Liza and her group at last start up the rutted path by the twisted cypress trees, through an area of dark woods, and now bright spring weeds. Someone, a man, seems camped out there. Liza sees a red blanket, a torn backpack, a dark and grizzled head propped up against a tree. A black man lying there, bearded, in ragged dark clothes. Whom Liza automatically labels A Homeless Person. And she remembers Caroline's fantasy, the homeless all over the parks, armies of homeless, taking over all the "lovely homes," reclaiming space for themselves. Reclaiming this last lovely city for their own.

The man stirs, shifts his face slightly, so that for one instant Liza has a terrifying sense of recognition: could it possibly be John Lee, this derelict?

In the next instant she thinks that of course it could be, but most probably is not. However, despite herself she finds that she is hurrying faster, rushing against the possibility that this man could be someone she knows.

"I really think she must have been drunk. Maybe not totally plastered but close to it, I *know* she'd been drinking. And the venom. It was really scary, the kids were very scared, they'd never seen anything like that, and actually I was scared too. I mean, I don't suppose she's a violent person but these days anyone could be, couldn't they. You read so much about violence. Random—"

"Yes." Saul's tone as always is fairly neutral, noncommittal, but he seems to wait for her to continue.

Having decided that she should tell Saul all this about Joanne Gallo (and besides she wants to, she needs the reassurance of his listening), Liza goes on. "So nutty all around. Roland keeping the tapes of his intimate phone calls, having them in his house. What vanity!"

"Condoms in the sock drawer."

"Exactly, but a lot more cruel. And so crazy, Joanne assuming it was me she heard. God, I barely know the guy. It's got to have been Jill or Fiona, and I rather think Fiona, don't you?"

"I don't know. But you're right, you do sound incredibly alike. You all. And not like anyone else."

"There was some craziness about making love in Palermo. Is Roland a Sicilian? I suppose he is. But honestly, the poor woman. My feeling is, and of course I could be making this up, in some accidental way she played that particular tape, and it more or less pushed her over the edge. It must have been a couple of weeks ago, she mentioned his not running for mayor. I mean, she's always seemed a little, uh, upset, but now she's really out of control. This is the first time I've seen her for a couple of weeks, come to think of it."

Frowning deeply, Saul makes an ambiguous sound. Liza would swear that he means (but would not say): I haven't seen her either.

"I just don't know what to do," says Liza, vaguely. She has decided not to mention the possible John Lee to Saul.

"About anything," Saul gloomily agrees. And then, decisively, "Excuse me, I have to go phone."

"Leave me some money, will you?"

"Here's all I have on me."

Early the next morning Liza gets a phone call (it is not so early in New York, it is 10). From Kathy, the editor at *You*. "It's sort of odd the way this happened," Kathy tells her. "But it's really good news, I think. Anyway, last night my boyfriend, he's an editor at T & T, was fooling around with some stuff on the coffee table—I'm afraid I don't put things away. He picked up the galleys of your story, he's a compulsive reader by the way, and he really flipped out halfway through. The greatest Sixties stuff he's read. You've really got the tone, he went on and on. He says you've got to write a novel. This could be the first chapter, he says. And get this, he thinks he could get you an advance on what you have so far. You guys must be about the same age?"

"I'm thirty-five."

"So's he, and really suffering over it. I guess I should be more sympathetic." Kathy laughs, giving Liza to understand that she, Kathy, is of course considerably younger. Maybe just thirty.

"Well, that's really great," Liza tells Kathy.

"Well, it is, I've honestly never heard him go on like that, he's a very restrained type. You know, New England."

"But really, a novel?"

Seated at her desk, in the screened-off corner of her bedroom that she has designated as her study, the idea of a novel begins to seem slightly less implausible to Liza. There are after all these notebooks, these pages and pages of scribbling, done when that was all she had time for, she thought. Those random jottings. Random, but there they are.

She picks up one of the big loose-leaf books and, opening it, begins to skip through, not exactly reading but catching a sentence here and there that makes her smile, or frown, remembering something.

Absorbed in such contemplation, in speculations, Liza at first does not quite take in the fact that the front door downstairs has opened and closed, and that someone (it must be Saul) is hurrying toward her, hurrying upstairs. This is not unusual: when he has a cancellation or just a free hour Saul does occasionally come home. (Liza does wish he had not chosen just this moment to do so, and she scolds herself for that wish.)

Saul looks elated, and out of breath. "We have to talk," he says, as he sometimes does, positioning himself on the corner of the bed that is nearest Liza's desk. Nearest Liza.

He is very excited: can he be going to announce that he has fallen in love with someone? Liza for one instant wonders this, and in the next she castigates herself. What a vulgar, low, obvious mind I have, she thinks.

"You remember the team of doctors I told you about?" Saul asks, right off. "The medical aid in Central America? Well—"

He wants to join up. To go there to help, for a year. He had thought they did not need a psychiatrist, but it turns out that they do, very much. To help people who have been imprisoned, maybe tortured. Or maybe just very upset people. "And you know I'm very good at first aid too," Saul reminds his wife. He also reminds her, unnecessarily, of how often he has expressed frustration at what he has felt as his total uselessness, his near-despair at doing "nothing": seeing middle-class neurotics in such a needy world. "I suppose this is a form of middle-aged angst," Saul says.

"It could be a lot worse." Liza smiles. And with an odd sense of permissiveness, of motherliness, even, she thinks, Is this what women come to, finally, with men? Do they inevitably, one way or another, turn us into their mothers?

On the other hand, she very much means it, she does agree with Saul that for every reason he should go. Wherever. Ideologically and emotionally, he is right, and she is with him, supporting.

He asks, "You're not afraid I'll run off with some Salvadoran guerrilla woman?"

"No, not really. Do you want me to be? But you know how smug I am, at least according to my sisters."

Also, Liza is thinking, with Saul away she will get more writing done. She simply, surely will. One less person in her immediate orbit will make a lot of difference. She can write at night. Saul is not an especially demanding man; on the other hand, in his way he is—quite demanding.

"I'm afraid this pretty much takes care of our Mexico trip," Saul then tells her.

He sounds so rueful, so guilty-boy, that Liza can only laugh at him—as she would at a child. "Such a surprise," she tells him.

Saul grins, reprieved, and he begins to tell her more about the plans. When they will go (next month). He tells her that he thinks she should hire more help for herself. He is full of plans for them both.

And Liza listens, taking in all that he says, but mostly she is thinking, Now I can write my novel.

Twenty-eight

"You're not Fiona, what is this?" Thus speaks an angry Roland, on a black and stormy San Francisco spring night, as he strides into Fiona's penthouse boudoir—where he finds a thin blonde woman in a new pale-blue silk peignoir. A woman with very short hair, who looks unfamiliar.

"You asshole, of course it's me," Fiona tells him, with a pleased crowing laugh.

"Same foul mouth, but for all I know your sister talks the same. You must be Jill."

"In point of fact Jill does talk a lot like me, but I'm not Jill. Roland, come over here. It's me. Look at me—"

He has stopped at her door, and now he just stands there, frowning.

And since it was she who called him ("I'm frightened of all this wind," Fiona said, "I need to see you") Fiona is loath to plead further. "Desperate women have their hair cut, don't you know that?" She laughs a little.

In Fiona's house, which is almost a hundred years old, the creaking and rattling from that ferocious wind have been loud indeed, and menacing, even to Fiona, who has lived there for years. Could this be a much worse than usual storm, be actually dangerous? Or is she simply in not very good shape? Or, are both those things true: the storm indeed is formidable, such powerful winds, and beating, pelting rain—*and* she herself is vulnerable, at low ebb?

Certainly nothing lately has gone very well for her, Fiona thinks. She saw no alternative to selling Fiona's; all her instincts informed her that this was the moment, and even Jill agreed that the offered price was good. But Fiona does not know now what to do with all that money, how to make it work best for her. Nor where to live, when she has to move out.

And besides (so irritating!) there was no way for Stevie not to get a huge chunk of it, thanks to their original agreement, when he lent her a sum that now seems very minor: clever Stevie, insisting on a percentage and a high-powered contract.

And then, just when she needed him, Roland has been evasive— for months. God knows he has problems of his own right now, but so does she. He had all that mess about that creep Buck Fister, and not running for mayor after all (Fiona was very glad: who needs that kind of attention all the time?). And always crazy, drunk Joanne in the picture. Still.

"What you need now is a terrific new haircut," was Jill's advice (Jill is now living temporarily downstairs, Fiona hopes it's temporary; Jill is getting her own shit together). Jill sent Fiona to her own great stylist. "The price will knock you on your ass," Jill warned. "But it's just about the same as an hour with a first-class shrink, think of it that way." And so Fiona did, and she came out looking wonderful, she thought. Not much like Jill at all.

"You're right, this is some storm," agrees Roland, now advancing toward her bed. "This old house really creaks, it's good you're moving. God knows what an earthquake would do to it." Sitting beside her, he picks up her hand and begins to kiss it, but sexily, using his tongue. "You are my Fiona," he tells her, "I know your taste. But, my darling, it's not like you to be afraid of a storm."

Please stop talking. I just want to be fucked. Fiona would like to say that but of course she does not.

She smiles, though, and twists toward him, reaching to curl her fingers around his wrist, pulling him very gently, and thinking: How I dislike him, this bald old man, with his big fat pink-gray cock, its droopy foreskin. How can I want such a man? And then, as he begins to kiss her mouth, But I do want him, a lot.

"My darling, I seem not to be myself," explains Roland, some ten or fifteen minutes later, as they lie nakedly and unhappily enmeshed. "Would you believe that this has never happened to me before?"

"Sure." Fiona does not believe him: she takes him to mean that he is only infrequently so disabled, which she knows to be true. Surprisingly (Fiona is surprised), she is not angry, she feels quite tender toward him, the poor old bastard. "Tell me how you've been," she says. "Somehow we never talk. We could now."

Roland sighs. "My soap-opera life." Like a beached whale he turns over on his back—but this is unfair, thinks Fiona; he is large but not fat.

"Most recently," continues Roland, "Joanne has decided to leave me for Betty Ford. The drinking had got a lot worse. All morning, drunk. So she quit. Went down there. But I'm supposed to show up for interviews. They like what they call the total picture."

As Roland talks—and it is quite true that they have never had a conversation—Fiona listens, and strokes his muscular stomach lightly, twisting body hairs gently, affectionately.

He should never have married Joanne, now says Roland. And he did so for the oldest, most chivalrously foolish reason of all: Joanne was pregnant. "And over thirty, she thought she might never conceive again."

"Why didn't you marry Sage, do you think?"

"It would have wrecked her life. I believe she sees that now. But I knew it then, I could see it. A brilliant and talented woman should never marry an old Sicilian pol like me."

"Of course you're absolutely right." Fiona wonders just when this version was invented; probably some years after his breakup with Sage, she imagines. "How smart of you to have seen that," she tells Roland.

"Lucky for Sage that I did."

"Oh, right." But you could marry me, that would work out perfectly for both of us. We could more or less retire together. Buy something big but dignified, really elegant, in Hillsborough, or maybe up in Ross, with a pool and maybe horses. Just live in a nice quiet elegant way, we could look like a Ralph Lauren ad. I could learn to cook, at last (Fiona as she thinks this enjoys the nice irony). Maybe even have a couple of kids, she thinks, and the little girl, whatever her name is, could come and stay sometimes. Not too often, she should be with her mother. Joanne would be all out of Betty Ford, graduated and okay, recovered.

Fiona herself is surprised by the total correctness of this picture. Odd that she had never thought of it before.

She murmurs, "Shall I kiss you?"

"Mmm."

She does so, moving slowly down to him, taking him in.

"You're the greatest in the world," she tells him, somewhat later.

"You're a very dear girl," says Roland.

Hearing some new note in his voice, something not exactly madly in love, Fiona chooses to ignore it: she has her own plans. "How awful of you to look at your watch," she says, for that is what he has just surreptitiously done.

"My dearest, I told you, Joanne is in very bad shape. I gave her some excuse about a meeting, but this is not a time to upset her more."

"I thought—Betty Ford—"

"That's tomorrow." He looks at his watch—again. "And now it's late," he says. "But the storm is over, you won't be frightened any more."

"Roland, I really wanted to talk."

"But love, we have talked."

"Roland, I insist on ten minutes more of your time."

Roland smiles his most appeasing, most political-Sicilian smile. "My darling, I grant you ten minutes."

"Roland, I think we should get married."

He stares. "You can't be serious. That's terribly sweet and flattering, but you must not be serious."

"I am." She stares into his eyes. "It's the most perfect idea."

"You must be mad."

"I am not mad. I want us to get married. Have a house. I know of one in Ross, with a pool. Stables. We could have children." She smiles.

"You are mad. I thought you were a sensible woman."

"I am not a sensible woman. I just want to be married. To you."

"For one thing, you seem to forget that I am married."

"I didn't forget. But Jesus, you're a lawyer."

Roland begins to get out of bed, at the same time reaching toward his clothes. "While Joanne is at Betty Ford I will go to Sicily with my daughter, to collect ourselves, so to speak. And to visit my mother."

"Your mother!"

Pulling up boxer shorts (an old-fashioned touch that Fiona has always appreciated, that crisp Sea Island cotton), and then long black socks, with some dignity Roland tells her, "My mother is ninety-seven. A most marvellous woman. I do not see her only out of duty."

"I couldn't believe it," Fiona tells Jill. "First he asks me to marry him, and then in the next breath he tells me that his mother is coming over from Sicily to live with him, with *us,* and she is *ninety-seven.* Not to mention his creepy daughter."

"What a jerk." Jill, who is smoking heavily these days (one among many things about her that are driving Fiona crazy), now lights another cigarette, her fourth during breakfast; Fiona counts.

"And he wants to stay right there in his house on Pacific, you know, right across from horrible Julius Kahn, where Liza used to go and smoke dope all the time and God knows what else, with those black guys. You'd think he'd know that it's time to get out of town."

Having hit on this version of her conversation with Roland, Fiona is finding it more and more plausible. He did more or less say that he couldn't get married now because he was going to see his mother, didn't he? Fiona has almost convinced herself that he did.

Fiona has a truly remarkable capacity for self-deception; and she believes her stories. She could very easily have fallen into a black and painful despondency, over Roland—but instead she managed to think, How dare he? and she made up this story to try out on Jill, a story that in time she will come to believe herself—almost.

"I'd really like to get back at him somehow," in a musing way she says to Jill.

"Why not?"

Jill is not really paying attention, but Fiona is used to that with her sister, these days. Jill is still not at all in good shape, though at least she has started back to work, she is not around the house all

day, as at first she was. And Fiona assumes that soon Jill will move
back to her own apartment.

"He thought I was you at first," Fiona tells Jill. "My new short
hair. Maybe you could pretend to be me, maybe we could get at
him that way."

"My call-girl time could come in handy."

"WHAT?"

Jill laughs. "I used to turn tricks." As she says this her look at
Fiona is speculative; she is wondering (Fiona thinks) if Fiona will
believe her. "I used to get a thousand bucks."

"Such a liar, you really are. Honestly, Jill."

"Okay, I'm a liar. But I might as well have, if you see what I
mean."

"You wouldn't dare turn tricks. Jesus. AIDS."

"Okay, you're right, I wouldn't dare. But what does this famous
Roland like best?"

"You mean in the sack?"

"Of course."

Fiona studies this question for a moment, then mentions an act
that she is fairly certain Roland would find abhorrent; he is actually
far more conventional than she would like Jill to believe.

"Yuck, who does he think he is, Norman Mailer?"

Fiona laughs, feeling obscurely that she has won some contest
with Roland. "Well, you asked," she says.

"Well, in that case I won't."

"Okay, it was just an idea." The relief that she now feels informs
Fiona of just how much she did not want Jill in bed with Roland,
doing *anything.* And at the same time (not quite coincidentally) she
observes how very much better her sister looks today. After last
night's wild rains the air is now washed and fresh, and even in that
very hard light Jill's skin is clear and pale, and her eyes are bright—
as though in the night she had come upon some cheering information. Maybe a phone call, turning her life around.

And so it is not entirely surprising when Jill then says, "Today's
the day, I know you'll be happy to hear. I'm off at last."

"Well, I'm not all that happy."

"Oh, come on, Fi, don't overdo. You've been great, you really
have. A true pal in need. In fact a sister."

"I guess it is time you went back there, though."

"To Telegraph Hill? But I'm not, I'm heading out to Stinson again. I really like it there."

"You don't mind the beach by yourself?"

"Well, I could always head over to Bolinas and check out our baby Ports, couldn't I?"

"You mean the heiress. She's probably all wrapped up in her Bernal digs. With that creepy Polish lawyer."

"Lebanese. Probably. But no. One, I don't mind Stinson alone, I sort of like it. And two, this time I don't plan to be alone there." And Jill gives a satisfied smile.

Fiona smiles too, having learned what she had already intuited from her sister's whole demeanor. From her skin.

Having Jill gone is not exactly the improvement in Fiona's life that she thought it would be, though. The lack of her sister, who is not at the moment available even for phone calls (something about the people who own the place not paying their bill), simply underlines and emphasizes all the other lacks in Fiona's life: she is suddenly without significant occupation, the restaurant is more or less running by itself. And she is also without any lover—a condition relatively new to her, and entirely unpleasant.

Twenty-nine

The Stinson Beach house is now for sale and stripped almost bare; as well as there being no phone, there is almost no furniture. Just basics: the bed, kitchen table, two chairs and the long hard living-room sofa. The heavy things. No draperies or curtains or lamps, just overhead lights. Not a great place to be alone in any more, Jill thinks—good that Noel is coming out.

"Of course you know where it is," she told him, calling at last, on the stormy night when she was still at Fiona's. While Fiona was upstairs fucking Roland Gallo, probably. "I saw you there at Stinson, the day you came after me," she said to Noel.

"Jesus, you did? Why didn't you come out from wherever you were? Jesus, what a bitch!"

"I didn't feel like seeing you right then."

"But you do now?"

"Now I really do. I told you."

"Well, just hold on for a couple of days. There's some stuff I have to pull together. I'll be out Tuesday night."

How like him to put her off for a while, Jill thinks. There's always more than a little power play with Noel. And maybe with me? She asks herself this question, does not answer.

In any case, on Tuesday, she hopes he gets there before dark—an hour or so from now. For one thing, the road out there is dangerous in some places, skirting the slopes of Tamalpais, winding and winding high up above steep gorges. Jill herself has just come in from a sunset beach walk, rather hoping that Noel would have shown up while she was out; that would be very good for him, she thought. But of course he did not—and there she sits in the foggy cool gray dusk. Somewhat worried.

Also, anyone passing can see right into the house; this too seems a little risky. Getting up to turn off lights, Jill is gratified at the thought of giving Noel just a little more trouble: he will have to come looking for her, all through the darkened house.

She wishes, though, that she did not know all those dizzying curves of the road by heart; it is far too easy to imagine Noel rounding each one of them, and at last not quite making it. Over-confident Noel at the wheel.

And then it occurs to Jill that there is absolutely nothing in the house to eat. All she has, she remembers, is some very fancy cigarettes that a man at work laid on her some time back ("Doctored—they've been through the Mayo Clinic," said their donor). She had thought she and Noel might try them out, but let's hope they don't make us hungry, Jill adds to herself; this is not exactly blind-munchy time. I don't even think there're any cornflakes.

There is, Jill observes to herself, a kind of woman for whom laying in food supplies, special goodies, is very much a part of getting ready to be visited by a man; she remembers a friend who at the end of a significant romance complained, "There I was with a refrigerator full of smoked salmon, which I don't even like very much." And there was always Caroline, bountifully feeding men (searching out Tex-Mex recipes, all that bean stuff that Ralph really loved). But Jill's own view of romantic protocol is at variance with all that: in her imagination a really super lover would himself arrive with a great big hamper of food, a basket of crazy, marvellous stuff, and some really good wine.

And that is almost exactly what Noel does. From her perch in the living room Jill hears and recognizes his car (no one else brakes like that) and then in a moment she sees him rounding the corner of her patio, and sees that he is burdened by a very large hamper. At that moment (not only because of the hamper, though it does seem a very good sign) Jill believes that this will be one of the greatest nights of her life. Even if Noel has only cornflakes in his hamper.

She rewards him by rushing out, not making him look around

for her after all, as she had more or less planned. She wraps herself against him, prolonging their kiss.

Running his free hand down her thigh, "You're *really* skinny now," Noel tells her. "I brought some cholesterol booster for you."

"Great. I have some high-powered cigarettes, but I paid the earth for them." Might as well make him think that she too went to a little trouble, big expense.

"Well, super. I have a little wheeze."

Possibly because she hadn't seen him for a while Noel looks, to Jill, extremely beautiful. Slightly flushed from the exertion of the drive (and possibly the excitement of her, he is excited) his skin is fine and fresh, his narrow eyes are brilliant and his thick dark hair, as always a little long, is becomingly disheveled.

"I walked out and saw the sunset," Jill tells him, and they both just stand there on the patio for a minute, in the fading light from the glowing reddish sky. Looking at Noel, at the thin perfect line of his nose and his perfectly curved mouth, Jill has the odd thought that this is the most beautiful moment of his life. Forever after this his handsomeness will blur, will steadily, very slowly decline.

She says, "Well, come on in. I can't wait to see all your goodies."

What Noel has brought is: Bread and cheese and wine. And some apples and grapes and pears. Big brownies.

A little ordinary, Jill thinks. But she appreciates his effort; he meant to please, to be nice to her. He is just not a very sophisticated person. Not original.

Once they are settled on the sofa with all their supplies, it then becomes hard to choose—what to do first, to eat or drink or smoke. Or snort. And so for a time they just sit there, while their eyes run over everything before them.

Sage has thrown him out of the house, Noel says. Their house. "Jesus, the work I put into that place. For that broad."

Noel has boasted that he was the first dropout from Mission High, and he has never mentioned parents; no relatives came to his wedding, just a few offbeat carpenter friends; one might suspect that if he has any people he is not exactly proud of them. But all that is evident in the way he talks, Jill muses: lack of education, lack of family. As she also thinks, God, I sound like my grandmother. Social class is really what it all comes down to, though, which no one ever mentions and which you are not supposed to think about, but there it is, everyone thinks of it all the time or at least is aware of it.

And she could never marry Noel, never, never, for just those reasons. This realization, never before quite so clear to her, gives Jill a certain feeling of power, in terms of their connection. She wants absolutely nothing from Noel, which means that she can do anything she wants to, with him.

"How about a smoke?" she now asks. "Chuck, who sold me this stuff, said it was really wild."

Noel laughs. "Well, okay, let's get wild." He has a good laugh, if very slightly phony; it is deep and controlled, a lot better than his speaking voice.

First they do a very little coke, then they light up.

Whatever is in the long fat doctored cigarettes at first makes them cough, and cough again, both Noel and Jill; they are laughing and coughing, bent forward on the huge sofa.

There was something powerful in that first hit, though. Jill feels somewhat unreal, and maybe Noel does too. She sees a slight confusion on his face, he looks disoriented, mildly.

"Okay," Noel says, "let's go for wild. I'm ready, are you?"

"Well, I think so."

They toke again, in silence. There is only, from the beach, the darkness, the heavy rhythmic periodic crash of waves, both loud and very remote. As though the waves were breaking in some cold dark other country.

Then Jill says, "What I am is hungry, I'm starving."

"Me too. I haven't eaten for a couple of years, I feel like. Not anything."

As they put out all that food, unceremoniously spread on the floor at their feet, as they bend, picking up things, eating ravenously, messily, somewhere in a corner of Jill's mind is the observation that they are not falling upon each other, Christ, they are not even kissing. Whatever this is it does not seem to be a sex drug. Or, not so far.

They eat all the food, each small scrap of bread, each grape, and they finish off both bottles of wine, only stopping occasionally to take more drags from the magic cigarettes.

Outside in the night a thin sharp wind has come up, it tears through this flimsy summer house, as boards creak, and windows rattle.

Noel says, "I wish we had a little plane, or a chopper."

"Oh yes, to be up in the wind. Or a boat."

"Yes, the sea. The rough."

"Yes, wind!"

"Birds!"

Crazy. And at the same time as they are having this loopy exchange they are also, as though unaware of what they are doing, kissing and removing their clothes, and then coupling, there on the hard cold bare floor.

A little later, or possibly several hours later, it is Jill who says, "God, I'm so cold."

"Let's make a fire. I am too. Freezing."

"But there's no wood. No nothing."

"Rotten people."

And then Jill says, "Oh, but I know where there's a wonderful warm fireplace. And it's near here."

"Great. Then we won't have to burn the furniture. Or burn the house down."

"There's no furniture here to burn, you silly fool."

"Well, Jesus. Let's go. But first a little snort."

Not locking, barely closing the door, they run out into the night, to Jill's car. Noel wants to drive.

"But you don't know where we're going."

"I do. I will. You just think of it real hard and I'll receive your message. Directions."

They skid out of the *calle* and onto the bumpy dirt road, fast past those dumb middle-class houses, past night walkers who skitter off the sides of the road like birds. And on, on to the main road, where they take a left, around the lagoon.

Where—ah!—Noel makes the car fly over the water! although that is quite impossible, anyone knows a car would sink, no matter who was driving, but even many months later, by which time God knows she is straight and sober, that is what Jill remembers: her wild yellow Mercedes winging fleet across the slick black water. Water shining below them, shining ahead.

She does not remember the accident: the explosion and fire that almost killed them both—in Bolinas, near Portia's house, their presumable destination.

Thirty

"One of the first things I'm going to do is join AA. For one thing, I hear it's the greatest for meeting people. The new singles scene," says Jill, from her narrow white bed.

Portia smiles, then remembers that, since Jill cannot turn to see her, she has to speak. "Probably a good idea," she says.

"Well, I have abused a few substances in my time." And then, "Do you think Sage will come to see me?"

"Probably," Portia repeats.

"Shit. How I wish she wouldn't. What an impossible conversation, the one we'd have to have."

"I could ask her not to for a while."

"Would you really, Ports? That would be most kind of you."

Jill's hair is lank, a darker blonde than usual, and her un-made-up skin is sallow, yellowish. Her face was not burned in the accident, no bandages, but her upper body is still immobilized; she suffered some burns there, and in falling backwards (no one can quite account for this fall, least of all Jill) she fractured both arms and shoulders. She thus can only look straight ahead, generally she keeps her eyes closed. Portia, her most frequent visitor, has made note of this, but she still tends to forget that Jill does not see her. "Sage will understand," she now says. "I doubt if she's exactly dying to have that conversation either."

"Is she, uh, pretty upset about Noel?" Jill seems not to remember that she has asked this several times. On the other hand, she may be on painkilling drugs that affect her recall. Or, Portia has thought, she may be questioning her own feelings about the near-death of Noel, his undoubted terrible burns, and scars. (Noel somehow had himself transferred from Ross General, where they were taken, that night, up to another hospital, in Grass Valley.)

"She's not as upset as she might be if she weren't so busy," Portia tells Jill.

"Well, that's good. I guess."

It is not clear to Portia just why most of the hospital duty with Jill has fallen to her. "You think that, since she was hurt while engaged in driving toward your house, you owe her perpetual care," Hilda has said, with unusual asperity, only modified by one of her mysterious, oblique dark smiles.

"Well, you're right, that would be my kind of logic," Portia agrees, half laughing.

Somewhat closer to the truth (Portia believes) is the simple fact that no one else is around: Caroline has suddenly and most surprisingly gone to Europe—at the moment she is in Paris, having left the day before the accident. Informed of what happened, she now telephones, and Portia has reassured her that no, she does not have to come home, Jill is doing well, Sage is all right. And although all that is quite true (Sage is indeed quite all right), because of Noel, Sage seems hardly the person to care for Jill. Besides, she is much too busy.

Liza comes to see Jill, but her visits are never long, with Saul away (he is in some sort of training camp, in Chiapas, Mexico, near the Guatemalan border) Liza is extremely busy with her children, as well as with trying to write. Fiona is in New York and in various parts of New England, being interviewed by various business schools; she wants to get a degree in corporation management, or corporation something—Portia is unable to follow this plan. Fiona wants to get out of San Francisco.

And that leaves Portia, who is still here, and spending most of her time with Jill.

And, when not with Jill, she is at home with Hilda. Absorbing, listening to, laughing with—simply enjoying Hilda, who moved to Bernal Heights, to Portia's house, during the week before the accident.

Knowing each other at once so intimately and in other ways not at all has made for some difficulties; both Portia and Hilda have had to acknowledge this to each other. They are, and have been since their first dinner together, "in love"; however, their eating and sleeping habits, those boring but irrefutably demanding basics, are vastly different. Portia, a California girl with certain distant Texan roots, is essentially a day person—up early, instantly vigorous, hungry for breakfast. Whereas Hilda wakes slowly from a troubled sleep, from whatever Middle Eastern dreams of violence; she is not quite herself until noon. And then by nightfall she is vividly alive, prepared to listen to music, talk, prepared for anything, including love, until long past midnight.

Portia tends toward healthy California food, whereas Hilda, whose girlhood was spent in Paris, Tangier, Beirut, likes richer, much more exotic fare. In tiny portions.

All this has still to be resolved, and so far, at times, the results have been somewhat dismaying: there was Portia's perfect fresh grilled swordfish—which Hilda topped with a (perfect) *crème fraîche*-cilantro sauce. And there were Hilda's exquisite *profiteroles,* produced to accompany Portia's first-of-season raspberries, from Real Food.

Not to mention the prolonged and intense political discussions: the threats of war in Iraq-Iran-Lebanon. The true character of Arafat. And what should be done, really, with the West Bank?

On the first night that Hilda finally came to dinner (Portia had called on the day after her father's death, which occurred on the night of the day they met)—after that dinner, at which Portia had talked more than she meant to of Ralph, sometimes with tears but more often in an intense effort to get across to this new friend, Hilda, some sense of what he was like, this waterfront man from Texas—after all that talk it was Hilda who simply rose and came over to lean down to Portia for a kiss, and then to say, "And now you must please let me take you to bed."

Which she did. For Portia, there was amazing revelation, and former confusions clarified. For Hilda, the more experienced, there was also revelation, of love. "I find myself astounded," she said to Portia, with a laugh of disbelief. "My terrible war-torn cynical self. In love."

And so it is Portia who sits beside Jill's tight white hospital bed (the same hospital, Presbyterian, that both Molly Blair and then Ralph were in); she sits there longing for Hilda, looking forward to Hilda. Talking, in her secret mind, to Hilda.

As Jill, who is getting better fast, talks more and more. "Needless to say I do feel the most horrendous guilt." She repeats this sentence, with variations, frequently. "Screwing your sister's husband, even a half-sister's, that's got to be the worst. And the terrible thing is—Portia, you must never tell this to anyone—I really didn't like him all that much. Oh, at first I was sort of crazy about him, but I never really wanted him for me. I would never have married Noel, he has absolutely no class." And then, "Oh Jesus, it's all so horrible. I can't wait to get into AA."

Once she asks, "Do you mean you're really in love with this woman, this Hilda Daid, the lawyer?"

"Well yes, you could put it like that."

"Tell me something, is it simpler with women? I mean just getting along?"

"I honestly don't know, I've had so little experience with men. Or for that matter with women either." Portia makes an effort to examine what she is saying. "I wouldn't say that things with Hilda are exactly simple. Just, uh, very good."

Jim McAndrew's visits to his daughter are brief and awkward, so that Portia, who is usually there when he comes, is for the first time aware of what Caroline has sometimes complained of; Jim's entire capacity for affection and for intimacy is directed toward his patients, has been Caroline's claim.

Caroline's Daughters

Jim and Jill discuss her symptoms, the stiffness and burn pain—since she is not a patient, but just his daughter, Jill's most frequent sentence to her father is simply, "When am I getting out of here?" Which Portia often takes as a cue to leave.

But Jim in his stiff white lab coat is far more impressive than in the old Brooks garb that Portia has usually seen him wear, on those infrequent occasions when they have met at all. (He must feel quite odd about her, Portia believes; she would be for him the product of his wife's adulterous love. Or perhaps he does not think in those terms at all.) Portia has never understood Jim's great attraction for Sage, except in the most rudimentary "Freudian" terms. Nor can she really understand why Caroline was ever sufficiently attracted to marry Jim. In any case, though, Jim as "the doctor" is clearer, more in focus and more confident than in the discarded-husband, uneasy-guest roles in which Portia has seen him before.

"Don't let me force you out of here, now, please, Portia," Jim tells her, flashing his doctor smile, which is quick and confident. Then, checking his watch, "I've just got a couple of minutes."

"No, I really have to get home. Dinner," Portia murmurs. "Okay, Jill. See you tomorrow."

"Ports, you really don't have to come every day. But of course I love it when you do," Jill tells her.

This grateful Jill is quite a new person, to Portia. (Even Caroline has been heard to complain that Jill has never thanked anyone, for anything.) And she still looks quite unlike herself, with her short unwashed hair plastered down to her skull, her staring eyes no longer dark-rimmed, fringed. And Portia wonders, how will Jill be when she really gets all better, and gets into AA, as she insists that her plan is?

"What is it about doctors, really? Why are so many women turned on by them? I wonder if men are." Portia, at dinner, asks these questions more of herself than as someone expecting an answer. And as soon as she has voiced them she rather wishes that she had not—or, that she had waited until she and Hilda were alone: at the moment they have two guests, Sage and Stevie.

Hilda, though, emerging from the shyness with which she has so far been stricken, takes it up. "I think it has to do with power," she says. "The old equation of power and sexuality."

Stevie: "That's extremely interesting. I bet you're right. Not, as commonly supposed, so much their access to forbidden body parts."

Hilda: "That too, but less so, I believe."

Stevie: "Terrible, isn't it. An equation of total power over your life, which is far from always benign—with sex."

Hilda: "Indeed."

Stevie: "Of course, to be totally fair, I have to say that we're ignoring the helping aspect of doctors."

Hilda: "Yes, there is that, but I don't think that's what's sexy."

Pleased that the guests are getting along, and rather surprised at this dialogue which she herself seems to have instigated, Portia for the moment simply listens. She is also pleased that the whole implication of her remark was not apparent: she was speaking of course of Jim McAndrew, and she could just as well have said, Just what does anyone see in Jim McAndrew?

"Sometimes I think I only like gay men," is Sage's contribution. And then, with a small ambiguous laugh in the direction of her friend, "No offense, Stevie."

Good-naturedly he tells her, "Well, actually me too. At least half my friends are gay, which can be more than a little sad these days. Four lost already this year."

At which they all say yes, fervently, and then are quiet for a while.

"And the other half are women," Stevie next says, successfully breaking that moment of mourning. "I really like women friends."

This is visibly true, if the present moment is a sample of how Stevie "relates" to women. In the company of this somewhat heterogeneous trio, he is clearly much at ease. His plump soft body even seems to enlarge, to expand, as he sits so relaxed in Portia's (Mrs. Kaltenborn's) largest shabby leather chair, which creaks a little as he shifts his considerable weight.

They are having coffee, after an extremely good if slightly eccentric dinner—combined efforts by Portia and Hilda, their Middle Eastern–Texas–California cuisine.

"I really could not have got through the last few weeks without Calvin Crome," says Sage. "What a kind and really magic person in my life."

"You're forgiving him for making you so rich?" Stevie asks this with great affection, as though the question were familiar, one often repeated between them. And then he says, more or less to everyone, "Sage and I are the perfect example of what happens to old hippies. We get rich. If not conservative."

"Yes, but we really didn't mean to," Sage tells him. "You didn't know that Fiona would ever sell Fiona's."

"No, not really. But I saw to it that I had a very clever contract, so maybe in some sense I did know."

"You're too hard on yourself, you know that?"

"Unlike you." He laughs at her.

Sage then says, "Ports, I guess I do have to go and see Jill?" This was actually a question.

"Well, not necessarily," Portia tells her, somewhat guardedly.

"You think not? You're probably right, she could be dreading it too. Dreading me."

"Well, sure."

"And I have to admit, I am pretty angry. Which I might as well not say to Jill," Sage continues. "But of all the sleaze, getting it on with your sister's husband."

Stevie asks, "Did it ever come out what her connection was with that Buck Fister?"

"Not really," Sage tells him. "I suppose it might have if he hadn't got himself offed. By the Mafia, probably. And probably Jill was one of his girls, turning tricks for him."

"Oh, Sage."

"Sage, really."

"Sage, you're too harsh, really."

"Well, I've got some reason to be mad at her, don't you think? And even if she wasn't turning tricks, Fister is a very suspect person to have as a friend. I think Jill is basically dreadful!" Sage cries out, suddenly unleashed. "I've really had it with her, with her hundred-dollar panty hose—"

"How on earth do you know that?"

"She told me once. Actually boasting. And twice a week a masseur and three times comb-outs and every other day a manicure. Jesus, I hate yuppies. They're immoral. Hundred-dollar panty hose is immoral." In her passion Sage's voice trembles, edged with tears.

Stevie pours some red wine into her glass—a beautiful Mexican swirled blue, Mrs. Kaltenborn's glasses. "Baby, we all hate yuppies," he tells her. "Even yuppies hate yuppies. But you're right, they consort with the enemy, they're bad."

Sage is crying now, tears streaming down, and her voice is uncontrolled, but still she is trying to talk, to say something. "Well, you can see that my going to visit Jill is not such a great idea," she gets out. Her laugh is a croak. "I must be drunk, I think. Stevie, take me home?"

"Would you say that Stevie is gay? Is that what Sage meant?" Hilda asks this of Portia as together they try to clean up their disordered kitchen. Lively Hilda and sleepy, failing Portia.

"Well, I don't know. She could have meant that, I guess."

"Or is he possibly one of those men who are quite at peace with their feminine natures? Their animas. Often such men seem to be gay but are not, in all ways they are deeply fond of women."

"Well, I guess. Hilda, don't you think we could get a dishwasher? Everyone has them."

"Would not Sage then accuse us of yuppiness? My darling, for this night you have a dishwasher, who is myself. And now would you please go up to bed?"

Thirty-one

Waking in Ravello, an hour or so south of Naples, on the morning after a very late and somewhat problematic arrival at this inaccessible, mountaintop hotel, Caroline sees the slits of sunlight between the louvers, in the long wide windows. She sees and feels that indeed it must be morning, and so she gets up, she goes to open a shutter, and she sees what she never could have imagined: a bright vista of small steep olive fields, bordered by gray stone fences; tiny houses with sloping red-tiled roofs, gardens, everywhere trees and flowers; a miniature woman, blue-aproned, in her doorway; a man with a wheelbarrow; a horse and a goat; and far off in the shimmering pale-blue silver distance the sea, the Mediterranean. Caroline gasps and almost laughs with the sheer surprise of it all, of what she sees, the amazing beauty. A painter's dream of a morning, she thinks to herself.

She arrived the night before at a darkened entrance: a gate, a terrace, steps and a massive, barely illuminated door with a big brass plate. Bearing a name. A bellboy mysteriously appeared, opened her car door and took in her bags—there seemed no question as to her destination.

Quite punchy with fatigue, Caroline stood beside her pile of luggage in the entrance hall, on a black-and-white marble floor, noting a broad carpeted staircase with intricately carved banisters—leading upstairs? to beds?—as she watched the bellboy in some sort of conference, or argument, with a sleekly white-haired, rather corpulent person behind the desk. They both were gesturing, scowling, as Caroline was acutely aware of a longing to be in any bed at all.

She was allowed, though, only to wash up (in a surprisingly institutional, utilitarian, large bathroom, on the ground floor) before being ushered into what she could dimly make out to be a magnificent dining room: deep-drawn draperies, presumably over windows that looked out to some sort of view. And a dozen or so small round white-clothed tables, above one and only one of which a delicate crystal-hung chandelier shone down.

Seated alone in such splendor, she was soon served by a young blond white-coated waiter, who brought her a chilled green bottle of wine. Then cold chicken, a plate of sliced tomatoes. Some cheese and bread and butter.

Feeling drunk from her first sip of wine, which was dry and delicious, heady, Caroline said to the white-haired owner, "This is the most elegant supper I've ever had." He had appeared discreetly to inquire.

He bowed and smiled, reminding her suddenly but imprecisely of someone, someone—and then, as the smile receded, she saw that it was Roland. For a single exhausted and quite unnerving moment Caroline felt that Roland had followed her there—disguised, in a white wig, an affable innkeeper manner.

In the morning, though, waking to that view, and to no Roland, to her own wide restful private bed, Caroline thinks, How ridiculous, how very silly I do get, sometimes when I'm tired. Roland Gallo has undoubtedly propositioned at least several women since me, and no doubt with large success, his turn-downs must be as rare as hen's teeth.

"How brave you are, going all the way off to Italy by yourself." Almost everyone said that to Caroline, with a few individual variations. Even her daughters said it. And Saul, the favorite, reliable son-in-law, surprised her by asking, privately and highly seriously, "Caroline, are you really sure you want to do this?"

"It's actually much easier and much less brave than staying at home." That is what Caroline would have liked to say, and what she felt to be true. But she did not say that. Staying at home was indeed far harder to do; there were whole lists of simple and highly complicated demands, from people and from the house itself, enough to fill all her time.

And there at home was where she missed Ralph most. At many times, in many corners—in bed—at times intolerably.

But in Italy, and especially in Rome, Caroline walked all day, savoring the crowds and sheer foreignness, the frenetic bustle of streets, the rare shadowed peace of gardens. She was not thinking at all, she believed—she was simply enjoying the privilege, rare in her life, of being all alone.

At night, alone, she went out to restaurants, dressed up in her best (each night a new restaurant, but the same fairly old best dress). She held her head high, and shamelessly eavesdropped on all possible conversations. She ate pasta and marvellous veal and beautiful fruits and cheeses—and did not gain weight. She drank a lot of wine.

One day, in the Villa Julia, at a distance, Caroline noticed a smartly dressed American woman, navy silk with big white polka dots, who strongly reminded her of someone, somewhere—or was she only a type, from the mold of upper-class women everywhere—especially during the Fifties, all those women in their silks and hats and gloves, seemingly going underground or elsewhere in the Sixties and most of the Seventies, to resurface with bells on, so to speak, in the super-rich Eighties. And then Caroline thought, It is Mary Higgins Lord, who did not, after all, become a homeless, chanting bag lady.

On closer viewing, though, the polka-dot woman is far too young to be Higgsie Lord, and her eyes are dark, not pale yellow. She is neither a type nor a recognized person, then, but a very young, very proper, slightly overdressed young woman, whose moist upper lip betrays some crucial error: she has worn too much silk for the day, which is very hot.

She will have to call Jim McAndrew as soon as she gets

home, Caroline determines. Perhaps Caroline can find Higgsie herself.

In the meantime she simply wanders about Ravello, through gardens with sudden, breathtaking views of the sea, past courtyards of white stone statuary, sometimes stopping at a small open café for coffee, or an apéritif. A woman alone, testing waters—though Caroline herself would probably describe her activities as resting.

Tomaso, her white-haired host, remains discreetly, availably helpful. Would she like a trip to Capri, to Paestum or to Pompei? Any or all of those could be most easily arranged. But Caroline thinks not, actually (she has been to all those places with Ralph, on one of their Italian tours—though not to Ravello, which was one fact that brought her here). Caroline has the sense too that should she show the slightest interest Tomaso would also make himself available to her, a very temporary, probably very thoughtful lover. But she lacks that interest—entirely.

It is Tomaso, though, who wakes her from a longer-than-usual siesta—to announce, of all things, a phone call. (No room phones: she must come downstairs to take it.)

"From the States?" Caroline has thought first, of course, of her daughters, of some possible new disaster in any of their lives.

"No, it comes in fact from Palermo. Much less far." Tomaso smiles, secretly.

Hurrying toward the phone, Caroline is thinking, Roland, of course, but however did he—? And then in an instant she decides that since he could only have got her number from one of her daughters, with all of whom she leaves itineraries, she does not want to know which daughter, how, why.

"Well, here I am in Palermo," Roland tells her, quite as though from the next room. "I've tracked you down!"

Sensing that he would like to be asked how he did so, Caroline again decides not to ask, and only comments, "You sound much closer."

A laugh. "Well, actually I could be, but I'm not quite as tricky as all that. Palermo is absolutely marvellous, though." He pauses, lightly clears his throat. "In fact I have high hopes of persuading you to join me here."

"Roland, really—"

"What you would do, my dear Caroline, is to go down to Naples, easy enough by car, Tomaso could handle it for you, and from Naples a most pleasant overnight boat to Palermo, where, in the morning, I greet you. You see? It is almost all arranged."

But I don't want to come to Palermo, is what Caroline would have liked to say. Instead she temporizes, "How nice of you to have thought it all out."

"It's as good as done," Roland tells her, somewhat too emphatically. "I have the hotel reservation for you, can you stay a week, two weeks?"

"My dear Roland, actually I can't come to Palermo at all, nice as it sounds. I'm meeting a friend in Madrid next week. An old school friend."

"You fly to Madrid from Naples?"

"Uh, yes." *Can* one fly to Madrid from Naples? Caroline very much hopes so.

"Well, in that case, a slight detour to Palermo. Perfecto."

"Roland, I'm sorry, but I honestly cannot come to Palermo."

A pause. "Then perhaps I should come to you there."

"I think not, on the whole. Thanks, though."

"But, my dear Caroline, I had at least two things of the utmost importance to say to you."

But I don't want you here, Caroline does not say. However, she does manage, "I have to tell you, Roland, that I'm much enjoying being by myself. You know, I've had rather little of that in my life, and I value it now."

A long, no doubt expensive pause. "In that case I must come to you there."

"No, Roland, honestly. Please don't. Really. Please."

Roland arrives about mid-morning of the following day, having taken the Palermo–Naples boat and driven (surely madly) up from Naples.

Seemingly not wishing to commit themselves to a single place, any venue for what must be a difficult conversation, for an hour or so they simply walk about, Roland and Caroline. Each, perhaps, playing for time.

It is over Camparis at Caroline's small café that Roland, as though from the blue, begins to talk about Buck Fister.

"It is true that we were friends," Roland tells her, earnestly. "I talked to him, I don't know, something about him seemed to invite certain conversations. As you have no doubt observed, ordinarily men do not have conversations with each other."

"Yes, it seems very sad for them."

"Indeed so. In any case I did find myself talking to Buck, we had enjoyable lunches, though not with great frequency. It always seemed that it was I who talked, though. I had not noticed this, I had not thought of it, not giving it much attention. And then—" Roland scowls, as his voice simultaneously deepens and strains, as though he now speaks from great dark depths, with great effort. "And then one day he talked to me," Roland with difficulty says, "and he told me in some detail of what he was doing. His business—his business with girls."

"Girls?" Tired Caroline is not picking up the threads of this conversation.

"His, uh, traffic. The prostitution."

"Oh." But why are we talking about this, and why now? Caroline would like to know.

"But not with prostitutes. With *nice girls.* The prostitution of nice girls." Roland brings these last words out heavily, large stones on the table between them. Ugly stones, repellent. "I knew already that he had an interest in some houses," Roland continues, "but the houses were quite another thing from these girls. Girls even from families that you might know, sent out to hotels. Businessmen from wherever, even doctors, of course many lawyers." Roland pauses, staring across the table at Caroline, almost accusingly. "He mentioned one girl, and then I had to end it. I made a certain phone call. Concerning Buck. To certain people."

He is telling me that Jill was involved with acts of prostitution, thinks Caroline, her mind reeling. That Jill went to hotels for money, with strangers, and that for that reason he caused Buck Fister to be murdered. Caroline receives this dizzily, it almost makes her faint. Closing her eyes against it, beginning to deny it, "I am tired," is all Caroline said.

A moment later, opening her eyes, revived to a degree perhaps by sheer curiosity, she asks him, "But how did you know—to call—?"

"How did I come to be involved with such people? My darling, this is a very long Italian story, very Sicilian, commencing with the youngest sister of my grandfather. I will tell you at a later time."

It is enough—just for an instant—to make Caroline believe that she might never return to San Francisco, nor to her daughters. How selfish they all are, really—beautiful, selfish, spoiled and greedy girls, San Francisco girls, perfect products of that spoiled and lovely city. She almost wishes that an earthquake might overtake them all, so that San Francisco, like Pompei, like Paestum, would be historical.

Thirty-two

"Stevie, I have something to tell you. I've fallen in love with you. Really. I'm sorry, but there it is. I love you."

"Uh, Stevie, instead of going out why don't we just take some dope and go up to bed? I'll cook something later."

"Uh, Stevie, have you ever given much thought to how you, uh, feel about me?"

"Stevie, something really sort of amazing has happened."

Sage, who is having considerable trouble getting to work, is saying all that to Stevie, all those nutty sentences, in her mind. They are to have dinner together tonight, and it is true, she is in love with Stevie. Tremendously. She realized it only this morning.

And how wonderful, really, to fall in love with an old and trusted friend, good kind smart dear Stevie. It struck her like a whirlwind, as, at breakfast, she began to think of the coming night. Of seeing Stevie. And then the feeling went on and on, as she tried to work.

How very surprised he will be to hear this, though. But since they are indeed friends, Sage feels a clear compulsion to tell him of her feelings, just as she would if she were in some way angry at him. The problem is how to put it so that Stevie will not be embarrassed. He is such a gentle, on-the-whole quiet person.

Strong mid-afternoon sunlight, strained through the streaky windowpanes, illuminates all the comforts of Sage's studio: the broken-down but still comfortable leather sofa; the small bookcase, holding some favorite poetry (what Sage reads when she really cannot work): Neruda, D. Levertov, Auden, Chaucer, Yeats. A. Rich. A Bible, and several green Michelin guides. Two bentwood chairs, her worktable, the radio—turned always to the classical music station, which is just now playing some Brahms, familiar, stirringly melodic, undoubtedly contributing to Sage's mood, all that lavish lonely love. The haunting cello, tremulous violins. Enough to make anyone believe herself in love.

But despite the support of such surroundings, the sunlight and the music, Sage is getting nowhere with her work.

Her fingers dig into the clay, and her delving, shaping tools form and re-form and shift its small mass, but whatever she had in mind does not come forth. (She had Stevie in mind actually: not literally Stevie but a tall heavy man like Stevie with a group of less defined small children. Very interesting, she thought—and whatever is that all about?)

Sometime later, though, an hour, maybe two, there on Sage's table is a small intricately and delicately fashioned naked man, far more detailed than most of her figures: she had shaped his shoulder blades, rib cage, loins, penis and long muscled legs. He stands in repose, his head just bent, his hair too long. And Sage sees that it is Noel. It is far more clearly Noel than if she had meant to portray him. With a painful accuracy she has re-created Noel, strong and intense and very beautiful.

All she has heard from him is a postcard from Grass Valley: "Burned out. (Joke.) Divorce me. I'll sign." And a box number.

Sometimes, unexpectedly, she has wept for Noel. His lost beauty, the sheer waste of their life together. She does so now, there in the sunny studio that he made for her, as from her radio still come the lovely rippling trembling piano runs. More Brahms.

Sage weeps until she realizes that she is enjoying the tears, along with the music—and then she stops, and gets back to work.

"We celebrate today the birthday of Johannes Brahms," says that unctuous voice. "Over a hundred and fifty years ago today, in Frankfurt, Germany. His mother, already in her early forties, his much younger, by seventeen years, father—" (Which explains what all that Brahms was about.)

As Sage thinks, Amazing! And, That's not a bad life plan, marry a much younger man when you're in your forties, and then produce a genius.

"I wonder what on earth my mother's doing in Italy," Sage muses aloud to Stevie, that night, as she not very successfully tries to grate fresh ginger into a marinade. They are both in her kitchen, which, since Noel, Sage has tried to finish up: with a butcherblock table, a Cuisinart and a microwave, all attesting to considerable money spent ("My nouveau riche cuisine," Sage has earlier remarked to Stevie). Plus some blue-and-white toile curtains, and a Barcelona chair, in which Stevie now comfortably lounges.

"What she says is most likely the truth," he tells Sage. "I'd imagine she's having a very good time, like she says. And probably not really wishing you all were with her."

"I guess. Oh shit!" Sage has just grated her thumb, which she now protectively sucks.

Getting up, unwinding, "Here, let me do that," Stevie tells her. "I must say, for a sculptor—"

"I know, clumsy fingers. Noel always said that."

"Which I did not. Give me credit."

"Dear Stevie, I do. Well, I hope she's just having a good time. Caroline."

"What on earth else would she be doing? Why are you so suspicious of your mother? An unusually nice woman, as you know."

"I do know. She's so nice that I get suspicious. And she is staying a lot longer than she said."

"A good sign, I'd think."

"I guess." Sage frowns dubiously, and then she says, "But, Stevie, you haven't said what you're up to now. You were going to tell me."

Dextrously chopping—he too has had to give up grating the very moist and fibrous root—Stevie pauses before he tells her, "I do have a plan. I don't know why I feel a little silly telling you about it."

"It's not a silly plan?"

"Well, no."

Stevie's plan, which he at first somewhat ironically refers to as his free-food place, has actually been worked out in considerable detail. He describes it to Sage over dinner, their gingered swordfish, and wine.

"You remember Tony Navarro? That nice Mexican kid we knew in the Movement, came to all the sit-ins and stuff, from Mission High? I ran into him again in the restaurant business, we used some of the same people. His folks had a place out on Mission that he inherited, which has put him more or less in the same position that I'm in now. Some dough to use, and a lot of experience in food. Purveyors, storage, all that. Plus our sentimental Sixties good intentions."

He and Sage exchange a look, a wry smile. And then Stevie goes on and on, describing a plan that basically combines restaurant food overloads, the goodwill (and a few other emotions) of restaurant owners—and human need. The needs of the homeless, people with AIDS, the impoverished old.

"Anyway, that's what I'm mostly up to now," he says, as they come to the end of dinner, and apparently of his recital. "Plus a not-so-good relationship that's winding down, I think," he adds.

"Oh really?" Sage, her spirits suddenly and considerably lowered, does not ask, as she would like to, Who? Why winding down?

"I don't know," Stevie tells her, "it just seems really hard to work things out these days. The women I meet are so terrifically distrustful. Not that I blame them, but they are."

"I guess so. I mean, I guess we are." Sage still feels a certain apprehension about the direction that this talk is taking.

"I meet two kinds of women," says Stevie, with a little sigh. "The first ones had a really bad experience, sometimes it's a marriage—have you noticed how many people our age have already been married, some of them more than once?—and the bad time was a few years back, but they still don't really want to get into anything. And the second group wants to get married tomorrow and have a lot of children the following week."

Sage laughs, as she knows Stevie meant her to, but she feels her own laugh as a little dishonest: she would like to get married next week, to Stevie, and have children as soon as they could. "Your current friend must be in the second group," she says.

"No, actually in the first, the bad-marriage group. The trouble is, she seems to be changing her mind at the same time that I'm changing mine. I know, it sounds a lot funnier than it is. I feel like I've been not quite honest with her, I mean I didn't really want her all that much, it turns out. But maybe I should have known that in the first place."

Sage cannot prevent or control the small wave of relief that rises within her. "It's mostly that you care about women much more than most men do," she tells him. "You're responsible."

"I do? I am? Well, I guess. It seems a problem for me. The energy involved in just not hurting, or getting hurt."

How lucky that she did not at any earlier point in the evening declare her great new love for Stevie! That would have been so entirely wrong, Sage now sees. And possibly it is not even *really* true. It even seems a little crazy, those violent emotions applied to Stevie. Slightly hysterical (a version of that terrible, still-embarrassing scene with Jim McAndrew).

Perhaps after all what she does feel for Stevie is the most affectionate friendship, the sort that never needs a declaration.

"Well, if I ever decide that I'm dying to have children next week you'll be the first to know," she tells him.

And they both laugh. Good old friends.

Thirty-three

S imojoval de Allende, high in the mountains of Chiapas, near
the border that separates Mexico from Guatemala, is not
what Liza ever envisioned when she thought the word "Mexico." She had, rather, pictured some aspect of Mexico City, the
Anthropology Museum, or teeming, exotic streets, and crowds, and
wild-colored flowers. Or, a tropical beach, a slick-magazine scene of
sexy smooth white sand, and green clear shallow water, gently rippling. A stand of palms.

Not an almost new but already showing wear, one-story California-
ranch-style motel. Rutted, muddy, unpaved streets, and a restaurant
that serves burned beans and tepid beer. And not much else. Nevertheless, that is where they are, she and Saul, for their Mexican
reunion—where, as he has reminded her once too often, she always
wanted to go.

Nearby there is marvellous scenery, deep gorges and waterfalls;
and in several neighboring towns and small cities, most notably San
Cristóbal de las Casas, there is architecture of a Baroque beauty
almost unsurpassed in colonial Mexico. But this is the rainy season,
and although it only rains in the afternoons the roads are very slick,
almost impassable. There was a horrifying bus accident the week
before, thirty-nine people over a cliff, no survivors. A Third Class
bus: "Naturally," Saul and Liza muttered to each other, in an infrequent moment of agreement, on this trip.

Also ("to make everything quite perfect," as Liza puts it to
herself), Saul has crab lice, and not only that but he has run out of

the DDT powder that would have controlled their incursions into the deepest follicle of each hair on his body. Saul is not an exceptionally hairy person, he has none on his back (he now thanks God), only in the ordinary male places for hair, but he now feels himself most horrendously hirsute. Everywhere itches, he feels dirty and disgusting, asexual and full of guilt—and a guilt that will not let him speak its name. Because Liza insists on his innocence.

"Darling, I've had crabs too, once I picked them up or, rather, they picked me up in jail, that time in Santa Rita. I know how easily you can get them," she tells him affably. "And it's not as easy to get rid of them as they say. Easier for women, I guess, with less hair."

"You'll get them from me."

"Sweetie, of course I will. But isn't that what reunions are all about? Funny sex? Things not quite working out?"

Saul has not been in jail, but he has been living in "substandard" conditions, huts and slapped-up dirt-floored shacks, mostly along the coast of Honduras. However, he did not get crabs from those anonymous conditions but from a nurse, fervent skinny Lorna Cassidy, from Michigan. With whom Saul has been fornicating (that is the word that comes to his mind; he could also say that they had been fucking their socks off) at every available opportunity.

Liza in her cheerful way seems to assume that no such thing could ever be possible. And it is not possible: Saul, the good doctor, the good Jewish son and husband, quite passionately and permanently in love with his wife, with lovely blonde Liza, he could never do such a thing. But that is just what he has been doing, fucking Lorna, whom he does not even love, he just likes her. Doing it every time they have found ten minutes of privacy, or less, anywhere at all. Several times standing in a closet. In improvised bathrooms.

In a way Saul would like to tell Liza all this; for one thing she would find it very interesting. She likes stories that involve a lot of sexual goings-on. But Saul admits to himself that telling Liza, for whatever reasons, ostensibly moral and honest, would in fact be a cruel sort of boasting, and so he does not.

In any case there they are, drinking too much tasteless beer, and talking in more or less opposite directions.

Liza is in fact grappling with a moral problem (she sees its essence as moral) of quite a different sort from that which so distracts and disturbs poor faithless Saul. What obsesses Liza is the fact that she sent a story to the largest and reputedly the richest of the so-called women's magazines, and they have called to say that they "love" the story, it is "wonderful." So much strong feeling, they say, which is so rare these days. They would love to publish it—if only. If only she could make things a little more clear, here and there. And perhaps the lover need not after all be Polish? They mean, why Polish? And the scene in bed, well, just a little too long? And then there's the ending: possibly a little more explanation, a little what you might call lightening up?

"In other words, totally change my original story. To meet their specifications," Liza concludes her recital. "I'm surprised they didn't want me to put everyone in Ralph Lauren clothes."

"You're sure?"

"No, I'm not sure. Some other inner voice is saying they could be right, you know, they're not all dummies. They could be really improving the story. And then it all gets more confused because of the money. Of course I'd like it, even if I know we don't need it. But, you know, trips?"

At that word they both smile feebly; in their present hot, damp and dubiously clean surroundings the word "trip" is not exactly magic.

"So I don't know quite what to do." About anything, Liza could continue, including us. How terrifically lonely I feel, now that we're together. How much closer, really, I felt when I was in San Francisco and you in Honduras, or wherever. Thinking of you, I felt much closer than I do now.

Maybe I'm supposed to live alone? Liza wonders. Maybe that's better for writers? But how can I, with three children?

The proprietor of this bar, and at the moment its sole other occupant, is a very thin and sad-faced, very dark young woman, her high-boned face a mask, her clothes dark and drab, anonymous. But despite her Mayan (Olmec? Zapotec?) features, she could easily be a California Mexican woman—and this bar could be in some remote High Sierra hamlet, to which the woman's family had in some way been displaced, from the valley. The calendar on the wall advertises Pepsi, the radio plays Mantovani.

"I wish I could have met you at some beach." Saul apologizes with a gesture that includes the whole of their surroundings: The ugly room, and the speechless sorrows of the woman who served them warm beer. The mud and the dripping trees outside. His crabs.

"This is like northern California," Liza tells him.

Saul brightens. "Quite a lot." And then, "You don't know how much I've missed you. And the kids. Less them, though." He smiles.

"Well, that's good."

"It's strange," he says. "I feel more troubled by the people I've been treating here, Christ, I mean trying to treat, than I ever did back in the States. And I don't think it's only because they're worse, worse troubles, I mean. But. There I am with some guy whose life could not be less like mine, we're just barely communicating, I have to say that my Spanish is not as great as I thought it was. And his pain really gets to me. It gets through." He pauses. "I'm not really making sense, am I."

"Sure you are."

In fact this is their moment of greatest rapport, so far. Looking at each other across the stained, once-white table cover, Liza and Saul both know this, and they smile, acknowledging the moment. But they are unable to sustain it, and their fragile connection sags.

"I think I don't know what I'm talking about." Saul sighs, and stretches—and reaches to scratch, he can't not.

Saul looks more sad than Liza has ever seen him, the lines in his long lean face are deeper and darker, his large dark eyes are downcast. And not quite meeting hers? Liza has this sense of him, of some private, harrowing pain, or guilt—a sense for the moment she suppresses.

Or, almost suppresses, as she wonders, Can he be so foolish as to feel guilty, still, over having left me more or less alone, while he went off to the wars, so to speak?

Or, can he possibly be so foolish as to have screwed some nurse, or someone, who gave him crabs? And she thinks, If he did I just pray he doesn't tell me about it, I can't stand confessions.

Nevertheless she says, "I sure hope it wasn't really some sexy nurse who gave you crabs."

Saul scowls. "Of course not."

"Well, good."

There is a tiny pause, during which Liza, incredulous, receives the clearly intuited information—his whole face is telling her this, and the way he slumps in his chair—that Saul did indeed screw someone. Saul unfaithful, the one thing she never expected. It makes her rattle: "I do wonder about my mother in Italy. She's staying such a long time."

"Isn't that a good sign? She's having fun?" Saul indeed looks relieved at the change of subject—as well he might.

"Oh, I suppose. But in some terrible way everything seems to fall apart when she's out of town."

"We weathered the years in Portugal," Saul reminds her.

"Well, did we, really? You and I were too busy having kids to notice. And that's when Sage went crazy over Roland Gallo, and then married Noel, and God knows what Fiona and Jill were really up to. Or what they're up to now, for that matter."

She simply does not want that sort of confrontation with Saul, Liza believes, at the moment. It would only be damaging, and besides, she could be quite wrong? Her literary imagination running away with itself?

But maybe later on she will bring it up, and Saul will deny it, and they will have a terrific fight—something they never do, but it might clear the air between them. Now.

She says, "I'm worried about this black guy I keep seeing in the park. At first I thought he was someone I used to know, but he's not, he's just this guy living in the park. I tried to give him some money but he wouldn't take it, and I brought him some food but I don't think he ate any."

"If he were rich we'd call that a clinical depression. And try Lithium. Or shock."

"As it is he's just a street crazy."

"I could see him if you want, when I get home."

"Darling, where? He'd never go to your office. You'd see him in the park?"

"Why not? I need to broaden the scope of my practice. I see that now."

On schedule the rain begins again. Torrential green rains, through which all the leaves shimmer brightly, brilliantly, every green leaf, every shade of green, alive and tremulous. Through a cracked open window comes the smell of rain and leaves, and damped-down dust, and dung, and garbage.

"Well, here we are in Mexico," Saul says, with a somewhat forced laugh.

"Okay." Liza's throat tightens—is very dry. "Now do you want to tell me how you really got those crabs?"

Thirty-four

In Boston it is raining, a dark warm relentless summer rain; it both accelerates and strangles the city's pace. People and cars move faster and to less effect, and in both cases they end up jammed in crowds, wet and snarling. Tremont Street looks like Hong Kong, or Delhi. In the quieter sections, around Beacon Hill, the dead white blossoms' huge petals are spattered against the dark and ancient brick of houses and walkways, flattened on sidewalks and narrow winding streets, in the unbelievably warm wet black air.

Hurrying along those venerable small streets, in her long red plastic raincoat, from California, Fiona imagines that if she should be accepted at the Business School, at Harvard, she would live around here. In one of these very tall narrow brick houses, with a high flight of worn brick stairs leading up to a shiny black door that is flanked by bevelled glass panels. A big bright brass plate, with her name. And inside there would be a series of high white narrow rooms, with tinted lavender windows looking out to a garden.

To dead flowers smeared on the old dark earth. God, how she really hates Boston!

On the other hand, she does very much like the Ritz Hotel, where she is staying, and toward which she now is hurrying through the rain. The Ritz is Fiona's idea of what a hotel really should be. Quietly luxurious. Discreetly comforting.

. . .

Seated somewhat later in the hotel's dining room, at her corner table with its view of both the Public Gardens and Newbury Street, Fiona has a sudden vision of herself for the next few years or more, living at the Ritz. It has a nice sound to it, for starters:

"Have you been able to find an apartment yet?"

"No, actually I didn't even try. I'm living at the Ritz."

Or:

"Could I take you home? You live around here?"

"No, actually I'm living at the Ritz."

However.

However, living at the Ritz, even in just a room, not a suite, would cost her three or four thousand a month, Fiona quickly calculates, the price of a hefty mortgage, at least in California, and not all deductible. As Jill would quickly point out, if asked. For that money I could be buying something really ravishing up in Napa, Fiona reminds herself.

Besides, she doesn't even like it in Boston, outside of the Ritz.

Besides, she won't necessarily even be admitted to the Business School.

New York is worse, although it isn't raining there. Unspeakably hot, in the upper 90s, and thick with smells, the multiple odors of dirty people with half their clothes off. And so many street people, everywhere beggars, sick-looking, crazed. She could be in Calcutta.

Over the phone Jill tells her, "I must say, it's great out here. These rare summer days. I know it won't last, but it's gorgeous."

"I remember."

"Like some terrific slam-bam love affair, which I must say I wish I were having."

"I can't even think about sex in this filthy city. Or clothes. They're getting in the fall collections, already, and I can't even look at them."

"Tell yourself that it's all in a good cause, your being there. Really, Fi, we've got to work out a sensible plan for all that money of yours."

"We could go into business together."

"Doing what? Running a so-called house? That's not a sensible plan."

"Has Caroline called anyone yet?"

"Not that I know of. But then as usual I haven't talked to Sage. Or Ports. And Liza's in Mexico."

"Whatever could Caroline be doing in Italy all this time?"

"Having fun. Getting fat. Getting laid? I guess she could be."

"Honestly, Jill."

"I know, that's all I think about. Well, actually it isn't." A pause. "I guess it's up to me to do something about talking to Sage? Effecting a rapprochement?"

"If you think so. I don't know. Poor you."

"I'm going to AA next week, my first meeting. Everyone says it's really neat. You see everyone you know."

"Oh, great."

"Well, maybe they'll tell me what to do."

"I hope."

Hanging up, Fiona realizes that talking to her sister has afflicted her with a terrific homesickness. She longs for California passionately, sensually. She has not felt so bereft since the early days of missing Roland Gallo.

And in New York she does not like her hotel. The Plaza. The lobby is jammed with tacky people in awful Midwestern clothes, and out in front she can't even get a taxi, it's so crowded with gray or white stretch limousines. One *pink*. The only good thing that happens to her in the Plaza is that one night in the Palm Court (of all incredibly tacky places) the waiter brings her the wrong check; he brings her a check for one glass of wine, whereas actually she had two glasses and a lobster salad. Well, screw them, a free drink and a free lobster; big deal, her present from the Plaza.

She has interviews at Columbia and NYU, Princeton and Pennsylvania. Which on the whole go quite well.

"It's hard to tell with New Yorkers, though, they're so goddam rude," Fiona tells Jill, on the phone.

"They are that. But it works out, their rudeness makes them think we're terrifically nice. So friendly and open."

Fiona laughs. "Right, I could feel them thinking that. Thinking,

What a nice friendly open woman, we want her around. My hunch is that I'll be accepted at least in a couple of places."

"You're probably right. It may be a problem for you. Choosing."

"Probably."

On her next-to-last night in the Plaza, Fiona is invited to dinner by an old school friend, Pipper Harmon, and her husband, Jack Matting. Pipper, a literary agent, and Jack, a show-biz lawyer, live on upper Park, in the 90s. A wonderful building, Fiona sees that right away. It is huge, a great fortress built around a central courtyard, and guarded by not one but three very tall doormen, gnarled old Irishmen, with brogues, and red noses, and smart gold-trimmed uniforms.

The apartment too is impressive. Long low rooms, and fireplaces, and halls, and big windows looking down to the street, then back to the courtyard. All done in pale silky fabrics, pinks and sands, pale turquoise; very smart, Fiona recognizes the style.

The other guests are literary rather than show biz, somewhat to Fiona's disappointment (too bad her sister Liza the writer is not here, instead of her). There is a famous writer whose name she knows but whom she has not read, and his wife, a doctor; a newspaper-writer couple; and a young actor whose name Fiona has never heard, who is very cute and possibly gay; he is Pipper's gesture toward inviting "someone for Fiona."

All these people seem to know each other very well indeed; happy to see each other, they talk a lot, so that Fiona is barely required to make any social effort, not even to explain where she comes from or why she is there. Until the famous writer at her side asks her if she could possibly be connected to the marvellous San Francisco restaurant of which they have all read so much. And so Fiona explains all that. Everyone seems to find it really impressive that she once owned a trendy restaurant, and they all agree that it was even more clever to sell out when she did. (What a bunch of morons, is what Fiona thinks.)

Al, the blond and bearded famous writer, tells Fiona that actually he comes to San Francisco from time to time. He went to Stanford, he got his start in the creative-writing program there: "great bunch of guys." He would like to call her, could they meet for a drink?

Well, why not? Fiona tells him, but with as little interest as he himself has actually shown in her.

Unfortunately, the only really attractive man in the room is her host, Jack Matting, lawyer, husband of Pipper. With his dark wise look of experience, his narrow white face and thin sexy mouth, Jack is a prize, getting more attractive with age and success; quite probably he knows this, and undoubtedly Pipper does. Pipper is or was extremely good-looking too, a small frothy blonde, but she has put on weight, and she drinks too much. And from Jack Fiona is getting serious flirtation signals; for one thing he is extremely discreet about it, which he would not be if he were not serious. But: Do I really need a new romance with a married man? And with an old friend's husband, for Christ's sake? That's almost as bad as Jill with Noel, really, Fiona decides.

She shares a cab ride home with the cute young actor, who also says that he would like to call her when he comes to San Francisco. Fiona says yes, sure, why not? He is gay, she is sure of that.

"You mean New York would be okay if you could live on upper Park? Do you have any idea what those places cost?" It is early still in California, when Fiona, late at night, gets back to the Plaza and dials her sister, and finds Jill lively, wide awake.

"No." Tired, with a little too much wine, Fiona listens to Jill and feels homesick, for California quite as much as if not more than for her favorite sister.

"Well," Jill tells her, "I've heard that these days in New York a million means less than nothing, maybe some fixer-upper on the West Side. And a place like that, well, I just don't think it's for you, dear Fi."

From the terrace behind the house, beneath the pure blue vaulting California sky, the view is all green, of hills and vineyards, a low-lying, flowing meadow, and farther hills, all green, here and there darkened with the shifting, irregular shapes of shadows of clouds.

Even the small lake nestled into the valley looks green, a jewel of cool green water, reflecting leaves.

"Actually the house that goes with this is quite nice too. Come on up and see it." The real-estate agent, a sharp-eyed, hoarse-voiced Marin County "socialite," a recovering alcoholic, has noted Fiona's total bemusement, her dazed look of someone in love, in love with that view. It is a look that Lil, the agent, has seen before, and so she knows that it does not necessarily mean closure.

"Nice" is not quite the word for that house; even dazzled Fiona, who has already decided to buy it, finds the structure quite peculiar: the downstairs area is conventional enough, a huge glassed-in living room (facing that view), and at one end a galley–dining room. But for going upstairs, to any one of the seven or eight quite sizable bedrooms, there is a separate staircase. Eight staircases, each partially concealed by some very tricky panelling.

"Actually a local architect I've talked to told me he could take out all those steps and put in a balcony, and just one flight, no problem," says Lil, who is dying for a cigarette.

"Well. I don't know. It's sort of fun like this. I'll have to show it to my sister. The practical one."

"Fine with me, any time you want to bring her by. But what on earth do you think the builder had in mind?"

"A whorehouse, probably."

Lil laughs raucously, although that is exactly what everyone who has seen the house has said.

"A mansion in Napa? You really are quite nuts, do you know that?" Jill scolds. "I know, you're going to start a new restaurant up there. The new thing, a country inn."

"That was last year's new thing, remember? Actually solitary splendor is what I'm thinking."

"Baby, you can't afford it, not with that mortgage."

"I could rent it out part-time and take off for somewhere cheap, like Mexico."

"Liza hated it there, she said. She even lost weight."

They snicker familiarly, and then Jill continues to chide. "Fiona, you're not being practical, and you have to. This is like some new addiction you've come up with."

"Oh God, are you going to start talking like that?"

"Probably I am."

However, as Fiona thinks of it, she has to admit some truth to Jill's rather clinical view of her purchase: she did fall in love with that view, and what love really means is (this flashes across her mind): I have to have this, now.

Thirty-five

"My turning tricks, if that's what you want to call it, had nothing to do with low self-esteem. I do not have low self-esteem, and I'm so tired of reading that that's why people do it. Trick. I did it because I got a thousand bucks a shot, and I knew I was worth it, and getting all that money helped me keep on thinking I'm terrific. Like buying hundred-buck panty hose and two-fifty haircuts. I love all that stuff, and the thousand-dollar tricks were part of it."

No one is clapping, although Jill has been told that at AA meetings everyone claps when you talk; she was looking forward to that, she now realizes, she was thinking of all the clapping even as she dressed in her new red Go-Silk clothes to come to this Tuesday-night meeting, in this somewhat dingy church basement.

But the faces she sees out there are not at all responsive; they are sad, lost-looking faces, not quite getting her drift. These people are heavy and pale, a lot of them with bad skin. They look puzzled, and surely she sees real disapproval, here and there? Surprising; you're not supposed to disapprove of other people in AA, Jill feels sure of that. Perhaps they expected her to talk more about drinking, using drugs? Well, she's coming to that.

This meeting, though, did not begin with any drink or drug talk. There was a prayer about serenity, and then some talk about Steps (Jill had heard of the Steps, at least), and traditions, and then the woman who seemed to be in charge, a fat dowdy type who looked quite crazy to Jill—this woman, who had earlier introduced herself as Britt, asked that everyone say his or her name. "And maybe some people would like to tell us why they came here tonight."

And so Jill got up. "I'm Jill," at which everyone clapped for the first and only time, and they all said, Hi, Jill.

And then she told about her job, the lucky hostile takeover, all the money, and what a good time she had with her Mercedes and the place on Telegraph Hill. And then Buck coming up with the idea of dates, paid dates. The Game.

They are not really sympathetic to all this. Jill sees thin lines of disapproval down those faces, slightly narrowed eyes, even looks of impatience, of questioning. Some people seem to wonder what she is doing up there, talking on and on about herself. But isn't this what you're supposed to do? Everyone said so. "You'll love it," everyone said.

Britt is standing up, about to interrupt, but Jill does not want to be interrupted. She is just now coming to the good part, the why-she's-here part. "And then I got involved with this guy who was doing a lot of drugs, and drank a lot." (This is something of an exaggeration: Noel's drink and drug use were not remarkable, not until that ultimate night, in Stinson Beach, and Bolinas.) "One of the problems was that he was married to my sister. My half-sister—" This sounds like a broken record, and Jill pauses there.

At which Britt jumps in. "We all thank Jackie very much for sharing—"

"Jill. My name is Jill."

"Oh, sorry. Jill. We all thank Jill for her very interesting share, and now, if there are any other first-timers—"

And so Jill sits down, and a dark young woman in a motorcycle outfit, black jersey and leather tights, gets up. The guy she lives with is in jail now, she says; he was caught dealing crack and there was a big stash of money in their house that got stolen. She has two children, she's pretty sure that she's pregnant again. Her husband was really nice, before all the wine and dope and then the crack. They'd grown up together in Fredericksburg, Texas. They came out here together, and then—

Overcome by tears, she cannot continue. Several people near her hurry to her side, with big hugs.

What is all this about what fun AA meetings are? Jill is wondering that. All she has heard about the neat people you meet there, how everyone loves you at AA meetings. Do you have to cry to get that love? turn yourself into some sort of junkie sobber?

After a while, during which Jill does not pay much attention, having decided that she does not like it there, not at all—they all stand up and join hands to pray. More about serenity. And then the meeting is over.

But no, not over. Another part seems to have only begun. Everyone gets up and goes over to another person, they greet each other, and hug (to Jill the hugging looks rather unnecessarily prolonged). And then they talk very seriously, sometimes with more tears.

A long way from the door, Jill hopes to get out without an encounter of that sort; she begins to sidle in the direction of the exit, with what she hopes is a passable smile on her face. But she is wrong again: a man whom she had not noticed, possibly because he is exceptionally small, about five feet, Jill guesses—this man comes up to her out of nowhere. "Hi, I'm Morry," he says, and reaches up to be hugged.

And Jill obediently reaches down. If she did not, she believes that all the gooey love in that room would congeal into stony rage; they would all turn and look and start yelling at her. Hitting her, maybe.

"I was really interested in your share," says Morry, once they disentangle. He looks up at her with tiny button-black eyes, appraising eyes, old eyes, the skin around them is slack and yellow. Morry looks like a very old child—could he be a dwarf? He is not shaped like most dwarfs are, though, he is just very small. He smiles up at Jill, expectantly.

"Well, I somehow didn't feel I was saying the right thing," she tells him. "I mean I wasn't talking about my, uh, drinking."

Startlingly, Morry laughs at this, a curious small wheezing sound. And then he says, "You meant to come to an AA meeting, is that right?"

"Of course. Yes."

"And you've come to Al-Anon instead. And you know how I know? Because I did exactly the same thing myself, other way around. Meant to go to Al-Anon, found myself in AA instead."

"Al-Anon?"

"Folks related to drinkers, living with them. Parents of them. Married to. Trouble those kinds of ways."

"Oh Jesus."

"First way you know is how happy they all are over to AA. All laughing and clapping at each other's stories. And smoking, you never saw so much heavy smoke in all your days."

"God." Later Jill supposes she will find this funny, a good story to tell around. How she tried and failed to go to an AA meeting. But just now she does not.

"What I wondered," says Morry, looking up at her with those hard little eyes, "I wondered did you ever think of starting up one of those *houses?* Hearing your share, I just wondered over that. Not anything bad but just someplace that so-called singles could go to on their own, and maybe the management would come up with some sort of a friend. Like when you go out to a restaurant without a tie, and they lend you one."

Leaning down, as clearly as she can, Jill whispers, "You're out of your fucking mind." And then, no longer caring what anyone in that room might do or say, Jill bolts, she is out of there within one minute. For good.

After that, but certainly no thanks to that meeting, that accidental brush with Al-Anon, things do improve considerably for Jill. Back at work, her world seems after all not to have fallen apart; it is in fact very much the same as it always was, or as it has been during this decade, the elegant Eighties.

"It looks like the Eighties will go on forever," a broker friend remarks, during a chance breakfast encounter at Maxine's, one unusually bright summer morning.

"The market looks good."

"Yeah. Big surprise. So much for the doom-and-gloomers."

"I have to admit, I was a little surprised."

"There you go. Hey, you're looking great these days, babe. Dinner some night?"

"Sure, why not?" Why not is that this creep is very married, with

a big house down in Burlingame, to which he is known for returning very late.

As Jill is leaving, at the end of the counter she passes someone
who is, really, the dead spit of Buck. Very startled, she then sees
that it is not Buck, of course not, and she remembers that a lot of
people look like Buck, they always did. That was one of the points
about him: Buck looked like everyone.

On that same day, on an impulse, Jill does what she has meant
to do for some time: she calls Sage and suggests that they have
dinner.

"Not especially to talk," Jill tells her sister—half-sister. "I'm sure
you know pretty much how bad I feel. Just to have dinner."

"Well, sure. Where?"

They settle on Greens, in Fort Mason, with the view of the yacht
harbor, and the Golden Gate.

"It should be really beautiful there tonight," says Sage. "It's so
clear."

And it is, unbelievably beautiful. Immediately outside their window are the clustered masts of small boats, matchsticks on toys, and
the blue-black, flat, reflective water. And then the gate, the broad
passage out to the vast Pacific, spanned by the soaring bridge—
now all veiled by thin white fog. The bridge and the sea below are
fogged, and the rising hills of Marin. Everything is drawn very
faintly, like an Oriental painting. So delicate. Unreal.

"Interesting that the greatest pieces of real estate in this city be-
long to the Army," Jill says to Sage. "This and the Presidio. If they
ever pull out, wow. Watch out."

Sage asks, "Do you think they will?" This is the sort of thing she
would expect Jill to know about.

"There're always rumors."

Sipping wine, they both turn back to the view.

What on earth do you say to your sister when you've fucked her
husband and then really (almost) caused his death? You say nothing,
Jill has decided. You have dinner together and say almost nothing
at all. The surprising part is that it all seems okay, acceptable. Noel
gone, and their both knowing what they know, and not talking
about it.

Another surprise is how unlike herself, or any self that Jill can remember, Sage now looks. Sage, the thinnest of them all (Jill and Fiona used to speculate about bulimia), has really put on some weight. Everywhere. Her once-thin, almost sharp face is rounded, softer, and she is wearing her silk shirt outside her pants, unbelted and possibly concealing fat.

Just as Jill has made that observation, Sage's new weight, Sage remarks, "I think I'll have everything on the menu. It all looks so good, and I'm starving."

"Me too. But you look great, Sage," Jill lies.

"I've put on too much weight, the doctor says. You did know that I'm pregnant?"

"No. No, I didn't."

"Oh well. I thought someone would have told you, though I'm only just. This weight gain actually began before, though. Stevie's been cooking for me."

"Stevie?" A messy person from somewhere drifts vaguely toward Jill's mind.

"You remember, he was a friend of mine back in the Sixties, and then he worked with Fiona."

"Oh, that Stevie." The one who got so much money when Fiona sold out, Jill does not say. She is trying to work out how to ask what she most wants to know. But under the circumstances she can't just say, The child is Noel's? although she thinks that it must be. They did still have sex sometimes, Noel told her. She attempts, "I thought you were sort of involved with that dealer from New York. Art dealer, I mean."

"Well, I sort of am. But I don't think in the way you mean. He's gay, and the most terrific friend."

"Oh." This is something that everyone says, these days; women are always talking about what terrific friends gay guys are, but Jill does not actually have any gay friends. In fact she does not have a lot of friends, she now reflects, without sadness. Just people she knows.

"And then Stevie and I, well, fell in love is not exactly how it was, but our friendship changed." Sage laughs, as at some very private, very happy memory. "And then, when I turned up pregnant, there seemed no reason to have an abortion, to put it negatively. We just got more and more pleased." She laughs again. "In fact we're really excited. I know I'm too old, but we're all very hopeful. Me and Stevie and the doctor."

"Well Sage, that's absolutely great." That will be something to do with all the money you both have now, Jill is thinking. The costs of kids these days: it's amazing that anyone has them any more.

"Fiona, this place is truly, truly fabulous. The absolute greatest." Balancing her wineglass on the low stone edge of the terrace, Jill stares out at the view. "Of course you'll have to put in a pool, but still."

"Isn't it something? The very, very most beautiful. Honestly, when I think of all those sleazy places in New York. And *Boston*."

Both women are somewhat drunk. Having driven up to Napa, to Fiona's new house, quite early in the day, a Sunday, they have been sipping at some cool and festive Napa Chardonnay. And they have been snacking, or grazing, their mutually preferred method of food intake; they brought along some tomatoes and grapes, some radicchio-wrapped goat cheese and cold marinated eggplant. Nothing very substantial, or alcohol-retardant.

Now, toward the end of that long summer afternoon, the sky is streaked with strange gray-lavender clouds, and the hills are shadowed with large odd-shaped patches of darkness. At the most distant horizon are dark fogbanks, gradually encroaching, building to black. Leaves tremble in a silver-green stand of aspen, near the terrace, stirred by a slight breeze in which there is more than a hint of fall. Which neither Jill nor Fiona has so far mentioned, or noticed.

"When I went to that supposed AA meeting," Jill now tells her sister, "this tiny little man did say something that was actually quite funny. He said, why didn't I open a house for singles? A whorehouse is what he damn well meant. But he said a house that'd supply a person for people who came there alone. Sort of like restaurants handing out neckties, he said."

"Well, that really is quite wonderful."

"Like handing out ties. So marvellous, when you think of it."

They giggle together for quite a while, each one's laughter re-infusing the other's.

When at last they come out of it, Jill says, "And actually not the dumbest idea in the world. A place where singles would go, and know there'd be someone. Supplied by the management."

"Jesus, do you think we actually could? And get away with it?"

"Well, why not? The most discreet, most elegant operation in the world."

"How rich we'd get."

"You mean, how richer."

"Oh, right."

Thirty-six

"I could never tell you how really beautiful Lebanon is. Beirut." Wistfully Hilda sighs, and gives up, gazing silently out across the Mission District—the view from their house, from their deck, hers and Portia's. Once Mrs. Kaltenborn's.

"What we should have done, I guess, is find out more about roses before we went and bought all these," muses Portia. She adds, as though joking, "I wish Caroline were here. I need my mom!"

"The roses in Lebanon become enormous," Hilda tells her. "My mother's roses."

"Do you remember how she did it? I mean, were there tricks for growing them?"

"I don't know but I'll ask her. Remind me."

Hilda has suddenly (to Portia it seemed very sudden indeed) accepted a fellowship at the law school of the American University in Beirut. "There was a law school when it was Roman, fifteen hundred years ago," Hilda has said, as though that explained everything.

The fellowship is only for a year (only!) and the plan is that Portia will go to visit at least twice—or, that they will meet in an intermediate place, like Paris, or Rome.

One of the things that Portia feels is that they do not know each other well enough for such a separation; their "relationship" may not be old enough or sufficiently established to bear it. Also, as she is unable not to say to Hilda fairly often, it's dangerous there.

"It's dangerous in San Francisco, and really dangerous in New York," has been Hilda's answer.

"Not the same way. No wars."

"Crack wars. Gangs."

"Still. It's not as dangerous," Portia repeats, feeling helpless, scared.

In the meantime, roses. Today, a Saturday, they have driven down to Watsonville to a place that specializes in old-fashioned varieties. "Caroline would go mad," remarked Portia, going a little mad herself.

The rose place turned out to be enormous, fields and hills of roses, all kinds, damasks and tea roses, ramblers and climbers, English roses, floribundas. Miniature roses, the only kind that Portia and Hilda could agree not to like, not to covet as they did almost all the rest, all those ravishing colors, velvet petals. A rich rose scent wafts delicately up through the cool blue air, of that California day.

They came home with a dozen cans of roses. Having chosen ten quite at random, not counting, they then said almost at once, "Oh well, in that case we might as well get a dozen," as though twelve were a magic number. The two final choices were of course the most difficult; they settled at last on the impractically lovely pale lavender Sterling Silver (a favorite of Caroline's) and an orange-pink hybrid tea, called Tenerife.

Other choices were various. Everything but white in fact, yellow to burnished gold, and every shade of pink, and deepest scarlet.

And so, on the deck of their house, in the declining sunlight, there sit Portia and Hilda, and their dozen cans of beautifully flowering roses. And their separate preoccupations.

"I don't even know whether we want to put them down in the garden or just have them up here in pots," continues Portia.

"Well, maybe some in both places." Saying this, Hilda frowns, as though judicially confronting the most serious problem in the world.

At which they both laugh, and Portia thinks, It's going to be all right, after all.

And then the phone rings.

"Want me to get it?"

"I will—"

"Okay, it's more likely for you."

It is indeed for Portia. It is Sage, saying that she and Stevie have just made some gravlax; they were in Sausalito the day before and bought some lovely fresh salmon. Could they bring it over? Maybe a picnic supper out on the deck?

In an almost automatic way Portia says yes, do come, what a great idea. And then, after hanging up, she begins to note the lowering of her own spirits. Odd: she loves Sage unreservedly, and Hilda likes both Sage and Stevie—and Portia takes such pleasure in all Sage's new happiness, and really she is very fond of Stevie too.

"I can't figure it out," she tells Hilda, having already developed the habit of telling Hilda most stray thoughts, most random reactions. "I really wish they weren't coming. And why?"

"Dear Portia, you think about it. I don't know."

And then of course it comes to Portia: she is remembering the night she had planned to cook for Sage, and came home to find Sage *and* Noel in the kitchen. And on that occasion too there was salmon involved: Noel turned her salmon steaks into an hors d'oeuvre, and cooked his own goddam pasta. And talked so much, was so *present*.

She tells Hilda all that; they have not talked about Noel much before.

"Such a complicated human," is Hilda's comment.

"Sage seems to go for that. Roland, I think, had even more contradictions."

"Which would possibly indicate that Stevie is more complex than he looks to be?"

"Probably. And if he's not it simply won't work out."

"But it has to. With the baby."

"Oh, has to. Hilda, what will I do when you're gone?"

Hilda smiles darkly, impenetrably. And then she says, very practical, "You'll find some work. It's the only solution, for anything."

"Oh, I know you're right. But what?"

By the time Sage and Stevie arrive, quite promptly at 7, both Portia and Hilda are very happy to see them.

"Someone sure has an eye for the greatest roses," Stevie exclaims as they reach the deck; there, in the continuing warmth, despite the clutter, they plan to have some wine and the now-chilling gravlax. Stevie goes slowly from bush to bush, less as an inspector than as a lover. He looks intently at each clump of blossoms, smiling at them, breathing them in. And then, standing up, he begins to laugh at himself. "I'm sorry, I'm really a rose nut," he explains. "Honestly, this is hog heaven."

"I did work in a nursery for a while." Portia seems to feel that her superior taste in roses requires explanation. "With, uh, what's-his-name."

None of them can remember the name of Portia's former co-worker, her semi-lover, until at last Portia comes out with "Harold."

"Which reminds me," Stevie says, "do you all remember Fiona's old flower purveyors, Lois and Bonnie? Lois was tall and black, Bonnie little and blonde."

"Not really," Sage tells him. "But then I never exactly spent a lot of time hanging out at Fiona's."

"I sort of do remember them, I think," lies Portia, the truth being that she remembers both those women with excruciating vividness; she used to be so (she finds no other way to put this) so turned on by them, by their persons and by the very idea of them: two forthright, uncloseted and apparently very happy lesbians. She was passionately curious about them, especially about Lois, the very tall, very beautiful black woman.

"Well, they broke up, remember?" (Portia does very clearly remember, and remembers certain fantasies of her own, concerning Lois). "And Lois, who's one terrific businesswoman," says Stevie, "or I guess that's what she is, Lois has this new nursery business over on Potrero, near where we used to be, the restaurant. And she's looking for someone. In case you hear of anyone interested in working with her."

"Why not in fact for you, Portia?" asks innocent Hilda. Or, is she after all so innocent? Can she have picked up something in the air from Portia, some breath of Portia's intense interest, and sensed its nature? It is hard to read anything so devious on Hilda's clear-featured pale-brown face, or in her luminous green-brown eyes.

And how possibly can she, Portia, even imagine anything with someone else? "Well, I don't know," she says. "It's true that I need to get into some kind of work, and it should be something I know about," she trails off, weakly.

Or, does subtle, very wise Hilda actually plan to stay in Lebanon, and does she (altruistically? managerially?) hope to leave Portia on the threshold of a new relationship? Impossible to tell, and certainly impossible at the moment to ask Hilda.

"Harold might be interested," says Portia. "He called the other day and sounded sort of at loose ends. Besides, I've been thinking that I might go back to school and get a teaching credential. Learn how to teach foreigners. Boat people. Children." She had in fact thought of this before, but not been sure that she would do it until she spoke—so definitely.

"Well, that's a most good idea." Hilda smiles.

And Sage, "Yes, good."

Sage is wearing a sort of maternity smock, something yellow, embroidered in red. It seems to Portia a little early for such a costume, but she can understand Sage's need to confirm it. "Are you going to have the test?" she asks Sage.

"No, I'm not." Sage is very clear, and defiant. "I know at my age I'm supposed to, but unless you're prepared to have an abortion, which I'm not, there's no point."

"We plan to take what we get," adds Stevie, smilingly.

"And we think our chances are great," Sage announces, and then she frowns. "I keep having to explain that this doesn't mean I'm anti-abortion, for God's sake. I plan to march and do everything I can if those morons overturn *Roe v. Wade.* It only has to do with this particular kid. Mine and Stevie's. Also, at my age I'm not all that likely to get pregnant again."

"You can't tell, this may be the first of many." Stevie laughs.

"Don't count on me for more," Sage tells him.

"It's certainly no one's business but yours," Portia tells her sister.

"Exactly, that's how I see it. Anyway, I really don't want to know its sex."

Hilda asks, "When does Caroline get home, exactly?"

Sage tells them, "Next week. Thursday morning. We should have a party for her, don't you think?"

"No, I don't think." Portia is thoughtful. "Really, can you imagine all of us together in a festive way? I mean, now?"

"Well, I guess not. You're right."

By now the fog has come in, obscuring the hills of the Mission, and cooling the air on the deck where they all still sit, among all those rusty cans of beautiful roses. Behind one of those cans the old cat, Pink, is hiding; from time to time she looks out malevolently, hating guests.

"In Lebanon—" Hilda begins, and then interrupts herself to say, "But I've already told you, I repeat myself. The roses of Lebanon are famous too." Her smile is gentle, mildly ironic.

"Caroline will tell us how to deal with all the roses," says Portia. "Is anyone cold now? Isn't it maybe time to go in?" And then she asks, "Where's Pink? Has anyone seen her?"

Thirty-seven

"T he thing is, I'm rather tired of my daughters," says Caroline to the woman on the bed, in a strange and creaky, dingy old hotel, in Seattle. "Not Sage and Portia," says Caroline, "and really not Liza, although she is awfully self-absorbed these days, going on and on about her writing. But I am terrifically tired of both Fiona and Jill, is the truth of it. I don't even want to hear about this new sort of inn in the Napa Valley. I'm sure there's something fishy about the whole operation, and I just don't want to know."

"Five daughters is quite a lot," says the woman on the bed, who has long yellow-white hair and strange light eyes.

"Yes, and I'm sure they'll do much better without me around. They're all much too old to have a mother so actively in their lives. I've been so *present*."

"Five daughters would have driven me crazy." The woman laughs, a soft, rusty sound, an old rocker of a laugh. She is very fat, a huge sausage mound in the tight white bed. "Not to mention all those husbands," she adds. "Four, did you say?"

"No, just three. But you're right, it was quite a lot. But I didn't set out that way. I only—"

"You're probably over-sexed."

"I guess. I could be."

"Always hated it myself, which kept me out of considerable trouble, is how I see it. Your daughters seem to have a lot the same problem, from the sound of it."

Not much wanting to go on in that way about her daughters, nor about sex generally, Caroline remarks, as she has several times before, on the several successive days that she has visited, "Your view is marvellous."

"I know, see it all the time." Again the creaky, gentle laugh.

This room is on the top floor of a building a few blocks from the Pike Place Market. From its long wide windows is the view, first, of water—Elliott Bay, Bainbridge Island. To the north, more water, and, eventually, the mysterious dark San Juans. Southward, water and more islands and, on very clear days, the mountains of the Olympic range. Just now there is a streaky, tattered sunset, bright remnants of color, mauves and faded pinks against an old ash-blue sky, reflected in all that dark smooth water.

On one of the streets below this hotel, down closer to the water, there is a newish building, lots of glass and steel, what look to be condominiums. What views they would have! Constantly, there would be those views. Caroline plans to go by and have a look at one the following day. Well, why not? She could easily sell her house and move to Seattle. Maybe that's what she most needs, a move. A real change.

To leave San Francisco.

A week or so earlier, in San Francisco, the following conversation took place:

"Caroline, please try to understand. Bayard Lord did everything in the world to get that woman off the streets. It wasn't just you who saw her and recognized her. Several people did and called Bayard about her."

"Jim dear, you sound as though that were the worst of it."

"Caroline—God in heaven. I did not mean that. You are always so determined—But you must admit, she made a point of choosing the neighborhoods—Well, the point is, Bayard sent a whole team of professionals—"

"What sort of 'professionals' do you mean?"

"Oh, a couple of social workers and an intern from Children's, I believe he was from Children's. Caroline, just a minute—"

This early-morning talk between Caroline and her former husband was interrupted then as Jim seemed to muffle the phone with his hand—as Caroline heard in the background an impatient, young and feminine voice: "Jim, for Christ's sake, come on—"

"Honey, I am—"

And then Jim's voice, back to her. "Professionals," he said again. "Honestly, Caroline, I appreciate your concern but you weren't exactly friends, as I remember you were pretty hard on old Higgsie in fact. Look, I really have to go—"

"I know, I know you do. But where is she now? Did they ever find her, these professionals?"

"Yes, they found her but after that I don't know. Caroline—"

"Jim, as a terrific favor, could you call Bayard? I honestly don't want to."

"Sure thing. I'll get back to you soon."

That last was what he always said to patients, Caroline reflected, hanging up. "I'll get back to you soon." As though that would cure everything. Cure Mary Higgins Lord of her madness, and now cure Caroline of all her uneasiness, her guilt and deep concern over the fate of this almost unknown woman.

However, Jim did in fact get back to her. Two days later a tiny note came from his office, in his own small cramped hand, which through long training Caroline can read. "Higgsie Lord okay and in Seattle."

Almost, though not quite content with that resolution, Caroline tries to put it from her mind, and to concentrate, metaphorically as well as actually, on tending her own garden. The girls, as she sometimes thinks of them, seem more or less "in place" (Ralph's old phrase for the rare times of peace among the daughters); she sees all of them somewhat less than usual. Instead she spends time with some long-neglected friends.

When she does think of Mary Higgins Lord, in either or both incarnations, the black-and-pearls doctor's wife, and the wild chanting street woman ("Three hundred sixty-five days a week, fire from dung"—Caroline will never forget her song), when she thinks of Mary Lord, Caroline almost rebukes herself for so much attention paid to a single woman. With the world so visibly coming apart, with every day more homeless, more AIDS, more pollution, more carcinogenic everything—how could she have worried in that obsessive way about one single damaged, maddened woman, terrible and deeply pitiable though her story was?

However.

However, one morning Sage calls to say that she is not feeling well. Nothing serious, nothing to do with her pregnancy, just a silly summer cold. But she does not feel like going up to Seattle with Stevie, as they were going to do, to see his parents. Would Caroline—possibly? Stevie knows a nice inn up there, right next to the Pike Place Market, which at least used to be wonderful.

And so Caroline took the plane to Seattle with Stevie. Well, why not? She has never been there, had always vaguely wanted to see the great Northwest. She checked into a small and pretty hotel, near the market. Into a room with a large view of water and islands.

The phone book yielded up no Mary Higgins Lord, in any form. There was, however, an M. Higgins, at a number which, after some hesitation, Caroline called; she got what seemed to be a hotel switchboard, operated by an Oriental-sounding elderly woman who seemed to understand very little, to grasp none of the names that Caroline mentioned until she said the magic: "Higgsie?" and then was volubly told, "Oh yes, our friend Higgsie. In Room 804. I think she sick today, not come down, maybe you come see her? Oh yes, all our guests like visitors, very much! More merrier!"

The hotel turned out to be only a couple of blocks from Caroline's hotel, but those blocks brought Caroline into a very different, menacing neighborhood. She walked down a wide, dirty street on which winos, druggy-looking people lounged about, or whispered on corners to each other. Some of them looked to be Indians, she thought; all looked desperately poor. She gave what change she had and a bill to a heavy dark woman on a blanket, with a very small cat—and she entered the hotel, a black massive structure, very dingy and old.

The lobby was bleak and bare: a few upright chairs, a decrepit, off-green sofa. Several very old, rather shabby people sitting there, all staring as she passed. Finding her way to what looked to be a reception desk, Caroline saw, indeed, an extremely wizened Chinese woman, with incongruously beautiful long gray hair, who grinned happily, and called up to "Higgsie" to announce a visitor. Who said again, "More merrier!"

The elevator was very large, all dingy brass, and it mounted with an incredible slowness. To the eighth floor, the top.

Caroline walked down a broad and barely illuminated hall, peering at numbers until she came to it. 804. She knocked, and a soft old voice told her to come right in.

And there, propped up among fancy pastel satin pillows, among boxes of Kleenex, cookie cartons, a few slick magazines—there lay a woman, huge and soft and fat, with long white hair, a woman who never in a million years could have been Higgsie the street woman, the woman who chanted so desperately about dung, and fire, and days. (Who never, probably, appeared at expensive parties in black and pearls, intimidatingly.) Despite her light-yellow eyes.

Caroline's heart irrationally plunged, and she understood then how much she had looked forward to seeing Higgsie *well:* that would have meant that everything was all right, after all, or would get better, somehow.

Much afraid that her disappointment and confusion would show, Caroline began to chatter: "I'm terribly sorry—I'm from San Francisco. And someone told me—another woman named Higgsie. I'm so sorry—"

The woman turned. Her whole massive body moved as those eyes came to rest on Caroline. Turning, she looked somehow powerful, very strong. But the voice that emerged was creaky as she said, "I guess you expected my sister, Mrs. Lord."

"Oh! Well yes, I did. Mary Higgins Lord. We used to call her Higgsie too." A pause. "Is she here in Seattle? I heard that her former husband, Bayard—"

"Yes indeed. He found her and threw her up here. Got her off the streets, all right."

"But what happened?"

"She died, of course. My name's Mavis, but you can call me Higgsie too, if you want to."

"Died?"

"Day she got here. Her heart gave out. Her and her 'escort' got off the plane and he brought her here, room next to mine here all ready for Mary. But I took one look and I knew it would be no go. Too far gone, she was, for retrieving."

All this information, this infinitely sad story lies there between them. Caroline would like to ask more, much more about Mary Higgins Lord, she would like the whole story of her life from this odd unlikely older sister, but at least for the moment she does not.

"Well, it's nice that you came to see me, dear," says this Higgsie. "Would you like a cookie? As they say downstairs, more merrier."

"Yes. Thanks." She might as well visit her every day while she's here, Caroline decides, this amiable, lonely and slightly loony woman with whom she has so accidentally become connected, and in a gradual way they can start to talk.

Between these visits, which are brief—Mavis's attention falters, she falls into light naps after half an hour or so—Caroline walks about the city, very much liking it. And comparing it, inevitably, with San Francisco.

The air is cleaner here, she thinks, and the architecture more straightforward, less pretentious. The people plainer, and also more straightforward. She finds, off Pioneer Square, a wonderful bookstore, one that has, apparently, everything, including a nice bricked-in downstairs café.

But it is mostly the air that she likes, its freshness, its cool. It seems new air, unused. And she loves the views of the dark smooth water, and islands.

She thinks, I could easily sell my house. I could buy a house up here for less than half the proceeds, and live on the rest. I might even be able to find some sort of job.

It is on her third visit to Mavis Higgins that the two women discuss Caroline's daughters.

"They all seem embarked on some definite course at the moment," is how Caroline sums it up. "But I seem to have said that before about them, and was wrong. In fact, I'm often wrong about my daughters."

"We'll all be better once the awful Eighties are over," Mavis tells her. "I'm just eighty-one myself. Friend of mine said the Nineties are going to be lots better."

Hearing this somewhat confusing sentence, Caroline wonders, Is

Mavis referring to the age of the century—the coming decade—or to her own great age? Either supposition could turn out to be true, she thinks. Caroline hopes that the Nineties of Mavis Higgins and those of the century will be a vast improvement, but she is not at all sure they will be.

A NOTE ON THE TYPE

The text of this book was set in Garamond No. 3, a modern
rendering of the type first cut by Claude Garamond (c. 1480–
1561). Garamond was a pupil of Geoffroy Tory and is believed to have based his letters on the Venetian models,
although he introduced a number of important differences,
and it is to him we owe the letter that we know as "old
style." He gave to his letters a certain elegance and a feeling
of movement that won for their creator an immediate reputation and the patronage of Francis I of France.

Composed by Creative Graphics, Inc.,
Allentown, Pennsylvania

Printed and bound by The Haddon Craftsmen, Inc.,
Scranton, Pennsylvania

Typography and binding design
by Dorothy Baker